Praise for

"I love this premise: Sara acci[...] vice versa, and the mistake t[...] [...]. So clever!"

—Alafair Burke, *New York Times* bestselling author

"Dynamic women with complicated lives take center stage in this twisty mystery about a rideshare mix-up which results in murder. Lalli is a fresh voice in the thriller genre and a writer to watch!"

—Wendy Walker, internationally bestselling author of *Don't Look for Me*

"A gripping, immersive read, S. C. Lalli has written a tightly woven thriller featuring my new favorite complicated female protagonist. Sara—Saraswati Bhaduri—is riveting as a struggling, savvy law student who becomes embroiled in a gritty murder mystery, while also tackling issues of race, class, and identity at her Ivy-league college. I couldn't put this book down, and neither will you!"

—Uzma Jalaluddin, bestselling author of *Hana Khan Carries On*

"*Are You Sara?* is a crackling spitfire of suspense. I read it in two sittings! And that delicious little twist at the very end is a brilliant depiction of just how cunning women can be."

—Wanda M. Morris, award-winning author of *All Her Little Secrets*

"Deliciously dark and twisted, *Are You Sara?* hits the ground running and never loses momentum. This book embraces the often messy, sometimes misguided, and always difficult compromises universally made on the path to success, weaving an un-put-downable story that is the perfect propulsive page turner for summer."

—Erica Katz, author of *The Boys' Club* and *Fake*

"It starts off with a nightmarishly riveting conceit: Two women with the same name accidentally switch cabs and one of them gets murdered at her wrong drop-off location. . . . *Are You Sara?* cogently navigates the duality of identity, what it says about social hierarchy, and the things people will do to survive. . . . S. C. Lalli's debut thriller is punchy and an introspective reminder that money and power always come with dangerous strings attached."

—NPR, Books We Love

THE PLUS ONE

Also by S. C. Lalli

Are You Sara?

THE PLUS ONE

A NOVEL

S. C. LALLI

WILLIAM MORROW
An Imprint of HarperCollins*Publishers*

For information, please email the Special Markets Department in the U.S. at SPsales@harpercollins.com or in Canada at HCOrder@harpercollins.com.

HarperCollins books may be purchased for educational, business, or sales promotional use. For information, please email the Special Markets Department at Spsales@harpercollins.com.

FIRST U.S. AND CANADIAN EDITIONS

Interior text design by Diahann Sturge-Campbell

Illustrations throughout © Annartlab/Stock.Adobe.com

Library of Congress Cataloging-in-Publication Data has been applied for.

Library and Archives Canada Cataloguing in Publication information is available upon request.

ISBN 978-0-06-322631-9
ISBN 978-1-4434-6703-2 (Canada)

24 25 26 27 28 LBC 5 4 3 2 1

For Annie

Mehndi Party

Welcome! We are absolutely thrilled to host you in the coastal paradise of Los Cabos to celebrate our destination wedding! If you haven't been to an Indian wedding before, then prepare yourselves. The next four days are going to be one wild ride.

We're kicking things off late this afternoon with the Mehndi Party. Henna artists will be on site for those interested in having their hands painted, followed by dinner and drinks. Blush's award-winning head chef has prepared a feast of traditional Baja fare, which pairs perfectly with tonight's spicy signature cocktail. Think passion fruit. Think habanero. You've got to try it. Trust us—it's to die for.

Love,
RAJ & RADHIKA

Location: The Beachside Terrace,
Blush Resort & Spa Los Cabos
Dress code: Resort Chic

P.S. In accordance with the nondisclosure agreement signed by all guests, we respectfully remind you to refrain from sharing your own photos or videos on social media throughout the festivities. Our team will email you approved content for posting within ten business days, after which you are required to use the hashtag #RajikhaWedding.

1.

Thursday, April 25
8:10 a.m.

Someone is coming for me.

I white-knuckle the handle of my suitcase and stop dead in my tracks. My right ankle wobbles on impact. I'm uncomfortable in heels, even low slingbacks like the ones I'm wearing now. Soft, almost hypnotic music sings through the overhead speakers, and as I take a deep breath in preparation, I notice the scent overpowering my nostrils. It's sweet and soapy, like freshly washed skin. It can't be me. I haven't showered since yesterday morning.

The woman charging at me is extremely pretty, late thirties or early forties, and impeccable top to tail. Her chocolate-brown hair is swept back in a graceful ponytail, and she's wearing a crisp white-collared shirt and navy-blue skirt and blazer. She plasters a friendly smile on her face as she draws closer. My stomach clenches as I brace myself.

"You must be Ms. Shaylee Kapoor!" she declares, hand extended for a firm shake.

I attempt a smile. "Guilty."

"My name is Daniela Munoz. *Welcome* to Blush Resort & Spa Los Cabos." She beams. "How was your journey?"

Before I can answer, she glances down at my suitcase and gasps.

"Did someone not take your bag, Ms. Kapoor? I am *so* sorry—"

"I wanted to carry it myself," I say quickly. I practically had to wrestle my suitcase and handbag away from three bellhops when my taxi pulled up a few minutes earlier.

"Of course." Daniela nods. "Whatever you wish, Ms.—"

"You can call me Shay." I smile. "Just Shay."

"'Just' *Shay.*" Daniela winks. "We are so pleased you have arrived."

A frosted glass of sparkling rosewater appears in my hand as Daniela leads me farther into the lobby, which has the feel and acoustics of a contemporary art museum. We sit on a plush magenta couch where she efficiently checks me in on an iPad and fastens a discreet plastic band around my wrist. Apparently, Daniela is the resort's events director and the mastermind behind this weekend's wedding festivities. She's attending to me personally because, in her words, I'm the plus one of a "VIP."

After check-in, Daniela tours me around the resort—pointing out the state-of-the-art spa and fitness facilities, shopping piazza, seven world-class restaurants, Parisian cafe, jazz bar, dance club, hookah lounge, conference center, and banquet halls. After, she leads me outside, and even though I googled the resort extensively before arriving, the view still makes my stomach flip-flop. Tucked into an oasis of palm trees is a lush garden of virgin-white daybeds and cabanas facing four swimming pools, the farthest of which is an infinity pool that spills out over the Pacific.

"Blush Los Cabos has been a long time coming." She sighs, waving her arm around. "It's now the crown jewel among Blush Continental's fourteen resorts in Baja, Jalisco, and Riviera Maya. Have you been to any of our other hotels?"

I shake my head, and she turns wistfully back to the view.

"*Well*. What do you think?"

Blush opened its doors only two months ago, has a rumored price tag of seven hundred million dollars, and according to a leading travel magazine, is the best ultra-luxury adults-only resort in the Americas.

What do *I* think?

What the hell am I *doing here?*

Of course, I don't say that out loud, and the grand tour continues. Daniela briefly points above and behind her, drawing my attention to the event spaces where some of the wedding festivities will take place. Above are seven floors of hotel rooms and suites, all of which have an unparalleled view of the ocean. But that's not where I'm staying. Next, she leads me past the swimming pools and through a canopy of palm trees toward the eastern, even more exclusive side of the resort.

The Blush Villas.

It's a half mile walk slightly uphill, and by the time I get there, I regret having declined Daniela's offer to have a golf cart drive us up. Panting quietly, I try not to gawk as she tours me through the community of thirty-two mini vacation homes and rattles off facts I've already read online. Each villa is at least three thousand square feet and—among other things—comes with its own infinity pool, rooftop terrace, and wellness room, as well as a private chef and butler on standby. I follow Daniela through a labyrinth of villas tucked among exotic flower beds, cactus gardens, and swooping palm trees, and suddenly, an ominous shiver runs up my spine.

For all its glitz and glamour, there's something not right about this place.

The plant life is too lush. Vibrant. Jarring harshly against its arid desert surroundings. The white marble footpaths reflect the already-hot sun. I can almost feel its heat through the soles of my shoes. We weave around a massive human-made waterfall and, as the sounds of trickling water fade away and all I can hear is the click-clack of my heels and the drag of my suitcase against the sandstone, my knees quake as it hits me.

There's no one else around. This place is a ghost town.

"In just a few hours, the Villas will be humming with life," Daniela says as if reading my mind. "The bride and groom reserved all thirty-two villas for their guests."

She lowers her voice to a loud whisper.

"As I'm sure you know, the invite list had to be cut *twice*."

I didn't know, but that tidbit doesn't surprise me.

"I've planned dozens of South Asian weddings over the years— but this one?" She makes the chef's kiss gesture. "I can't tell you how honored we are to host the happy couple's big day. This is by far the most *exclusive* wedding I've had the chance of being a part of."

I make a noncommittal sound and try not to trip. People keep telling me how "exclusive" this wedding is going to be, as if trying to impress on me how lucky I am to be attending. "Lucky" is one way to describe it. Depending on the villa, a single night costs between five and fifteen thousand American dollars, and I'm told the "happy couple" is footing the whole bill.

Finally, the maze comes to an end when Daniela stops short

in front of a villa—jaw-dropping but indistinguishable from the dozens of others we passed.

"The garden villas are lovely, but the VIPs have an ocean view." She sighs again. "This is one of my favorites. It's a generous one-bedroom, and your terrace is right on the cliffs." She points south. "Just behind, you'll find a staircase leading down to the beach. You and your neighbors will be able to access it without going back through the main resort."

I hold up my left wrist, to which she'd earlier fastened the plastic band. "And I just . . ."

"Wave your hand near the detectors by the front or back terrace doors. They will unlock."

I thank her and start wheeling my suitcase up the front path. When I realize Daniela hasn't followed me, I turn around. Her smile falters.

"I will leave you here." She nods curtly. "I have a meeting with the happy couple."

A lengthy pause. She doesn't make eye contact.

"Will that be all, Shay?"

She lingers, as if noticing my hesitation, and I wonder what else she can see. The drugstore makeup I slapdashed on my face in the taxi on the way over. The price tag poking out of my chichi jumpsuit, which I plan to return next week. The fact that, unlike my boyfriend, I'm not a "very important person."

I'm a big fat fraud.

* * *

THE VILLA APPEARS to be empty so I leave my bags in the bedroom and tour myself around. Everything about the place just screams money, like the bespoke furniture, ivory-white furnishings, and floor-to-ceiling windows, which give every room an uninterrupted view of the Pacific. On the ground floor there's a huge kitchen, living room, bedroom with an en suite, and an indoor-outdoor terrace with an infinity pool. Upstairs is the wellness space, which includes yoga mats, meditation pillows, a jacuzzi, and a surprisingly tasteful Buddha statue. The room leads out to an expansive rooftop deck with cushy lounge seating and—

I clock the hammock in the corner.

It's Caleb. He's passed out cold.

This morning he's wearing a neon-green tank top, Bermuda shorts, and Birkenstocks, and his hair, which is several inches longer than mine, is wet and pulled into a tight bun. You'd never know just by looking at him that he works in finance and has a sizable trust fund. That he was born and raised in high East Coast society. His legal name is Caleb Malcolm Prescott III.

"Shay?"

Caleb's eyes flutter open. Game face on, I join him in the hammock.

"Babe, you should have called me. I would have met you in the lobby." He grins lazily as he wraps his arm around me. "It's nice here, huh?"

I turn away from Caleb to take in the view. It's a gorgeous April morning, already a balmy eighty degrees, and there isn't a cloud in the sky. A single gust of wind whips off the water. It *is* nice. It's by far the nicest place I've ever been, that I'll likely ever go, and the thought makes my stomach churn even harder.

I'm only here because of Caleb. He's the best man in this weekend's production, and I—to quote the bride—am the "gold-digging whore" who snagged him.

"I missed you," he says.

"It's only been two days."

"And they've been the longest two days of my *life*."

Caleb kisses me then. Passionately. We go two or more days without seeing each other all the time, but he's romantic and prone to public displays of affection, sending flowers and saying things that make my eyes roll. By his count, we've been together for just over three months, although I tally it a little differently. He rolls me onto my back as we lock lips, and, reluctantly, I let him. I'm above average height for a South Asian woman, and still I feel tiny pressed up against him. When things start to heat up, I gently push him off.

"Where are the others?" I ask.

"Still sleeping, I imagine. We had a big one last night."

Hand in hand, we walk downstairs to the bedroom. Caleb squints at the unmade king. I'm worried he's going to suggest sex, but instead he asks me if I'd like to get breakfast.

"Sure. Let me use the bathroom first—"

As I start walking toward the en suite, Caleb darts in front of me and blocks my path.

"The maid hasn't come yet," he says quickly.

"So? I just have to pee."

He twists his neck around, eyes tracking the bathroom through the open door. "Oh. OK."

He swivels back. Is he sweating?

"Sorry about the mess."

After Caleb lets me by, I lock the door behind me. Except for the wet towels in the gigantic bathtub, the bathroom is spotless. It's also larger than my shitty rental in LA. After I use the toilet, I inspect the miniature bottles lined up on the vanity, rub some of the body butter on my knees and elbows. It has the same scent as the lobby.

"Shay, you good?" Caleb asks suddenly through the door. His voice is loud; he must be standing just on the other side.

"Yes," I call back. "Can I have a minute?"

"Of course. Sure."

I hear his footsteps as he drifts away from the door. Am I imagining it, or is Caleb acting strange? I put back the lotion and then peek in the shower.

"Sorry about the mess," he calls again.

Yep. Something's definitely off. I open all the drawers. They're empty, except for the bottom one, which contains Caleb's toiletries, shaving kit, and several prescription pill bottles. Next, I shake out the towels in the tub and, frowning, catch sight of the trash can beneath the sink. There's an empty bottle of Pacifico, tissues, and a half-eaten packet of the organic, gluten-free vegan seed chips Caleb loves.

I crouch down to get a better look, and my heart catches in my throat when I spot the "mess" he clearly doesn't want me to see.

The condom.

When Caleb calls out my name for the third time, I wash my hands and leave the en suite. He's sitting on the edge of the bed, elbows on knees. He blushes easily. His forehead is the color of a stop sign.

"Have you read through the program?" His voice is unusually high, and he won't meet my eye as he gestures at a stylishly decorated booklet on the bedside table. "Radhi was explaining some of the rituals to me." His eyes flit to the en suite and then back to the booklet. "Indian weddings are pretty elaborate, huh?"

He laughs awkwardly as I stare back at him blankly.

"And then they're doing it all over again in India . . ."

Caleb continues prattling on about the wedding: how this

all-inclusive Cabo vacation is only for immediate family and Raj and Radhika's closest friends, and the even more upscale wedding—with a two-thousand-person guest list—will take place in Mumbai in the fall. I already know all of this, but still I don't say anything, curious to see where Caleb will steer the conversation.

I've just arrived at my boyfriend's best friend's destination wedding, there's a used condom in his bathroom trash, and all I feel is numb.

I'm aware this isn't a normal girlfriend reaction. I find out Caleb cheated on me and I should be—what, exactly? Irate? Heartbroken? Vengeful? *Violent?* I spot a sea-glass vase in the corner. It looks heavy, not to mention expensive. Right now, that's the type of thing I should be chucking at his head.

"It's going to be an epic weekend," Caleb continues, standing up from the bed. He draws closer, sneaks his hands into mine.

"Are you—"

Caleb's voice changes as he suddenly tugs me closer and stares suspiciously at the wall to my left.

"Do you hear that?"

Huh? "What are you—"

Midsentence, my mouth falls open when I hear something too. It's muffled, and I can't be sure, but it sounded like a scream.

"What was that?" I whisper.

Goosebumps prickle my arms as we both approach the window. Beyond the terrace, all we can see is ocean and sky. There's nobody back there.

"Someone's television?" I suggest.

Caleb doesn't answer as he takes my hand again, leads me to the other side of the villa, and opens the front door. We go outside, and at first, I don't see anything. Caleb's villa is the last one on the row, just a thicket of palm trees and greenery to the west, an empty villa to the north. I turn to face the villa east of us, and that's when I see Daniela. She's on her knees, shaking, bent so far forward the end of her ponytail brushes the pavement.

"Daniela?" I call out.

There's a charge in the air, even though the forecast is pleasant. My ears ring as time slows down, my heartbeat nothing but a dull vibration in my chest.

Daniela's screaming now. Hysterical. Her speech garbled and incoherent.

I'm next to her, my hands holding her quaking body when I finally understand her words.

They're dead.

She's telling us the bride and groom are dead.

2.

The phone slipped down Shay's neck as she turned to get a better look.

The security guard stepped out first, holding the door open for an attractive thirtysomething pair. Shay tensed. The man had the build of an NBA player and a brownish-blond man-bun that jarred beautifully with his expensive suit. The woman, Hollywood gorgeous and alarmingly drunk, gripped his arm as they joined Shay on the sidewalk.

"Did you hear me? Are you there?"

Shay wedged her phone back between her ear and shoulder, having forgotten Lexie was still on the line. In the background, Lexie's two-year-old screamed bloody murder.

"No, I didn't," Shay said into the phone, lowering her voice. "Actually, can you hang on a sec?"

The music swelled from the restaurant, making it difficult for Shay to eavesdrop on the couple. She drifted closer and chanced another look. The man caught her staring and smirked.

"Mhm," Shay said enthusiastically into the phone. "Uh-huh. *Interesting.*"

"What's interesting?" Lexie answered suspiciously.

"Honestly, don't worry about it," Shay said to her, wondering if the man was still watching.

"I don't know what's going on over there," Lexie replied, "but I'm putting you on speaker."

"Brilliant," Shay said, and then laughed as if Lexie had said something funny.

A black car with an Uber sign in the windshield appeared at the curb, and Shay took a few steps back as the couple approached it. The drunk woman nearly tripped as she grabbed a fistful of the man's bottom.

"It was good to see you," Shay heard him say as he gently removed her hand and helped the woman into the backseat. "I'm going to head back inside."

The woman popped her head out, eyes wide. "Aren't you coming?"

"Can't. Sorry."

"But, then why did—"

"Get some sleep, OK?" He smiled, and then without waiting for a reply, shut the door in her startled face.

On the other end of the line, Lexie's toddler blew raspberries to a song on the radio. Harry Styles, Shay thought. The man watched the Uber drive off, and after a moment, turned his gaze on Shay, as if he knew she'd been watching. Uncomfortable, in need of something to pretend to do, she tucked the phone into the crook of her shoulder, rummaged around her purse for a cigarette, and lit it.

"Can I bum one?" the man asked.

Was he talking to her? Shay was tempted to look around and confirm as much, but she was the only one standing in his vicinity.

"I'll forgive you," Shay said into the phone, as if in midconversation with Lexie. With her free hand, she handed the man a cigarette. "Anyway, I've got to go. Talk soon."

Without waiting for Lexie to reply, Shay hung up and tucked her phone away. The man was standing close to her now, face-to-face. He smiled.

"I didn't mean to disturb you."

"You didn't." Shay blew smoke out of her nostrils and did her best not to fidget with the outfit Lexie had lent her—a stretchy black thing Lexie had made her promise to return. "Need a light?"

The man nodded, and so she held out her lighter in her palm. Stepping forward, he placed his whole hand over hers, squeezing lightly as he swiped it from her. "Are you here for the party?"

"What party?" Shay squinted at the restaurant from which he'd come. "Oh. No. I was supposed to meet a friend."

Lighting the cigarette, he asked, "A friend, or a date?"

"A friend." Shay smiled playfully, and then pointed indiscriminately at one of the several upscale bars and restaurants lining this part of Sunset. "We were going to grab a late dinner, but she can't make it."

"Her loss." He paused. "What's your name?"

"Shay."

"I'm Caleb." His eyes dropped briefly to her bare legs. "You're not from around here, are you?"

Shay cocked her head to the side and suppressed a smile. "How could you tell?"

He exhaled deeply, smoke billowing.

"Right. I'm a smoker." She made a face. "Nobody smokes in LA. I feel like an alien."

Caleb bent over and lifted up his left pant leg, revealing ET-branded trouser socks.

"Everyone here is an alien."

Shay laughed. With those eyes, that face, that objectively perfect SoCal physique, she hadn't expected him to make her laugh.

"And what distant universe did you come from, Caleb?"

"Connecticut."

"*Connecticut.* Ah. So let me guess. You're a lawyer?" she tried. "Management consultant?"

Caleb's cheeks reddened as he smiled. "I work in finance."

"Of course you do."

Smiling, Caleb took a long drag. She could feel him evaluating her.

"My turn," he said slowly. "I bet you're a . . . . *model.*"

"Good line."

"Did it work?" He grinned.

She avoided the question. "I'm a grad student. I grew up in Vancouver, but I moved around a lot in my twenties."

She could feel Caleb's eyes tracking her face, her physique; he was calculating her age.

"I moved here to study public policy," she continued, suddenly desperate to impress him. "At USC Price."

"Damn." Caleb's eyes widened. "You're smart."

"Going back to school at thirty? In *this* economy? I'm a fool."

Caleb snorted a laugh, which turned into a coughing fit.

"Well, that was embarrassing," he said after catching his breath.

"A little," Shay admitted. "Do you actually smoke, or did you just want to chat me up?"

His gaze seared, and Shay wondered where her confidence was coming from. How was she managing to chat up a guy who was freakishly out of her league? Shay tucked her hair behind her ear. And when was the last time she'd even flirted?

She hadn't.

"I don't smoke often," Caleb said wryly. "But after I've had a few drinks, I'll do pretty much anything."

Shay gestured at the street, where the Uber had just whisked away the other woman.

"Except take advantage of drunk women trying to get you into bed?"

He grinned, and she caught something light and weird fluttering in her stomach. Caleb took a step closer, his eyes dropping again. He smelled like cedarwood, rosemary, and red wine. He smelled rich.

He smelled good.

"You're not drunk, are you, Shay?"

He bit down on his bottom lip, his gaze moving up to her mouth. A man like Caleb got what he wanted, when he wanted, and Shay felt exhilarated and terrified in equal measure that she—however briefly his interest would last—was the object of his attention.

Smiling, she took a step back, putting distance and reason between them. "So, what's going on in there? Some fancy party?"

"You could say that."

"If you want to impress a newly minted LA girl, this is where you name-drop," she teased. "Who's inside? George and Amal? Priyanka and Nick?" She paused. "Blake and Ryan?"

"It's my best friend's engagement party. And it's more impressive if I don't name-drop, isn't it? But there are some heavy-weights in there."

"Wrestlers?" she deadpanned. "Or capitalists like yourself?"

Caleb scratched the scruff on his jaw, smirking at her attempt at a joke.

"His fiancée is an influencer, pretty successful at it too." He took another drag. "Not that she needs the money."

Shay inhaled her cigarette, her nerves catching up with her. After a beat she said, "And the groom?"

Caleb didn't respond. Instead, his eyes drifted behind her head, to the restaurant entrance. Shay swiveled around. Her mouth nearly fell open. Wafting through the door was a stunning South Asian woman, petite, sultry, and with curves that killed. Her gold gown shimmered as she sashayed toward Caleb.

"I was worried you left with . . ." the woman trailed off, noticing Shay standing there. "But you stayed."

"I stayed."

"I wonder why," she simpered, her eyes darting briefly in Shay's direction. "Have you seen Raj?"

"Yes," Caleb replied flatly, and a knowing glance passed between them. She rolled her eyes. "I'm a little busy right now—"

"You're busy with *my* engagement party. Could you please go check on him?"

Caleb's mouth twitched, and Shay wondered if it was a sign of annoyance or something else.

"Fine. I'll go check on him." Caleb dropped his cigarette and stepped on it. "When are we doing the toast?"

"As soon as he's presentable." Suddenly, the woman turned her attention to Shay. Her gaze pierced.

"I'm Radhika. And you are?"

"Shay," she replied, trying to keep her voice steady. "Shaylee Kapoor."

"This is the bride I was telling you about," Caleb said to her.

"Oh!" Shay nodded politely. "Congratulations."

Radhika blinked at Shay, unsmiling.

"When's the big day?"

When Radhika didn't respond, Caleb stepped in and cleared his throat. "End of April. Anyway, Radhi, this is Shay. Her friend stood her up for dinner. And then she was kind enough to lend me a cigarette."

"The kindness that kills," Radhika answered flatly.

"It's just a bit of fun."

"Everything's a bit of fun until you're *dead*, Caleb."

Shay, still smoking, stepped backward as her cheeks heated up.

"Radhi." Caleb grimaced.

"Do whatever you want," Radhika chided. "But *tobacco*? Jesus."

Shay tried to mumble an excuse as Radhika reamed Caleb out for smoking, racking her brain for the talking points she raised whenever under scrutiny.

Around my old coworkers, it was basically part of the job description.

It's a social thing.

It's a stress *thing.*

But Radhika wasn't interested in what Shay had to say. As she lectured Caleb, it was as if Shay wasn't there at all.

"OK, I'm done now." Radhika batted her eyelashes at Caleb, concluding, "You know I'm just a little protective."

"A little?" His voice was playful, but Shay could tell he wasn't impressed.

"Fine. I'm very protective." Her eyes turned pointedly to Shay. "But you give me *plenty* of reasons to be."

"Be nice," Caleb chided. "You don't even know Shay." Gently, he rested his hand on Shay's shoulder. "She's smart. She goes to USC Price."

Radhika's eyes narrowed. "Is *that* what she told you?"

"It's hard to get in there, Radhi. A buddy of mine was rejected, even after his dad donated a library."

Besides the fact that Caleb and Radhika were speaking as if Shay weren't even present, it felt mildly nice to be defended. Doll eyes wide, Radhika turned her chin to inspect Shay, as if to judge if she was worthy of Caleb's praise. Shay always thought herself above petty dramas and jealousies, but she couldn't help but feel about one inch tall in Lexie's Banana Republic little black dress, while Radhika, although short, towered high above, stylish and stutteringly gorgeous.

"We better go get Raj, then," Radhika said finally. Her eyes bored into Shay. "Would you like to join us inside?"

"I . . ." Shay's heart raced as beads of sweat formed at her temples. "I don't want to intrude."

"It's my engagement party. I get to decide if you're intruding."

Radhika's words failed to reassure her, and, stalling, Shay puffed her cigarette and blew the smoke over her shoulder.

"You might as well come in," Radhika pressed. "Caleb has a fetish for brown girls, and he's already slept with half of the ones inside—"

Caleb groaned. "Come on, Radhi."

"As if, Caleb, you totally do."

"And *you* have a penchant for embarrassing me."

Caleb turned to Shay and drew her closer. "Don't let her claws fool you. Radhi's a sweetheart deep down. She wouldn't invite you in if she didn't mean it."

Shay glanced over Caleb's shoulder at Radhika, who was now smiling and beckoning her inside.

"Are you sure?" Shay whispered to Caleb.

"Not at all." He laughed. "But I think I like you, and I want you to come inside anyway."

3.

'm chain-smoking out the window because I don't know what else to do.

Am I hallucinating? Is any of this real?

I only need to quiet my heavy breathing to realize that this *is* mind-numbingly real. Caleb's in the en suite bathroom, bawling. I can hear him right now. I tried comforting him earlier, but that only seemed to make him feel worse.

His best friend is dead. The bride and groom are dead. Raj Joshi and Radhika Singh, two very real human beings, are somehow *dead*.

I have traveled through war zones and lived through a bomb scare and a severe bout of typhoid, but never before have I experienced such profound chaos. I've stopped peeking through the curtains at the crime scene investigators, police, and hotel security buzzing outside Caleb's villa like carrion flies. It's a zoo out there. It's absolutely insane.

We have no information and have been instructed to stay in the villa until further notice. Earlier, several officers from the local police force barged in to interview us. Me in the bedroom. Caleb upstairs. They lost interest in me as soon as I told them I arrived at Blush less than an hour before Daniela found the bodies. Caleb's interview lasted quite a bit longer.

For a change of scenery, I go into the kitchen and hop up on the countertop. The AC is on full blast, and the marble feels frigid against my thighs. Is it weird that I'm not crying? I didn't know them that well; still, does it make me a monster?

I open Instagram on my phone and click through Radhika Singh's Instagram Stories. The bride. She posted seven times over the last twenty-four hours. Most are selfies of her, Raj, and Caleb at the resort's pool yesterday afternoon. The final one, timestamped to late last night, is a chaotic video of her dancing to EDM at a club. Little do her followers know—all two million of them—it's the last time she'll ever post.

My knees like jelly, I switch to Raj Joshi's private Instagram account. His bio tells his one thousand–odd followers that he's VP Biz Dev at his father's hotel empire, the Joshi Group, and #YOLO. When Raj accepted my follow request last month, I quickly grew to understand why he kept his profile on lockdown. He travels a lot for work and documents his day-to-day in painful detail, an occupational hazard when you're wealthy enough to have kidnap and ransom insurance. Quietly, I scroll through some of Raj's recent posts: photos of him in the penthouse suite at one of his father's hotels in Chicago or Amsterdam, obnoxious selfies of him remote-working from some unknown tropical paradise or wherever he was for business that week.

I hop off the counter, shivering and overwhelmingly cold. I can't call Raj obnoxious anymore, can I? Now that he's dead. Now that everything has changed.

I'm halfway through a can of Pringles I procured from the

snack bar when Caleb emerges from the bathroom. He appears to have aged a decade in the past few hours. His eyes are red and watery. His complexion is sallow, and there are deep grooves between his brows. I've been waiting for Caleb to come out of the bathroom so I could console him, but now that he's here, I have no clue what to say.

"Pringle?" I offer sheepishly.

Shaking his head, he pads toward me and throws his arms around my waist.

"You should really eat something," I try next, because that sounds like something a supportive girlfriend would say.

"I can't." He drops his head into the crook of my neck, sighing. "I'm sorry I disappeared on you, babe. I needed to be alone."

"Of course." I pause. "Is there anything I can do for you—"

Babe. It's on the tip of my tongue. But I bite it back before the word slips out.

"Actually, there is," Caleb says after a beat. "The Joshis are calling a family meeting."

"A family meeting," I echo.

"Will you come with me?" Caleb whispers into my hair. "I need you."

My chest tightens as I think of how to respond. It makes sense that Caleb would be invited, considering he spends every major holiday with Raj's family, not the Prescotts, and as of a few months ago is even employed by the Joshi Group. The Joshis are the family Caleb never had.

But me? I'm nothing to that family.

I'm less than nothing.

I don't think I should attend the meeting, but Caleb looks so fragile I fear he'll shatter to pieces if I say no. Once outside, police officers steer us past the villa next door, which is now sectioned off by yellow caution tape, to the next villa over. It's at least twice as large as Caleb's, a mansion among mansions. Stationed outside is a cumbersome-looking man who's a dead ringer for Hulk Hogan, except he's South Asian and sporting aggressive vacation apparel—khakis, a white linen shirt with the top two buttons popped, a sombrero, and aviator sunglasses. I give Caleb the eye, curious about his identity as this Brown Hulk Hogan ushers us inside with a nod. He's not wearing a staff uniform and doesn't look like police either.

"He's uncle's private security," Caleb whispers.

It shouldn't surprise me that Caleb calls Mr. Joshi "uncle," or that the man has a bodyguard. Mr. Narayan Joshi is the head of the family and chief executive officer of the Joshi Group, which isn't your average multibillion-dollar hotel group. It's the largest multinational hotel and resort empire in Asia—and expanding rapidly worldwide.

Anxiety swells in my throat as we enter the foyer, where Mr. Joshi is waiting. In photos online, Mr. Big-Time CEO is featured signing documents at the head of a boardroom table. Smiling thoughtfully while delivering a keynote. Walking the red carpet of a new Bollywood movie directed by or starring one of his close personal friends. But Mr. Joshi in the flesh is balding, has a paunch tightening the midsection of his golf polo, and exudes an eerily jolly, uncle-like vibe. If I didn't know this Mr. Joshi was *the* Mr. Joshi, I'd look right past him.

His hands are stuffed into his shorts pockets, and his eyes—bloodred and glassy—are cast down on the floor. When we're just a few feet in front of him, Caleb drops my hand and reaches for him. Only then does Mr. Joshi seem to notice we've arrived.

The two men embrace as I stand off to the side, trying to

use as little oxygen as possible. The grief hangs in the air, a thick, suffocating fog. Mr. Joshi seems small, even frail, in Caleb's arms. I hear a sob, a baby-like whimper. I wonder if it's the mourning sound of the father or the best friend.

Caleb pulls away first, wiping snot from his face as he gestures my way.

"Uncle, this is my girlfriend, Shaylee Kapoor."

Mr. Joshi frowns, and words escape me as we stand face-to-face, and the twisted fate that brought us together catches up with my nerves.

"I . . ."

I shouldn't have agreed to come. I shouldn't be here.

"I'm so sorry for your loss," I say softly, bowing my head in respect.

He hesitates. I'm not sure he heard me.

"You are Caleb's *girlfriend*?"

"Yes," Caleb answers on my behalf.

I can feel Mr. Joshi's eyes boring into me as he accompanies us into the living room.

He doesn't believe it. He doesn't see how a relationship between Caleb and a nobody like me makes sense.

He's sharp. I suppose he's the revered chief executive of a multibillion-dollar company for a reason.

* * *

IN A DREAMLIKE state, Caleb and I offer hugs and condolences to Mrs. Joshi, who's catatonic on the largest sofa next to Sean Joshi, Raj's cousin. Sean and Raj look so much alike that it's a bit shocking to see Sean right now. The two are cut from the same cloth, could easily be twins. Medium height with wiry builds, sharp noses, and wickedly handsome smiles. For obvious reasons, Sean isn't smiling today. He's off on another planet, staring at a lamp, and ignores me when I say hello and offer an awkward gesture of sympathy. I hover for a moment, trying to make eye contact, but he won't engage. I push down the embarrassment and shuffle after Caleb.

"Are we ready to begin?"

As Caleb and I sit down on another couch, a very tanned man with a clipboard enters through the terrace door, two uniformed police officers and Daniela trailing him. She looks like a ghost, her cheeks the same shade as her crisp collared shirt. She must still be in shock from having discovered Raj and Radhika's bodies.

"We are ready," Mr. Joshi answers blithely. "Unless anyone else in the Singh family is to be expected?"

He clears his throat, and in unison, everyone shifts their gaze to the billiards table in the far corner. Right in front of it is Radhika's older sister, Zara Singh. I don't know how I failed to notice her earlier. She's the most famous person in the room.

Zara's crumpled in an armchair, snot running out of her nose, which she wipes angrily with the sleeve of her sweatshirt. I've never seen her in loungewear before, or looking anything less than fabulous, and I find myself staring at her, searching for the sisterly resemblance. But unlike Raj and Sean's similarities, Zara looks nothing like Radhika. Zara is model-tall, slim, with a strong jaw and high "don't fuck with me" cheekbones. Radhika is tiny, voluptuous, pretty, with a suspiciously approachable face.

My heart gives a pang as I remember. Radhika *was*.

Radhika's *dead*.

"No one else is coming," Zara answers eventually. She stares at her hands thoughtfully. "Mom couldn't get out of bed. My brother and his wife stayed with her. So, yes, *everyone* is here."

"OK." The tanned man nods. "OK. Then for those of you who just arrived, my name is Tobias. Tobias Hall."

He goes to stand in front of the TV and immediately starts pacing. It's clear he's trying to act with authority, but it's hard to take him seriously with that ridiculous tan.

"I'm a foreign services specialist at the US consulate in San Jose," he continues somberly. "I will be your police liaison and will work closely with Blush management to make sure the next few days go as smoothly as possible."

He nods to himself, looks down at his clipboard while fishing a pen from his pocket.

"I understand Daniela Munoz and her staff have been hard at work all day, turning away guests and out-of-town vendors, and rebooking their flights back home. We're hoping to keep the news quiet as long as poss—"

"How about we get to the point, *hah*?"

We all turn to face Mr. Joshi, whose words are quiet yet commanding.

"My son is dead." He looks blankly at his watch. "I have had this information for over six hours, yet no one has informed me *how* this happened." His eyes track the room. "Tell us. Now."

Tobias stutters for a moment, dropping the pen. Mr. Joshi isn't even angry with me—may well have forgot my name the moment he heard it—and even I'm shitting my pants.

"I understand. My apologies, Mr. Joshi," Tobias stammers. "I will share everything I've been told."

"Please," Mr. Joshi says crisply.

"Early this morning, between the hours of three thirty and five in the morning . . ." Tobias falters. "I . . . I'll just get right to it, then. I'm sorry to say that Raj Joshi and Radhika Singh were murdered."

Quite suddenly, I feel as if I'm going to be violently ill. Gasps fill the living room, and my eyes cross as I scan the floor around me for something to catch my sick.

"It can't be. *No*." Caleb's voice. "Are you sure?"

"We're certain."

Tobias's voice.

I close my eyes and press my hands over my mouth as I gag.

"They were found in Raj's villa, in the ground-floor bedroom. They were unclothed. In bed. They appeared to have been sleeping. Both of them sustained fatal gunshot wounds."

I swallow everything down, but that just makes me sicker. I feel like I'm on a boat, at the mercy of the ocean's swell. Up and down and side to side, the movements unpredictable and relentless. I just barely register the pressure of Caleb's hand on my knee. The cries of Mrs. Joshi and Zara somehow have the quality of a faraway sound carried in on the wind.

The nausea is all-consuming, and for several long moments, I let my head rest against my knees. Vaguely, I think I hear Tobias ask the room if everyone's ready to continue, but my mind won't stop spinning at the thought that Raj and Radhika didn't just die. This wasn't an accident, an overdose.

They were *murdered*.

"Tell me this wasn't . . ."

Mr. Joshi's voice. It pulls me out of my head, and slowly I sit up to look at him.

Mr. Joshi grimaces. "A murder-suicide?"

Tobias bites his lip. He speaks slowly.

"Based on the evidence at the crime scene, investigators are certain: they were shot by a third party."

"I'll kill him." Caleb stands up and starts pacing. "I'll *kill* him. Who was it? Surely the bastard was caught on tape—"

"That's unlikely, Caleb," Daniela answers robotically. "Part of the appeal of the Blush Villas is the privacy. There are no security cameras on this side of the resort. Our mission was to make our guests feel at home."

"Not a *single* camera?"

Daniela shakes her head gloomily. Caleb sinks back into the couch, muttering under his breath.

"Could it have been some sort of thief?" Mr. Joshi clears his throat before continuing on. "Has anything been stolen?"

Tobias glances at his clipboard. "So far, everything has been accounted for except Radhika's cell phone." He looks up. "Does anyone know where that might be?"

Sean looks at Caleb, who glances at Zara. She simply shrugs.

"Radhi had it on her last night."

Caleb nods in agreement. "She asked me to carry it for a while—her purse was too small. But I gave it back after an hour or so."

"Maybe she lost it while we were out," Zara suggests. "Maybe—"

Tobias waves her off. "I suggest we refrain from speculation. As soon as I receive more information from the police—"

"Don't interrupt me," Zara snaps, standing up. "What else are we supposed to do *but* speculate?" She turns to Caleb. "What the hell happened last night?"

"Nothing." Caleb starts then stops. Sean doesn't say a word.

Zara scans the room, looking at everyone, even me. "We went out with them. Me, Caleb, and Sean. This ridiculous club in Cabo San Lucas. Radhi wanted to go"—she looks to Caleb for confirmation—"and it's her wedding. So we had to. But we all came home together."

"We were back at the resort by one thirty or so?" Caleb furrows his brow, thinking. "One thirty. Yeah."

"Radhi got a little too drunk," Zara says, blushing. "I walked her back to her villa to make sure she did her skin-care routine. None of her products were at Raj's, and I didn't want her to break out this week.

"But I was wiped. After I dragged her to the bathroom and saw she at least took off her makeup," Zara continues, "I kissed her on the forehead, went back to my own villa, and that's the last time I saw—"

Zara sits down abruptly and gently weeps. Zara now incapacitated, Mr. Joshi presses palms to thighs and takes over.

"What about you boys?" He turns to Sean. "I didn't hear you come in last night, *beta*. Were there any strange goings-on that we should know about?"

Sean explains to the group how he's staying in this villa with his uncle and aunt, while Raj was next door and Caleb in the villa beyond that one.

"The three of us walked back here together," Sean says, his eyes darting in Caleb's direction. "But I went straight to sleep. It was a long day."

"Did you hear anything through the window?" Zara asks him, sniffing. "Maybe the gunshots?" When Sean shakes his head, Zara scoffs and says, "I thought you had insomnia."

Sean hesitates before answering.

"Usually, yes. But I slept surprisingly well last night."

Zara waits a long beat before dragging her eyes to Caleb. "What about *you*?"

"I crashed right away," Caleb answers quickly. "And like I told the police, I didn't hear anything overnight."

Caleb's voice is so confident, so convincing, I nearly miss it.

There's a condom in his trash.

He didn't "crash" right away. He slept with someone else. Which means he's *lying*.

"I might suggest again we refrain from further discussion for the time being," Tobias says, taking charge of the room. "Crime scene investigators believe the perpetrator had placed a suppressor—or 'silencer'—on the weapon, so it's unlikely anyone would have heard the gun go off.

"Regardless, police are conducting extensive interviews and exploring all lines of inquiry. They've been interviewing staff and guests and are checking security footage from the main resort."

He then glances at the terrace door, jaw tight. "Although, it's worth noting the perpetrator didn't necessarily trespass through hotel grounds. The police are looking at the possibility they used the stair access from the beach, which is directly behind Mr. Prescott's villa."

Tobias lets his words hang there, and, after a singular pause, he points to his clipboard and continues with his bureaucrat's agenda.

Death certificates. Documentation. Repatriation of the remains.

I tune out. I shouldn't be here.

Raj and Radhika have just been murdered, and I shouldn't fucking be here.

My eyes close as I imagine bolting out the front door, pushing past Brown Hulk Hogan, and retrieving my passport from Caleb's villa. Leaving everything else behind, I picture myself running through the lobby, high heels clacking, and hopping in a taxi to the airport. Going home—away from all of this, these sad, rich aliens—safe and sound on the next flight back to Los Angeles.

Do it.

A little voice in my head whispers, a shiver up my neck.

Shay. Run.

My feet twitch at the ready, but when the moment comes—that lull in the conversation, that spike of adrenaline rushing—I freeze. I feel Caleb next to me.

I should leave him, I should leave all of them, but I can't. I won't.

Not yet.

Haldi Ceremony

Rise and shine, sleepyheads!

This morning's event begins at sunrise next to the big waterfall in the Villas. A ceremony held to cleanse and purify the bride and groom ahead of their wedding, family and friends will rub a haldi (turmeric) paste all over our faces and bodies.

This promises to be a fun, messy ritual that will set the tone for the coming celebrations. Siblings in particular can really get into the tradition, competing over who can stain the bride and groom the most.

Who do you think is going to win? First up is Zara Singh, Radhika's big sister and confidante, to be followed by Raj's Co-Best Men and "brothers from other mothers": Sean Joshi and Caleb Malcolm Prescott III. Get your bets in—and butts out of bed—early if you want to partake in the fun.

A light breakfast and mimosas to follow the ceremony, and then the rest of the day is yours. Shop, swim, spa, or feel free to explore Los Cabos. Just don't forget to be back at Blush before dusk. We have something else special planned today that you're not going to want to miss.

Love,

RAJ & RADHIKA

Location: Los Cascadas Gardens,
the Blush Villas Los Cabos
Dress code: White, turmeric yellow, or gold

4.

It's surprisingly chilly tonight. I'm tempted to grab a sweatshirt from the bedroom, but Caleb's only just fallen asleep and I don't want to risk waking him. I stretch out in the hammock on the rooftop deck, smoking, trying to enjoy the quiet before what promises to be another chaotic day. Bright and early, Caleb and Zara are meeting Tobias at the morgue to identify the bodies, the families will discuss how and when to announce the news to the public, and, hopefully, the Mexican and US governments will clear the families to fly the remains back to California.

The remains.

I know they're dead—that all of this is real—but I still can't quite believe it. And *murder?* Without having to say it out loud, upon first hearing the news, I think we all assumed they died from an overdose. Raj "partied" quite a bit—a term, since moving to LA, I'd come to learn usually included the intake of cocaine, molly, ketamine, or god knows what other party drug. Being wealthy doesn't make you invincible; a few too many micrograms of fentanyl laced into a party favor will kill anyone.

But Raj and Radhika are not simply tragic victims of the opioid epidemic. They were shot in the head. But *why*? Was this some sort of random attack? A burglary gone wrong? I shake my head, my chest tight. That doesn't make sense. Tobias said the only thing missing is Radhika's phone.

I find myself flicking endlessly between my news apps, Instagram, and TikTok, but there's no information to be found about the deaths online. I wonder what excuse Daniela and her team told wedding guests as they turned them away, and how long the US consulate and Mexican authorities will be able to keep this under wraps. Raj and Radhika are the children of two of the wealthiest, most influential South Asian families in America, had some *famous* people on their guest list, and it's only a matter of time until word spreads. I may have lost my VIP access to the *shaadi* of the decade, but all too soon, I'm going to have front-row tickets to an international media circus.

Restless, I clamber out of the hammock and position myself at the eastern railing. Just beyond is what used to be Raj's villa. The crime scene. There are three police officers on watch tonight; one at the rear, stationed at the top of the beach stairs, and two out front. Their presence should comfort me, but it only makes me feel as if they're waiting for someone.

As if there's a reason to be afraid.

Raj's villa partially obscures the one beyond it, where Mr. Joshi, Mrs. Joshi, and Sean are staying. The ground-floor windows are dark, but there's a light on the second floor. Sean's, likely. He said he was an insomniac. But after what just happened, I can't imagine that anyone is sleeping soundly tonight.

My first cigarette blazes to an end, and I immediately light another. I must be in shock, because I'm smoking too much and my mind isn't functioning the way it usually does. There's so much that doesn't make sense, and I don't even know how to begin to process the information I do have.

First things first. Caleb slept with someone else.

I've seen the looks he gets when we're walking down the pier. When we're in a crowded bar or restaurant in West Hollywood. When a stranger recognizes his family name. Caleb Malcolm Prescott III can have any woman he wants, whenever he wants, but, like a fool, I'd assumed he wanted only me.

I walked into this relationship with my eyes wide open, and I shouldn't be surprised by his infidelity, but for some reason, I am. I can't reconcile this behavior with the Caleb who always finds time to call me between meetings "just to check in"; who surprises me with an Uber Eats order when I'm studying late at night; who makes plans for us weeks, even months into the future. The Caleb who wears his whole big heart on his sleeve.

I smoke at an alarming rate and promise myself I'll stop ruminating the second my cigarette burns out. After what I've done to Caleb, I don't have the right to feel hurt or care who he slept with. Besides. It's not the act of cheating that should be bothering me right now; it's the fact that he lied to the police about it.

My thoughts are on a runaway train to nowhere logical or productive. Lexie will still be asleep, and I might wind up dead too if I wake up her toddler. I'm debating calling her anyway when I hear footsteps to my left. Quick. Light. I hurriedly stub out my cigarette and move to the northern edge of the balcony. After a moment, a figure appears on the footpath, walking briskly or maybe jogging. I squint, trying to make out who it could be. As they slow down and then stop right in front of Caleb's villa, I realize it's Radhika's sister, Zara.

I first read about Zara Singh, CEO and cofounder of Lustre,

last summer in the *Los Angeles Journal*, which awarded her their much-coveted accolade *Entrepreneur of the Year*. Front page of the business section, the article profiled the woman at the helm of the Silicon Valley darling whose skincare products promised to stop, and then reverse, the processes of aging. Consumers have been promised antiaging remedies for centuries, but apparently, Lustre actually works. Not that I would know. It's prohibitively expensive for everyone but the ultra-rich.

Although it was Zara and Radhika's mother, Dr. Simran Singh, who actually developed the revolutionary patented formula, according to the article Zara was the one to recognize its potential. She dropped out of her MBA program to launch the company, and within two months had secured their first investor. One year in, Zara had venture capitalists falling over themselves to get in on the action. Now, a decade later, Lustre is a household name, and Zara is an A-list celebrity.

I watch Zara closely as she jogs farther up the path, her high ponytail swishing back and forth with each step. I clock her sneakers, leggings, and sports bra. Is she exercising right now? It's not even four thirty in the morning, and her sister was just murdered. In *this* resort. I don't know how she's functioning right now, let alone working out.

Zara comes to a stop just out of view of the police officers patrolling the crime scene, and, after a moment, retrieves her phone from her back pocket. From my vantage point on the roof, I can just make out her face from the glow of her screen. The pouty lips. The furrowed brow. I lean farther over the railing as I study her, wondering what she's doing here. What she's looking at on her phone right now.

What she saw last night.

According to the official timeline, Raj, Radhika, Zara, Sean, and Caleb all returned to Blush around 1:30 a.m. early Thursday morning. Zara and Radhika went off to their respective villas in the far eastern side of the community, while Raj, Sean, and Caleb came back this way.

They all say they went straight to sleep, but at some point during the night, Radhika wandered over here to Raj's abode. And then, between 3:30 and 5:00 a.m., someone killed them. But *why*? And who—

Suddenly, Zara whips her head in my direction, toward Caleb's villa. Toward me.

I flinch. Can she see me watching her?

Zara's head tilts upward, fractionally, until her face disappears from view and her phone lights up only her neck and jaw.

I wave. A beat passes, and then I wave again, but it must be too dark. Zara backpedals, slowly at first, and then, with one last look toward Raj's villa, disappears down the path from which she came.

* * *

I MANAGE TWO hours of sleep before Caleb wakes me up and begs me to come with him and Zara to the morgue. Nobody else in the Joshi or Singh families have the heart to view the bodies—but neither do I. I tell Caleb I'll come, but that I'm staying in the car.

While Zara and Caleb disappear into a nondescript building in San Jose, I doodle in the margins of my notepad until our driver slides open the glass partition and introduces himself.

"Are you on vacation at Blush Resort & Spa Los Cabos?" he asks me in Spanish, after introducing himself as Isaac. I'm reluctant to embarrass myself with my basic knowledge of the language, and so I simply tell him yes. *Si.*

"What do you think of your hotel?"

I form the sentence in my head carefully before responding.

"It's very nice," I reply in Spanish, slowly. "Very beautiful."

"My friend works for the police," he says next. "She said there was a disturbance yesterday?"

It takes a moment for the wheels to turn, to truly register what he's getting at.

This is how it starts. Rumors turn into questions. Questions persist, and eventually, they lead to answers. If Isaac, our limo driver, knows that a "disturbance" occurred yesterday at Blush, then everyone in the area must be talking about it. The US consulate and Mexican authorities will only be able to suppress the news for so long. Whether it's a local who puts two and two together, or one of Raj and Radhika's famous friends who make the news public, the truth is going to come out.

It always does.

I play dumb in front of Isaac and change the subject, ask him to tell me about the resort I'm staying at. He explains to me that its parent company, Blush Continental, is a major employer in Baja, including for two of his three children, and how the hotel group now has three resorts in the region: an adults-only party hotel in the town of Cabo San Lucas, or Cabo; a family-friendly establishment in San Jose; and their newest property, from which he picked me up this morning. Blush Resort & Spa Los Cabos is located on the Tourist Corridor, halfway between Cabo and San Jose, among twenty miles of oceanfront resorts, hotels, and vacation villas that stretch between the towns.

Isaac happily explains how "Los Cabos" is the municipality that includes both towns and the Tourist Corridor. Just as he's telling me how, confusingly, most tourists colloquially refer to the whole region as simply "Cabo" as well, the limo door flies open.

Zara and Caleb are back.

Zara shoots a long leg into the car and then stares at me harshly until I realize I'm in her seat and scooch down. I try to meet Caleb's eye as he clambers in after her. But he won't look at me. It's clear they've both been crying.

"Can you tell him to shut up?" Zara says loudly over Isaac, who's still chatting. "Do you speak Spanish or something?"

My stomach squirms at her tone. "Sort of. But—"

"Whatever, I'll do it." Zara taps on the glass. "Hello? *Hola?*"

Isaac turns around cheerfully. "*Sí?*"

"*Quieres* be quiet *por favor?*"

I cringe as Zara smiles condescendingly and reaches for her phone.

"No 'talky-talky,' all right? Just 'drivey-drivey.'"

What.

The.

Fuck.

My cheeks heat up with shame as I try and make eye contact with Isaac in his rearview mirror, but his eyes are now fixed on the pavement ahead as he steers us out of the parking lot.

One thing the *Los Angeles Journal* failed to state in their profile is that Zara, quite famously, is an elitist bitch. What I didn't know is that she's also a racist. My eyes dart to Caleb, hoping he'll call her out, but he doesn't. Should I?

I want to. But she just identified her sister's dead body. Is it wrong to give her a pass?

The journey back to Blush is painful. Quiet. Cars and trucks groan as they barrel past us on the highway—the ocean to our south, the desert to the north. Twice we pass military personnel and vehicles stationed on the roadside. Zara's nails click rhythmically as she types on her phone, her gaze laser focused on her screen, and every so often sighing in exasperation. Is she actually *working* right now?

I watch her face carefully, flabbergasted by her ability to compartmentalize, as if she merely squeezed "view dead sister's body" into her schedule between her morning run and workday. She brushes flyaway hairs off her cheeks, and there's something almost robotic about the way she moves. Something not quite human.

"May I help you?"

I jump as Zara's gaze flicks my way. My face goes red.

"Sorry," I mumble, embarrassed she caught me staring. "I zoned out."

"Oh." Zara softens. "Been there."

She smiles at me then, and I'm caught off guard by how genuine it feels. It's not the one she sneered at Isaac, the help; it's kind. It's the smile she reserves for friends.

"Do you have a sister?" she asks me. After I shake my head, Zara adds, "Radhi was . . . something, wasn't she?"

Something.

"Influencing is the most saturated, hypercompetitive market out there. I thought she was crazy for trying to make it on social." Zara's eyes well up. "But she did it. And I was so proud of her. I should have told her that more often."

Zara is on the precipice of breaking down. Even though I'm still fuming about her treatment of Isaac, I lean forward, offer her my hand, and plaster a smile on my face I only hope comes across as genuine.

"Is there anything I can do?"

Zara laughs, almost cruelly. "Do you know you're the first

person who's asked me that?" She squeezes my hand once before pushing it away. "If I could delegate to you the task of holding the Singh family together, trust me, I would."

She runs her hands through her hair as tears suddenly fill her eyes. Suddenly, I feel bad for judging her for working and exercising today. She's in mourning; she's compartmentalizing because she has to.

"Do you know they were shot in the head?" Zara sobs.

I didn't. I feel Caleb shift beside me as I struggle to push the image from my brain.

"And at close range—"

"Stop it, Zara," Caleb interrupts harshly.

"You stop it." She whips toward Caleb, eyes red. "You heard what the examiner said. They were shot in the side of the head, one after the other. Just like—"

"Don't say it," Caleb warns, his tone menacing. I haven't heard him speak to anyone like that before.

"Don't say what?" I breathe.

Caleb shakes his head, his gaze fixed on the floor of the car.

"I won't say it," Zara continues after a moment. "I won't. But look at the facts, Caleb. And we're in *Mexico* for Christ's sake . . ."

A pit forms in my stomach as Zara's words register, and I realize what she's trying to get at: Raj and Radhika were shot in the head at close range, execution style. They were murdered in Mexico, ground zero for the American War on Drugs, the epicenter of narco-trafficking and violence.

She's saying Raj and Radhika might have been murdered by a drug cartel.

5.

You have a beautiful house."

Raj looked up from his phone just long enough for Shay to know that he heard her. When he didn't answer, she pulled nervously at the bottom of her denim skirt. She didn't know how to behave around him, or where to put her hands, or even what to talk about.

You have a beautiful house.

What a stupid thing to say, on more than one level.

It wasn't really Raj's house; it belonged to Mr. and Mrs. Joshi. And it wasn't just a house either. It was a forty-million-dollar Bel Air estate.

Shay had read all about it in an architectural and design magazine she found online. The "Avalon," which the Joshi family had purchased upon their arrival in the US three decades ago, had two kitchens, four bars, twelve bedrooms, sixteen bathrooms, seven living rooms, and three dining areas. That was just the indoors. Outside were two swimming pools, a tennis court, a sports/gym complex, and a temperature-controlled cellar, as well as a five-thousand-square-foot guest house.

Shay desperately wanted a tour, but nobody had offered her one. She hovered awkwardly next to the twenty-four-seater modular white couch on which Raj, Caleb, and Radhika sat idly on their phones, texting, scrolling, and posting. Waiting for the guests to arrive and tonight's party to start. Shay thought about joining them but stopped herself from sitting when she realized her skirt would ride up. It was short and exposed more leg than she was used to showing off.

"Are your parents home?" Shay asked Raj, trying again. Trying to make conversation. "I'd love to pay my respects."

"They're in Mumbai for the week," Radhika answered on his behalf. She sighed and tossed her sparkly diamond phone to the side with a huff. "Sorry, boys. I promise I'm done now. I was legally obligated to post that before midnight."

She eyed Shay and smiled broadly, as if just realizing Shay was here.

"Don't *you* look nice."

Shay squirmed under the spotlight, fairly confident that Radhika was making fun of her. She'd been told Raj was having a party, so she'd dressed up more than usual.

"Thanks." Shay smiled back at her.

"You have great skin. Do you use Lustre?"

Shay shook her head. She couldn't afford it.

"Zara's not coming tonight, is she?" Raj asked Radhika without looking up.

"No. She's busy." Radhika diverted her attention back to Shay. "So did you have the jackfruit tacos or those cauliflower ones for lunch?"

Shay tensed. "Pardon?"

"Caleb took you to my favorite taco truck on Melrose," Radhika explained impatiently. "You're a vegan like Caleb, right? So did you have the jackfruit or the cauliflower?"

"Oh." Shay cleared her throat. "Right. I got the jackfruit. They were great."

"You took your yoga teacher there too, didn't you, Caleb?" Her eyes still on Shay, Radhika raised a bare calf and toed Caleb on the shin. "Or was it the checkout girl from Whole Foods? Or that coworker you—"

"Radhi, can you not?" Caleb said evenly. His ears burned red as he set down his phone, and Shay tightened her lips into a casual smile. She sensed Radhika was testing her, and the best way to pass was to keep her mouth shut.

Radhika stared at Shay another beat, unblinking.

"Can I not what? I'm just trying to get to know the girl you're bringing to *my* wedding—"

"Radhi, what the *hell*!"

Shay's stomach lurched as Caleb sprang upright from the couch and the rest of his face went as scarlet as his ears. He threw Shay a pleading look, one that told her Radhika was telling the truth: Caleb was inviting her to the wedding.

Holy shit. Caleb was inviting her to *the* wedding.

"My bad," Radhika purred. "Have you not asked her yet?"

"No, I haven't asked her yet," Caleb spat. "God, you can be so immature sometimes."

Caleb sidled up to Shay and wrapped an arm around her waist, and even though she was majorly freaking out inside, she did her best to appear calm. Shay smiled back at Radhika and shrugged.

"That's very generous of you to offer Caleb a plus one," Shay said, overwhelmed by the idea of attending. "Are you sure? I remember you saying the guest list for the Cabo wedding only included immediate family and close friends."

Radhika waved her off playfully. "Plans changed. My sister is forcing me to invite a few 'key' investors. So if those old fogeys are coming, then *you* might as well tag along too."

Caleb saved Shay from further abuse by taking her aside and making her a cocktail. As Raj and Radhika whispered about something—probably Shay—Caleb squeezed her hand behind the bar, an apology for which he seemingly couldn't find the words. This wasn't the first time she'd seen Caleb react to one of Radhika's childish ploys. Last week at dinner, she caught him rolling his eyes when Radhika kept going on, and *on*, about the conversion and click-through rates on her latest sponsored post. And just two days ago, Caleb had FaceTimed Shay from his bedroom, livid, because Radhika had turned up uninvited to watch the Clippers game. Caleb had thought only Raj was coming over; he was hoping for a boys' night.

Their group dynamic was further complicated by the fact that Raj full-on ignored Shay, always speaking around her, through her, as if she were a piece of furniture or a paid staff member. Raj was, for all intents and purposes, a douchebag, and Shay thought he played the part of the only child to a preeminent billionaire beautifully. The clothes. The confidence. The charisma. He held court in every room he deigned to enter, surveying with mild disinterest, always making it perfectly clear he had somewhere better to be, with somebody more worth his precious time.

Shay found it odd Raj had approved of the idea of extending Shay a wedding invite; she wouldn't have been surprised if he didn't even know her name.

* * *

A SHORT TIME later, Raj and Caleb's coworkers at the Joshi Group's LA office started to turn up. It was their PR director's going-away party; after ten years, she was reluctantly leaving them for an international gig with a cruise line.

Shay wasn't sure what she should have expected attending a work function at a billionaire's house. Champagne and fancy hors d'oeuvres. Servers in penguinlike attire. Celebrity sightings. In reality, it was just a grossly extravagant house party. A living room that comfortably sat fifty, rather than five. A sound system that made you feel as if the music was playing inside you. Premium liquor. And enough cocaine to fuel Elon Musk's alleged mission to Mars.

Caleb could sense her discomfort, and when Shay finally owned up to it, he offered to refrain from partaking that evening. He even volunteered to take her home. But Caleb had only joined the Joshi Group a few months ago and had been looking forward to socializing with his new colleagues. And so she lied and told Caleb she didn't mind being around drug use, and for him to go ahead and enjoy himself.

Truthfully, Shay had a major problem with drugs and abstained for moral reasons more so than health or legal concerns. During a module on globalization and illicit trade, a passionate professor had woken her up to the amount of violence, murder, human rights abuses, and environmental and social harms it would have taken to get these privileged partygoers their party drug tonight. In the decade since she took that class, the consequences and evils of the drug trade had only worsened; she'd read in the news that many cartels now dabbled in methamphetamines, fentanyl, and other dangerous synthetics.

Shay did her best to laugh, and drink, and blend in with the crowd, but it didn't take long for her window of tolerance to slide closed. People on drugs were so loud. So *obnoxious*. So fucking oblivious. Having given up her attempt at modesty, Shay found herself becoming increasingly nauseated squeezed into the modular sofa next to Caleb, who was both caressing her bare thigh and screaming his other neighbor's ear off about capital markets. On Shay's other side was Raj, sloppily bragging to anyone within earshot about how he was "running point" on a confidential deal in the Americas for his father, that he was the one responsible for its success and his father should give him more credit. When Raj stood up on the couch and began to holler like a Neanderthal, Shay politely excused herself and slipped out of the room.

As soon as she entered the corridor, she felt like she could breathe again. Raj and Caleb's friends and coworkers were exhausting; it required Shay to code switch into a character she didn't even recognize. Leaving the muffled sounds of the party behind her, she walked down a long hallway leading toward the central part of the mansion and, treading lightly, navigated her way back to the dimly lit front foyer.

It was like being in a museum, a grand intersection of staircases, passageways, and halls, and Shay tried not to gawk as she stood at its center and pivoted on her heels, staring, *thinking*—

"Are you lost?" someone said.

She stumbled backward, hitting a marble pillar as her heart fell into her stomach. The lights were off and she blinked, looking for the person behind the voice, which was deep and slightly accented. After a long moment, the chandelier lights switched on, and she noticed a man sitting on a plush bench near the front doors. Her heart started to race.

It was Raj's cousin, Sean.

"You scared me," Shay stammered, grasping for words.

"I scared you in my own home." Sean's nose crinkled in amusement as he toed off his brown leather oxfords. "Funny, that."

"Sorry." Shay blushed. "I'm just looking for the restroom."

He regarded her as he loosened his tie, still seated.

"It's Sean, right?"

He nodded.

"I didn't realize you lived here."

Shay shook her head at the misstep, the presumption. As a key member of the Joshi Group empire, Sean's personal information was all over the internet. Shay knew he was thirty-eight, born and raised in Mumbai, and the only child of Mr. Joshi's elder brother, Jackie Joshi; Sean's parents died in a tragic car accident when Sean was sixteen, after which he was adopted by his uncle and brought over to live with him in LA.

What was the protocol for meeting celebrities and powerful figures? Was she supposed to play dumb about how much she already knew?

Because Shay knew a lot about Sean. She knew he studied at Cambridge, then the London School of Economics, and was now VP Operations at the Joshi Group in LA. She knew he co-headed that office with Raj, and that he was, technically, Caleb's boss. Shay even knew all about Sean's previous boyfriends; he was an attractive man, and during his five-year stint in the UK, British tabloids had him linked to a London stage actor, a Manchester United soccer player, and even a junior member of the royal family.

"I forgot about the work do." Sean gestured through the windows, at the many expensive cars in the driveway. "You're not one of our interns, are you?"

Shay shook her head.

"Then you're a friend of Raj's," he finished.

"My name's Shay," she answered, choosing not to clarify. "Shay-lee Kapoor."

"Kapoor! You're a Punjabi," Sean mused. "Do you speak the language, or, like my cousin, have you forgotten everything about our Mother India?"

"I know enough to get by," Shay said, on her guard, wondering why someone like Sean was being pleasant to her. "But I'm more confident in Hindi and Bengali."

"Bengali too?" His eyes widened. "Are you a linguist?"

She shook her head. "I used to work in India and Bangladesh."

Sean crossed his arms, as if impressed. "What kind of work?"

Vaguely, Shay explained how she used to work at various charities and international organizations, particularly with children.

"They're the ones who taught me to speak the languages. Honestly, I think I learned more from them than they did from—"

She stopped midsentence, cringing.

"God, that sounded corny. Sorry."

"The world can be a dark place. We could all use a little corny." Sean pulled his tie loose from his neck, smiling. "Do you miss the subcontinent?"

"Yes and no." Shay shrugged. "They're complicated countries."

"Extremely."

"It's a land full of extremes," Shay remarked, remembering monsoon season. "Like its climate."

"Its cultural diversity," added Sean.

"The extreme gap between the rich and poor—"

Shay bit her lip. Shit. That was another stupid thing to say, especially to a Joshi. But unexpectedly, he didn't become defensive or annoyed; nodding his agreement, he stood up and said it was the responsibility of companies like his own to do something about that.

"Truthfully, there's more I could be doing," Sean said, stuffing his hands into his pockets. "But there's only so much impact I can have on our corporate social responsibility strategy living here in LA. My uncle exclusively handles the business at our Mumbai headquarters. I haven't even been back to India since . . ."

Sean trailed off, his face paling slightly. Shay immediately felt terrible.

"I read about your parents," she blurted. "I'm so sorry."

"Hasn't everyone," Sean said tiredly. "But thank you. Most people are too afraid to mention them to me."

Their eyes locked, and Shay couldn't be sure, but she sensed a moment of tenderness pass between them. Like meeting like. It was the most genuine conversation she'd had all night, and despite her better judgment, Shay found herself warming to him. She hadn't expected to like any of the Joshis.

"I should let you go to bed," she said after she caught Sean yawning. "It's late—and a Wednesday."

They shared another smile as a high-pitched squeal erupted from the party.

"Unless you're planning to make an appearance?"

"It's never late when you're an insomniac." Sean checked his watch and nodded. "Sure. Why not. But I need a moment to decompress before I face that lot. They're not really my vibe."

Shay understood. They weren't Shay's vibe either. She backpedaled, ready to give him space, but then Sean gestured for her to follow him into the kitchen.

As they picked at cold leftovers and chatted at the island,

Shay nearly forgot she was sitting next to *the* Sean Joshi. She found him to be endearingly normal. Cultured, although not a snob. Intelligent, but not arrogant. Warmhearted, yet practical. How he and Raj were in the same family Shay had no idea.

"Can I ask you something personal?" Shay said after they'd bonded over their shared distaste for okra *subji* and love for *bhaingan bhartha*, both of which Mrs. Joshi had left plenty of in the fridge.

"Shoot," Sean said, spooning another helping into his bowl. "I'm an open book."

"You're a billionaire, right?"

Sean choked on a laugh, turning to Shay. She simply shrugged.

"I think you already know the answer." Sean smiled.

Shay didn't know the answer, actually. Mr. Joshi was a billionaire, but his son and nephew didn't necessarily fall into that bracket.

"Do you have a point to your personal question?" Sean mused.

Shay reached over him to grab a cold *naan*. "I'm just curious why you and Raj still live at home. You could live *literally* anywhere."

"Raj doesn't live here full-time. He's often at Radhi's and has a beautiful house in Santa Monica, but he bores easily and tends to come home when he needs the company or to throw parties." Sean paused. "And I . . . well. Shay, I'm Indian."

"Shut your mouth," Shay deadpanned, which made Sean laugh again.

"What I mean is I'm *traditional*. My uncle and aunt are my parents now. I owe them everything. I plan to be here as they get older and need care and companionship. If I settle down with a partner, *if* being the operative word, he would have to move in here with us too. My uncle and aunt have never treated me like a nephew, or even an adopted son. They treat me as their own. And I will always do the same for them."

Shay offered a timid smile, both in awe and embarrassment. Shay was Indian too, and not once had it crossed her mind what would happen when her parents got older and needed care.

"Besides," Sean continued, "this place is huge, *yaar*. I could sleep in a different bedroom every day of the week."

Shay grinned. "And do you? *Yaar*?"

"Should I?"

"Why not? I hear Caleb even has his own bedroom here . . ."

She trailed off as Sean's face changed. As something seemed to flash—and then darken rapidly—right before him.

"Who told you that?" Sean said warily. He set down his fork and stared at it. "Raj?"

"Yeah." Shay hesitated. "Caleb too."

Slowly, Sean rotated his chin to look at her. Blinking, he asked, "And how did you say you know them?"

This felt like a quiz. A trick multiple-choice question. An answer that would either be right or wrong.

"I'm dating Caleb," Shay said finally. "We've been going out for a month."

"I see."

Immediately, Shay knew that wasn't the answer he wanted to hear. Sean's mouth twitched, a movement that seemed to signal anger, bemusement, or maybe both. Leaving his dishes on the counter, Sean pulled himself up from the stool and sighed.

"I wish you the best luck with that, Shay," Sean said, his words dripping in sarcasm. His friendly demeanor vanishing before her eyes. "I'm off to bed. Do enjoy the party."

6.

Back at Blush, there's a media van trying to get into the property. Its driver is arguing with the gate attendant, holding up traffic. Eventually, an impatient security guard waves us around the van and ushers us through the gate. I'd bet a lot of money I don't have that the media van is here hoping to confirm the rumor of the "disturbance."

Inside the resort, it's almost disturbing to find everything business as usual. Guests waft through the lobby in fashionable swim coverups, elegant and day drunk. Management in navy suits and their staff in crisp beige or white uniforms walk briskly and with purpose, attending to guests' whims and whimsies with the happiest of smiles. There appears to be no extra security, no police activity, no enterprising journalists sneaking their way inside. Tobias mentioned that police and forensic investigators have been using a side road to get to and from the crime scene, that Blush is limiting their presence to the Villas. They say it's to "maintain the integrity of the investigation," but

I'm betting Blush doesn't want their other guests to find out there's a murderer on the loose.

It's only a matter of time. There's a media van outside, rumors swirling among the locals, and, the last time I checked Radhika's profile, dozens of her followers have commented on her latest post, asking questions.

Where are you, Radhika?

I thought you were getting married this week.

Why have you gone silent?

The answers to their questions are coming. Soon.

Back in our villa, Caleb disappears into the bathroom long enough for me to start to worry. But eventually he comes out, and then he stretches out on the bed and closes his eyes. I should sleep too. I'm exhausted. But I know that if I go lie down my head will spin harder than it already is. Instead, I pick at an elaborate cheese and fruit tray someone left for us in the kitchen and wait for him to fall asleep. I need to talk to Lexie. I still haven't had the space to call her, but I can feel things taking a turn from bad to worse and I need her advice. I need to download my brain. I need some perspective on—

"Shay?" Caleb calls out suddenly while I'm nibbling on a tropical fruit I've never seen before.

Dammit. He's still awake. There goes my chance to call Lexie.

I'm hungry so I bring the fruit and cheese tray with me, set it on the bedside table, and then slide in next to him. He hugs me tight and then turns around to be the little spoon. I can feel his chest rise and fall, rise and fall, and as I match his breath with my own, I realize that the bed is made. My eyes dart around the room. The whole villa is spotless.

Yesterday, the police barred housekeeping staff from the

Villas, but while we were out this morning, someone must have come through. I raise my neck until I catch sight of the garbage bin through the en suite door. It's empty; they took the condom, and all evidence of Caleb's affair, out with the trash.

"I don't deserve you," Caleb whispers into the pillow. "Do you know that?"

He rolls over to face me. In some parallel universe, it would have been all too easy to forget about Caleb's little transgression and continue burying my head in the sand. He says heartfelt, romantic things like "I don't deserve you." He's affectionate and attentive. Despite my better judgment, he makes me feel good.

But Caleb lied point-blank about his whereabouts the night of the murders, and I can't ignore how unsettling that is. I stare at the back of his neck, freckled and flushed pink from the sun, and ask myself why he would risk the consequences of covering up his affair from the police. It's a bad look not to be one thousand percent honest in a murder investigation. Was it only so I wouldn't find out he cheated? Or is there another reason why Caleb doesn't want anyone to know?

"I wouldn't blame you if you went back to LA," he says next. "This is a lot. I'm asking too much of you."

I massage the length of his forearm. "Do you want me to go?"

Caleb's nonresponse is his answer.

"Then I'm staying," I say, not realizing the implications of my words until the words are already out. "What do you need?"

"I need this." He cozies into me and sighs. "You know, Zara is such a bitch, so I never thought I'd say this, but I kind of feel bad for her. I can't believe her family is leaving her to handle Radhi's death alone."

His body tenses. A beat later, he adds, "You don't think she's right. Do you?"

"That Raj and Radhika were killed by a drug cartel?" I say mildly. "Of course I don't. Zara's grieving. She's looking for someone to blame."

"But those kinds of accusations are dangerous."

I smile. "They're not dangerous. They're absurd."

He gives me a look.

"This isn't *Breaking Bad*, Caleb. Or some problematic Hollywood action movie—"

"But they're dead. Someone shot them in the head." Caleb eyes me, his bottom lip wobbling. "If it wasn't the drug cartels who killed them, then who did?"

"I really don't know," I say calmly. "But the police are here. And they're going to figure out what happened."

Caleb scoffs as he flattens himself against the pillow. I can tell he wants me to pull his next thought out of him, and so I lightly run my fingers up and down his forearm until he speaks.

"I think Sean's lying to the police."

Like you're lying, Caleb?

"Ever since his parents died, Sean hasn't been able to sleep through the night. Sometimes, he doesn't sleep at all—Raj told me." Caleb scrunches his nose. "Yet on the night Raj and Radhi get killed *next door*, he 'slept surprisingly well'? Seems a little convenient if you ask me."

I chew my lip, unsure how to respond. It does seem convenient, but then again, I need to take Caleb's accusations against Sean with a grain of salt. Sean ghosted me the moment he found out I was Caleb's girlfriend. And the morning after the party, when I told Caleb how much I'd enjoyed hanging out with Sean . . .

Caleb shut the conversation down. He didn't want to talk about Sean either.

I don't know why they dislike each other. They were both close to Raj; maybe they're territorial. Or perhaps it's some disagreement at work. Whatever it is, I'm guessing it's big. Yesterday during the family meeting, Caleb and Sean didn't say two words to each other. Someone they both cared for deeply had just died, and they'd acted as if the other person didn't exist.

I think about asking Caleb if my hunch is correct, that he and Sean despise one another, but then I see something over Caleb's shoulder that gives me pause.

My computer.

"Did you move it?" I breathe, scrambling to get up.

Caleb slowly sits up next to me, eyes half closed, as I throw my legs over the side of the bed and point to the writing desk beneath the far window.

My laptop is out.

"I left it in my backpack." I walk toward the desk.

"Are you sure? I didn't move it."

I don't answer Caleb as I sit down at the desk. I enter my password and then quickly look through all the tabs I have open and my search history. As far as I can remember, it's exactly the way I left it last night.

"Do you think someone was in here?" I ask over my shoulder.

"Maybe the maid riffled through your bag," Caleb suggests. "The room's been cleaned since we left."

I click through my emails and recently downloaded documents. My password is a random combination of letters and numbers and would be difficult for anyone to guess. But if someone had gotten access . . .

"Are *you* missing anything?" I ask Caleb. "Maybe we got robbed."

"Wallet's in my pocket. Everything else is in the safe."

"I didn't know there was a safe."

"It's upstairs in the wellness room."

Nodding, I stand up and search my backpack and suitcase, but nothing else seems to have been tampered with. Next, I grab my crossbody bag, which I always keep on my person, and dump its contents onto the bed to take inventory.

"Missing anything?" Caleb asks, watching me.

Passport. Check. ID and credit cards. Check. Notepad and pen. Check.

"No." I shake my head. I haven't been robbed—everything's accounted for—but then why is my laptop out? Something that important I would never leave out in the open.

"You said there's a safe upstairs," I remind him. "Can I put my computer in it?"

He waits a beat before answering.

"It's full of my stuff."

"You don't have room for one—"

"No, I don't." Caleb sounds irritated, even though he's smiling at me with his eyes closed. "No one cares about a grad student's laptop."

"But—"

"You're freaking out for no reason, babe. Chill out, OK? It was just the maid."

Caleb pulls me back down on the bed. He wraps his arms around me and, suddenly craving the comfort of a warm body, I let him.

He must be right. I'm tired and pointlessly freaking out.

The housekeeper must have moved my computer. Who else could it have been?

7.

Y ou don't need to worry about getting food poisoning in a place like this."

Caleb ignores me as he rudely flags down our waiter. We've been at Blush's Oceanside Bistro for less than ten minutes, and I already regret having dragged him out for a meal. He's about to put in his third complaint since we arrived. The first was because there was a single crumb on our tablecloth when we sat down. The second: the bistro didn't have Caleb's preferred brand of sparkling bottled water.

Embarrassed, I keep my head down as Caleb reams out our waiter for failing to warn us the appetizers were raw and served cold, and condescends to him about the perils of E. coli and other waterborne illnesses. His behavior is cringeworthy, made worse by the fact that I'm hangry and haven't smoked a cigarette in four hours. I don't want to be here right now. I don't want to be around *this* Caleb.

You see, there are two versions of him. There's the gentleman who figured out my birthday and surprised me with a weekend getaway in Santa Barbara; who works hard and plays harder, but always prioritizes me and never plays games; who shows me his vulnerability, opens up to me about the fact he no longer speaks with his parents, about the distance he's put between himself and his clusterfuck of a family.

When he's that Caleb, it's easy to forget he was still raised to be a Prescott, belongs to a family that has owned large swaths of the East Coast since before the Civil War. *That* Caleb attended an elite boarding school, sometimes treats people he deems beneath himself like dirt, and can be just as big of a douchebag party bro as his best friend, Raj.

I've done a pretty good job avoiding that version of him the past few months, but unfortunately, he's sitting across from me right now.

"This is a nice place," I say, gritting my teeth. The waiter's come and gone, exchanged our appetizer for something more "acceptable," and still Caleb won't stop moaning. "We're not going to get food poisoning."

"If it was a nice place, then they would hire competent staff," Caleb snips. He retrieves a bottle from his left pocket, shakes a pill into his palm, and swallows it. He must have a headache, and before I can ask for one too, he adds, "And you can't be too careful in the third world."

Third world.

I physically bite my tongue to keep from snapping at him, and then take a sip of my water with ice cubes. Caleb stares at me accusingly; he'd refused ice cubes, even though the waiter ensured us they were made with filtered water. I let a cube fall into the back of my mouth and crunch purposefully on the ice.

"You want a real drink?" he asks me. "Should we order a bottle of wine?"

It's not yet noon. I'm tempted.

"Would you like to?"

"Sure." Caleb's face falls. "Actually, no."

"No?"

"I'd feel too guilty. Like . . ."

I feel myself softening as his eyes go moist.

"You're enjoying yourself without them?"

"Yeah." He laughs sadly. "Something like that."

I reach for his hand. With the flip of a switch, the other Caleb is back, and suddenly, both our moods slot back into place. When Lexie asked me to paint her a word picture, I described Caleb as that stereotypically hot guy in college who dumbs himself down and often acts like a shithead, but who everyone seems to love anyway. He's a manbaby in one breath, a fuckboy in the next, and a beat later, he's charming his way into your heart.

Because he does have a heart. A big one. Caleb smiles at me as a tear rolls down his cheek, and yet again, the condom in the trash flashes to mind and—

No.

I push away the image, breathe through the pang in my chest.

Betrayal goes both ways. He may have had sex with someone else, but I by far am the guiltier party.

When our food arrives, Caleb doesn't find a single thing to complain about, and, considering he hasn't eaten more than a piece of mango in twenty-four hours, I'm pleased he actually eats. Our meal is by far the best vegan tapas I've ever tasted. Garlic mushrooms and asparagus, white bean stew, *patatas bravas, pimientos de padrón, berenjenas con miel,* and a lot of various nuts and breads. I can tell Caleb's still thinking about Raj and Radhika, and so we eat our meal in silence and stare at the ocean.

We have one of the best tables at the restaurant, a beachside view, and as I watch lovers, friends, and families stroll along the sand, I feel my phone buzz.

It's Lexie.

I shovel another forkful of heaven into my mouth, mumble an excuse to Caleb, and answer the call on the fifth ring.

"Shay," she yells immediately, loudly enough I wince. "What in god's name is going on?"

"You heard," I whisper, speed walking away from the table. How did she hear already?

"*Yeah*, I did. What the fuck happened?"

My eyes on Caleb across the restaurant, as quickly as I can, I fill Lexie in. She's silent right up until the end.

"You're joking," she breathes. "They were *shot*? With a *gun*?"

"Crazy, right?" I pause, lowering my voice to a whisper as I furtively search the restaurant. "Zara wonders if it could have been a drug cartel—"

Lexie goes off on me then. I get a lecture for not calling her the minute it happened. And then another one for refusing to bail on Caleb and staying at the resort. It's too dangerous, she keeps saying. This isn't my family. They aren't even my friends.

I need to come home.

"This wasn't a drug cartel hit," I hiss at Lexie, hoping the table nearby can't hear me. "That would be nuts."

"What's *nuts* is two people are dead," Lexie cries. "You gotta get out of there. Especially before . . ."

Lexie sighs.

"Two of Radhika's influencer friends just posted about their deaths," she says somberly. "That's how I found out. This is going to be front-page news by the morning, Shay."

I tell Lexie to wait a moment as I shove in my AirPods and

open up Instagram. Within seconds, I find the posts, both of which went live in the last twenty minutes. The first is by a lifestyle influencer I met briefly at the bachelorette party, who put up selfies of her and Radhika together, with a slightly hysterical caption about how much she loved and will miss her friend. The second is a fitness influencer who posted a photo of herself looking blankly out a window, geotagged to the airport in San Jose. The caption paints herself as the center of the narrative, how much she'd been looking forward to Raj and Radhika's wedding, how tragic it is that their "beautiful love" was cut short by fate. She uses only one hashtag: #RIP.

"Are you reading them?" Lexie says, breathing heavily into my ears. "They don't seem to know they were murdered."

"No one knows." I pause. "Yet."

I glance back at Caleb across the restaurant. He's still staring blankly at the ocean.

"I'm worried about you," Lexie says after a moment.

"And I'm worried about Caleb."

I tell Lexie about his fragile emotional state, how he needed my support during the family meeting and the trip to the morgue. Lexie scoffs.

"Be careful, Shay. You're getting invested in the guy—"

"I am *not*," I say quickly. "But his friends just died, all right? What kind of person leaves at a time like this?"

Lexie coughs in a very irritating way. Abandoning Caleb right now wouldn't be the worst thing I've done to him, and we both know it.

"Apparently the bodies will be released soon," I say. "Maybe even today. I'll fly back with Caleb and the others."

Lexie stays quiet. She knows I've made up my mind.

"Whatever's going on here, I'm safe," I insist. "Last night, there were two police officers stationed next door. Besides, Caleb and the families are still here."

"But, what if the murderer is someone in the families, huh? What if it's . . ."

She trails off and lets the meaning hang there.

"Caleb's not involved," I say coolly. "He's a mess. There's no way."

I crack my neck and pad two steps back toward the restaurant. I'm done with this phone call. Caleb isn't perfect, but he's not a murderer.

"Look, we're in the middle of lunch. I should go."

"But—"

"I know," I interrupt, unwilling to have that conversation with Caleb fifty feet away. "We have lots to talk about, but not now. I'll call you as soon as I can."

I hang up and return to our table, unable to put my finger on what's bothering me. Caleb's finished all the small plates, but that's OK, because I'm not hungry anymore. I pretend to be invested in his decision on dessert, but my mind is elsewhere. It's nearly one, and the restaurant has filled up. A middle-aged white couple, sunburned to a crisp, is now seated next to us. I smile politely when I catch the woman staring at me.

"Crème brûlée?" Caleb asks, listing items from the menu. "Made with cashew milk."

I flick my eyes back at the red blobs in my peripheral vision. The woman is still gawking my way.

"Sure."

"Or how about the gelato?"

The woman, still staring, is now pointing me out to her

husband. I slide down in my chair and lower my voice. "What-ever you want."

Caleb senses my agitation. He cocks his head to the side, his face changing when he spots the woman weirding me out.

"May we help you?" he asks her politely.

Her eyes bulge as she smiles over at us.

"Oh. Hello!" She has a friendly country lilt. "I was just tell-ing hubby here that I remember seeing your girlfriend out the other night. Small world, huh? That we're seated next to each other at lunch too?"

"Excuse me?" I stammer. "I don't know what you mean."

"I'm not a stalker, honey. I just remember you, is all." She smacks her husband on the arm. "Two nights ago we were out in Cabo San Lucas for dinner. I saw you walking around."

"I'm sorry," I say, trying to keep my voice level. "That wasn't me."

"Nuh-uh. It was you." Again, she looks to her husband for confirmation, but he seems more interested in his piña colada. "Two nights ago. It was Wednesday, wasn't it? I remember, I do. You were wearing this black-and-white polka-dot dress. I re-member it because my son's little girlfriend has the same one. It's cute. For Old Navy."

My hands are clenched on my thighs, so tight I can feel my fingernails deep in my palms. I look to Caleb, who I can tell is thinking the same thing as me: Wednesday night—and early Thursday morning—was the night Raj and Radhika were mur-dered.

"You don't have a polka-dot dress?" The woman won't stop. "Think now, it was maybe eleven or so—"

"She was still in LA Wednesday night," Caleb snaps suddenly. "All South Asians look the same to you, huh?"

The woman's face goes scarlet as Caleb stands up from the table and yanks me with him.

"It wasn't her," he spits. "Now go bother someone else."

* * *

WE'RE ON OUR terrace behind the villa drinking coffee, passing time, staring at our respective phones. I told Caleb about the posts by Radhika's influencer friends, and, in the last few hours, seven more of her friends have shared news of the tragedy. #RajikhaWedding has been repurposed to spread word of a vigil.

"I'm going to have a dip," Caleb announces, sliding the patio door closed. I'd been so engrossed with monitoring Radhika's social media that I didn't notice him disappearing into the villa. With a half smile, he saunters up to me, plants a kiss on the top of my head, and perches on the end of my deck chair. Even though we've barely spoken, he seems more like himself the last few hours. Caleb suffers from bouts of white guilt, and I can tell he enjoyed playing the trump card on that woman from the restaurant; it seems to have temporarily dulled his pain.

I shade my eyes with my hand as I watch Caleb roll out his shoulders, preparing to dive into the pool. He's shirtless, and his tiny swimming shorts ride up his thighs.

"Do you want to join me?" His voice is a touch suggestive. Yep. He's definitely feeling a little better.

"Sure." I smile. "That would be nice."

A gust of wind blows up from the beach. Shivering, I stand up and start backpedaling toward the villa.

"I need to put on my bathing suit," I say, avoiding his gaze. "You go ahead. I'm right behind you."

From the bedroom window, I watch Caleb slide into the pool. When he dives deep and doesn't reappear, I squat down in front of my suitcase.

I retrieve my laptop from where I stashed it in my undergarments bag. Tied the knot in a careful bow, one so precise I'd know if it had been tampered with. I sigh in relief when I find the bow tied exactly how I left it. I set it to the side and then dig through my clothing.

My hands are shaking, even though I smoked a cigarette ten minutes ago. I rub my fingers along the edges of the fabric as I carefully set each garment aside. My new black bikini. The glittery *sari* I'd planned to wear to the Mehndi Party. The turmeric-color *bandhani lehenga* I borrowed for the Haldi.

Next, I pull out my Old Navy polka-dot dress.

I ball it up tight and then search the villa for a place to hide it.

Sangeet

The Sangeet is all about bringing family and friends together before the wedding to enjoy great music, dance, and make merry. So that's exactly what we're going to do!

Tonight's program will feature some of the world's best classical Indian musicians, *kathak* dancers, and the *bhangra* troupe who won last season's *America's Got Talent*. And then a certain Grammy Award–winning artist will be capping off the formal portion of the evening with a sneak preview from her not-yet-released sophomore album!

After, Radhika's favorite DJ (another surprise) will take center stage to keep the dance floor going until sunrise. Remember to pace yourself. It's only day two! But if you end up going a little too hard, a recovery kit will be waiting in your villa when you return. Himalayan hydration salts, junk food in adherence to your dietary restrictions, painkillers, and Lustre's bestselling "Overnight Rejuvenation" product line.

You'll have everything you need to catch your second wind. You're going to need it. #RajikhaWedding is only just getting started.

Love,

RAJ & RADHIKA

Location: The Grand Terrace, Blush Resort & Spa Los Cabos
Dress code: Bollywood Glamour

From: Eric Santos
To: Shaylee Kapoor
Time: 5:28 p.m.
Subject: Urgent

Call me?

Eric

8.

Who's Eric?"

My chest tightens as my eyes track to the outdoor bar, where Caleb is fetching us something to drink; I'd left my phone to charge on the fridge. Keeping my face neutral, I rise from my deck chair and pad over to him.

"He emailed you."

I nod, playing it cool, and reach for the phone. I heightened my security settings prior to the trip, and only the sender's name appears on my home screen—not the contents of the email. Turning away slightly, I quickly hold my phone to my face until it unlocks.

> Call me?

I smile in relief. Thank god, it's nothing incriminating.

"Do you have a secret boyfriend or something?" Caleb says, reading over my shoulder.

His comment feels like a gut punch, but I don't react. Instead, I toss my phone lazily to the side and wrap my arms around him.

"Yes, and he's *way* hotter than you."

"How dare you." Caleb grins, kissing me. "Should I be jealous?"

Although Caleb's tone is light, I sense an undercurrent of anxiety. *Is* he jealous? *Caleb* slept with someone else.

"Eric's a classmate," I lie breezily. "We're doing a paper together on housing segregation. You should be very jealous."

"Ha. Seriously, though, why is he emailing while you're on vacation?"

"I don't know," I say, bristling. There's a neediness to his tone that doesn't sit right with me. "I suppose because the paper's due next week—"

Suddenly, someone bangs loudly on the front door, startling us both. Hand in hand, I follow Caleb through the villa and stand to the side as he opens the front door. Four officers wearing bulletproof vests are outside.

"Mr. Prescott?" the biggest one asks him.

Caleb glances at me before nodding. Nervous, I sidle up to him and slip an arm around his waist.

"Yes, that's me."

The officers step inside, and one of them knocks shoulders with Caleb as he surveys the room, devoid of emotion.

"We need to ask you a few questions. Is there somewhere private we can talk?"

"I already answered your questions," Caleb stammers, looking at me for reassurance. "Yesterday—"

"What happened yesterday no longer matters," the officer says gravely, turning to face us. "Today matters."

"Do I need a lawyer?"

"Do you?" he asks, and immediately Caleb shakes his head.

Something about these police officers seems different. Yesterday, it felt as if they were here to protect us. But today . . .

They're dressed differently, for starters. Their uniforms look military. I flit my eyes from the leader of the pack to the three officers behind him. Even their badges—

"Who are you?" I ask, clocking the "GN."

The leader turns to me and frowns.

"Who are you?" I repeat, and after a moment, he speaks.

"We are with the Guardia Nacional," he answers, gesturing to his colleagues. "We are now in charge of this investigation."

I nod, an article I read several years ago suddenly flashing to mind. Mexico's National Guard is a relatively new security force that absorbed the former Federal Police (Federales) and certain military enforcement organizations. But why would they be here? What happened to the local police?

"Do you have a card?" I ask anxiously. The leader obliges, but then immediately kicks me out of the villa for Caleb's interview. Only after I've grabbed my phone, a pair of flip-flops, and have headed out onto the terrace do I stop to read the card.

It's in Spanish, and there's not much there. Not the officer's name, rank, or phone number. And right beneath the words *Guardia Nacional*—

My mouth hangs open in disbelief. Loosely translated, the text reads "task force against the drug cartels."

Shit.

Shit!

Lightheaded, I dart toward the beach stairs behind Caleb's villa, but I'm suddenly having trouble seeing straight. I stop and press my hand against my chest. This morning, Zara's suggestion that a drug cartel killed Raj and Radhika had seemed wild and unreasonable. But now that a drug cartel task force has taken over the case, I don't know what to believe.

I need to walk. I need to think. I start my descent toward the beach, wondering if I shouldn't venture too far, if the National Guard will want to speak with me too.

Wondering if they'll catch me in my lie.

It wasn't a lie of consequence, but it was an untruth, none-theless. Yesterday during my brief interview with local police, an officer asked me when I arrived at Blush, and I told them approximately 8:30 a.m. on Thursday, April 25. The thing is, I failed to clarify that I flew down to Cabo a day earlier. I may not have been at this resort, but I was in town the night of the murders.

Holding the railing tight, I descend slowly, which feels treacherous in my years-old flip-flops. The switchback stairs hang off the steep cliffs like weeds, but I swallow my nerves and take it one step at a time.

The view is spectacular. It must be early evening by now because the sky and ocean are starting to flush with color, the golden sun obscured by patches of clouds. Halfway down the staircase, I pull out my phone and sit down. Under different circumstances, I would take a photo. Instead, I text Lexie.

> Are you there? Can we talk? It's important.

She replies right away.

> In meeting. Text me.

I palm my jaw, restless and tempted to just call her anyway. A breeze is billowing in from the ocean. Even though it's warm, I shiver.

> A Guardia Nacional drug cartel task force has taken over the investigation!!

I set my phone on my thighs and stare at it as I wait for Lexie's response. I don't need to spell out the rest for her.

> Holy shit. That's HUGE.

Understatement of the century.

I hear someone on the stairs above me, footsteps muted by the crashing waves below. I stand up and wait for them to pass. A beat later, my phone chimes again.

> You think, or you know?

> I know. The officer interviewing Caleb right now gave me this card.

After I text her a picture of the card, I quickly glance up the stairs. The footsteps have quieted. I look back at my phone.

> Can you get out of the meeting? I really need to talk, Lex. I'm starting to freak out.

Normally, I'm quite good in a crisis, but right now my head feels like a pressure cooker on the verge of exploding. I stare at my phone, willing Lexie to call or text, and I grow more and more impatient as time ticks by. I should be tolerant. Lexie is a working mother. Her days are long, her time precious. But right now, I need her. I need—

My eyes lift as I hear something.

Pebbles. Sand.

I hear it spilling down the wooden stairs, gravity pulling them toward their inevitable fate. Slowly, I exhale, waiting for the person on the stairs above me to show themself.

"Hello?" I call, when no one appears.

A shiver runs down my spine as I look up, the force of my hand splintering the railing.

When did it become so dark? The sun has nearly set, the sky a bruised purple with the faded glow of the night's most eager stars. I brush my fingers along the weathered wood of the banister as I climb back up a few steps.

"Is someone there?" I call again.

Nothing.

I'm at the top of a landing. Waiting with bated breath, I peer around the corner of the switchback.

"*Hello?*" I say, even more loudly.

Nobody's there, but there was someone before. I know it. I heard the footsteps. The pebbles and sand crumbling down the stairs. Fear stabs me in the ribs as I rest my weight against the railing, lean to the side, and crane my neck to try and get a view of the landing above. As I push off, my left foot leaves the ground. My flip-flop slides off.

I watch as it teeters and then, as if in slow motion, topples over the edge.

I gasp.

It falls through the air, weightless, hanging on the breeze.

An eternity passes as I wait for it to hit the rocks below. I expect a crunch. But from up here, it doesn't make a sound.

* * *

AFTER I CLIMB back up the stairs, Caleb's waiting for me on the back terrace. He catches sight of my left foot and frowns.

"You're missing a shoe."

I make a face but don't explain. I never bothered to retrieve my flip-flop from the beach. Night has officially fallen, and I was too spooked to go down there.

"Did you see someone back here?" I ask him, looking over my shoulder. From where we're standing, the beach stairs and the cliffside path stretching behind the Villas are just barely visible. If someone was watching me from the stairs above, maybe Caleb saw who it was. Could Zara have been out jogging again? Or maybe it was one of the Joshis, or that hulk of a security guard; their villa is just two doors down.

"When?" I hear Caleb ask me.

"Earlier." I turn back around. "I don't know. Did anyone use the stairs while I was out?"

Caleb stares at me blankly.

"I was a little busy."

"Right." I pause guiltily, remembering his interview. "How was it?"

When he doesn't respond, I show him the officer's card and translate the text. "The National Guard are investigating Raj and Radhika's murders as a drug-related offence! Zara was right—"

"I know," he grunts, his face reddening. "I figured it out during their questioning. But we're going to have to talk about that later. Uncle just texted. Tobias is on his way. Maybe he can tell us what the fuck is going on."

I sigh in relief.

Hopefully, Tobias will also have news from the consulate that the paperwork is complete and we're all clear to get ourselves and Raj and Radhika's bodies the hell out of Cabo. If the drug cartel is involved in these murders, I don't want to be anywhere near here.

Caleb tells me I have ten minutes to get ready. I lock the en suite, turn on the shower, and then dial Lexie's cell. I need to talk to her—not because of work, not because of what I came here to do—but because she's my friend and I need to hear her voice. I need someone to tell me it's all going to be OK. To reassure me I'll be going home soon.

Thirty-six-hours ago, I was a woman with an agenda, a heavy conscience, and an invite to Raj Joshi and Radhika Singh's exclusive destination wedding.

And now? They're dead. But why would the cartel want to kill either of them?

Lexie doesn't pick up. I take a quick shower, cranking the temperature and water pressure to the max. After, I try her cell again. There's still no response.

I stare at the phone as I change into dry clothes and towel dry my hair. It's strange that Lexie hasn't called me back or returned my texts, that she's gone silent after I told her what at first seemed unimaginable has suddenly become real.

When Lexie doesn't pick up for the third time, I try her office phone number out of desperation.

She's the only person in my life who knows I'm in Cabo. Who knows why I'm here. Who knows I'm dating Caleb—

Dating.

I shake my head as her office line rings and keeps on ringing.

Caleb and I aren't really dating, though, are we? Our relationship is a lie—and our chance meeting wasn't fate.

No. I'm not a "gold-digging whore." I was never after Caleb's money.

But I was after his friends.

"Hello!"

My heart drops into my stomach when the answering machine abruptly picks up and Lexie's bubbly receptionist delivers the automated greeting into my ear.

"I'm sorry we can't take your call right now," he says loudly. "Please leave your name and number, and someone here at the *Los Angeles Journal* editorial desk will call you right back."

9.

How the hell did you get in here?" was the first thing Lexie said when she found Shay waiting in her office. She leaned against the doorframe, eyes wide in disbelief as she studied Shay from head to toe. Shay stood up and gawked in return.

"Lex," Shay breathed, too stunned to answer her question. "What's it been . . . Eight, nine years?"

Lexie crossed her arms, regarding Shay skeptically.

"Look at you," Shay tried next, smiling nervously. She gestured to the downtown skyline through the floor-to-ceiling windows, to a *Los Angeles Journal* pennant haphazardly pinned behind the desk. "You made it."

Shay looked Lexie up and down and playfully gave her the eye.

"And you haven't changed a bit."

"That's a lie," Lexie warned. "But I'll take it. Seriously, how did you get up here?"

Shay stammered an excuse about Lexie's receptionist having discovered Shay in the lobby, trying and failing to get a visitor's pass for the prestigious newspaper.

"Remind me to fire him," Lexie said after.

Even though Shay knew she was joking—that she was *probably* joking—she shook her head apologetically. "Don't. I told him I was your best friend from college."

"That's true," Lexie agreed mildly. "*Was* being the operative word."

Lexie sat down at her desk while Shay's cheeks heated up with shame. Shay deserved that. And she shouldn't have been surprised by Lexie's frosty greeting; it was Shay's fault they'd drifted apart.

They'd met in freshman year, both determined to be the top student in their journalism program, and quickly became the best friend neither of them had ever had. Competitive, passionate, and radical, Shay and Lexie were a force to be reckoned with, were equally hellbent on changing the world for the better. So it came as a shock to Shay when, a few weeks before the end of their program, Lexie told her she'd taken an entry-level reporting job at a top-tier *right-leaning* newspaper in New York. Shay hadn't even known Lexie applied.

After graduation, Shay took unpaid internship after unpaid internship, unwilling to apply for any job that would compromise her values, even if it would have gotten her foot in the door. One year later, tired of the job search, frustrated by the lack of opportunities, she signed up for a term position at a human rights multilateral agency in Dhaka. The job was journalism-adjacent, something she thought would pad her résumé with international work experience. But the longer she spent in Bangladesh, the more she realized that she could make more of an impact working overseas. *This* was where she would find meaning.

After Dhaka came Hyderabad. Then Chennai. Bengaluru.

Chittagong. Pune. Every few months or years, Shay picked up and moved to join a new project or nonprofit, and slowly but surely, her wild passion to "change the world" matured. She specialized in economic development, realizing that job creation in sustainable industries, microfinancing, and trade bolstered the communities she was trying to help. She acquired a nuanced understanding of South Asia's market economies, governance structures, labor laws, and the system risks that undermined progress. The last two and a half years she'd specialized even further, joining a human rights watchdog in Mumbai that investigated economic justice, corporate accountability, and corruption. Her interest in reporting the truth evolved.

At first, she'd tried to keep up contact with Lexie. But promises to Skype every Sunday were quietly broken. Facebook message updates were sent further and further apart, and then, one day, Shay simply stopped responding. She met Lexie's overtures to maintain the friendship with total silence.

It made sense at the time. Lexie had turned into someone Shay didn't recognize, and grew to represent the stupidly trivial life Shay had left behind. Lexie posted photos of her and her roommates' nights out in the East Village, selfies with her new boyfriend, shared memes about the hottest new Netflix series. She'd also become a beat reporter on Wall Street for that right-leaning paper, worked for and reported on the one percent who controlled half the world's wealth and sucked it dry.

Shay had thought Lexie was a sellout, and she was angry. Angry enough to let their friendship crumble into ruins.

But now?

"You're probably wondering why I'm here," Shay said, after

several awkward, obligatory minutes of small talk. "I have a story for you."

"So *that's* what this is about," Lexie said bitterly. "You need something from me, huh? What do you want—a job?"

Shay's lungs burned, and although she was tempted to clap back, she kept her cool. "No, I don't want a job." Doomscrolling a few weeks ago, Shay had stumbled upon an old classmate's Instagram post, which led her to discover that Lexie had moved with her new husband to LA. That she was now a senior editor at the prestigious *Los Angeles Journal*. That Lexie could *help*.

"Lex, I should have been better about keeping in touch. I would love to be friends again—"

"No one calls me 'Lex' anymore and, honestly, I have enough friends. Real friends." She sat up straight. "So if you have a story for me, then pitch it. I have a million other things I should be doing."

Nodding, Shay pushed down the embarrassment, reached into her backpack, and pulled out a printed copy of the report she and her colleagues at the human rights watchdog had spent over two years scrupulously investigating.

"What do you know about the Joshi Group?"

Lexie said she didn't know much, and so Shay tossed her the papers and started from the beginning.

In the mid 1970s, Mr. Narayan Joshi and his brother Jackie used family money to purchase and renovate a crumbling hotel in the historic Colaba district of Mumbai. The hotel was a success, prompting them to open several more in the city, and by the time their respective sons Sean and Raj were born, they owned dozens all over South Asia.

From there, the empire only grew. Narayan Joshi emigrated with his wife and Raj, only a toddler, to the United States to expand the business in Europe and the Americas, while his brother Jackie stayed back in Mumbai. Jackie focused on acquiring hotels and growing the business throughout the rest of Asia.

Their global strategy worked, and Raj and Sean Joshi were the children of billionaire brothers before they hit puberty. After Sean's parents were killed in a car crash when he was sixteen, Mr. Joshi adopted him and brought him over to the US.

"And how is this a story?" Lexie interrupted, picking her nails.

Shay grimaced. "Give me a second. I'm getting there."

Worried Lexie would lose patience, Shay sped up the story, speaking more quickly. She told Lexie how Mr. Joshi was hungrier than his brother, cared more about the bottom line than his workers. Prestige and profit over doing what was right.

Because of the surviving Mr. Joshi's business tactics, the Joshi Group was already on several watchlists for a long list of corporate crimes when Shay joined the human rights watchdog in Mumbai three years ago. Fraud. Bribery. Collusion. Violating environmental regulations, human rights, and labor laws. Of course, nothing that could be proven in a court of law. Nothing that other companies around the world weren't doing either. Shay was at a desk pushing paper, compiling research about the Joshi Group, and wishing she could actually make a difference in the world, when the unthinkable happened. In April 2021, during the height of India's second COVID wave, there was a fire at the construction site of a Joshi-owned hotel in a growing suburb in Mumbai. The half-built convention center and fifteen hundred hotel rooms above it went up in flames, taking everything and everyone with it. Eighteen workers died.

Five of them were only children.

"It felt a little too convenient," Shay, who now had Lexie's undivided attention, said slowly. "The global hospitality sector took a huge hit during the pandemic. Nobody was traveling or going to conferences. At the time, the Joshi Group wasn't going to benefit from opening another big hotel."

She crossed her arms, smiling over at Lexie.

"But they did benefit from the insurance payout for the fire."

Shay flipped to the relevant page of the report and handed it back to Lexie. From that moment on, day in and day out, she explained, she and her colleagues at the human rights watchdog dedicated themselves to investigating the Joshi Group, finding a way to hold them accountable. They pored over every available public record and government filing, and conducted extensive interviews with construction workers and Joshi Group employees, as well as confidential sources at the insurance company that wrote the check.

Eventually they found the evidence they needed. Damning evidence. The Joshi Group had been operating in the red long before COVID, and, motivated to cut spending and by the hefty insurance payout, Mr. Joshi gave the orders to burn down the half-built hotel.

"How do you know Joshi himself is involved?" Lexie interjected. "A lot of these company heads get their minions to do the dirty work in secret for plausible deniability."

Shay pointed out the testimony from four separate witnesses who saw Mr. Joshi on-site moments before the fire. "Mr. Joshi's directly responsible. He gave the order. And he's a notorious control freak. He lives in Mumbai half the time, and according to many sources, he oversees the day-to-day operations of every aspect of the India business."

Shay returned to the story. How everyone at the watchdog had high hopes that their work would lead to action, but when they finally published their report, nothing happened. No more than a handful of bloggers and minor newspapers covered the report—an afterthought in a single news cycle. Nobody cared. Or if they did, their boss's boss was in Mr. Joshi's pocket. He was getting away with it the same way bad actors the world over have always gotten away with it. *Money*. Bribes that appeased the bureaucrats. Made certain politicians look the other way. Payouts to the affected families in order to shush them before anything reached the courts.

"Joshi has too much power to go through the government or the courts," Shay said after, her mouth parched. "This runs too deep."

"So you need media attention to nail this guy," Lexie said flatly.

"*International* media attention," Shay clarified. "If we want the authorities to take our accusations seriously, then we need an eminent publication like the *Los Angeles Journal* to expose him."

An eminent publication. Shay jiggled her leg, and for some reason, couldn't look Lexie in the eye. When she first took that job at the right-leaning paper, Lexie had gone on, and *on*, about how the job was only a means to an end. So she could gain a foothold in journalism.

Lexie's plan had worked. Yes, she'd sold out for a while, but now she edited the type of publication Shay had always dreamed of working for.

"I'll think about it," Lexie said, flipping idly through the report. "But I don't want to get your hopes up. I don't think I want to take this on."

"What? Why not?"

"The fire happened in another country. *Years* ago. Our readership simply doesn't care—"

"They should care. The fire is just the tip of the iceberg. Like I said, the Joshi Group is under suspicion for fraud, labor and human rights violations, enviro . . ."

Shay trailed off when Lexie raised her eyebrows.

"Come on," Lexie said quietly. "Those crimes aren't exactly uncommon. A lot of the shit we buy isn't ethically produced, Shay. Soda, chocolate bars, baby formula, palm oil, cars—"

"I get it."

"—pharmaceuticals. Half the companies we rely on, including American ones, have international rap sheets longer than—"

"I said, I get it!" Shay sighed, exasperated, tired of hearing the same old argument. If everyone does it, then it's OK. It's the status quo. It's *no big deal*.

"This kind of stuff is still important to me," Lexie said after a moment. "Your report is incredible work, Shay, and I wish I could help, but—"

"News media is dying," Shay said dryly. "All you washed-up hacks care about are the clicks?"

Shay worried her half-joke would hit a little too close to home, but then Lexie grinned, and for a moment they were back in their dorm room, cowriting an open letter to student administration about decolonizing the history department's curriculum, or whatever cause had lit the fire in their bellies that week. But a beat later, Lexie's face darkened, as if remembering how much Shay had hurt her. And as Lexie looked back at Shay like a stranger, Shay realized that this amazing woman—who she'd known as a feisty freshman, who had beat the odds among journalism grads everywhere, whose wedding invite she hadn't even bothered to respond to—years later, was still the closest thing she had to a friend.

"I'm sorry," Lexie said coolly. "If only there was a more personal angle, something else to bring our specific readership into the story, then maybe there's something I could do."

"The Joshis live in LA," Shay responded professionally, even though Lexie's tone made her feel like crying. "They're American citizens. Ostensibly, they pay taxes here—"

"That's not enough. I need something else."

Long ago, Shay had promised herself she would do whatever it took to bring Mr. Joshi down. That's why, upon discovering that Lexie was an editor at the *Los Angeles Journal*, she took a hiatus from her job at the watchdog and depleted her savings to fly to LA to meet with her. That's why Shay was blatantly sucking up to the former best friend she'd wronged and who didn't owe her any favors. That's why, even though she hadn't wanted to *go there*, she was going to give Lexie what she asked for.

"Mr. Joshi's son, Raj," Shay said, staring at the ceiling. "He recently proposed to his girlfriend, Radhika Singh."

"Radhika Singh?"

She sat up straight and caught Lexie staring.

"Why does that name sound familiar?"

"Because she's a successful influencer." Shay swallowed. "And Zara Singh's little sister."

Lexie's mouth dropped. "As in—"

"Yes," Shay said, reminding Lexie about her newspaper's recent profile. "Mr. Joshi's son is marrying the younger sister of your *Los Angeles Journal*'s 'Entrepreneur of the Year.'"

10.

Friday, April 26
7:49 p.m.

Hand in hand, Caleb and I walk over to the Joshis' villa, both of us too frazzled to speak. Fingers crossed, Tobias will announce the bodies are being released, Mr. Joshi will let me board his private plane, and I'll be back in LA before midnight. Never in a million years could I have imagined a scenario where I'd be willing to board a private plane—let alone one funded by the Joshi Group. But desperate times call for desperate measures. And right now, I'm fucking desperate.

A day after my first meeting with Lexie, the *Los Angeles Journal* commissioned me to write a follow-up to their profile of Zara Singh, an investigative piece on what kind of family her little sister was about to marry into. The contrast between the two wealthy South Asian families, Lexie kept saying, would have everyone shaking their head. The admirable Singhs, the creators of Lustre who had pulled themselves up by their bootstraps, were about to climb into bed with the family headed by the reprehensible Mr. Joshi?

This wasn't a merger of two Indian American dynasties. It was a hostile takeover.

I wasn't thrilled about the angle. I wanted to focus on the Joshi Group, the fire, and the litany of corporate crimes the company had been accused of. In particular, I wanted to hang Mr. Joshi out to dry. But I had to write the article the way Lexie wanted, because I knew I had to get the news out there any way I could: big media attention of any kind creates impact. A piece in the *Los Angeles Journal* shedding light on Mr. Joshi's actions had the power to marshal US, Indian, and international regulators to hold him accountable.

I hold my breath as we approach the Joshis' villa, clutching the man I've been betraying these past few months. The man I've been using as a means to an end.

Lexie and I were taking a break from going over my research that Saturday evening in January when she happened to scroll past a photo of Raj, Radhika, and Caleb posted by celebrity gossip blog *The Scoop*, which had been Lexie's guilty pleasure since college. The paparazzi photo, posted just minutes earlier, showed the trio walking into one of the trendiest restaurants on Sunset. A source claimed Raj and Radhika's engagement party was about to kick off.

Before I knew it, Lexie was shoving me into her little black dress and sending me out to do some recon. I recognized Caleb from the paparazzi photo, and when he asked me for a cigarette, the most I hoped for was a bit of background for my article—*maybe* a quote. But when Radhika and Caleb invited me into that party, the chance to actually meet and spend time with members of the Joshi family was an opportunity too good to pass up. And then who would have thought Caleb would end up flirting with me the whole night, track me down on social media the following morning, and insist we go out for coffee? How could I have predicted that one—then two, then *three*—innocent little dates would turn into a full-blown relationship?

Lexie encouraged me to go for it too—thrilled that the *Los Angeles Journal* would have the inside scoop—and I grew accustomed to lying to Caleb and his friends, pretending I was a grad student at USC, and eavesdropping when they thought I wasn't paying attention. I even started snooping. That night during Raj's party at the Joshi mansion, I wasn't in search of a bathroom when I ran into Sean; I was looking for Mr. Joshi's home office.

Speaking of Sean . . .

When we're in front of the Joshis' villa, I catch sight of him barreling down the footpath from the opposite direction. He's looking at something on his phone and shoves it into his back pocket the moment he clocks us. I smile. He doesn't smile back.

It was hard not to wonder at first if Raj and Sean were complicit in the Mumbai fire; they were in leaderships positions, the son and nephew of Mr. Joshi, and rumor was that one of them would ultimately take over as CEO. But all the evidence we found back at the watchdog pointed to Mr. Joshi alone.

He was infamously controlling, enforced information silos between different parts of the business, and frequently made decisions without board knowledge or approval. Moreover, we discovered that he kept Raj, Sean, and the others in LA at arm's length from the Asian side of the business, leaving them to focus on Europe and the Americas. If there was blood on anybody else's hands, we would have found a trace of it.

Sean's nostrils flare as he makes his approach, his icy stare fixated on Caleb, and then it dawns on me. Raj and Sean may not have had a hand in the fire that killed eighteen of their workers, but that doesn't mean they're innocent. Could there have been a reason the cartel wanted Raj *dead*?

"Out for a stroll?" Caleb snips as Sean draws closer. His tone is off, and suddenly, you can cut the tension between the two men with a knife. My suspicion was right. Caleb and Sean despise each other.

"Something like that," Sean answers.

"Where were you?"

I squeeze Caleb's hand. As curious as I am about why the two dislike one another, where this conversation might go, the family meeting is about to start. And, more than anything, right now I want to go home.

"Last time I checked, the finance department reports to me." Sean meets Caleb's gaze with equal fury. "I get to know your whereabouts, not the other way around."

"You wouldn't be hiding anything from us, now, would you, buddy?" Caleb smiles meanly. "Maybe about having miraculously slept—"

"Caleb!" I start.

"—through the night?" Caleb finishes, ignoring me. "We all know you have insomnia."

Caleb drops my hand and takes a step forward. He's not much taller than Sean, but he's wider. Denser. He looks like he could crush Sean with his bare hand.

"You know something about their murders, don't you?" Caleb hisses. "What are you hiding?"

Sean smiles in response and, staying composed, simply crosses his arms.

"Didn't your mommy and daddy teach you not to throw stones inside a glass house?" Sean says, his voice mocking. "I'm not hiding anything, Caleb."

Sean moves closer. He stops when their foreheads are just inches apart.

"Are you? *Bud*?"

They stare at each other for a long moment, and, both fearful and irritated, I start to wonder if I would be strong enough to break the two of them up in a fight. They're both grieving. Raj, someone they both loved as their brother, has just been murdered, yet they're both acting like total dickheads.

Caleb leans into Sean too, chest puffed. He looks like he's about to punch him in the face.

"That's enough," I snap, hooking my arm through Caleb's before he can do anything he'll regret. "It's time for the meeting."

I feel Caleb's forearm pulse once, and then twice, as he clenches his fist. And just when I'm thinking about calling someone out to help, he shakes me off and storms away.

* * *

CRISIS AVERTED, WE all head into the villa. Mr. Joshi is in the foyer again, waiting, his bodyguard Brown Hulk Hogan standing at the ready. I must have been in shock yesterday, because today I can feel my body viscerally react to Mr. Joshi's presence. His pastel golf polo and potbelly. His tired smile and swollen red eyes.

Yes, he's a grieving father, but he won't get my sympathy. The man is still Satan incarnate, and he deserves to be in prison.

In the living room, Sean and Mr. Joshi join Mrs. Joshi on the largest couch, where she is silently weeping into her hands. As Caleb and I take our seats, I notice Zara tucked away by the billiards table, behind which stand several members of the National Guard, still as statues, watching our every move. Brown Hulk Hogan stands solemnly in the corner. Last night, when the time was right, I casually asked Caleb again what he knew about the bodyguard; he'd never come up in my research of Mr. Joshi. But Caleb didn't know a thing about him either, not even Brown Hulk Hogan's name. All he said was that Mr. Joshi had hired him back in India, and that he'd been his loyal bodyguard for nearly twenty years.

The air conditioning is off, and as we wait for Tobias to arrive in the hot muggy silence, I find myself wondering what is going to happen to my article now that Raj and Radhika are dead. The article's angle would have to change, and we'd have to wait until the families had officially given statements to the press. Until a respectable amount of time had passed for the Singhs and Joshis to mourn. But surely the *Los Angeles Journal* would still publish *something*, right? I'd still get my chance at exposing Mr. Joshi?

Finally, Tobias arrives, Daniela on his tail. She looks tired, worryingly so. Her face is gray, makeup-free, and, by the wrinkles in her uniform, my guess is she's still in yesterday's clothing. While Tobias sets himself up in front of the television, she lingers in the foyer. I make room for her on the couch between me and Caleb and wave her over.

"Do you want some water?" I whisper. But she shakes her head and smiles politely. Even though she looks like she's about to throw up, Daniela remains standing.

"Thank you for your patience," Tobias says, calling my attention back to him. He taps twice on his clipboard. "I'll get right to it."

He clears his throat and, with a nod at Mr. Joshi, continues. "The first update is one you may have already guessed. A *Guardia Nacional* drug enforcement task force has taken over the investigation. Some of you would have met with them this afternoon—"

"*Met?*" Caleb mutters angrily. Everyone turns to face him.

"Was I the only one to get the third degree?"

I turn to look at him, shocked. He never mentioned the interview was hostile. I'll need to ask him more about that later.

"They hassled Sean and me too," Zara adds. "I can't help but think—"

"Zara," Caleb warns.

Mr. Joshi looks between the two of them. "What are you two talking about?"

Zara blushes before responding.

"Mr. Joshi, you know how much I respect you and your family. And I would never—"

"Speak freely. Please."

Zara nods once. "Then let's look at the facts, all right? One. A National Guard *drug* team is here. Two. Raj and Radhi were shot in the head, execution style, which is the same MO as countless cartel hits—"

"Hold on, young lady—" Mr. Joshi starts, but she stands up and waves him off.

"I'm not a *young lady*, and you asked me to speak freely, Mr. Joshi, so let me finish." She takes a deep breath and straightens her shoulders.

"Three."

Zara's gaze flits around the room, tears brimming in her eyes.

"Radhi told me Raj had been flying down to Cabo every month for over a year. He said he was doing business with some Mexican, but never gave her any details." Zara pauses. "I'm sorry to suggest this, but I'm starting to wonder if Raj had some secret 'business' with a cartel."

I balk, looking at Caleb. Then Mr. Joshi. Then Sean. They all seem equally horrified.

The room falls into silence, and I take deep breaths until my pulse returns to its normal rate. Although it may be tempting to jump to conclusions right now, my professional training doesn't allow me to do that. Raj's monthly work trips certainly raise new questions, but Zara's suggestion that any business dealings in Mexico must be related to the drug trade is downright racist.

"I can't believe you would say that," Caleb says icily. "Even for you, that's cruel."

"Then explain to me why Raj was coming here so much—"

"Raj travels for work constantly, Zara. I never know where he's running off to. I had no idea he had business in Cabo." Caleb turns to Sean. He clears his throat. "Did you?"

Sean waits a beat before answering. "Yes, we knew. Raj briefed me on all his meetings. He wanted the Joshi Group to partner with—"

"*Beta*," Mr. Joshi interrupts harshly. "*Bus.* This is not the time for business talk."

"I think this *is* the time," Zara declares. "Tell us, Sean. What was Raj doing here?"

Sean's eyes dart to his uncle, who's shaking his head at him. Sean's Adam's apple bobs up and down, and then, as if unable to resist, he keeps talking.

"Raj thought we needed to expand our luxury brand offerings in Central and South America," Sean says, turning his head away from Mr. Joshi. "He wanted us to partner with Blush Continental and invest in their forthcoming resorts."

Blush Continental. The hotel group that owns the resort we're in now.

"Is that true?" Zara asks Mr. Joshi, her voice dripping in skepticism. When he nods, Zara sighs in relief.

"Oh, thank god. I was worried . . ." She shakes her head at a silent thought. "Maybe this is just some terrible mistake. Do you have copies of his notes? Dates and locations of these meetings? *Names?*"

"Of course," Sean says evenly. "And if the National Guard requests that information, I'll happily hand it over. His meetings with Hector—"

"Are we done with this now?" Mr. Joshi interrupts again, his voice booming. "*Hah*, Zara?"

He places his hand on Sean's shoulder, squeezes, and then turns to Tobias.

"Answer this now: Why are these men here? Do they really believe a cartel is involved in my son's murder?"

Tobias shifts uncomfortably. "They aren't at liberty to confirm that at the moment."

"Of course they aren't." Zara rolls her eyes, and then smiles rudely at the closest National Guard officer.

Mr. Joshi shoots daggers at her, and Zara, straightening her shoulders, glares right back. As much as I don't like her, I admire she has the guts to stand up to powerful men.

"Right, then," Zara says, looking away first. "If that's the only update, can we leave? I want to take Radhi home tonight."

Mr. Joshi nods. "I have to agree. My plane is on standby at the San Jose airport."

"No, no. Not so fast," Tobias says, cheeks flushing. "I'm afraid that won't be possible."

"Make it possible," Zara hisses. "My mother is a disaster. My brother's wife is expecting. We all need to go home. We need to have a funeral. For fuck's sakes, we need to grieve—"

"I must clarify, Ms. Singh. Your mother, brother, and sister-in-law can return to the US at any time," Tobias stammers. "Mr.

and Mrs. Joshi"—his eyes move from them to me—"Ms. Kapoor. You three are free to go as well. The paperwork is ready for signatures, and you may repatriate the remains tonight—"

"Wait a second." Sean's voice cracks as he stands up too. "Are you implying that Zara, Caleb, and I are not 'free to go'?"

"Yes," Tobias answers severely. "This brings me to our second and final update."

He swallows hard.

"Ms. Singh, Mr. Prescott, and Mr. Sean Joshi, I'm sorry to inform you that you are indefinitely prohibited from leaving the municipality of Los Cabos. *Guardia Nacional* has marked you three as persons of interest in the investigation."

The room erupts with Mrs. Joshi's moans, Sean's frustration, Zara's anger, and Mr. Joshi's threats of legal action. Caleb remains quiet. I keep my mouth shut too, even though I want to scream.

What the actual fuck? My legs shake uncontrollably as I flick my eyes over to Daniela, sitting next to me. She's staring at the ground, her face vacant. My stomach twitches. She's the only person in the room who doesn't seem surprised.

"Quiet," Mr. Joshi barks, after he returns from taking his wife to the other room to lie down. His presence is so powerful, even the National Guard officers whispering in the corner shut up.

"Sean. Caleb." Mr. Joshi takes center stage, arms crossed. "I have texted my lawyers. Zara, I suggest you contact yours as well. I am confident we will have this straightened out by the morning. In the meantime—"

He wags a stubby finger at Tobias.

"—if you are forbidding them from leaving the country, they have a right to know what evidence you have against them."

"I'm not forbidding anything, Mr. Joshi," Tobias says. "I work for the US ambassador, and we cannot intervene in a sovereign government's criminal investigation. I'm just the messenger, and I'm here to help your family as best I can.

"As for the evidence against them," Tobias continues, turning to face the rest of us. "With Ms. Singh, Mr. Sean Joshi, and Mr. Prescott's agreement, I'm happy to lay out in the open the circumstances that led them to being persons of interest."

Zara, Sean, and Caleb nod warily. Tobias continues.

"The Villas are equipped with state-of-the-art locks. When the 'do not disturb' function is activated, Blush housekeeping staff and security are unable to use their master keys to enter. Only those who have been assigned access via their wristbands can unlock the doors."

"Hotel security systems confirm that, on the night in question, the 'do not disturb' function in Mr. Raj Joshi's villa was switched on at 2:14 a.m. That's forty-five minutes after the group"—Tobias points at Sean, Caleb, then Zara—"returned to the resort. And more than an hour before the window for the time of death.

"Everyone's wristband is intact," Tobias continues. "And the 'do not disturb' function was still on when the victims were found yesterday morning. Given their unclothed nature, and that they were likely sleeping at the time, the police believe—"

"The murderer also had access to Raj's villa," Sean finishes quietly.

"And, let me guess," Zara whispers. "Sean, Caleb, and I had been given access?"

I surreptitiously take a look at each of their Blush wristbands. Indeed, all three are intact. They're made of hard plastic, can only be removed with a pair of sharp scissors, and the gravity of this fact presses me firmly to my seat. Raj and Radhika may not have been killed by a stranger, but by someone they trusted enough to give access to the villa. By Zara, Sean, *Caleb*—

"What about Daniela?"

My chest tightens when I hear my own voice. When I realize I'm the one asking the question.

"What about Daniela?" Caleb echoes slowly.

"She found them," I point out, my eyes drifting to her apologetically. Thursday morning, *Daniela* discovered Raj and Radhika's dead bodies. "That means you had access to Raj's villa too. Doesn't it?"

"Ms. Munoz has an alibi," Tobias interjects quickly. "Although she had been granted special access via her staff wristband, law enforcement has ruled her out as a suspect."

"So you're saying that Zara, Sean, and Caleb are *suspects*," I retort, shocked yet again to hear myself speak in this crowd. "A moment ago, you said they were persons of interest."

Before Tobias can clarify further, all hell breaks loose as Mr. Joshi demands to know Daniela's alibi and then threatens the Mexican authorities with political and legal action. I lean into the couch, back into my place, as my disbelief gets drowned out by the others.

This doesn't make any sense. A drug enforcement task force has taken over, yet they're also suggesting that Raj and Radhika were murdered by someone who loved them. By Zara, Sean, or *Caleb*.

My heart races as a prickling sensation descends down my body telling me to fight or to flee. Telling me it's time to run.

Do it.

All at once, I feel something on my lap. Moist, and cold. Gasping for breath, I look down and find Caleb's hand on my leg, searching for my palm. For comfort. For the support of his girlfriend.

As I thread my fingers through his, cautiously, I turn my head to get a better look. Caleb's eyes are teary and downcast, and he's hunched forward, his lean bulk contorted in an unflattering light.

Shay. Run.

Now might be the time to finally listen to that little voice inside of me. To my instincts. For all I know, right now, I might be holding hands with the murderer.

Wedding Ceremony

Today is the day. And—fair warning—
it's going to be a long one.

Traditionally, Hindu weddings can last several days, but we'll
do our best to have it wrapped up in a few hours. As the
ceremony will take place entirely in the ancient language of
Sanskrit, here's a primer on the key rituals to watch out for:

❋ The Bharat, in which Raj, his groomsmen, and
family dance their way to the ceremony

❋ The exchange of *jai mala* (flower garlands)
to proclaim mutual love and respect

❋ Raj places the *mangalsutra* around Radhika's neck,
symbolizing the sacred union between them

❋ Raj and Radhika take seven revolutions around
the sacred fire, representing the seven vows of
nourishment, strength, prosperity, family, progeny,
health and happiness, and finally, love and friendship.

There's going to be a lot going on, and we totally
understand if you need to take a break, make a phone
call, or go grab coffee throughout the lengthy ceremony.
And if you have no idea what's going on . . . don't feel
bad! Neither will we. Your guess will be as good as ours.

Love,

RAJ & RADHIKA

Location: Atlantis Banquet Room,
Blush Resort & Spa Los Cabos
Dress code: Traditional Indian Attire

11.

At dawn, I go up to the rooftop deck with a single cigarette. The cool morning air hits my face, and, for the first time all night, I feel like I can breathe. Even though it's early, I try calling Lexie again, and I curse under my breath when it goes straight to voicemail. She still hasn't returned any of my texts or calls.

My back to the ocean, I take a drag and watch the sky slowly brighten. Down below, two National Guard officers are on duty, walking the circumference of the crime scene. I watch them for a while, smoking and standing far enough away from the railing to stay out of sight. One loop around Raj's villa seems to take them about five minutes. They linger and chat out front for about ninety seconds, and then they bend out of view as they walk the path between Raj's villa and the Joshis'. Thirty-odd seconds later, I catch sight of them moving south along Raj's back terrace, before they turn right and head back to the front, walking between Raj's villa and Caleb's.

It's nice knowing there are law enforcement officers with

heavy artillery nearby. Still, if I was a sane and intelligent person, the news that Caleb might be a cold-blooded killer should have sent me packing already. Instead, last night I allowed him to rest his head against my chest as his tears and snot drenched my T-shirt. I didn't force him to explain what the National Guard "grilled" him on during his interview, after he told me he was too upset to talk about it. Instead, I held him; I practically rocked the guy to sleep.

What the hell was I thinking?

I wasn't. I was terrified, and despite everything, I couldn't bring myself to leave.

Even now, with a few hours' sleep under my belt, I'm still unable to think clearly when it comes to Caleb. I simply can't believe he'd hurt them. Raj and the Joshis were Caleb's chosen family, and even though Radhika irritated Caleb to no end, he cared about her too. On the other hand, I can't deny how suspicious it is that Caleb lied about his whereabouts the night of the murder. What if he isn't just covering up his affair? What if he did something exponentially worse?

Restless, I pad around the deck as I recall his strange altercation with Sean. Caleb had accused Sean of lying to the police right before he nearly punched him out, although Sean had quickly turned the tables around and asked Caleb what *he* was hiding. Does Sean know something I don't?

And I can't forget how cagey Caleb acted when I asked him to store my laptop in the villa safe. My breath shallow, I tiptoe into the wellness room and try to open it, but, unable to guess the combination, eventually I give up. What else is Caleb hiding?

I return to the deck and, taking a deep calming breath, remind myself that he isn't the only "person of interest," that he wasn't the only one who had access to Raj's villa. The "do not disturb" function was switched on, so if we trust Tobias's claim that Daniela has an alibi, then the only other people who could have killed them are Zara and Sean.

I liked Sean the first time we met, but I don't know him. I don't know his heart, his motives, or why he and Caleb seem to despise each other. And then there's Zara. Could she have done it? The fact that she's been exercising and even working while grieving her sister's death sets my nerves on edge. There's something almost robotic about Zara, something cold, even horrible. But she wasn't horrible to Radhika. I saw it with my own eyes: Zara *loved* her.

But, if the authorities believe someone close to them is the murderer, then why has a drug enforcement task force taken over? Of course. Raj's business trips to Cabo!

Raj worked in business development for the Joshi Group, and globetrotting to attend meetings with other hoteliers and potential business partners was part of his job description; he was away on business as often as he was in LA. Sean's claim that Raj was meeting with Blush Continental to discuss an investment is perfectly plausible.

But it's no secret that a major drug cartel operates in the region, and Zara's right: read another way, Raj's travels here are suspicious. I wring my hands, frustrated by the limited information. During the family meeting, Sean had started telling the room about Raj's business contact "Hector" at Blush Continental; if only Mr. Joshi hadn't interrupted him, then maybe I could have confirmed what the hell Raj had been doing in Cabo.

I can feel myself spinning out. The last few days, I've been drifting in a fog of disbelief. Suspended in time and place, it's as if I was waiting for this nightmare to be over so I could get back to what really mattered: finishing the article for the *Los*

Angeles Journal and bringing Mr. Joshi to justice. But now I know I can't wake up from this. I can't keep punting my indecision down the road. I can't keep sleeping in the same bed as a man who very well may be a murderer. I have to do something.

But what?

It's just shy of six thirty, and I already regret having only brought one cigarette with me up to the roof. I'm thinking about going back down to fetch another one when the porch light flickers on two villas over at the Joshis. I press my weight against the guardrail in the northeast corner. Raj's villa partially obscures my view, and so I lean over as far as I can to see around it. I don't have to wait long. A beat later, Mr. Joshi, Sean, and Brown Hulk Hogan emerge.

I quickly crouch down so they don't spot me, and, squatting on my heels, I watch as Mr. Joshi gently closes the front door. A beat later, he turns around and says something to Sean and to his hulk of a security guard. Both of them nod obediently.

In spite of his unassuming appearance, there's something about Mr. Joshi that makes my skin crawl. Even if I didn't know who he is and what he'd done, I'd be able to tell there was something evil about the way he carries himself. The way he talks, and walks, and moves about the world.

I'd be able to tell that *he* is the boss.

My eyes fixed on Mr. Joshi, I watch him collect himself and start walking down the footpath toward the main resort, the other two a few steps behind. Right now, they must be off to cause a fuss at the consulate in San Jose. Before the family meeting broke up last night, I heard him reassuring Zara, Sean, and Caleb that he and his lawyers would figure out a way to get them back to the US. With the type of powermongers he surely has on payroll to cover his long list of crimes, I have no doubt that's the case.

I grind my teeth in anger, and the downright hatred I feel toward Mr. Joshi takes over my brain. If Raj was meeting with the cartel, and that's a big *if*, then there's no way he was there on his own accord; from what I understood, the man wasn't all that intelligent and partied harder than he actually worked. And what was it Raj drunkenly bragged about at his house party? I inhale tightly. He was "running point" on a confidential deal in the Americas for his father.

Yes. Raj would have been flying down to Cabo at his father's bidding. Drug money is a dirty business, but it's lucrative, and the exponential growth the Joshi Group experienced in the nineties and two thousands had already plateaued when the pandemic hit and global tourism took a nosedive. Maybe Mr. Joshi found an opportunity to work with the cartel to save his empire and further line his pockets. He had no qualms about lighting a hotel on fire and killing eighteen people for personal gain. Entering the drug trade and committing the untold evils required to support it—for a man like him—would be a walk in the fucking park.

Silently, I return to the bedroom, where Caleb is still fast asleep. And, before I fully realize what I'm doing, I grab my sneakers, phone, and crossbody bag and slip out through the terrace door. Out back, I plop down in a deck chair and stretch out my calves. After a few minutes, the officers appear to my left during their patrol around Raj's villa, and I lean down to tie my shoes and pretend not to notice them. I watch them in my peripheral vision, and as soon as they're out of sight and heading up the path back to the front, I spring upright and break into a jog.

I bypass the crime scene and head to the terrace behind the Joshis' villa. With Mr. Joshi, Sean, and Brown Hulk Hogan out for the day, I know no one's here; Mrs. Joshi flew out late last night, along with Zara's mother, brother, and sister-in-law, to repatriate the remains. Holding my breath, I tiptoe across the marble expanse and duck behind a cabana, as if waiting for someone to stop me. To smack me across the back of the head. To tell me that this is a very bad idea.

What am I even doing here?

Before I come to an answer, I catch sight of the terrace door. It's open.

Squatting low, I creep toward it, double checking to make sure the officers haven't returned. When I confirm no one is around, I slide the screen door open, slip through, and then slide it closed behind me.

Once inside, my heart rate slows down and, my jaw clenched, I set out through the villa. I do a quick walk-through of the kitchen and then the large living area, where we've been gathering for family meetings. When I don't find anything of note in the cupboards, drawers, or on any surfaces, I move into the larger of the two ground-floor bedrooms.

The layout in this villa is different from Caleb's. The primary bedroom is gigantic and features a California king bed at its very center, the foot facing out toward the floor-to-ceiling view of the Pacific. The bed is unmade, and there are two midnight-black socks hanging neatly over the back of a chair. The initials *NJ* are embroidered on the ankle.

Mr. *Narayan Joshi*. I'm in *his* bedroom.

It's hot in here, and I wipe the sweat forming on my upper lip with my sleeve. What am I doing here? What am I even looking for?

Adrenaline spikes through me as I rifle through the bedside drawers. When I find them empty, I go to the grand walk-in closet. On the left are Mr. Joshi's western suits, *kurtas*, and *sherwanis*. On the right are Mrs. Joshi's fine silk saris, designer *lehenghas*, and even a Valentino gown. There were only four days of events planned for the wedding, but they've brought enough clothing with them to change outfits every hour. Mrs. Joshi especially, who also brought a dozen pairs of shoes and nearly as many purses.

I quickly go through their clothing, searching all the pockets, and then move to the deep drawers beneath the vanity at the back. The top one contains various watches, three matching Cartier silver bracelets, and a Roja Dove Haute perfume. The bottom two drawers—

My mouth drops a little at the sight of it.

The drawers are overflowing with solid-gold jewelry.

Gold bangles, chokers, anklets, *jhumkas*, and rings. Heavy gold necklace sets with matching four-inch earrings, *tikkas*, and nose and belly chains. Gold encrusted with emeralds, rubies, diamonds, and sapphires. Gold, gold, and more fucking gold.

Traditionally, gold plays a huge role in Indian weddings—at least for those who have the means. The bride is gifted it in vast amounts and adorned like a Christmas tree. They say it's auspicious, a blessing, but it's also a marker of social status. This amount of gold is surely worth hundreds of thousands of dollars, maybe even millions. The fact the Joshis have left it lying around only further proves they're at the very top of their hierarchy.

The very sight of all this gold—this useless material good that stands against so much that I believe in—makes my stomach sour, but I feel myself softening when I spot a small necklace in the back corner of the bottom drawer. It's plain, compared to the rest of the jewelry. I pick it up and let it hang from my pinky finger. The chain has three threads of gold and black beads, and the pendant is solid gold, carved with a very desi, very distinctive design.

It's a *mangalsutra*. An ornament placed on a bride during her wedding, one which will forever signal her as a married woman.

I wonder if this is Mrs. Joshi's *mangalsutra*, from her wedding day, or if it was meant for Radhika, and the mother of the groom was storing it for safekeeping. The pendant spins on its axis, and a dizzying realization hits me: in an alternate universe, Raj would have clasped this necklace on Radhika's neck today. In just a few hours from now, they would have been husband and wife.

The Joshis didn't have a daughter; were they looking forward to this union? To welcoming Radhika into their family?

Suddenly, a wave of melancholy hits me with such force I'm nearly tempted to sit down. I didn't like Radhika, but she was just a girl of twenty-four. She had her whole life ahead of her. She didn't deserve to die. And, whatever Raj was doing here in Cabo, regardless of whose son he had the misfortune of being, he didn't deserve the end he got either.

After I put away the *mangalsutra*, I go through the other ground-floor bedroom, which I quickly discern is occupied by Brown Hulk Hogan and contains nothing of note. Next, I sneak upstairs. There's a rooftop terrace and a wellness room much like in Caleb's villa; I search for a safe, but if there's one here too, I can't find it.

Next door, there's another large bedroom and en suite. Immediately, I know it's Sean's room because the collared shirt he wore yesterday is in the pile of clothes on the floor. Quickly, quietly, I scavenge the drawers, his wardrobe, and as I look under the mattress, I find myself wondering how Sean fits into all of this. If Mr. Joshi and Raj are involved with a drug cartel, then does that mean Sean is too?

Sean knew about Raj's trips to Cabo and defended them, claimed he was doing business development with this Hector at Blush Continental. But he could have been covering up the truth. Sean is an obedient nephew, still lives at home, and is open about the fact that he'd take care of Mr. and Mrs. Joshi as they grew older. Even if he wasn't supportive of Mr. Joshi's and Raj's alleged endeavors with the cartel, would he have the guts to go against the grain?

I come up empty-handed in Sean's bedroom, and disheartened, I slink back downstairs. I'm not even sure what I was looking for in here: a smoking gun? Some piece of evidence one of the Joshis conveniently left lying around that would make sense of this whole mess?

I almost laugh at myself for being so stupid, so impulsive. Still, when I return to the ground floor, I decide to take one last look in Mr. Joshi's bedroom. Standing at the head of the massive bed, I survey the room—

Beep.

My stomach drops at the familiar sound. The front door to the villa has just been unlocked.

I drop down to hands and knees and crawl to the far side of the bed, out of view from the doorway.

Fuck.

Someone's here.

Is it housekeeping? The National Guard? I hear footsteps in the front room, slow, deliberate. My stomach flush to my thighs, I curl into a ball against the ground.

"You're right," someone says in Hindi. "We left the back door open."

The voice is masculine, gruff, but I can't place it. I swallow hard as heavy footsteps reverberate through the villa. After a moment, I hear the terrace door slide closed.

"I've locked it now, sir," the voice says. There is only one set of footsteps, so the person must be talking on the phone. "Would you like me to turn on the AC?"

The air conditioning. The thermostat is in the primary bedroom. In *here*. I press my hand over my mouth, screaming on the inside as two loafers suddenly appear in the doorway.

It's not the authorities, housekeeping, or another intruder. It's Mr. Joshi's giant security guard, Brown Hulk Hogan; Mr. Joshi must have sent him back.

The bed is too low for me to crawl under, and there's nowhere else for me to hide. I contort my body to make it as small and soundless as possible as the loafers disappear from view. I listen breathlessly as Brown Hulk Hogan enters the room, tracks along the opposite side of the bed. My heart is beating so hard I swear he can hear it. If he comes even a foot closer, I'm done.

My hands shake as Brown Hulk Hogan moves toward the thermostat, from which he'll have a direct view of my hiding spot. I inch backward, slowly, and as his large frame appears in front of me, I log roll out of view behind the foot of the bed.

The only problem is that now I'm next to the floor-to-ceiling window that looks over the back terrace. If the National Guard times their patrol correctly, then I'm screwed hiding here too.

My mind is in a frenzy as Brown Hulk Hogan fiddles with the thermostat. He takes his time, turning all the dials. Pushing all the buttons. Finally, I hear the air conditioning power on, feel the cool blast from the vent touching my calf. After Brown Hulk Hogan retreats from the bedroom, I slowly uncoil my body and combat crawl out of view from the window.

That was close. *Too* close.

A minute passes, and then another. Brown Hulk Hogan is still somewhere in the villa. Curious, unable to stop myself, I crawl toward the bedroom door. What is he still doing here?

I hold my breath as I approach the doorway and drop my butt back to my heels. Did he go upstairs? Inch by inch, I lean forward and peer through the doorway.

Brown Hulk Hogan is in the foyer facing away from me, his thick neck popping from his collar as he looks at something on his phone. I study his form, curious who this man is, and what he knows. How much his loyalty costs. Despite my extensive research into Mr. Joshi and his company, this man never appeared on my radar. I don't even know his name.

Suddenly, Brown Hulk Hogan locks his phone and then returns it to his back pocket. As his meaty forearm brushes the fabric of his shirt, I catch sight of a bulge tucked into his trousers by his right hip.

My heart catches in my throat. It's not the smoking gun I hoped to find.

But it's a gun. A real one.

12.

The moment Brown Hulk Hogan leaves, I shakily pick my-self up from the ground and race out the terrace door. When I'm safely on the path overlooking the cliffs, I scan my surroundings. There's no one around. Luckily, those officers didn't catch me on their patrol.

The lights are still off in Caleb's villa. I jog toward the beach stairs just behind it, adrenaline pumping, sweat dripping down my back. Of course Mr. Joshi's bodyguard has a fucking gun. A gun that I very much doubt the National Guard and Mexico's border security are aware of.

Briefly, I wonder if it's the murder weapon, if *he* could have murdered Raj and Radhika at Mr. Joshi's bidding. Immediately I shake my head. No. Mr. Joshi may be a murderer, but I simply can't believe he'd kill his own son. In our culture, everything parents do is for the benefit of their children's future and security, particularly when they're boys. Even if Mr. Joshi is a narcissist, he would still view Raj as an extension of himself. Moreover, logically there's no way he could have killed them; neither

Mr. Joshi nor his bodyguard had access to Raj's villa. And who in their right mind would hold on to a murder weapon?

Yet, when the son of someone as evil as Mr. Joshi is murdered in cold blood, it can't be a coincidence. What if there *is* a link between Mr. Joshi and the murders? I don't want to jump to conclusions, but the only clues available to me suggest that the Joshi Group is in bed with the cartels—doing what, I have no idea—and is using their supposed investment in Blush Continental as a cover. Mr. Joshi could have been sending Raj down to Cabo as the go-between, and then something happened. Something that got Raj and his new bride murdered. Did Raj mess up? Steal from them? Maybe. But why then are Zara, Caleb, and Sean under suspicion too?

Down on the beach, I kick off my shoes and walk barefoot until the cold waves lap at my toes. I sit down, unperturbed by the wet sand. The National Guard must believe that one of them is also involved in this conspiracy or, at the very least, used their wristband to allow a cartel assassin entry into Raj's villa. *Yes.* That must be it. I still can't believe that Zara, Sean, or Caleb could have decisively killed someone they loved in cold blood. But maybe one of them has a reason for wanting someone else to do the dirty work.

My head wanders in a fog as I debate whether or not to go straight back up the stairs and confess everything to the National Guard. I could tell them about Brown Hulk Hogan's gun, that I'm here as an undercover journalist, and what I know about Mr. Joshi, Raj, and their company's poor financial state of affairs. If the Joshis are in league with the cartel, and that involvement somehow precipitated the murders, then maybe I know something that could be helpful for the investigation.

But can I trust the National Guard? Corruption among

Mexico's law enforcement isn't a prejudice; it's a fact. And the drug cartels are no joke; what happens if the wrong person finds out I'm cooperating?

I breathe in the salty air, overwhelmed by indecision over my next move, and kicking myself about my last one. It was reckless to break into the Joshis' villa. Pointless too. I should have booked that flight and left already for the airport. Sticking around, putting myself in harm's way; what am I even trying to accomplish?

Eventually, I stand up and meander toward the main resort. I haven't come this way before and it's quite peaceful, only a handful of other tourists and joggers out this early. The Blush Villas community sits atop a cliff at least two hundred feet above the beach, but the terrain levels off quickly during the half-mile journey west. The beach behind the main resort is flush with its outdoor spaces: swimming pools, bars, restaurants, and seating areas.

The sand over here has been scraped into smooth, concentric circles, on top of which sit ivory-white beach chairs and daybeds. Several guests are already lounging, sipping mimosas and iced coffees. One man is obnoxiously taking a business call while typing away on his laptop. A pair of young lovers is holding hands.

A Blush beach attendant in a beige uniform waves from his post, grabs a towel from his cart, and then bounces toward me. He's in his early twenties and looks like a Backstreet Boy with those frosted tips. I've noted that staff here is a mix of locals and Americans. This one's American, his accent a touch West Coast. After he leads me to a beach chair and takes my coffee order, I ask him for his name so I can tip him later. I don't have any cash. He waves me off with a cheeky grin and tells me to enjoy the beach.

Enjoy the beach.

Ha.

Drumming my fingers on my thighs, I try to calm my nerves by enjoying the view, but my idyllic surroundings only increase my discomfort. I shouldn't be here, pretending to relax, as if this is some kind of paradise. As if I'm not delaying the inevitable.

I have to face Caleb and tell him the truth about our relationship. And, more than anything, I have to make sure that Raj and Radhika's murders don't thwart my chance to take Mr. Joshi down. Their deaths are a tragedy, but they're also proving to be a distraction. I came here for one reason and one reason only: Mr. Joshi. And just because his son is dead, just because he's grieving, doesn't mean justice won't be served ice-cold.

* * *

THE MORNING PASSES, and I go back to basics. On my phone, I pore over all my research on the Joshi Group, which I have backed up to the cloud, looking for some clue I might have missed. A nudge in the right direction. Backstreet Boy keeps interrupting my work to flirt or bring me fresh iced coffees, and I accept the latter because I forgot my cigarettes in Caleb's villa. I get the caffeine shakes, and, as my mind whizzes a mile a minute, in a million different directions, I also can't shake the feeling that I'm being watched. I think of my laptop open in the villa, and then that creepy moment on the beach stairs when I saw pebbles and sand trickle down the steps above. But I know I'm just being paranoid. Nobody knows why I'm really here. Nobody's following or watching me.

Right?

Guests come and go. A few local vendors stroll up the beach, selling sombreros, ponchos, bracelets, ceramic bowls, and cigars they carry on their person. Although they're barred from entering the resort's premises, the beach itself is public and so they're allowed to be here. The wealth disparity between the locals and tourists is uncomfortable, yet frustratingly familiar to me. As I glance up and down the sand, wondering how many miles the vendors would have had to travel by foot, I suddenly remember what Tobias said in the family meeting: the murderer could have arrived at Blush via the public beach. They could have accessed Raj's villa using the stairs behind the Villas, where there are no security cameras, rather than going through Blush's main resort. The murderer could have slipped in and out without a trace.

After I fail to find a lead in my own research, I turn to Eric's.

Call me?

When he emailed me yesterday, I lied to Caleb when I said he's a classmate. Eric Santos is a prominent freelance journalist, and the reason I'd secretly flown down to Cabo a day early.

Lexie had set up the meeting. She and Eric had become friends while they were living in New York, both junior reporters at the right-leaning paper; when I laid eyes on him at our meeting place, a dive bar he suggested in Cabo San Lucas, I recognized him from Lexie's years-old Instagram posts.

I'd been reluctant to share my investigation with a total stranger, but Lexie said she trusted him implicitly and that I could too. Eric wrote extensively about the economics and infrastructure underpinning Mexico's tourism industry, and she asked him to provide me with background on Blush Continental for my article. One editorial question for which I never found an answer was why did Raj and Radhika choose Blush Los Cabos Resort & Spa for their wedding? Other couples with similar wealth and status tended to marry in French châteaus, or on private tropical islands. Lexie didn't accept my explanation that many South Asians in Canada and the US these days opted for destination weddings south of the border; neither the Joshis nor the Singhs were your average Indian American family.

My meeting with Eric lasted the time it took each of us to drink a cold bottle of Dos Equis. He briefed me on the history of Blush Continental, told me how they were both loved and hated by the community; although they were an important employer in the region, they were known to treat their workers unfairly. Eric then handed me a thumb drive with all his research, and I'd simply dumped the files onto my cloud and watched *You've Got Mail* in Spanish in my one-star hotel room next door; the southern woman from the Oceanside Bistro must have clocked me and my Old Navy polka-dot dress during my late-night taco run.

My gut twists with regret. At the time, I didn't know Raj had been flying down monthly supposedly to meet with Blush Continental. And I definitely didn't know, less than twenty-four hours later, he and Radhika would wind up dead.

I sit up straight as I try calling Eric back, but it goes straight to voicemail. I wonder why he called me yesterday, what was so "important." I wasn't thinking clearly; I'm still not. I should have found a way to ditch Caleb and called Eric back immediately.

I've been running on the assumption the Joshi Group's supposed partnership deal with Blush Continental was a cover for Raj's meetings, but what if they factor into this too? What if Raj and Radhika chose Blush's resort in Los Cabos for a reason?

Shading the sun from my eyes, I enter my cloud password and start scrolling through Eric's files on Blush Continental. There are folders containing information on the history of the company, a timeline of its resorts openings, financials, and stats on and biographies of the company's executives and board of directors. Wondering if one of them might be Raj's contact Hector, I sift through the names carefully, but I don't find any matches. After, I search through another folder containing articles about the grand opening of Blush Resort & Spa Los Cabos two months ago. Dammit. I've read all of them before.

Even though I'm running out of hope of finding a lead, I force myself to click on the very last folder, which is titled *Miscellaneous*. At first, I don't understand what I'm reading. My head is groggy; I'm in desperate need of a cigarette. The file contains countless PDFs of jumbled text files, and eventually I realize I'm looking at Reddit threads Eric must have downloaded from the internet.

Leaning forward, I read as carefully and quickly as I can. The conversations among posters touch on all sort of subjects. Whether or not Blush's resort in Tulum or Puerto Vallarta is friendlier to swingers. A rant by an unsatisfied customer who claimed he found a pubic hair in his Acapulco resort bed. A post about—

I gasp as I read:

u/angelgirl222

Posted seven months ago

DO NOT STAY AT BLUSH RESORTS!!!

Guyzzzz. If you go to Mexico, WHICH YOU SHOULDN'T BECAUSE WE NEED TO SPEND OUR HARD-EARNED DOLLARS ON AMERICAN SOIL, then definitely avoid all resorts owned by Blush Continental.

Story time. My boyfriend's sister is a travel agent. She told us one of her rich CHINESE clients is obsessed with Blush. It's a Mexican company (red flag!) with loads of super fancy resorts. Anyway, this China Woman has been to all the Blush resorts except one, Blush El Paraíso, which apparently is out in the middle of nowhere and is super expensive and "boutique." It's several hundred miles away from Cabo. I don't know why China Woman is so desperate to go, but every time she asks my boyfriend's sister to make her a booking, it's always full. Always! Even when they try a YEAR ahead of time.

So this past winter China Woman decides to just show up. (Fucking immigrants thinking they can go wherever they want.) She flies to Cabo. She hires a Mexican to drive her hundreds of miles to the Blush El Paraíso address and apparently is just bursting with excitement when they pull up to this beautiful resort. But guess what she finds when she goes inside?

Nothing. No staff. No guests. And although the exterior of the resort is all grand and impressive, the insides look like a half-finished construction site!!

As funny as it is that China Woman got stranded in the middle of nowhere, that's totally messed up right? Ever since my boyfriend's sister told me the story, I've been obsessed with figuring out what happened. And, based on my research, here's what I think: Blush is totally laundering money for some drug cartel!

Apparently, there are these things called "BLACK HOTELS."

There are no real guests, but if someone calls and asks for a room, the hotel tells them its full. Meanwhile, the hotel is COOKING THE BOOKS with fake guest names and claim they're paying in cash.

And, guess what, that cash is the CARTEL'S DRUG MONEY! THE HOTEL IS LAUNDERING THEIR DIRTY MONEY!

Sound familiar?

13.

Blinking, I read the Reddit post two more times, my heartbeat pounding in my ears. Blush Continental is an award-winning, internationally recognized hotel group. It caters to the ultra-rich, and if they were so blatantly operating a "black hotel," surely someone other than angelgirl222 would have noticed.

Right?

Licking my lips, I take a deep, calming breath and then scroll down to read all the comments. There are over a hundred, but nothing sheds more light on the original poster's accusations. Dozens merely piggyback off the poster's racist remarks and add colorful ones of their own. Others debate her view that Americans should only support US tourism. And the comments that do focus on her theory that Blush El Paraíso is a "black hotel" all sound like they've been written by avid conspiracy theorists.

I set down my phone and close my eyes, thinking. Angelgirl222's allegations could be just that, a conspiracy theory.

Anyone can post anything on Reddit. The idea that Blush Continental cleans up drug money could be complete and total crap.

But a cartel may have just killed Raj and Radhika on a Blush Continental property. What if Blush's involvement with the cartel isn't just a conspiracy theory, and the Joshi Group is laundering money for them too?

It would make perfect sense. The Joshi Group runs hundreds of hostels, hotels, and resorts around Asia, some of them in countries rampant with corruption, with fewer regulations and less government oversight, where black hotels would more easily slip under the radar. Maybe this "Hector" from Blush Continental was showing Raj the ropes on how to clean up dirty money through a black hotel, and then something happened that triggered the murders. Betrayal comes to mind first. Mr. Joshi's business tactics are bullish and opportunistic. Maybe the Joshi Group was undercutting or stealing from the cartel, taking a larger share than what was due. Maybe the cartel killed Raj (and Radhika) as a warning, and Mr. Joshi himself is now in danger.

Before I lose track of my thoughts, I pull out my notepad and pen and start to jot everything down. Dammit, Lexie. Why haven't you called me back? I need my editor right now. I can't think straight; I need my *friend.*

I'm scribbling so fast I can barely read my own handwriting and only look up from the page when a group of boisterous guests suddenly splash into the infinity pool, the edge of which is just a few feet behind me. Their voices are loud, and male. Obnoxious. Without looking over my shoulder, I can already tell what kind of men they are. Frat boys and hedge fund managers.

Finance bros. I set down my pen, unable to help myself from eavesdropping when two of them start to debate fixed-income securities and another waves over a beach vendor. Leans over the edge of the infinity pool, tries on a sombrero, and delivers a sermon about how the vendor would get more business if he accepted Venmo.

Cringing, I reluctantly turn around to look. There are seven of them in the pool, all of them white, tall, fit. All of them devilishly good-looking. They are horsing around like they own the place, and, after a loudspeaker starts blaring mariachi music, the assholes even start singing.

Enchiladas. Piña coladas. Salsa verde. Salsa dancing.

It all sounds and tastes and feels the same to them, doesn't it? I want to scream as I watch them shimmy around the infinity pool, waving their arms to the beat, belting nonsense over the Spanish lyrics. One of them shouts "*arriba*" at the top of his lungs as he shotguns a beer. It's nine in the morning, and you'd think one of the other guests would say something, but nobody does. Not even me.

Shame flushes my face as I stare at them from down below. I don't know what I feel more mortified by: their behavior, or because these men remind me exactly of Caleb.

How could I have so easily faked a relationship with a man like that, but can barely stand to breathe the same air as the ones acting like fools right in front of me?

There are two Calebs. I've known this from the beginning, and I chose to see his good side, his sweetness, but I can't deny there's a part of him that I don't understand. Even that I despise.

Caleb—*my* Caleb—did not kill Raj and Radhika. But what about Caleb Malcolm Prescott III? He cares about money, and status, and is obliviously happy for others to stay down so they can continue propping him up. What does this Caleb want? What is *he* capable of?

"Check out the legs on that one," I hear one of the Pool Bros say, snapping me back to the present. I glance over as he points and gawks at a woman, while his friend wrestles him into a headlock.

"She's all yours," the friend says. "You know I only do blondes."

"Your loss, buddy. Should I call her over?" The first one scoffs, and then his face breaks into a wide grin. "Wait—*shit*. I know her."

"No way—"

"I do," he insists. "That's the chick who started Lustre."

My mouth drops to an O as I stand up and backpedal in the sand to get a better view. My eyes track across the pool in the direction of their gaze. I lean forward, squinting. They're right. It's Zara.

Quickly, I gather my things as the Pool Bros debate whether they should approach her. Ultimately, they decide against it—convinced that the infamous Zara Singh will be too much of a "ballbuster"—which is good for me. I'm heading that way now.

I don't know why exactly. I don't know if I can trust Zara; she's under suspicion for murder too. But she's not a member of the Joshi family, doesn't work for the Joshi Group, and something in my gut tells me I need to talk to her. Radhika told Zara about Raj's frequent visits to Cabo, his meetings with a Mexican businessman. Maybe Zara knows more than she's letting on. Maybe she could tell me something—anything—that will help me with my next move.

I hustle up the beach, and with a wave goodbye to the Backstreet Boy beach attendant, I head toward Zara. She's lounging in a cabana, her identity almost shielded by an extraordinarily large floppy hat and sunglasses. I can tell immediately why the Pool Bros noticed her among the dozen or so other beautiful women in their vicinity; Zara's not just gorgeous. She has presence. There's something about her that simply screams *celebrity*.

My nerves catch up with me as I draw closer. She's so hot and cold, she might not even be willing to speak to me. But I place one foot in front of the other, and I'm nearly standing right in front of her when her phone goes off.

I don't catch the name on her screen in time. She answers it too quickly. And as she brings the phone to her ear, I halt my approach and freeze.

"What do *you* want?"

Her tone is sharp, rude. I recoil backward even though I know she isn't speaking to me. Even though she has no idea I'm standing six feet away from her.

"Oh really?" After a moment, she adds," You're pissing me off too, but fine. *Whatever.*"

Who's pissing her off? Who is she talking to?

"*Fine,*" she repeats. She brushes her hair out of her face and adds, "Jesus! All right, I said I'd be right there!"

Zara violently tosses her cell into her white leather tote and throws her legs over the side of her deck chair. Fluidly, I spin on my heels and squat down in a seat facing away from her, keeping my head down. Behind me, she mutters under her breath as she gathers her things. When I can't hear her anymore, I peek behind me. She's hustling down the path toward the main resort.

I bolt after her, curious. A little suspicious too. Zara sounded annoyed by the caller, although there was a sense of familiarity to her tone. It felt like she knew them well. Caleb hasn't texted me yet, which means he's still asleep. Mr. Joshi and Sean are at the consulate. And the rest of the Singh family already left. Then who was she talking to just now; who is here at Blush that she's going to see?

I stay on Zara's tail as she catwalks through the maze of outdoor pools, bars, and seating areas, and as she picks up speed, I struggle both to keep up with her and stay at a safe distance. Once at the main resort, I follow her through the doors leading into the shopping piazza, which is on the ground floor. At the end of the corridor, right before the entrance to the spa and gym, Zara takes the staircase leading up to the second level.

I don't want her to see me on the stairs, and so I wait thirty seconds and then race up after her. I'm out of breath when I get to the top and find myself in the far end of the lobby, past the concierge, at an intersection of corridors that fan out to several of the restaurants, banks of elevators, and other amenities. Taking a few hesitant steps forward, I search the faces of all the guests coming and going, but I don't see her.

My shoulders slump. I lost her.

* * *

A PACK OF smokes from the gift shop costs three times what they do in LA. Feeling defiant, I charge it to Caleb's villa and then track down an outdoor deck where I'm actually allowed to smoke.

Immediately, I can feel my head clear, my body release. Taking a long, sweet inhalation, I hang over the railing and scan the horizon. From up here, I have a panoramic view of the ocean, and it's fucking breathtaking. The water is the color of gemstones, sparkling, lapping against a sliver of white sandy beach. Before giant hotel groups like Blush Continental developed this land, it would have been beautiful. It would have been, truly, a paradise.

My lips tightly pinch the cigarette as I pull up Blush Continental's website and click through to the page for Blush El Paraíso, the supposed black hotel. The cover photo features the grand exterior of the resort. It's designed hacienda style, with a clay roof, light stucco, and wooden beams. There's a sign reading "Blush El Paraíso" above the veranda. I stare at the cover photo and, quite suddenly, something fires in my brain, a neural pathway abruptly becomes unlocked. Something about this photo feels familiar. But what?

Unsettled, I continue scrolling through gallery photos. They showcase everything from guests having romantic beachside dinners, to luxury king-size hotel rooms, to spa and fitness centers, but there are no pictures specifically of Blush El Paraíso's interiors; they're stock photos used to advertise all of the hotel group's resorts. Could angelgirl222's accusation that Blush El Paraíso isn't fully constructed be true?

Her other Reddit allegation in my mind, I try to make an online booking. Just before checkout, the webpage reads "error" and requests I call to make a reservation. When I do, the man on the phone tells me the Blush El Paraíso is booked up for the foreseeable future and requests my information so they can "let me know" when they have availability.

I hang up the call and, my shoulders tense with suspicion, I return to the gallery photo. The clay roof. The hacienda architecture. It feels so familiar, almost like—

My heart falls as it hits me. I rush to open up Instagram and click on Raj's profile. I don't have to scroll long. Just four months ago, he posted a selfie on that same veranda, beneath that same "Blush El Paraíso" sign.

Raj visited the Blush Continental alleged black hotel.

My stomach sours as I feel my reality shift around me. This isn't a conspiracy theory; there are too many coincidences. The Joshi Group must be working with Blush Continental and the cartels!

Down below, the Pool Bros continue to wreak havoc in the infinity pool, and, as I watch them, and the rush of tobacco further clears my head, suddenly, my next move becomes crystal clear.

When I set out to expose Mr. Joshi, at most I thought my report on the fire would lead to his public shaming, lawsuits, and government inquiries. Years and years of expensive red tape. But if I can prove that his company is part of an international drug ring? And, by sending Raj to do the dirty work, he put his son and future daughter-in-law in harm's way? The bastard's going to get what he really deserves.

Prison.

I'm not a Mexican police officer or local journalist; I don't have the resources, connections, or language skills to unearth enough further evidence to expose the drug ring or determine why the cartel wanted Raj dead. But right now, I'm uniquely positioned on the inside. And I might be able to figure out who let the killer into the villa.

The National Guard would not have barred Zara, Sean, and Caleb from leaving Cabo without a very good reason. Only they had access to Raj's villa—and only one of them could have betrayed him and Radhika to the cartel.

Yes, they loved them, but more is going on here than what I can see on the surface. All three of them had the means, and maybe one of them had motive too.

Sean ran the LA office with Raj and is part of the Joshi family. Did Mr. Joshi and Raj keep Sean in the dark about the conspiracy, or was he equally involved? Did Sean have something to gain by giving up Raj to the cartel? Did *Caleb*? He claimed he didn't know Raj had been flying to Cabo, but that could just be another one of his lies. He's been working at the Joshi Group for months now; he might be in on the game too.

A vibrant blur down below catches my eyes, and I lean over the railing, wondering if it's Zara. The figure sashays toward the jacuzzi, and as I watch the figure strip down and enter the water, I realize it's someone else. I don't know where Zara is, where she disappeared in the resort.

And I don't know what she's capable of either.

Sighing deeply, I turn and press my back into the railing. Zara may not be part of the Joshi clan or have alleged cartel connections, but I know she's hiding something. I take another drag of my cigarette, remembering how she was up at five in the morning, jogging, the day after her sister's murder.

It could be nothing; she's a hardworking woman dedicated to her routine. But what if she wasn't merely exercising when I saw her earlier? She'd stopped in front of Caleb's villa, just before she came in view of the police officers patrolling the crime scene next door. Why was she there? And why, moments ago, did she run off to meet that mysterious caller? A woman like her must have secrets. Big ones. But are they related to the murders?

I finger my Blush wristband, which has temporarily granted me access into this exclusive world. Nobody here knows I'm a journalist—I hope. I *think*. I need to make the most of the time I have left and do what I must to get the people behind these high walls to talk.

What happened that night, in the hours leading up to Raj and Radhika's tragic demise?

Zara. Sean. Caleb. One of them sold out Raj and Radhika to the cartel; one of them is just as guilty as whichever cartel member pulled the trigger. And, come hell or high water, I'm going to figure out which one of them is responsible.

From: Shaylee Kapoor
To: Eric Santos
Time: 9:36 a.m.
Subject: Re: URGENT

Hi Eric,

I tried calling you back but it went straight to voicemail.

Can we connect ASAP? I'm not sure how much I should put in writing, but the reason for my being in Cabo has drastically changed and now I'm desperate for more information on Blush Continental. I looked through your files and saw a Reddit accusation that they're operating their El Paraíso resort as a black hotel for the cartel. Can you confirm? I'm working an angle that the Joshi Group is involved too.

See attached screenshot of Raj Joshi at Blush El Paraíso four months ago. He posted it to his Instagram. Apparently, he's been visiting Cabo monthly and taking business meetings with someone at Blush Continental nicknamed Hector. Any idea who this person is?

I'll explain more when I can. Much appreciated,

Shay

14.

The gentleman at the concierge desk tells me Daniela is in "Atlantis" at the western edge of the resort. He offers to have someone escort me over, but I decline and decide to make my own way. I need time to gather my thoughts—and I definitely need to speak with Daniela in private. She found the bodies, had access to Raj's villa, planned their wedding, and works for Blush Continental, which may be working with the Joshi Group and the cartel. I need to question her and, just as importantly, I have to confirm her alibi.

I walk slowly, purposefully, keeping my eyes peeled—and my theory of the case open. I need to be objective, and I can't make snap judgments either. While I try and figure out why Zara, Sean, or Caleb might have facilitated the murders on behalf of the cartel, I also need further evidence to support my central premise: that the Joshi Group is in fact laundering money for the cartel. As of yet, I have nothing concrete. Maybe Eric can help me with that. I hope he emails me back soon.

At the far end of the resort, I climb three sets of stairs and find myself in a grand empty corridor. It's so quiet up here I can hear the pounding of my own heart, and a shiver runs down my spine as I follow the signage toward Atlantis. I tread past the desolate dance club and conference center, note the security cameras above the doors. I should take comfort knowing there are cameras spread around the main resort, even though there are none in the Villas. No matter what happens today, as long as I stay in public, within reach of help should I unfortunately need it, I'm hoping I'll be OK.

I hang a left at the end of the corridor, and, up ahead, my chest tightens when I spot Atlantis. It's unlike any banquet hall I've ever seen before, lit up with thousands upon thousands of fairy lights, its floor-to-ceiling glass walls providing a panoramic view of the ocean. This is where Raj and Radhika's wedding ceremony was supposed to take place; even without the highfalutin guests, the flowers, the fanfare, I can almost imagine it. Raj looking handsome in a regal jewel-toned *sherwani*. Radhika, his beautiful bride, adorned with *mehendhi*, gold, and a *lenengha* fit for a queen.

I draw closer, and the vision fades when I spot Daniela at one of the round central tables. She's sipping champagne.

"I see you, Shay."

The hairs on the back of my neck stand upright as Daniela slowly rotates her chin to face me. Eyes locked on mine, she smiles vaguely and sips her champagne.

"Welcome to the *party*."

I hesitate, uncomfortable by her tone. The directness of her gaze.

"Have you seen Zara?" I ask for starters, still unsure where she disappeared to earlier.

"I have not." Daniela's tone brightens. "Drink?"

She gestures at the champagne, a vintage Dom older than me. Without waiting for my answer, she fills a flute to its brim and pushes it toward me.

"Try it," Daniela says happily, taking a swig from the bottle. "Don't be shy. It's really not that bad."

She laughs at her own joke, a gurgle at the back of her throat. Is Daniela drunk? My stomach queasy, I awkwardly pull out the chair, sit down, and reach for the champagne. But the flute is too full, and when I lean down to slurp liquid from the lip, Daniela cackles.

"Should we play champagne pong, Shay? I could wrestle up the equipment."

Carefully, I swallow the drink and don't respond. The composed, elegant, intelligent woman who greeted me upon my arrival and proudly gave me a tour of the resort has vanished into thin air. Not that I blame her, but this version of Daniela is a total mess.

"How are you holding up?" I ask quietly after she catches her breath.

Her lips bend into a frown.

"Daniela." I hesitate briefly but force myself to push on. "You found two people *dead*. Why are you working right now? You should be at home."

And getting help from a mental health professional. But I don't say that part out loud.

Daniela sets down her glass, eyeing me.

"Would you like to know something funny?" She smiles. "I forgot to tell the baker!"

She throws a thumb over her left shoulder. Reluctantly, I follow it with my gaze. Set up against the southern wall is an over-the-top three-tiered wedding cake.

"We flew him in business from Paris," Daniela says dreamily. "Did the happy couple tell you?"

After I shake my head, she says a French name I don't recognize, tells me he has over five million followers on TikTok. How he was going to bake his viral Sunshine Vanilla and Caramel Latte Cheesecake for the wedding ceremony and reception respectively.

"We rented an industrial kitchen in San Jose for his personal use, hired him three assistants, sourced the ingredients to his *precise* specifications." She laughs. "He dropped off that eyesore this morning, hoped to have a word with the bride and groom."

Daniela's face darkens as she starts to pant.

"What the hell am I going to do with it?"

"Eat it?" I offer, hoping a joke might help. Her tight lips curl upward and she rises from her seat.

"I wasn't serious—"

"I know, but it's a good idea." She beams. "My career is over anyway."

My jaw hangs low as I watch Daniela carve into the giant cake and return with an enormous slice of Sunshine Vanilla and two forks. She examines one of them for a moment before viciously stabbing it into a lifelike frosted lily.

"Your career isn't over," I say gently. "Surely."

"You do realize, Blush hasn't yet fired me because they need me to handle—what's the phrase?" She pops a piece of cake into her mouth and chews. "This *shit show?*"

"You won't be fired for forgetting to cancel one vendor, Daniela."

"No," she quips, her mouth full. "I'll be fired because the bride and groom *I* was responsible for were shot in the head—"

She stops abruptly and moans.

"Honestly, Shay, this is heaven. You must have a bite."

I accept her offer to be polite, so I have something to do with my hands, and, together, we eat for a few moments in blissful silence. The cake is moist, not too sweet, an explosion of flavors that land on my tastebuds in all the right places. At one point, Daniela and I try and dig our forks into the same lump of cake. She uses hers as a sword, swatting mine away, smiling.

My appetite vanishes.

What was I doing here, eating dessert, acting as if nothing is wrong? As if every second doesn't count?

"Daniela, I need to ask you a few questions."

Her expression clouds over as she shovels another bite into her mouth. When she doesn't respond, I keep going.

"I need to know what happened that night. I need to know if my boyfriend *killed* Raj and Radhika."

I watch Daniela's face carefully. I'm gambling right now, but continuing to pretend to be Caleb's supportive girlfriend is the best strategy I have to get everyone here to open up to me. Even a supportive girlfriend would have questions, wouldn't she?

"How am I supposed to know if Caleb did it?" Daniela says after a beat, her jaw tight. "I don't know anything."

"I just want to know what you saw that night, your side of the story—"

"*My* side of the story?"

She doubles over, her loose ponytail nearly catching on the cake as her head whips forward. Even though I'm frustrated, I'm also becoming increasingly concerned about her well-being. She had her whole world ripped apart when she came face-to-face with two dead bodies, yet here she is. At *work*. When was the last time she slept? Or even changed her clothes?

"Where were you Wednesday night?" I ask, trying to remain

patient. She's still laughing, sucking air as if she's sprinted a marathon. I tense.

"Daniela?"

"Yes?" She takes a moment to compose herself. I wait for her to calm down, and then I repeat the question.

"I was here at Blush," she says plainly, returning to normal. "In my office."

"All night?"

"I had a million things to do before the guests arrived. I always work 24/7 ahead of marquee events. It's part of the job."

"And you stayed in your office the whole night."

She hesitates, seemingly understanding the real meaning behind my question: I want confirmation of her alibi. After a moment, she gestures indiscriminately in the direction of the resort.

"There are security cameras that vouch for my whereabouts during the hours the bride and groom were killed," she says robotically. Then she holds up her wrist, on which is fastened a Blush wristband identical to mine. "The bride and groom granted me special access to the villa too. I used this to get in when . . ."

She trails off. When she found their bodies Thursday morning.

"As you can see, the wristband is still intact." Daniela drops her arm theatrically. "My alibi is not in dispute, Shay. If it was, I would have been arrested by now. The authorities would have loved to pick off the low-hanging fruit and keep the Americans out of this."

"Low-hanging fruit?" I say, even though I know what she's getting at. It would be much easier to blame the local, the employee. If it was a matter of her word against Zara, Sean, and Caleb's, Daniela wouldn't stand a chance.

"Don't look so wounded," Daniela says suddenly. "None of this concerns you. Leave Caleb. Go *home*."

I sit back in my chair, surprised by her frankness. "I can't."

"Because you love that man?"

"Are you sure nobody else had access to the villa?" I ask, evading the question. "Surely, someone—"

Daniela waves me off.

"I am confident. During major events, I personally attend to all matters relating to the happy couple, their families, and their VIPs. No one could have been granted access to that villa without my knowing."

"Wait, did Radhika have a key to Raj's villa?" Could she have given access to a third party?

"Of course." Daniela nods. "But she and the groom were both wearing their wristbands when . . ."

Her words falter again, and I move on when the Joshis' terrace door suddenly comes to mind; they'd mistakenly left it open, and I'd taken advantage and broke into their villa. But when I suggest the murderer entered Raj's villa the same way, Daniela shakes her head and tells me that's not possible; when she arrived that morning, all the windows and doors were locked from the inside.

"Still," I insist. "Surely there is another explanation for how the killer entered Raj's villa *without* a key?"

Daniela gives me a look, blinking.

"I've been thinking about this too."

She purses her lip, weighing her words.

"On Thursday morning, right before I left you in front of Caleb's villa, I came *here* to wait for the happy couple." She taps on the table with her pointer finger. "We had scheduled a nine a.m. meeting, but when they didn't show up and neither of them answered their cellphones—"

"You went to Raj's."

"They were out late the night before. I didn't want them to get behind schedule. I thought I would wake them up."

My shoulders tighten. "You knew they'd both be in Raj's?" That Radhika wouldn't be staying in her own accommodation that night?

"Of course," Daniela says. "The bride hired her own villa for appearances only. She wanted to appease a few of her mother's more traditional guests, but the happy couple was so in love. Inseparable. I believe they always spent their nights together."

Daniela pauses, and I take the quiet moment to process. If Daniela knew that Radhika would spend the night with Raj, then Zara, Sean, and Caleb would have known too. The murderer *knew* Raj wouldn't be alone; that killing him meant taking out Radhika too.

"When I found them," Daniela goes on, "they were in the bed, naked, as you've been told. The blood—" She swallows as if she's going to throw up. "I won't go into those details.

"I saw the security logs on my own computer. The 'do not disturb' function was indeed switched on the whole night. The only way someone could have entered the villa without a key is if . . ."

My breath hitches, understanding.

"Raj or Radhika let them in."

Either way, the killer was someone they knew. They'd given them access to their villa, or let them inside voluntarily. But how did that make sense? Raj and Radhika were sleeping when they were killed. They were naked. Were they involved romantically or sexually with a third person? I shudder. With *Caleb*? I never understood their dynamic; maybe it was more complicated than I imagined.

Or—I backtrack from the thought—maybe they invited a guest in, offered them a couch to crash on. But if that was the case, wouldn't there be DNA or other physical evidence left behind that law enforcement would have told us about?

"This is so fucked up," I breathe, lost in thought.

Daniela throws me a sidelong glance. "Tell me about it."

I smile at her, feeling bad for manipulating her in this state. It's clear as day; Daniela's not doing well, underslept and a touch delirious. She needs someone, but I don't have it in me to be that person right now. The clock is ticking. I need to find out everything I can about what she saw that night, and if any of the clues point to Zara, Sean, or Caleb.

I need to say and do whatever it takes to bring Mr. Joshi down.

"So, how long have you worked for Blush Continental?" I ask vaguely.

She sucks air through her teeth. "Ten years? I used to work at their resort in Cabo San Lucas. I was promoted to run the events show here when they opened up a few months ago. There were over a hundred other applicants." Laughing, she adds, "Aren't *I* lucky."

"Is Blush a good employer?" I ask next, even though what I really want to ask is: *Does your employer launder money for the cartel?* And, *Do you know someone named Hector?*

"Sure." Daniela shovels another piece of cake into her mouth. I think she's going to say something else, but after a long moment, it becomes clear she isn't.

"It's a beautiful resort," I try next. "I can see why Raj and

Radhika chose it. Raj must have fallen in love with the place during all of those business trips to Cabo."

When she doesn't take the bait, I add, "Although, I'm surprised they didn't pick Blush El Paraíso."

Daniela's features freeze. "Why . . . why do you say that?"

"Well," I say, my pulse quickening, "Raj went to visit. He kept going on and on about how much he loved Blush El Paraíso."

Neither one of us speaks, or even dares to move, and I hold Daniela's gaze. Persistent. Forceful. What does she know? What isn't she saying? But, before I can get it out of her, the connection breaks when something buzzes. Instinctively, we both reach for our phones. When I realize it's not mine, I look back up. All the blood has drained from Daniela's face.

"What is it?"

She doesn't answer. Bending forward, her hands shake as she taps on her phone and places it on the table between us. A beat later, a video flashes on screen. It's a local news station featuring a live, aerial view of Blush Resort & Spa Los Cabos. Of *this* resort. Loosely translated, the caption reads "Wealthy Americans Murdered on Wedding Eve."

"Oh my god," I whisper as Daniela turns up the volume.

It's finally happened. The news is out. I squeeze Daniela's forearm, and together we listen to the anchor's voiceover, her Spanish clipped and clear. I don't understand everything, but she knows Raj and Radhika's names. She seems to know that they were about to be married, the stature and fame of their respective families. My body clenches. She even knows the National Guard is investigating the murders as a drug-related crime.

Abruptly, the video switches to the resort's front gate, where more than a dozen media vans and their crews have amassed.

But what the anchor says next confuses me, because it can't be true.

A knot tightens in the pit of my stomach as I try to decipher her words. I must be misunderstanding.

The news anchor seems to be repeating information the channel learned just ten minutes ago when the *Los Angeles Journal* broke the story of Raj and Radhika's murders. I think she's quoting directly from their article, a source close to the families.

I think she's quoting *me*.

15.

love how you draw a parallel between the likely success of Raj and Radhika's marriage, and the future of their families' companies," Lexie said as she went over her notes for Shay's sixth—no, seventh—draft of the article. "Well done."

Shay grimaced as Lexie rocked back and forth in her swivel chair in anticipation. Lexie's editorial style was to precede tough questions or criticism with a compliment.

"But . . ."

There it was.

"I want more insight into whether this marriage will affect the leadership of Lustre and the Joshi Group." Lexie paused. "Zara's clearly going to stay in charge at Lustre, but have you found out whether or not Radhika plans to get involved with the company in some capacity? You'd think a beauty-slash-lifestyle influencer like Radhika would want in."

"I'm not sure," Shay said vaguely, although the truth was Radhika's ambitions of working at Lustre hadn't even crossed her mind. "I'll look into it?"

"Definitely. Remember this article is really about *Zara* and Lustre, so you—"

"I remember," Shay grunted. "Vividly."

Lexie made one of her irritating *hmmm* noises before switching gears.

"OK. What about the future of the Joshi Group?" she asked next. "Joshi is in his seventies. Do you think he'll tap Raj or Sean as the next CEO when he retires?"

"The man's not going to retire. He's a powermonger. A tyrant. On paper, Raj and Sean run the Americas and Europe business, but Caleb tells me he breathes down their necks and basically runs the show in LA too."

"OK. When Joshi dies, or goes to prison, or whatever." Lexie paused. "Who takes over? Raj or Sean?"

"I'll ask again." She'd tried to float the question to Caleb a few times, but he never gave her a straight answer.

"My money's on Sean," Lexie mused. "He seems like he's got his shit together." She raised an eyebrow at Shay and added, "although he isn't the biological son."

Shay's eyes glazed over as Lexie continued to steadfastly go through her notes on the latest draft. Lexie's annoying habits had only become more pronounced since their university days at McGill. Nearly a decade later, Lexie still bugged out those wide, judgmental eyes whenever she spotted a dangling modifier or partially fleshed-out argument. She continued to spill her lunches on Shay's drafts, loudly picked food out of her teeth with her tongue while she read them. And then there was that low-pitched *hmmm* she always made at random intervals; that *really* drove Shay up the wall.

In college, Shay used to crack jokes about Lexie's mannerisms, and eyes still on the page, Lexie would respond with the middle finger. They used to show one another their bitchiest, most emotionally volatile selves—declare World War Three over whose days-old fried rice was stinking up the fridge—and then make up in time for class. But that was before Shay moved abroad. That was back when they were friends.

"Let's talk headlines," Lexie said after finishing her notes. "I polled a few of my colleagues. What do you think about playing off the Romeo and Juliet angle?"

Shay made a face. Here she thought she'd been commissioned to write a piece of hard-hitting journalism, not a pseudo-journalistic *soap opera* painting the Singhs as the Montagues and the Joshis as the Capulets.

"Fine. What about 'Crazy Rich *South* Asians'?"

"Why don't we keep it simple," Shay deadpanned, "and just call it 'Clickbait.'"

Seething, she started stuffing her belongings into her backpack and mentally preparing herself for the long drive through traffic back to her Airbnb. Caleb was busy tonight, and so she actually had to sleep at that shithole she was calling home these days; it was the only thing she could afford in the vicinity of the USC campus. Caleb rarely came over to hers, but when he did, she still needed him to believe she was actually a grad student.

Shay looked up and found that Lexie was watching her intently. "What?" she snapped.

"I know you think I'm a sellout. You've thought that about me since I took that job in New York."

Shay tried to keep her face neutral, even though she wanted to say *yes*. That's exactly what she was thinking. Lexie had sacrificed everything she claimed to believe in to accept that highly coveted job at the right-leaning newspaper. And, even now that she was here, an editor at a newspaper at which they'd both dreamed of working back in college, she was *still* a sellout.

This article was supposed to be about what was best for the public interest: holding a bad man accountable for his crimes. Not *clickbait*.

"Don't give me that look," Lexie chided. "Zara Singh and her Lustre miracle cure are what our readership cares about right now, and so we have to frame this as a follow-up to *Zara's* profile, one that exposes the type of family *her* baby sister is marrying into.

"Joshi's criminal actions can't be the primary focus," Lexie continued. "The article needs to delve more into Radhika's relationship with Raj, the wedding, the fanfare. It needs to paint a picture of their wealth and excess. It just needs *more!*"

Shay scoffed. *More.*

More gossip. More titillation. More newspapers sold.

"I know this article isn't turning out how you envisioned it," Lexie said, "but come on, Shay. People don't care about human rights abuses. People don't care about injustices in an Asian country they've never been to."

She threw Shay a wry look.

"Do you know what they care about?"

"Sex, drugs, and rock and roll," Shay grumbled.

"Exactly—"

"Then they should watch HBO!"

"Get off your high horse," Lexie snapped, her voice rising for the first time. "This is the real world. And doing this my way is the best chance you've got to expose Joshi. Do you want to take it, or not?"

Shay kept her mouth shut. Of course she wanted to take it. She knew with every fiber of her being that Mr. Joshi was a cheating, lying, murderous criminal. Shay had to take it. She had to do everything in her power to serve him his just deserts, even if it meant being just like Lexie. If it meant selling out too.

"Good." Lexie smiled, correctly interpreting Shay's silence. "Because there's one more thing we need to talk about."

Lexie crossed her arms, her voice dropping low.

"Caleb."

Shay held her breath as they both sat down in their chairs. "What about him?"

"I need you to explain to me why you never told me about his family."

Shay's heart dropped into her stomach as Lexie calmly reamed her out for keeping quiet about the Prescotts, how she randomly stumbled upon the latest Prescott scandal while scrolling *The Scoop*. Lexie was aware Caleb was part of the East Coast society family that had been real estate moguls since the end of the Civil War, but Shay had failed to clarify that Caleb's particular branch were a group of degenerates. His grandfather had a tragic rockstar death by overdose, Caleb's mother practically lived at an exclusive high-stakes casino, and Caleb's father and half-siblings were all alcoholics or drug users, in and out of rehab as often as they were featured on *The Scoop*, *TMZ*, or Perez Hilton. Caleb's only full sibling, a sister who had been cut off from the family for stealing from the family trust, was currently serving time for her fourth DUI.

As Lexie spoke to her about journalistic integrity as if she was a freshman, Shay felt herself shutting down. Her defenses going up. She didn't know how to answer Lexie's question without betraying Caleb, without giving up a piece of him she hadn't meant to find.

After their first night together, Caleb had held her tight beneath the sheets and told Shay his biggest fear in life was turning into his father and grandfather. That his wealth would make him similarly aimless, and bored, that he'd follow in their footsteps and choose pleasure over purpose. Himself over all others. There was a reason Caleb followed Raj to LA after college, worked hard in his career in finance, and claimed the Joshi family as his own. He didn't want to be a Prescott.

"I didn't think Caleb's family history was important," Shay replied evenly, after Lexie said her piece. "Besides, Caleb talked to me about that stuff in confidence."

"Confidence," Lexie scoffed.

Shay backtracked. "I meant I would have written about the Prescotts if it was *relevant*, Lex. You said it yourself: this profile is about Zara Singh and her family. About the Joshis. If I wrote about Caleb's family drama too, the article would lose focus."

"The Joshis think of Caleb as a son," Lexie reminded her. "And he works for them. How is his position in that family, and the fact that he's estranged from his own, not *relevant*?"

Before Shay could think of a reply, Lexie turned off her computer and fished her car keys out of her purse.

"Look. Your article barely mentions Caleb, and considering your *unconventional* investigative methods, I can't help but think you've lost your partiality here. And I can't in good conscience publish a biased article."

Shay started to protest, but Lexie waved her off.

"What happened, Shay? Did you get a taste for the good life?" Lexie cocked her head to the side.

"Or is it simpler than that? Caught feelings, have we?"

"No!"

Shay closed her mouth, surprised by her outburst. Red-faced, she hefted up her bag and stood up. As she reminded herself why she was here in the first place: Mr. Joshi.

"No?" Lexie goaded.

"I'll write about Caleb's family," Shay said, her voice clear. She couldn't lose sight, not now. Not so close to the finish line. "I'll write whatever you want about him. If that's what it'll take to get the article published, consider it done."

16.

Saturday, April 27
10:45 a.m.

Daniela metamorphoses from tipsy to sober in an instant. She straightens her collar, pops a mint, and, before I can string two words together, takes off for somewhere in the resort.

Reeling, I open the *Los Angeles Journal* app on my phone, down-swipe until the page refreshes. My hand shakes as the top story appears. It's an article breaking the news that Raj and Radhika were murdered.

I read every word, twice, my body humming. After, my cheeks on fire, I pick up my phone and text Lexie.

Shay: Are you fucking kidding me?

So, this is why she went silent. As I wait for her to reply—this time, she *will* reply—I'm tempted to hurl my phone across Atlantis. Ram my fists into that delicious, hideous wedding cake. Lexie used me. She took *my* research into the Joshi and Singh families and handed it off to a staff journalist to report on the murders.

I can't believe she would do that to me. Her journalist cherry-picked the shiniest details about Raj and Radhika from my draft article and repurposed them into a sensationalist report about star-crossed lovers murdered in paradise. He even paraphrased from the text message I sent Lexie yesterday, in which I told her a National Guard drug enforcement task force had taken over the investigation, suggesting actual cartel involvement. My breath sharpens. In Lexie's last text, she asked me to clarify if I "thought" or I "knew" about the change in investigators. Is that the exact moment she decided to screw me over? That I stopped being her journalist and became her fucking "source close to the families"?

My phone rings a few minutes later. I wait ten seconds before answering, and then I go in hot.

"Do you remember that time I had to bail you out of jail because you chained yourself to an old-growth tree about to be cut down?" I snarl. "What happened to her?"

Lexie doesn't respond. The other end of the line is so quiet I can hear the soft rhythm of her breathing. No crying baby, no LA traffic, just the faint crackle of landline on speakerphone; she must be at work.

"What happened to her?" I ask viciously.

Lexie sighs theatrically before responding. "Shay, the free-lance contract you signed with us is very broad. It gave us permission to utilize your research however we wanted—"

"And you wanted to be the one to break the news that two famous people got offed, huh? I always knew you were a sellout, Lex. I just didn't know you'd sell me out too—"

I hear muttering on the other end of the line. I stiffen.

"What did you say?"

"I said, kind of like you sold *me* out?" Lexie snaps. "Jesus,

Shay. We used to be best friends. You didn't even RSVP to my wedding. You moved away and then I just never heard from you again!

"I'm so sorry that I stopped living by your very superior moral code, but don't you dare try and convince yourself that you dropped our friendship because I 'sold out.' Everybody in our class, including you, would have taken that job in New York. You dropped me because you were *jealous*."

I swallow hard, her words echoing around my body as tears well in my eyes. She's wrong. She's *wrong*. I open my mouth to shout back—to tell her she's out of her mind, that she's misplacing the blame—but a lump grows in the back of my throat. It renders me speechless.

"You still can't admit it, can you?"

I press my palm over my face as the tears spill down. *No*. I wipe them away, I shake myself off. I don't have time for this. I can't waste another moment.

"You wanted to get even with me," I say finally. "Is this sufficient? Can we call it a draw?"

Lexie sighs. "Look. I had to make a tough decision very quickly, and ultimately, I prioritized my job over your self-righteous vendetta against Joshi. But I should have called you and given you a heads-up. I was a coward, and for that, I'm sorry."

"No, you're not." I slam my fist against the table. "And I didn't call you so you could assuage your guilt. I want to know what's happening with my article."

I push past the anger and, as quickly as I can, pitch Lexie on a new angle. I tell her about my working theory that Blush Continental and the Joshi Group are laundering money for the cartels, Raj's "business" trips to Cabo, and the picture he posted at a rumored black hotel.

"It'll be a takedown piece on Mr. Joshi, and it won't just talk about the Mumbai fire. It'll connect him to an international drug ring and Raj and Radhika's murders!" I whisper. But before I can explain to her the role Zara, Sean, or Caleb must have played too, Lexie interrupts me.

"Once you're back, I'll schedule a meeting with the editorial board," Lexie says worriedly. "But if you're right, then this thing with Mr. Joshi is way bigger than you or I ever thought. The authorities are likely going to ask us not to publish anything that interferes with an ongoing criminal investigation. And even if they don't, our lawyers are conservative these days and might advise—"

"But—"

"But nothing," Lexie says, her tone final. "You want Joshi to face justice, right? That's what this whole crusade of yours has been about?

"The murders of his son and future daughter-in-law are going to put him under the microscope. This is too hot and too expensive for you and for the paper. You've done what you can, and now it's time to let the authorities take it from here. It's time to step aside, Shay. I'm spiking your article."

I place my phone on the table and stare at it while bile rises in my throat. I put my life in Mumbai on pause, left the watchdog, and moved to LA for *this*, and the *Los Angeles Journal* is canning my article. Lexie is trying to tell me it's over.

Since the murders, a part of me must have known this would happen, because, strangely, I don't feel as surprised as I should. Deep down, I must have already known I'd have to finish this on my own.

It's not over. Until Mr. Joshi faces justice, to me, it will never be over.

"Are you safe?" Lexie asks after a long pause.

"I'm safe."

"And you're coming home?"

A part of me wants to tell her the truth: No. I'm not coming home. And it doesn't matter that she's pulled out, because I will never let this go. I will never stop chasing Mr. Joshi. And I won't leave Cabo until I find another way to bring him to justice. All too soon, the entire Joshi family will get the all clear to retreat to their fortress high up in the hills, surrounded by walls and security and lawyers and red tape. Raj and Radhika's deaths would become a distant tragedy, and Mr. Joshi would be able to fight off any allegations with his billion-dollar fortune.

But if I stay?

Maybe I can find out whether it was Zara, Sean, or Caleb who betrayed Raj and Radhika and let the killer into the villa. Maybe I can find out how the murders are related to the cartel, to Blush Continental and the Joshi Group.

Maybe I can find something that will hold Mr. Joshi accountable once and for all.

I open my mouth to explain this to Lexie, but then I shut it when I remember I'm on speakerphone. I have a hunch that her boss is in her office with her, listening in, making sure Lexie says the right thing.

I'm on my own in this. Lexie needs to do her job. And I need to do mine.

"I'll be back soon," I tell her vaguely.

"OK. Text me when you land."

"I will," I say. "And Lex?"

I breathe in slowly, and then out, struggling to speak.

I want to say that I'm sorry too. For disappearing on her. For ghosting on our friendship. I want to tell her that she's maybe right. Maybe I am jealous. But I'm also fucking furious. And, before I can say a word, she tells me she has to go and hangs up.

* * *

I SPRINT DOWN the empty corridor away from Atlantis, my chest tight from the exertion. From my phone call with Lexie. When I reach the top of the stairwell leading down to the lobby, I place my hand on my sternum and breathe through the pain. I need to keep going. It won't take long for the others here to start suspecting I'm the "source." I don't have much time left to get to the bottom of this.

Caleb texted four times while I was on the phone. He's awake now and majorly freaking out about the news and is getting worried that something might have happened to me too. I don't want him to send out a search party, but I'm not ready to face him with my questions either.

Are you *the murderer, Caleb?*

Have you been lying to me this whole time, just like I've been lying to you?

I don't know if I trust myself around him, so, to buy myself a bit more time, I give him the most nonconfrontational excuse I can think of. I tell him I'm going to a yoga class.

OK. Now what, Shay?

I start running the stairs, my tread heavy on the carpet. Now I need to speak with Zara or Sean. I'm aware one of them may well be the killer, but equally, they could also be a key witness; they may know something that will help keep me going.

The friendly concierge who told me Daniela's whereabouts won't extend the same courtesy about their VIPs' locations, even though I tell him I'm staying in the Villas too. Deflated, I find an empty seat in the lobby and try to regroup.

The vibe in here is busy this morning, eerie. There are three sets of couples, two families with adult children, and a group of women my age standing impatiently in line at reception with their suitcases. By the ghostlike looks on their faces, I can tell they've seen the news, unlike the other guests who blissfully waft through the lobby, dazed, clearly unaware of the reason there are camera vans and journalists parked behind the resort's gate.

Is Blush going to make a statement now that the news is out?

Two guests murdered is bad for business, which begs the question: if the cartel is using Blush Continental to launder their money, why would they kill two people at one of their resorts? Wouldn't they know that the bad publicity might drive guests away, put their business partner's finances in jeopardy?

As I sit in the lobby, I try and stay focused. I don't know anything about the cartel, and I shouldn't waste my energy on posing questions I'll never be able to answer. My best shot at unravelling this mess is finding out why Zara, Sean, or Caleb might have wanted to cooperate with a cartel behind the others' backs, and what happened the night Raj and Radhika were killed. Create a timeline. A patchwork of versions of events for the evening. And pull at the threads.

Daniela claims that security footage vouches for her whereabouts during the hours the murders occurred. If only I had access to that footage. There's so much I don't know about that fateful night. Did everyone go straight to sleep like they claimed? And what was their behavior like on their way to and from the club in Cabo San Lucas?

I tap my feet against the floor, wondering what I've missed. Where else I have my blind spots. I'm getting restless, and I'm almost ready to go look for Zara and Sean in the Villas when I spot the beach attendant I failed to tip earlier this morning, the one with frosted tips who looks like a Backstreet Boy. He slows down his pace as he spots me, runs a palm against the side of his wrinkled beige uniform.

"Hey, it's you." He grins, his tone straddling the border between flirtatious and friendly. "Why are you always by yourself?"

"I still owe you a tip," I answer politely, changing the subject. "But all my cash is back in the villa."

His face changes as he studies me.

"You're staying in the Villas?"

My cheeks heat up.

"Yes." I hesitate. "I came for that wedding."

"Fuck me." He scoffs, brushing a hand through his hair. "What are you still doing here? This place is a zoo. I heard Blush is all over the news."

I flick my gaze to the concierge desk. At least ten more guests have joined the line to check out. I look back at the beach attendant.

"Are you . . ." He clears his throat, not meeting my eye. "*Were* you a friend of theirs?"

"Not really," I say. "I'm dating the best man."

"I thought Sean was gay."

He flinches just as I process what he's said.

"The other best man," I say carefully. "Wait. Do you know Sean?"

"Why would I know Sean?" He smiles again, but this one doesn't seem as genuine. "No. I don't know him. I don't know any of them. He's a VIP. The managers make us memorize their names. This Sean guy is one of those rich Joshis, isn't he?"

I nod slowly, wondering why he's acting so strangely. My eyes drift to his left collarbone. Unlike the other staff members, he's not wearing a name tag.

"What's your name?" I ask.

"Why?" He winks. "You want my number?"

"Just your name." I smile.

"Just my *name*?" He presses his hand on his chest, hurt. "In that case, lady, you can call me whatever you—"

I stand up and wave him off. I don't have time for this game.

"Actually," I say quietly, hoping no one at concierge can overhear us. "If you know who the VIPs are, can you help me find one of them?"

"Why can't you just call them?"

"My phone is dead," I lie. "Please, can you help me? Her name is Zara Singh. She's Indian. Really pretty. Tall. Midthirties, although she looks a lot young—"

"There aren't a lot of Indian people here right now," he interjects, frowning. "So I think I know who you're talking about. I saw her by the pool earlier."

"What time?"

"Nine-ish?"

Dammit. That's around the time I saw Zara too, right before she disappeared into the resort.

"What about Sean?" I try next. "He was out earlier this morning but—"

"Yeah, I just saw him actually."

My eyes widen. Sean's back from the consulate?

"Where?" I whisper. "When?"

"He was walking into the spa. Maybe about half an hour ago? Yeah, a half hour ago."

My pulse rising, I check my watch. The *Los Angeles Journal* published their article on Raj and Radhika thirty-six minutes ago. If I'm lucky, Sean doesn't have his phone on him and hasn't seen the news. He won't be on guard for the "source" who sold out his family.

And, if I'm really lucky, he might just be willing to talk.

From: Eric Santos
To: Shaylee Kapoor
Time: 11:15 a.m.
Subject: Re: Urgent

Shay,

I called you yesterday because rumors were circling about a double homicide at Blush Los Cabos and I was concerned for your safety. I have now seen the tragic news about Raj Joshi and Radhika Singh, who I know are the subjects of your article. My concern for you is growing by the second.

Between you and me, the cartel's control of Blush Continental is an open secret and I have been attempting to expose them for years. I have documents that suggest several of Blush's owners are involved in a money-laundering operation with the cartel. Is one of them this "Hector"? I don't know. I will need his real name to verify.

The alarming photo you shared of Raj Joshi at Blush El Paraíso certainly suggests that the Joshi Group might be involved too. I visited the resort earlier this year and it's nothing more than a skeleton structure. When I questioned my contacts at Blush Continental, each gave me a different answer. Several told me the building was deemed unsafe due to water damage or other causes and is frequently closed for repairs. Others said the issue was pandemic related. Nonetheless, I remain convinced it's a "black hotel."

Please send me further identifying information on Hector if you find it, and, in the meantime, I advise you to exercise a high degree of caution. This is not your country. And going after the cartel is more dangerous than you can possibly imagine. I strongly suggest you fly back to the US immediately and continue your investigation from safety.

Regards,
Eric Santos

17.

The spa's thermal baths are designed to feel like another world, a cavernous underwater sanctuary. Classical piano music plays on the overhead speakers, barely audible over the soothing sounds of the waterfall lazily flowing into the coldest plunge pool. I dip my feet into one of the hotter baths and slowly lower my torso as it adjusts to the temperature. I sigh as my body starts to unclench.

This isn't the worst place in the world for a stakeout.

After informing me all their massage therapists and facialists were booked solid, the spa's receptionist handed me a Blush-branded bathing suit and pointed me toward the thermal pools. She also confiscated my cell phone. If the Backstreet Boy told me the truth, and Sean's here too, I'm hoping he still hasn't heard about the *Los Angeles Journal* article.

Casually, I pretend to stretch out my neck and survey the baths. The space is massive and contains eleven different pools of various temperatures and sizes, but there are only two other guests here right now. An elderly couple taking deep, invigorating breaths as they prepare to launch themselves into a cold pool. I've never been to a Nordic-style spa before and think about giving the hot-cold circuit a try but decide against it. I angle myself toward the changing-room doors twenty feet away. I need to keep a lookout for Sean.

As the steam rises off the water, and still reeling from Eric's email, I find myself spinning scenario after scenario trying to solve how Sean might factor into this mess. If the Joshi Group is in bed with the cartels, then there's a good chance Sean's involved too. But why then would Sean betray his family and give the assassin access to Raj's villa? What would Sean have to gain?

I shake my head in frustration as I let my body slide farther into the bath. When the hot water burns the tips of my ears, Lexie's editorial question about the future of the Joshi Group niggles into my brain, and then it dawns on me. I sit back up a little straighter.

Do you think Mr. Joshi will tap Raj or Sean as the next CEO when he retires?

I lick my lips, which taste like chlorine and sweat. How could I have missed such an obvious motive: could Sean have betrayed his cousin, so he could ultimately take control of their family's company? So he could be the sole heir to the Joshi Group fortune? Mr. Joshi and Sean's father, Jackie Joshi, built the company together; when Sean became an orphan, Mr. Joshi adopted him, claimed him as his own. It's a beautiful story, but is it the truth?

In my peripheral vision, the elderly couple, having thrashed around in the cold pool, is toweling off by the changing-room door, and suddenly, I'm terrified. What if Sean's the murderer? What do I even say to him right now if he walks in?

I can't ask about the power dynamics among his family members, Blush El Paraíso, or what else he knows about Raj's business meetings with Hector; that would be too obvious, and Sean might be dangerous. I need to stick to the plan: pretend to be Caleb's wounded girlfriend desperate for answers. I could ask Sean what happened during their night out in Cabo San Lucas, and how he managed to sleep straight through the night, even though he suffers from insomnia. Sean's bedroom on the second floor of the Joshi's villa faces west—toward Raj's villa. Sean would have had a clear view of who came and went. Could I simply suggest that he may have seen more than he's letting on?

Suddenly, as if I willed him into existence, Sean pushes through the changing-room doors. My body goes stiff as I take him in and prepare myself. He's wearing Blush-branded swimming shorts and has a towel draped over his broad shoulders. His face is hard, even angry, and fleetingly, I fear he's somehow heard the news and knows I'm the source. He doesn't look up as the elderly couple brushes past into the changing room. I tense up as I realize we're alone in here.

Still, I sit up straight, trying to make myself more visible as he throws his towel on a deck chair and rolls his shoulders forward and back, cracks his neck vigorously from side to side. He must have just gotten a massage. Eventually, Sean turns around and scans the pools. His face drops when he spots me.

"Sean?" I call out, feigning surprise.

He regards me skeptically for a moment. His ripped torso is glistening from all the massage oils, and I force myself not to stare or say something stupid that will make him turn around and leave. From his body language, I can tell he wants to.

"Don't worry," I say, taking a chance. "Caleb's not here."

Just as I suspected, Sean's face relaxes.

"Do you want me to leave? If you want to be alone—"

"It's fine." Sean sniffs, stepping forward. "I'm not the only one who needs to relax."

He dives into the coldest of the plunge pools and swims a few short laps before making his way into the pool I'm in.

"How was the consulate?" I say breezily.

"I decided not to go." Sean shakes water out of his left ear. "My uncle should be back after lunch, so we'll find out what's happening then."

Sean was at Blush this whole time? Could Zara have been speaking to him on the phone when I overheard her this morning?

When Sean doesn't volunteer any further information, I decide not to press him. I need to tread lightly, let him come to me. This is the most he's spoken to me since he found out I was dating Caleb.

I lay my head back on the edge of the pool and close my eyes, breathe through the sweltering discomfort. A few minutes later, Sean asks me how I'm doing. I inhale tightly, sitting up.

This is it.

"Not great." I smile at him limply. "Although I'm guessing I'm doing a lot better than you."

"I suppose." Sean frowns. "The massage helped for about two minutes there."

As I try and think of what to say, Sean sits forward in the pool and stares at me.

"Why are you still here? You should have left last night with my *chachiji* and the Singhs. There was no need for you stay."

Yet another person telling me to go home, but I can't tell if he's sympathizing with or admonishing me. I wait a beat before answering, trying to figure out how best to keep the conversation going, veer it back toward Sean.

"I know I should go," I say finally. "I tell myself I'm sticking around to support Caleb, but I don't even know why anymore." I catch Sean's eye. "What if Caleb . . . What if he . . ."

I close my mouth, letting Sean fill in the blanks himself. Hoping that if he believes I suspect Caleb's behind this, then he'll air his grievances about him too.

"I don't think I know him as well as I thought."

Sean doesn't respond; am I being too transparent?

"I'm so sorry," I say quickly. "You lost your cousin, and here I am complaining about my boyfriend—"

"I lost my brother," Sean corrects me quietly. "Raj was my brother."

In the family meetings, Sean was nothing short of stoic; he didn't shed a tear. Now, his eyes mist as he tells me what it was like immigrating to the US at the age of sixteen, a recent orphan, moving in with his new adopted family.

"You saw the house. It has enough bedrooms to host our entire extended family, yet Raj insisted on bunk beds." Sean smiles to himself, blinking. "It's like he knew I needed the companionship. We shared a room until I left for college."

Sean massages the back of his neck, wincing as if in pain. "I'm aware the man was no saint. We all knew how he carried on. He wasn't the most responsible, or thoughtful. He wasn't a lot of things."

Sean swallows hard.

"But he was a good brother," Sean finishes, his voice shaky. "The best. Raj made me feel like I still had a family."

My lips tremble as I try and think of what to say, and suddenly, I'm overcome with doubt about my theory that Sean had Raj killed over a rivalry. I don't deny Sean's heartbreak right now. I can feel it, palpably. But is that because he's innocent, or he's overcome with guilt?

"What was it like working together?" I ask, hoping my question comes off nostalgic rather than invasive. "You and Raj ran the LA office together, didn't you?"

"We did. And we worked pretty well together too." Sean nods, smiling. "I've been trying to implement a new operational plan that will transform the company. Not all the executives agree with it—Christ, my own uncle doesn't agree with it—but Raj stuck up for me. Uncle and I don't always see eye to eye."

My heart stops as Sean palms the scruff along his jaw, slowly. Deliberately. The heated pool is overbearing now, burning my skin.

"What sort of operational plan?" I ask carefully.

Sean shrugs. "The usual. How to make our policies more environmentally friendly, our operations more sustainable and in line with international best practices. The typical corporate nonsense."

"That doesn't sound like nonsense."

"From the mouth of a public policy student," Sean quips. "Of course you would agree. Meanwhile, the corporate world prefers to make decisions that line their own pockets. Funny, that."

"How has it been?" I ask playfully. "Dismantling capitalism from the inside?"

"Do you know my father studied public policy too?" Sean says vaguely. "Who knows if the plan will work. I'm just trying to make him proud."

Sean dips his head back into the water and it takes every ounce of willpower not to pry further about the operational plan and why he and his uncle don't see "eye to eye." If Mr. Joshi is laundering money for the cartels, maybe he knew his nephew wouldn't be on board and shielded Sean from finding out about their company's criminal practices. It's possible that Sean has nothing to do with this.

That notion fits with my initial judgment about Sean as a human being. When we first met, he warmed to me the moment we talked about the Joshi Group's corporate social responsibility, when I realized our values might be closer than I thought and that in different circumstances, we very well could have been friends. But even though he seems like a lovely guy with solid values, as far as I know, Sean is the only one who stood to gain from Raj's murder; he's now the sole heir and future chief executive of the Joshi Group. I can't let my personal feelings get in the way of logic.

After Sean resurfaces, he shakes water out of his ear and smiles. I can feel him relaxing around me. Now's the time. I've got to throw my Hail Mary.

"Why don't you and Caleb like each other?" I ask suddenly.

Sean freezes, taken aback. He shakes his head and asks, "What makes you think that?"

I give him the side-eye, a look that reminds him about their fight yesterday that I nearly had to break up.

"If you know something I don't, you need to tell me. I'm sleeping in the guy's bed."

Sean waves his hands through the water, staring at them a beat. "You said earlier you don't think you know him as well as you thought. I agree, Shay. You don't know him."

I tense, and my body no longer able to take the heat, I stand up in the pool.

"Caleb cheated on me. Is that what you mean? He's unfaithful?"

Sean stays silent. Then says, "That doesn't surprise me."

"You didn't know?"

Sean shakes his head. My stomach lurches. If Sean didn't know, then what mystery about Caleb was he just referring to?

"*You* know," Sean says slowly. "And yet you stay with him."

"I didn't really have a choice," I say defensively, hopping up onto the edge of the pool. "I found a condom in the trash when I arrived at Blush, just moments before all hell broke loose."

Sean joins me on the ledge of the pool. "Are you honestly that surprised? You're a smart woman. Surely you know Caleb's love life is a revolving door."

Caleb has a fetish for brown girls . . . he's already slept with half the ones inside.

His yoga teacher. The checkout girl from Whole Foods. His coworker.

I cross my arms tightly over my chest, avoiding Sean's gaze. Of course I knew what Caleb was like; both Raj and Radhika had warned me, teased him right front of me. Yet . . .

"Are you going to stay with him?" Sean asks.

"What's it to you?" I snap, regretting my attitude immediately.

Reading between the lines, the wrinkles etched around his eyes, there's something Sean isn't telling me. Something about Caleb. There's a thread here, and although I'm anxious to pull at it, I don't. If I push too hard, veer too far off course, Sean will shut down.

"I guess it depends who he slept with," I say, with a quiver in my voice, returning to the role as the supportive, oblivious girl-friend. "I think it happened after you returned from the club Wednesday night." I pause. "Do you know who he slept with?"

"Does it really matter?"

"As his girlfriend, yes, it matters," I insist. "And considering we're all witness to Raj and Radhika's murders, *yes*, it matters. If Caleb's lying about what happened that night, then maybe there's a reason. Maybe I should tell the National Guard."

I watch Sean's face like a hawk. If he's guilty, shouldn't the threat of police frighten him? Instead, he shakes his head gravely and taps his toes against the water.

"I don't know who he slept with. Go talk to them if you feel you should, but I'm not coming with you. I've told them every-thing I know."

"You haven't told *me*," I say quietly, hoping he'll buy my curi-osity as that of a jilted girlfriend. "What happened at the club that night?"

Sean waits a beat before answering.

"It was fairly boring on my end. I was distracted." He hesi-tates. "With business. But Caleb, Raj, Radhika, and even Zara were partying hard. I think there was cocaine, by the way they were acting, but I didn't see it so I can't be sure. Raj knows not to offer it to me. I'm too old for hard drugs."

I'm tempted to ask about his "business." Instead, I say, "Was Caleb talking to or dancing with anyone in particular?"

Shaking his head, Sean stretches out his calves. "It was just the five of us."

Just the five of them. My stomach somersaults. Was Zara the one Caleb slept with? Was it *Radhika*?

I take a deep breath, parking the thought. There are so many questions I want to ask, like if he remembers who had Radhika's missing cellphone, but I don't want to veer off track and raise any red flags.

"So, what happened after you got back to Blush? Anything unusual?"

"No," Sean says. I can tell he's getting irritated. "Radhi and Zara went off together. Raj, Caleb, and I walked back to our respective villas. And, like I said, I went straight to sleep—"

"But you suffer from insomnia."

Sean freezes.

"I do."

"I'm just wondering if you heard something through your window," I say quickly. Innocently.

"Occasionally, I take something to help me relax," Sean said slowly, chewing his words. "Like that night. So I didn't hear anything, unfortunately. The last time I saw Caleb that night"—Sean's voice breaks—"was the last time I ever laid eyes on Raj. They were chatting outside Raj's villa."

I swallow hard. So *Caleb* was the last person to see Raj alive?

"What were they talking about?" I breathe.

"I . . ."

"Sean?" I press.

"I don't know, honestly. I'd the feeling they were waiting for me to leave to discuss something."

Sean shifts in his seat. I can feel his guard going up.

"Caleb was probably plotting on how best to sneak some girl into his room," I say lightly.

"I don't think so."

Oh?

"Raj seemed to be the one confiding in Caleb, now that I think about it." Sean runs his hand through wet hair. "God knows about what. Raj had been pulling away from me for weeks."

Another thread. Bright red, and within reach. I'm desperate to yank at it, and I'm about to, when Sean stands up and yawns.

"I'm hot. Are you hot?"

Dammit.

"Very."

Sean extends his hand to me, smiling. "Then, shall we?"

18.

The spa has its own bistro, an eight-table nook behind the waterfall that serves things like ginger tea and lavender scones. I'm still famished, having consumed nothing but iced coffees and a few bites of wedding cake, and I try not to eat too fast as Sean and I lounge around together in plushy bathrobes. The conversation naturally drifts to more neutral subjects, like the weather and where we went to college. When we arrive at the topic of the resort's amenities, I sit up a little and shoot my shot.

"I need to go meet Caleb soon," I say with a sigh. "And I *think* I need to leave him."

"Good," Sean says smiling. "You do that."

"I might need someone to push me." I reach for my tea. "Please, Sean. If there's something I don't know, tell me. Why do you hate him so much?"

"'Hate' is a strong word."

"Despise, then. Don't pretend otherwise. I'm not an idiot."

Sean uncrosses his legs and reclines farther back in his chair.

After a long moment, he continues. "If you're breaking up with him, then I might as well be honest with you. I don't trust him, and I don't like that my uncle and Raj all but forced me to give him a job. Caleb's toxic and has always been a horrible influence on Raj. I thought that even before I found out about his drug problem—"

My whole body goes rigid. Sean shuts his mouth in response.

"Wait. You don't know?"

My pulse pounds in my ears as Sean reaches for my hand, as I try to process the words he's just told me.

"What are you talking about?" I gasp, my voice hoarse. "Caleb doesn't have a drug problem!"

"I'm sorry, Shay. He hides it well. From Raj. Even from himself—"

"You're wrong." I laugh, emotion inexplicably rising in my chest. "He's not a drug addict. He's not . . ."

He's not like his family.

"There's no way. Caleb's so smart and works hard," I insist desperately, tugging on Sean's hand. "How can he be? He puts in seventy hours a week at work. Sure, he also parties a lot with Raj, but everyone in LA *parties.*"

"Shay," Sean starts.

I wave him off.

"And Caleb's so active. He surfs, he goes running, he lifts weights. Also he *reads.*"

"He's high functioning, I'll give him that. But he's always on coke, pills, *something.*" Sean gently tightens his grip around my palm. "I'm so sorry, love. I didn't mean to spring this on you. I thought you knew."

He pauses, ruefully, then looks me in the eye.

"I really thought you were capable of seeing past that facade."
His facade? No.

No.

"You're wrong," I stammer, even though I suddenly don't know what to believe. Caleb was so honest about his family's history with substance abuse, so transparent about—and seemingly in control of—his lifestyle, it never even occurred to me that he might have a problem too.

"But if you're right about this—" I swallow the bile rising in my throat. "*If.* That means Caleb's sick. He needs help, not our judgment."

"Of course I agree with you. But, *Shay.* You need to prioritize your own well-being."

Sean exhales deeply before going on.

"Look. About ten years ago, Raj, Caleb, and loads of their friends attended a music festival. Caleb was off his rocker that night. No one knows what he took, but, as Raj explained it to me, Caleb became unhinged. Someone spilled a drink on him. Words were exchanged, and a fight broke out. Caleb beat up another man to within an inch of his life.

"The bloke was in the intensive care unit for four days," Sean continues as I struggle to breathe. To internalize what I'm hearing. "He was lucky to make it out alive. And Caleb—well, he doesn't even remember throwing a punch."

"He blacked out?" I whisper.

Sean nods. "My uncle flew out and bailed him out of jail. He paid off the man's family to drop the charges, and Caleb told all of us he'd do better, but nothing's changed. Caleb has had a problem for a long time, Shay. He's not well, like you say. And, in the wrong set of circumstances, he can also be very dangerous."

I drop Sean's hand as my heart jumps into my throat.

"You think he killed Raj and Radhika," I snap. "Is that what you're saying? Why would he do that?"

"You tell me," Sean replies gently. "Why would he nearly kill a man over a spilled drink?"

I take a deep breath, and then another, while I try to bring myself back to center. I've been lying to and manipulating Sean to extract information about who might have killed Raj and Radhika. But wasn't I convinced the evidence would point me to Zara or Sean? Not *Caleb*.

Before I can say anything further, Sean's gaze moves behind me. He smiles politely. A beat later, I feel something on my shoulder. I turn my head slowly as goosebumps run over my body.

It's Brown Hulk Hogan.

"Sahib would like to speak with you."

Sahib. As in his boss, Mr. Joshi.

Brown Hulk Hogan's even larger standing right next to me, three times as wide and seemingly twice as tall. His cologne is overpowering up close, so pungent I feel as if I might be sick. Still reeling from the news about Caleb, I push my chair away from him and drop my eyes to Hulk's back pocket. To his gun.

"Any news from the consulate?" Sean asks, rising from his chair. Brown Hulk Hogan shakes his head gravely.

"No news," Sean echoes. "Right, then. I'll just pop in the shower. Tell my uncle I can come speak to him in fifteen minutes."

"That won't be necessary, sir," Brown Hulk Hogan says, his eyes landing on me. "It's Shaylee Kapoor with whom he'd like to speak."

Brown Hulk Hogan's eyes land on me just as my gut twists in terror.

"Ma'am, will you follow me?"

* * *

"Oh good, you're here!" Mr. Joshi calls down from the porch.

As if I had a choice. As if Brown Hulk Hogan wouldn't have dragged me here kicking and screaming if I'd tried to resist.

I watch Mr. Joshi closely as I slow my pace. He's no longer in the suit he wore to the consulate and looks dangerously friendly with that smile, salmon-pink shorts, and *chappals.*

"What do you want?" I say icily, even though I know exactly why I've been summoned.

He knows I'm the source. My time undercover with the Joshis has come to its bitter end.

"*Aaja,*" he says spritely. "Please, come inside. There's someone else we need to speak with."

Fuck.

I drag my feet across his porch, sullen, shooting daggers at the back of Mr. Joshi's head as I follow him into the villa. I wonder who's waiting for me in there. One of his lawyers, probably, ready to hit me across the head with a defamation lawsuit. It doesn't even matter if Mr. Joshi's suit is viable; the bastard has the power to tie me up in litigation for the rest of my life.

It wasn't supposed to be like this. I was supposed to bring Mr. Joshi right on this *one* thing in a world built upon wrongs. This can't be how it ends. Here in Cabo. Mr. Joshi, smug, in those fucking salmon-pink shorts. Me still wearing a wet bathing suit. Tailing Mr. Joshi, I round the corner into the kitchen and—

My stomach bottoms out. It's not Mr. Joshi's lawyers.

It's Caleb.

He's hunched over the kitchen island stuffing guac and chips into his mouth. His eyes light up as he spots me.

"Hey, how was yoga?" he asks brightly.

Caleb has no idea. Mr. Joshi still hasn't told him.

My body shaking, I go and stand next to him in the kitchen. He plants a tender kiss on my forehead and regards me. "You OK, babe?"

Sunlight pours in through windows, washing out Caleb's soft complexion, and I blink as I regard him in this new off-kilter light. As he is—and not the version I wanted to see.

"What's going on, Shay?" Caleb asks earnestly. "Why did Mr. Joshi call us here?"

It wasn't supposed to be like this.

I brace myself as Mr. Joshi leans on the kitchen island across from us. He sighs and gestures at me tiredly.

"Shaylee, would you like to explain?"

Blood drains from my face as my body goes cold. Out of the corner of my eye, I spot Caleb's hand resting on the counter. Caleb may be a drug addict. Caleb may very well be the *murderer.* Still, knowing it'll be the last time, I take his hand and squeeze it.

"Shaylee has not been honest with us," Mr. Joshi declares. "My dear girl, would you like to tell him who you are, or shall I?"

"I . . ."

I close my mouth, my tongue heavy like lead. I can't count the number of times I imagined facing off with Mr. Narayan Joshi, the preeminent chief executive of the Joshi Group, but never did I imagine it would go down like this. That my emotions would render me tongue-tied.

That I'd *lose.*

This is it. I gave it all I had. I'd shot my shot, and I'd blown it.

"What's he talking about?" Caleb asks me, still gazing over at me fondly.

I don't answer. I can't.

"Shaylee used you, Caleb," Joshi answers instead. "To get to *me*."

"I never meant it to get this far," I whisper, my eyes smarting as I turn to Caleb. "I swear. That night we met—"

Mr. Joshi cuts me off.

"Are you or are you not the 'source' quoted by the *Los Angeles Journal*?"

Instantly, Caleb's face goes dark. I feel as if I'm about to throw up.

"Caleb . . ."

He waves me off, drops my hand. I reach for it again, but he just shrugs me away.

"I can explain," I plead quietly. My voice cracks. "I didn't know—"

"You worm your way into our lives," Joshi's voice booms as Caleb backs farther away from me. "And then at our darkest hour—my son *gone*—you sell our story to a newspaper? You provide the media with sensationalist details about our lives? Our home? Our family? The murder of my *son*—"

"It wasn't supposed to be like this," I snap, losing my cool. "I swear it, Caleb. I didn't want to destroy anyone's life but *his*."

I point at Mr. Joshi, my hand trembling.

"Do you know who he is?" My voice shakes. "He's a criminal—"

"Caleb is a son to me, Shaylee, and let me be clear, my sons know me much better than you." Mr. Joshi places his hand on his brow and sighs theatrically. "Caleb, I was just informed that

Shaylee is a journalist by training, and her time in India included several years with a little 'human rights' operation whose sole mission, for reasons I don't fully understand, is to *hang* me—"

"Do you know why?" I say fiercely, searching Caleb's face, but he won't look at me. "He's responsible for the death of—"

"As I have explained to the relevant authorities and regulators, we were horrified about the unfortunate fire—"

"Bullshit," I spit.

"—on my building site." Mr. Joshi sighs, gazing at me as if I were a buzzing insect, a mere irritant. The patronizing son of a bitch.

"Your time with us is over, Shaylee," he continues. "If you or any of your journalist friends would like a comment the next time you hurl false accusations in my direction, I would request you call my office and set up an appointment. Preferably, after I have had time to mourn the death of my son."

Mr. Joshi pauses, summoning Brown Hulk Hogan out of the corner with a flick of his finger. "Find the butler and ask him to pack this woman's belongings. She will be checking out immediately."

As I shake frozen in place, Mr. Joshi then turns to Caleb.

"I am sorry about this, my boy. But we will have to discuss this unhappy matter in more detail later. If you could run along too. The butler will require your permission to enter your villa."

Caleb nods obediently, and his face stiff, he finally turns to look at me.

"Caleb—"

He waves me off, his face like stone.

"You used me."

His words drip with anger. And, for a moment, I see a flash of the violent man Sean warned me about.

"You fucking *used* me."

"I . . ."

It wasn't supposed to be like this.

My throat closes in as words fail me. And a small piece of my heart, a morsel I wasn't fully aware belonged to him, shatters when he turns to leave.

19.

"This isn't her real bachelorette party, you know." Mei Lin, who had already pointed out twice she was Radhika's childhood best friend, lowered her voice to a whisper. "A few of us just got back from Miami."

The other women standing in their group smiled at Mei Lin through tight lips. Shay shimmied her way farther into the circle and gasped indulgently.

"Miami," Shay exclaimed. "That's so cool."

Mei Lin beamed and then briefly flicked her eyes at the influencer-focused bachelorette party raging behind them. "It was more low-key than this, you know? Just a few of Radhi's closest friends. Zara, of course. Super intimate, super fun—"

"Was it, though?"

Another woman in the group, a different noninfluencer friend of Radhika's, widened her eyes sardonically.

"I heard one of the girls got food poisoning, Radhi had bad PMS, and Zara had to deal with some investor problem and left early," she continued blandly. "Didn't you end up watching *The Office* the whole time?"

Cheeks coloring, Mei Lin shot her daggers from across the circle.

"Not the whole time," she replied icily. "It was still an amazing trip."

The other woman's eyes bulged, and her tone dripping in sarcasm, said, "More *amazing* than *this?*"

Mei Lin scoffed. "What is that supposed to mean?"

The other woman froze.

"Radhi's successful," Mei Lin snapped at her. "And she's marrying a guy who really loves her. Why can't you just be happy for her?"

The other girl pursed her lips. "I am happy for her."

"Good," cooed Mei Lin. "So. Am. I."

Shay had migrated to Radhika's group of noninfluencer friends because she thought she'd feel more at ease, but was finding this conversation as uncomfortable as the ones she'd had earlier. Avoiding the awkwardness, Shay glanced over Mei Lin's shoulder to admire the house. Radhika's West Hollywood home had been transformed into something straight out of a '90s Bollywood film. Thousands of flower garlands adorned with fresh marigolds, roses, and jasmine strewn across every square inch of the house and backyard. A Pakistani American DJ made TikTok-famous was set up on the far side of the pool, strobe lights thrashing to the beat. Photo booths equipped with professional photographers, lighting, and desi-style props. Custom cocktails sponsored by a trending small-batch distillery in Huntington Beach. A gifting suite, fully stocked with pretty brand executives and goodie bags containing everything from makeup to coffee, designer swimwear to restaurant gift cards.

And then there was the pièce de résistance. Radhika's event

planner had had a field day with this part: a stretch of her back lawn had been transformed into a makeshift film set. White floors. Draping white fabric. Giant clay pots of brightly colored powders. Studio lighting. At the appointed hour, Radhika would invite everyone to join her so the party could really begin. The hired crew could capture the action, and all the influencers in attendance could create content for their socials.

"Holi" Shit. Radhika's getting hitched!

Shay was shook when Radhika emailed her the invite. Radhika wasn't just hosting her bachelorette; she had combined it with a celebration of the Festival of Colors, or Holi, during which families, friends, and neighbors traditionally wore white and gathered jovially on the streets for a color war. A few years ago, most people outside of India and the diaspora had never heard of Holi, but now desi culture was everywhere, especially on Instagram and TikTok. The glitz and the glamour of it all, Shay supposed, lent itself well to social media.

Mei Lin and the woman she'd called out were still glaring at each other, but none of their friends seemed interested in intervening. Shay glanced at her watch. It was still early; she couldn't leave yet. She'd promised Lexie she'd try and gather more background on the Singhs (preferably juicy) for the article.

"So how do you all know Radhika?" she blurted to the group. No one had spoken for a solid minute. "I'm—uh—dating one of her friends," Shay prompted again. "Raj's best friend, Caleb."

There was an audible gasp from somewhere in the circle. Shay's eyes darted in its direction, noted two of the women's cheeks had gone scarlet. Radhika had mentioned, more than once, that Caleb had slept with several of her friends. Shay wondered mildly if these two were on his list of conquests.

"Oh, I know who you are," Mei Lin said cheerfully, giving the woman standing next to her a look Shay couldn't read. "You're the grad student."

Shay flinched at her tone but decided to push on.

"And how do you know Radhika?" Shay asked instead. "Are you guys friends from school—"

"No." Mei Lin gestured at a few others in the circle. "We all met in math camp."

Shay laughed. "*Math* camp?"

Her jaw dropped a little as Mei Lin told her about the selective summer camp in Palo Alto that was a "must" for any child or teen with mathematical aptitude and ambitions, how it was a feeder program to the top programs such as those at MIT, Princeton, and Stanford, which was where most of them went.

"Wait." Shay shook her head in disbelief. "Radhika wanted to be a mathematician?"

"She *is* a mathematician," Mei Lin said coolly. "Why do you sound so surprised?"

"I'm not," Shay lied. "I just had no idea—"

"There's a lot you don't know." Mei Lin rolled her eyes slowly away from Shay, back toward the rest of the group. "As I was saying. *Miami . . .*"

Her face hot, Shay waited until Mei Lin was twenty seconds into her soliloquy about their stay at Soho Beach House before slipping away. She found a quiet corridor away from the noise, googled Radhika's name, and very quickly discovered that Mei Lin was right. All she had to do was scroll past the dozens upon dozens of higher-ranked links that mentioned Radhika as an adjunct to Zara, their mother, and Lustre before finding information about Radhika herself.

She'd graduated from her selective Bay Area private school at the age of sixteen, and then from MIT with top honors at nineteen. She'd coauthored two papers that were published in elite mathematics journals, placed second in a high-profile robotics competition, and was the youngest-ever presenter at an international symposium on applied mathematics in Oslo. Her résumé dropped off four years ago, around the time she started to go viral and moved to LA.

Shay tucked her phone away as she meandered back toward the party, feeling slightly off center. How had she missed this? She'd researched everyone else in the Joshi and Singh families so thoroughly—but not Radhika. She'd been all too willing to believe the influencer was who she presented herself to be. Shallow. Nonthreatening. Happy to post selfies in the fading limelight, while her fiancé and celebrity big sister took center stage.

In reality, Radhika wasn't just intelligent; she was a mathematical prodigy. The girl was a freaking genius.

It was a warm night, and most of the guests were in the backyard, dancing and filming themselves dancing to a remixed version of "Bole Chudiyan." Inside, guests were clustered into small groups around various pieces of furniture, speaking in low, familiar voices. On the living room sectional talking to Radhika and Zara were three well-known celebrities, including the hot new actor costarring in that Priyanka Chopra movie.

Shay ordered another drink from the bar and tucked herself away in the corner, watching them all, wondering how someone like Radhika could be happy with her hologram-like existence. Four years ago, she was at the top of her field and had the whole world ahead of her; how could she stand living like this? And why would she choose a man like Raj? Radhika was way too good for him.

As Shay sipped on the dregs of her drink, the celebrities excused themselves, leaving Radhika and Zara alone on the couch. They both looked beautiful tonight. Zara, tall and chic, in a rose gold *anaarkali*. Next to her was Radhika, tiny and maidenlike, in an off-white fusion sari. Soft curls framed her round, pretty face.

A weird pang formed in Shay's chest as she watched the sisters together. The way they whispered in each other's ear as one of them discreetly pointed at one of the guests across the room. The way they drunkenly held each other's hands, and touched the other's cheek, and said something to make the other laugh—

"No."

Shay snapped to attention, noting a palpable shift in Radhika's body language. The shape of her lips as she rebuked Zara. The way she pushed away Zara's hand, an attempt at comfort.

Were they fighting? About what? But just as she started drifting closer to their conversation, Radhika stormed off, followed closely by Zara.

Curiosity got the better of her, and Shay waited a moment before following them down a long, dimly lit corridor with several doors on each side. The last one on the left was ajar, and Shay held her breath as she crept forward and caught sight of Radhika and Zara's reflection in the bathroom mirror.

They were holding each other. Rocking back and forth. Radhika was in tears. But, whatever it was that had made her cry, the two sisters had already made up.

A few minutes later, after Zara left the bathroom, Shay hesitantly knocked on the door, which was slightly ajar. Radhika, who was fixing her makeup in the mirror, didn't look over.

"Hey," Shay faltered, unsure what to say. Or of her motives. "I wanted to check if you were OK."

Radhika didn't respond as she feathered a mascara brush

through her lashes. Her eyes were still red, slightly puffy. Shay leaned her weight against the doorframe.

"Are you all right?"

Radhika blinked at her reflection in the mirror. Her eyes locked on herself, she said, "What are you even doing here?"

Shay froze. "You invited me."

"Not here." Radhika switched to the other eye. "*Here*. With Caleb. With us."

She set down the mascara, picked up her phone, and lazily read a message that had popped up on her home screen. The sparkly diamond backing glittered in the light.

"Caleb's very passionate. Very emotionally available. Isn't he?" Radhika asked blandly as she returned to her makeup. "At first, I thought you were just another gold-digging whore who mistakenly believed you won the lottery."

Shay's nostrils flared.

"But the way you act around us. Around all of this"—Radhika continued, gesturing behind them toward the party—"I'm not so sure anymore."

"The way I act?" Shay said curtly.

"Holier than thou. Too good for us. Too smart for us. As if people like us couldn't also be intelligent."

Radhika flashed Shay a smile in the mirror.

"Or good at—I don't know—*math*?"

Shay cringed with embarrassment. Mei Lin must have already told her all about their conversation in the kitchen.

"A lot of people underestimate me," Radhika said to her reflection as she reapplied dark gloss to her lips. "Do you know I could be developing advanced algorithms for aerospace and defense contractors if I wanted? I could be creating cryptographic keys for Big Tech if I wanted. I could be running the data science team at Lustre *if* I wanted."

Radhika turned to face Shay, her voice rising.

"I could be president, Shay, if I wanted. But I don't. And you and everyone else just need to back the hell off and accept that *this* makes me happy. All right?"

Shay nodded, dumbfounded, and decided to stay quiet. She had a feeling Radhika's tirade wasn't just about her.

"And you know who else you underestimate?" Radhika said next, wagging her lip gloss at her. "Caleb!"

"He's used to dating bimbos. It's quite a novelty for him to be with someone who's almost as smart as he is." She smiled at Shay ruthlessly. "I don't know what you want from him, but, very soon, he's going to see right through you and toss you aside like the others. You think you're so good, so pure, but you're a hypocrite, Shay."

She gritted her teeth in anger as Radhika turned around and met her gaze. "You think I'm a *hypocrite*?"

"Come on. You go on and on to Caleb about your work abroad 'saving the children,' but you smoke *tobacco*. You're not just killing yourself. You of all people should know that tobacco contributes to deforestation, which is killing off those children's planet."

Shay inhaled tightly.

"And that organic locally produced almond milk Caleb says you just *have* to have in your coffee every morning? Do you know how much fresh water it takes to grow almonds and how harmful it is to bees?" Radhika scoffed. "And don't get me started on that gas-guzzling, decade-old car of yours—"

"I'm trying my best," Shay interrupted, her voice rising. "I'm doing my part. You, on the other hand, use your privilege and platform to earn the trust of impressionable kids, and then you abuse that trust by selling them useless products from your highest bidder."

Radhika laughed, leaning against the sink.

"Maybe, but the way I see it, you're as big of a fraud as the rest of us." Radhika glowered. "At least I'm honest about who I am."

Shay took a step forward, anger hot and red flushing on her skin.

"You dumb yourself down to be more palatable for social media," Shay spat. "I don't think you're being honest at all."

Shay clenched her jaw, glaring.

"In fact," Shay said, regretting the following words the moment they left her lips, "I'm starting to think the only reason you don't like me is because of who I'm dating."

20.

Twelve couples, four families with adult children, and the Pool Bros are ahead of me in the checkout line. I've been standing here for fifteen minutes and have only moved a few places in the queue. I can overhear the conversations between front-desk staff and guests, as the former try to convince the latter to remain at Blush. That, despite what they're hearing on the news, the resort is very safe. They are issuing promises of extra security, upgrades, and comps. It's partly working. About half of the guests attempting to check out reluctantly give in and stay.

I wish I could stay. The realization that I'm going home, that I've been found out and my plan here failed spectacularly, hasn't quite sunk in. I flick my eyes across the chaotic lobby toward Brown Hulk Hogan. Mr. Joshi asked him to escort me off the premises, but I've been in the checkout line so long that he's stopped paying such close attention to me. He's on the phone with someone, pacing back and forth. The couple ahead of me moves up, and, sighing, I follow the queue and drag my suitcase one spot forward.

You still can't admit it, can you? You're jealous.

Lexie's voice rings suddenly in my ears. Her words on the phone earlier this morning.

You're a hypocrite. You're as big of a fraud as the rest of us.

I cringe, hearing Radhika next. Their words come together, echo in unison. When Radhika called me out at her bachelor-ette party, I barely registered her accusations, chalked them up to the words of a jealous, threatened younger woman. But she and Lexie are right, aren't they?

I *am* a hypocrite.

I've written myself a neat little narrative in which I'm a hero who makes the required sacrifices to do her part to save the world. Who tackles head-on all those socioeconomic, political, and environmental injustices she'd read about in her textbooks. Who does what she must to help bring the big bad wolves of the world—like Mr. Joshi—to justice.

I run my hands through my wet hair, shivering under the blast of the air conditioning. But there's so much I left out of that story. Like how indignant I felt when I wasn't offered a high-profile journalism job, even though I was just as talented as peo-ple like Lexie who managed to get one. How the longer I lived and worked abroad, the more inequities I sought to solve, the less I felt my actions and beliefs were accomplishing anything: for every win, there were a thousand losses. There were an infi-nite number of injustices left to fight.

I felt stupid and demoralized, and when I joined the human rights watchdog in Mumbai three years ago, I was desperate for *something* to keep me going. A reason to believe I hadn't wasted my twenties and the opportunities afforded to me by privilege, trying to unbreak a world that couldn't be fixed.

Then the fire happened, and I threw myself into my investigation of the Joshi Group. Mr. Joshi came to represent every bad actor in politics and the corporate world, all of the puppet masters who helped the rich get richer and left the rest of humanity behind. He was a concrete example of what was wrong, and, as the evidence against him mounted, I became hell-bent on making at least *this* right.

I close my eyes and see the grief-stricken family of the twelve-year-old girl killed in the fire. I'd interviewed them several times and gotten to know them well. I'd so wholly convinced myself that holding the man who harmed them accountable was why I was here. Why I lied to Caleb, why I compromised my journalistic integrity and even my morals.

But is that even true?

My stomach sours as I let the realization sink in.

No, it's not. I'd started off my career wanting to do a little good in this fucked-up world, and somewhere along the way, my "crusade" had become all about me. What I could do. How I could help. What difference *I* could make.

I didn't just become obsessed with bringing Mr. Joshi to justice, but also with the idea that I could be the one to do it. That the recognition that came from bringing him down would also lift *me* up.

The line moves again. As I roll my suitcase forward, tears threatening to spill, suddenly, I hear someone calling out my name. I scan my surroundings, hoping it might be Caleb, but it's not. It's Daniela. She's speed walking toward me.

"Daniela?" I call.

She shakes her head, presses her pointer finger to her lips. Then, when she's just inches away, she grabs my elbow and whispers, "Follow me."

My mouth drops as I spin around and watch her hurry past

me in the lobby. Did I just hallucinate that encounter? No. Without slowing down, she rotates her head to look at me. Her eyes bulge, and once again, she gestures for me to follow.

What does she want? I don't know. But there's a steady stream of guests passing between me and Brown Hulk Hogan at this very moment. I can't see him, which means he isn't able to watch me either.

It's now or never.

And so, on an impulse, I spin on my heels and race after Daniela.

I jog through the lobby, pulling along my heavy suitcase as fast as I can. Up ahead, Daniela changes directions and abruptly darts into a corridor. When I'm safely around the corner, I stop, hoping to catch my breath, but Daniela's still rushing forward at full speed.

I keep up a good pace, sucking air, following her past the gift shop and two banks of elevators, checking over my shoulder every few seconds to make sure Brown Hulk Hogan isn't on my tail.

Where's Daniela taking me?

Adrenaline courses through me as I follow her into a smaller passageway of ground-floor hotel suites. She stops in front of the last door on the left, her face tense as she waits for me to catch up with her.

"Daniela," I pant. I need to stop smoking. "What's going on?"

"Quickly, Shay. Inside." She waves her wristband in front of the lock and pushes open the door. "I can't let you leave."

21.

I let the door swing closed behind me as Daniela crosses the room and peers through the blinds. We're level with the resort's outdoor area; just past this suite's private deck is a straight view of one of the swimming pools.

"You can stay here, but you must keep a low profile."

Daniela draws the blinds closed and, confused, I watch her pull a pair of scissors from her back pocket and move toward me. She cuts off my wristband, unearths a new one from another pocket, and then locks it around my wrist.

"Keep your 'do not disturb' function on at all times. Do not use room service. When you eat, do so quickly, but avoid the French and Japanese restaurants. Mr. Joshi has a taste for finer dining."

"I . . ."

She waves me off. "You don't have to pay. No one will know you're here except me and a trusted friend in housekeeping."

I have no idea what to say. I have no idea what the hell is going on.

"Why are you doing this?" I manage finally, meeting Daniela's eyes. Her mouth twists into a frown.

"There's something not right about that family, isn't there?"

When I don't say anything, Daniela goes on.

"Mr. Joshi's butler overheard everything." She hesitates, staring at me. "You're a journalist. You lied to Caleb and leaked the story to that newspaper. Why? Because Mr. Joshi is some sort of criminal?"

I nod, but don't explain. Chewing her lips, she steps backward and perches on the edge of the bed.

"Is he a criminal who works for the cartel?"

"Why would you ask me that?" I say carefully.

"It's why *Guardia Nacional* is here, is it not?" Daniela sighs. "It's why you brought up Blush El Paraíso to me earlier this morning. I've lived in Los Cabos all my life. I have worked for Blush Continental for more than ten years—"

"Meaning . . ."

"Meaning." Her voice gives out. "I know Blush does not always follow the law."

I sit down next to her on the bed as I think back on Daniela's startled face when I brought up Blush El Paraíso. My driver Isaac's curiosity about the hotel. Eric's email earlier today.

The cartel's control of Blush Continental is an open secret.

Everyone here knows. And no one can do a thing about it.

"One of the owners dropped by a few hours after I found the bride and groom," Daniela continues. "He made it clear to me that my priority is to maintain the company's reputation, and under no circumstances was I to cooperate with the authorities."

"How did he make it clear, exactly?"

"By threatening me, of course." Daniela laughs. "He reminded me that my three cousins, older brother, and uncle are all on *his* payroll. Hector said—"

My stomach bottoms out.

"—I'll 'pay' if I don't keep quiet."

Hector.

I stand up and start pacing, Daniela's words ringing in my ear. Hector is an owner of Blush Continental?

"What's his full name?" I ask in a panic. "Is Hector his given name or surname?"

"I'm not sure." Daniela regards me. "It's a nickname. Why?"

I make a split-second decision to trust Daniela, and, as quickly as I can, tell her about how I was dating Caleb in order to prove my allegations against Mr. Joshi. How I now suspect the Joshi Group's criminal wrongdoings go much further than I ever imagined: that, like Blush Continental, the Joshi Group is laundering money for the cartel. Mr. Joshi had been sending Raj down to Cabo to do his dirty work, to meet with her boss, *Hector.*

"I think Hector is the missing link that connects the Joshi Group to the cartel," I explain. "Raj and Hector had been meeting every month for the past year. If only I could prove Hector himself is involved in the cartel—"

"Then you can connect Mr. Joshi to the murders," Daniela finishes eagerly. "Let's do it! I'll help you."

My hands trembling, I turn to get a better look at her. She looks just as tired and disheveled as she'd appeared this morning, but her eyes are clearer. Brighter. She's one hundred percent serious.

"Mr. Joshi didn't actually kill Raj and Radhika," I say, gently backtracking. "He may have put them in harm's way, but—"

"He's still a criminal. He deserves to be punished for the role he played in the happy couple's demise."

Daniela's staring at me hungrily. She's so eager. She wants to help me take down Mr. Joshi. Just over an hour ago, I would have jumped at the opportunity, but now, I don't know what to do—or what's right. What would it mean if I stayed here and tried to finish this?

What would it mean if I *didn't*?

"This is the responsibility of law enforcement," I say, my voice small. "I should never have gotten involved."

Daniela scoffs and runs a hand through her dirty hair. "And how do you know they're not in the cartel's pocket too? *Guardia Nacional* have a bad reputation just like their predecessors, Shay. They might sweep this under the rug, and then we'll never get to the bottom of this.

"You're a journalist," Daniela continues somberly. "And two people have just been murdered. Is it not *your* job to tell the public the truth?"

Her words knock the air out of my lungs. She's right. I've been so hell-bent on holding Mr. Joshi responsible, and on my own scheming, that I've been forgetting what really matters. Two people are *dead*.

"It would be risky," I say to Daniela as my head falls to my hands. "You and your relatives could lose your jobs—or worse."

"I know," I hear her say. "But I'm tired of those mobsters having control over my life, my family. I'm tired of the violence. I'm tired of what the American War on Drugs has done to us. If there is an opportunity to help change the situation in my country, I have to try, Shay. I have to help make this right."

Make this right.

Doing what's "right" is the reason I wanted to be a journalist, and, as much as I'm tempted by Daniela's offer to help, it also doesn't feel right to put an innocent woman in danger.

I sigh deeply as I consider the fork in the road.

I could go home right now. End this chapter of my life, start a new one fresh, and keep Daniela out of this too. Or, risking her safety and mine, we could try and crack this case. Not for validation, or credit, but because two people were killed. Because Raj and Radhika deserve justice—and, like Daniela reminded me—the public deserves the truth.

I open my eyes when I feel Daniela's hand gently squeeze my forearm.

Do I leave—or do I stay. Both options seem equally right and wrong, and for the first time—maybe ever—I wonder if there is no right or wrong. Good or bad. Virtuous or evil. Whatever choice anyone makes, there will always be consequences.

"OK," I say, sitting up abruptly. "Let's do this."

Daniela grins widely and pulls me into her arms. Instinctively, I tense, but eventually let go and hug her back.

"But we do it my way," I say, pulling away. "We're not going to do anything that puts you in danger. We're not going to go after Hector."

And raise the cartel's alarm bells.

"There's another way."

I explain to Daniela the angle I was working before Mr. Joshi kicked me to the curb. "Besides yours, there are only three wristbands that could have opened the door to Raj's villa," I remind her. "Which means Zara, Sean, or Caleb must have betrayed them."

Daniela nods, catching on. "Yes. Of *course*. We must find the traitor first. They'll lead us back to Mr. Joshi and the cartel."

She crosses the room and rummages around in her purse

with great conviction. At first, I don't know what Daniela's doing, but when she returns to the bed with her phone and her screen flashes to life . . .

"You have access to the hotel's security footage?" I breathe. When Daniela nods, I cry out happily in disbelief. "I think this warrants another bottle of champagne."

* * *

"THAT'S ME," DANIELA says a few minutes later, after I've snuck a cigarette outside and she's pulled up footage from Wednesday night. From a camera angled above a corridor of offices on the third floor of the resort.

Although the video picture is small, it's clearly her. Daniela's uniform and gait, her long ponytail and striking features. We watch Daniela tread down the hall, enter an office, and then leave the door ajar. From the angle, I can just make out her sitting down at a desk and turning on the computer. I note the timestamp in the bottom right corner of her phone. It's Thursday morning at 2:28 a.m.

Next, Daniela fast-forwards the footage to 6:16 a.m. She doesn't move from her desk the entire time. Back at normal speed, after a few seconds, Daniela stands up, stretches her arms up over her head, and walks out of the office.

"That's why the police dismissed me so quickly," she says, pointing at herself. "I worked all night."

I exhale in relief as I grab my notepad and jot down the times Daniela entered and left her office. She was there during Raj and Radhika's window of death, 3:30 to 5:00 a.m. Her alibi is solid.

I take a few minutes to fill in a timeline. In the family meeting, Tobias said the "do not disturb" function was switched on in Raj's villa at 2:14 a.m., which means, after that point, unless he or Radhika opened the door themselves, the murderer must have been granted special access to get in.

Next, I check the taxi receipt in my wallet. I arrived at Blush at 8:10 a.m. Thursday morning, and, considering Daniela gave me a good half-hour tour of the resort, I couldn't have arrived at Caleb's villa until 8:40 a.m. at the earliest. After that, Daniela went to the Atlantis Banquet Room for her 9:00 a.m. meeting with Raj and Radhika—the one they failed to show up for; she shows me the footage to confirm as much. I also make a best guess at the time Caleb returned from his walk, and when we heard Daniela scream upon her finding the bodies next door.

"What's next?" Daniela asks, reading over my shoulder. "Should I pull up another camera?"

Nodding, I flick my eyes up and down the page. I've jotted down everything I know for certain. The rest of the timeline— the part leading up to and following the murders—I'll hopefully be able to discern from the security footage.

"The group returned from the club in Cabo San Lucas around one thirty a.m., right?"

Daniela hesitates before confirming with a nod.

"I believe so."

"If only Blush had security cameras *inside* the Villas community," I sigh. "Oh well. Let's try the lobby cameras next? I assume they had to walk through it to get back to their villas."

I rub my hand up and down my thighs in anticipation as I think about what the next video might reveal: What was their dynamic like that night? Was anyone fighting? Did Zara and Radhika really go off on their own, ahead of the guys? Getting impatient, I flick my eyes toward Daniela, but she's placed her phone on the bed between us. Chewing on a hangnail, her eyes are fixated on the ground.

"Can I see the lobby camera?" I prompt.

Her face flushes a deep red as she drops her hand. Confused, I wait for her to look over at me. There's something she isn't saying. There's something she doesn't want me to see.

Trembling, she finally turns her gaze toward me, and finally, it hits me. The answer to one of the questions hanging over my head.

"It was you, wasn't it?"

Her face gives her away, and I'm not sure how I missed it.

The way Daniela spent thirty minutes of her valuable time touring me around the whole resort but refused to take me inside Caleb's villa. Earlier today, the way she evaded answering my question about what else she got up to the night of the murders. The way she calls Raj and Radhika the "bride and groom" or "happy couple," and formally refers to all guests as *Mr.* and *Ms.* except for me, because I requested it, and *Caleb* . . .

My chest tightens, a dull burn spreads up my neck and flushes my cheeks.

"You're the one he slept with," I whisper.

Daniela nods once, and then she starts to cry.

22.

t's OK," I insist, after Daniela apologizes for the millionth time. "Our relationship wasn't real. There's no reason to feel bad."

My voice comes off false, even though I'm trying to sound sincere. Hiccuping, she blinks at me, as if trying to decide whether or not to believe me. When I smile at her reassuringly, she bursts into another wave of tears.

"It's still not right." Daniela sniffs. "I should have known he had a girlfriend. I was in charge of the guest list. I must have known there was someone else assigned to his villa. But Caleb never mentioned you."

She wipes her nose with her sleeve as I try not to dwell, force myself to push down the hurt feelings.

"I'd been running on fumes. I've barely slept in weeks." She turns to me and grips my hand. "I've never done anything so stupid. I was risking my job, my integrity. I was just so burnt out, Shay. And Caleb's so . . ."

She trails off, and I nod at her because I get it. I never intended to have sex with Caleb either.

It first happened only a few weeks into the "relationship." Caleb had wined and dined me and then invited me back to his house. He was thoughtful and sweet. Passionate, but not pushy. I got lost in the moment. One thing led to another. It was just another milestone in our fake relationship.

I crossed so many ethical lines with Caleb that I stopped keeping count. I told myself it was for the story, for the sake of my vendetta against Mr. Joshi, but that's only half the truth. I've been single most of my adult life, and it felt good to be with someone—especially someone like Caleb. Attractive. Wealthy. White. He glided through life with ease and grace, and didn't I enjoy swimming in his wake? Didn't I relish the perks of dating a *Prescott?*

We're different people with very different values, and I'm under no illusions about the depth of our feelings. I don't love him, but I do like him, and, like an idiot, I thought he liked me too. At least I thought he liked me enough not to cheat.

"I feel so humiliated, Shay," Daniela adds a moment later.

You and me both, Daniela.

How many times had Raj and Radhika poked fun at Caleb's promiscuity right in front of me? And how many times did I choose to blind myself to the truth?

"I never told the police I went to the Villas to see him that night," Daniela continues. "What if they catch me in my lie?"

"It'll be OK," I say, my voice firm and final. I don't want to picture her and Caleb together. "Let's just get this over with, shall we?"

Wiping her face, Daniela pulls up footage from a lobby camera that has a near bird's-eye view of the entrance, valet desk, and concierge.

"I was in the lobby when they returned that night," Daniela says, rewinding to early Thursday morning at 1:35 a.m. "I'll show you everything."

At normal speed, I watch Daniela on screen chatting to another staff member at the concierge desk. She appears to be giving him instructions while he listens and types something out on the computer. The lobby is otherwise empty. Just before 1:36 a.m., the front doors to Blush slide open.

"Here they come," Daniela breathes. I lean in to get a better look.

Caleb walks in first. My fists clench. Immediately, I can tell he's high by the way he shuffles through the door, his limbs slow and uncoordinated, and the way his jaw practically hangs off his face. I've seen him in this state so many times before, but this time feels different. I watch as he sloppily rubs the back of his hand across his face, and, palming my tight jaw, I ask myself how the hell I never saw it before: Caleb has a problem with drugs.

Sean's right. He's fucking right. Lungs burning, I think of the rows of prescription pill bottles in Caleb's medicine cabinet and toiletry bag, which I always saw but never noticed. The pills he sometimes popped, which I assumed were Tylenol. His intense and unpredictable mood swings. His family history. The red flags, the glaring neon signs, that I never wanted to see.

But how could I have seen it? So stuck in my sheltered preconceptions about what addiction does and does not look like. So naive, having been the "good girl" who stayed out late at the library, not clubs. With overachievers, not partiers. The only experience I had with drugs came secondhand from TV shows like *The Wire* and *Euphoria*.

I trusted Caleb at face value. I thought I knew him, but as I observe him through a camera, it's as if I'm watching a stranger on television. The man he is for his audience is not the man he is inside.

And I don't know this man at all.

Caleb halts in the lobby, unsteady on his feet, and just as he looks back through the doorway, Radhika and Zara stumble through. They're laughing gregariously, and Zara's arms are wrapped tight around Radhika, as if to keep her upright. She's so young—only twenty-four—and my heart feels a pang as I think of how harsh I was to her at her bachelorette. How, right now, walking through that hotel lobby, she only has a few more hours to live.

I never gave Radhika enough credit while she was alive. I was petty, perhaps a little jealous of her starring role in Caleb's life, even though she annoyed him. But my judgments were wrong and just as shallow as the behavior I accused her of displaying. I pause the footage on Daniela's phone, my eyes tracking over Radhika, who looks so tiny next to her sister. Radhika's absolutely stunning, but there's always been more to her than her beauty. I should never have brushed her aside so quickly, and right now, I shouldn't dismiss her ability to have played a role in this mess either.

She was young and immature, sure, but she was also a genius. Emotionally intelligent. Observant. She was the only one who, rightfully so, mistrusted my intentions with Caleb. If Raj really was the go-between for his father, Blush Continental, and the cartel, it would have been difficult for him to hide his double life from Radhika. Could she have known what he was up to?

I hold my breath, weighing another possibility.

What if Radhika didn't just know; what if she was criminally involved with the Joshis too?

"May I keep going?" I hear Daniela ask suddenly. I nod blankly, and when she restarts the footage, Raj walks into the frame. A beat later, Sean follows.

I temporarily set aside my thoughts about Radhika and make a note on the timeline. It's 1:36 a.m. Thursday morning.

"What is Radhika saying to you?" I ask as we watch the group walk over to Daniela on screen. She's all smiles for them and has stepped away from concierge to greet them.

"I just asked them about their night," she explains. "The bride is telling me a story about how the club's bouncer nearly kicked them out, but she was quite drunk, and I couldn't make heads or tails of it."

As Radhika chatters away, I play the footage at half speed and carefully study everyone for clues. No one appears to be fighting or in distress, although perhaps it's a little odd that Caleb, Sean, and Raj are standing so far apart. Caleb's clearly high, laughing at whatever it is Radhika's saying; Sean's on his phone, perhaps working like he claimed; and Raj sways quietly, a little less obnoxious than usual.

Why would security nearly have tossed them from the club? Maybe it was harmless. Or does it have to do with the murders?

"What's she saying now?" I ask, pointing at Radhika. Abandoning Zara's support, she wraps her arms lovingly around Daniela.

"The bride just told me"—Daniela smiles sadly—"it was very sweet. She said I was her fairy godmother. And *I* said, 'Then it's time for my Cinderella to go to bed.'"

Reluctantly, Radhika lets go of Daniela and then effortlessly hops up onto Zara's back, piggyback style. They look comfortable together, as if they're used to Radhika hitching a ride from her big sister. Zara cranes her neck around and sloppily kisses Radhika's cheek.

Daniela and I rewatch the same footage from a different camera, which has a view of the back of the lobby. From this angle, I still can't make sense of Raj's atypical quietness. I also look carefully to see if Radhika or anyone else was carrying her missing phone with her signature sparkly phone case, but I don't see it anywhere.

We continue watching as the group leaves the lobby, drifting toward the large doors that lead to Blush's outdoor area and the path toward the Villas. Zara and Radhika go first, followed by Raj, who walks several steps in front of Sean. My body clenches as I remember what Sean said in the spa: that Raj had been pulling away from him over the past month. Is there a reason they're not walking side by side or speaking to each other? What was causing Raj to keep his distance, to act uncharacteristically quiet?

Before I can think on it too hard, I feel Daniela squeeze my forearm. On screen, Caleb's hanging back to speak with her.

"What's he saying to you?" I ask, my mouth suddenly dry.

"He's asking me if I'm his Prince Charming. If I was going to put him to bed—I'm sorry." Daniela stops. "Do you really want to hear this?"

My stomach churns, but I ignore it.

"Yes. I do."

Together, we watch Caleb's eyes drift up and down her body, the same way he inspected me the first time we met. We watch Daniela succumb to the weight of his flattery, the way he affected me too. I lick my lips, my tongue a sheet of sandpaper as a wave of emotions roils through me.

He cheated on me. He's a drug addict. He might be a *murderer.* So why does this hurt so much?

"What's happening right now?" I ask. My voice cracks but I cover it with a cough. On screen, Caleb backpedals away after the group, although his eyes are still on Daniela.

"Are you sure you want to know all the details? I hate myself for—"

"I'm not exactly one to judge you," I interrupt, turning back to the phone. "Just tell me."

Daniela nods. "Caleb made it clear that he wanted me to visit him. I told him I would after I sorted out a guest's airport transfer."

Daniela fast-forwards the video until the timestamp reads 1:58 a.m. At that point, she leaves the concierge desk and starts walking through the lobby.

"There," she declares. "I've just finished my task, and now I'm going over to . . ."

Caleb's.

I feign a smile as Daniela in the video disappears through the back doors, in the direction of the Villas.

"And what time were you—"

God this is awkward.

"Finished?"

Daniela goes red. "It didn't last long. He was very high, and not very . . . I regretted it immediately and left as soon as I could."

Next, Daniela fast-forwards through the lobby footage to the point she returns from her rendezvous with Caleb. 2:26 a.m.

I make a note of it in the timeline. Daniela entered her office two minutes later, at 2:28 a.m. After she was with Caleb, she went straight back to work.

Shaking off my feelings, I take a deep breath and press onward.

"I learned recently that Caleb has the capacity to be quite violent when he's on drugs," I tell Daniela. "I think you're right that he was high that night." And if Caleb was in an extreme altered state, then he could have killed Raj and Radhika without fully realizing what he was doing.

"Did you feel unsafe with him?" I ask Daniela, unable to articulate fully what's on my mind.

"No." She furrows her brows. "I didn't find his behavior any worse than half the other American men who come to Cabo to party."

"Was he asleep when you left?"

"No. I slipped out when he was using the bathroom."

So Caleb was still awake nearly an hour after they returned to Blush, and shortly before someone killed Raj and Radhika. He very well could have been the one to betray them to the cartel.

I wander over to my purse to check my phone. Caleb hasn't texted or called, but later, once the shock and anger have worn off, he might be willing to speak to me. He's not used to being the one betrayed; he'll want an explanation, and when the time comes, I'm going to demand one from him too. I'm going to confront him about his drug problem and ask him to account for his whereabouts Wednesday night and Thursday morning. I'll ask him to tell me what else he's kept hidden from me, like what he has locked in his villa's safe, or secrets he keeps for the Joshis.

Will he tell me the truth?

Maybe not. And maybe I don't know—and could never know—the multitudes that make up Caleb Malcolm Prescott III. But something tells me that when I look into his eyes, his face will give me the answers I need.

Sunset Sailing

Tonight we're boarding a sunset cruise to Land's End where we'll visit Lover's Beach, Divorce Beach, and the iconic Arch of Cabo San Lucas. We've been on dry land all weekend, and now it's time to take a step backward and enjoy the scenic coastline from a different angle.

The ocean can be rough this time of year, even on a mega-yacht, so come prepared for all weather. You never know what's going to happen on the high seas.

Our photographers will be taking advantage of golden hour to shoot group wedding photos for our "First Look" cover deal with *People* magazine, so tonight's attendance is mandatory. We warned you it was going to be a long day. There's no rest for the wicked.

Love,
RAJ & RADHIKA

Location: Marina Del Rey, Cabo San Lucas
Dress code: Elevated Nautical

23.

> Meeting running long. I'll bring my
> laptop to your room within the hour.

> Perfect. Thanks, Daniela!

Bleary-eyed, I look up from my phone and peek through the blinds. The sun has yet to set, but there are ominous clouds obscuring the western half of the sky and it feels darker outside than it should. I return to my makeshift workstation on the bed, where I've spent the better part of the afternoon. I have the television on in the background. Nearly every news channel, Mexican and American, is airing stories about Raj and Radhika's murders, citing the *Los Angeles Journal* article. Nobody else has dug up new information; the authorities and the Joshi and Singh families have officially declined to comment.

Daniela and I spent another hour together combing through security footage, and I added everything relevant to my timeline.

Around 9:20 a.m., Sean was seen having a heated phone call outside Blush's spa, after which he went inside for an appointment. Raj, Radhika, and Caleb worked out together at the gym around 11:00 a.m., and around the same time, Zara attended brunch with her mother, brother, and sister-in-law. I paid particularly close attention to Zara's movements for any further signs of suspicious behavior and meetups; I still don't know who she went to see earlier this morning when she disappeared into the resort.

At 8:03 p.m. on Wednesday, Sean appeared in the lobby by himself and worked from his phone until, five minutes later, Zara, Radhika, Raj, and Caleb showed up and the five of them left for the night. At precisely 9:00 p.m., Mr. and Mrs. Joshi entered Blush's Japanese restaurant and ate a late dinner together, after which they retreated to the Villas. Brown Hulk Hogan wasn't with them. I didn't catch him on camera all day.

I reorganize my papers, feeling impatient. I hope Daniela's team meeting doesn't run much longer. She's bringing her laptop, on which we'll be able to access security footage from the resort's outdoor cameras. I hope she hurries back; I'm running out of leads.

Sighing, I return to my current task: I had Daniela email me a list of all the wedding guests and I'm eighty percent through completing their background checks. So far, I haven't found any links between guests and Blush Continental or the cartels. And no one has a criminal record. Not even Caleb.

If Sean is telling me the truth about Caleb's violent altercation at a music festival, that means Mr. Joshi effectively expunged the arrest from Caleb's record. Did the act buy Caleb's loyalty? Did he join the Joshi Group for a reason? If the company is laundering money for the cartel, out of respect and obligation to Mr. Joshi, Caleb, their new finance director, may have been helping them. He might be the one cooking the books.

But even if that's true, it doesn't mean Caleb sold out Raj and Radhika to the cartel, does it? And why would he? Caleb is rich in his own right; he has nothing to gain from committing such a betrayal.

On the other hand, Sean had plenty to gain. He and Raj were in competition to take over the Joshi Group. I think back to our conversation in the spa earlier. His commitment to corporate social responsibility seemed so genuine, especially when he told me he inherited his sense of ethics from his father. I grimace as I entertain my next thought, which seems so far-fetched it could almost be true: What if Sean initially didn't know the Joshi Group was laundering money for the cartel and, when he found out, decided he'd had enough of his uncle's criminal business practices? What if Sean sold out Raj so one day he could take charge of the Joshi Group and fulfill his father's legacy?

My mind humming with uncertainty, I return to running background checks on the guests, and just as I'm crossing off another name, my phone buzzes.

> She's in the lobby. Go now.

Smiling, I grab my floppy hat and a pair of sunglasses and dart into the corridor. Daniela asked her team to keep an eye out for Zara, but after several hours I'd nearly given up hope we'd track her down. I hustle toward the lobby, hoping my accessories will adequately disguise me should I run into the Joshis or Brown Hulk Hogan.

By now, Zara will have heard that I'm the leak. She'll be furious with me. But if she's innocent in all of this, won't she still want to help? Wouldn't she do everything in her power to help bring her sister's killer to justice? In the family meeting, Zara was the one who first spoke up about Raj's frequent business trips to Cabo and implied that he could have been working with a cartel. Zara could know more than she's letting on.

I hurry toward the lobby, breathless. It's even more chaotic than it was earlier today, but it doesn't take me long to find Zara, who towers over most of the other guests. She's speaking with someone at concierge, her body language sharp, as if she's telling them off. I scan her surroundings, but she appears to be alone. After a few minutes, she throws her hands in the air and stalks off.

Where is she going? Not back to the Villas; she'd be heading in the opposite direction. My heart beats wildly as I trail her, determined not to lose her this time. I follow her to a bank of elevators that take guests up to their suites. I hang back behind a pillar as I watch her chat idly with the elevator attendant, feeling slightly nauseated. Does she have another room here? Or is she going to see someone? Maybe it's the same person she was speaking to on the phone this morning.

After Zara disappears into the elevator, I go up to the attendant and fake the hiccups. He offers me a gentlemanly smile, asks me if I'm all right and on which floor I'm staying. I giggle like I'm drunk and tell him I forget.

"My—uh—sister was right in front of me," I slur, hoping I'm not being too obvious. "Maybe you remember what floor she selected?"

The attendant smiles patiently. "Your sister, ma'am?"

"She came through just a minute ago." I stretch my hand up high above my head. "She's very tall. Wearing white, I think—"

"Of course." He summons an elevator and then holds open

the door. "Your sister selected the eighth floor. I can accompany you if you'd—"

"That won't be necessary," I say, rushing inside. "But thank you!"

As soon as the doors close, I drop the charade, my pulse pounding with the uncertainty of what I have to do when they open again. After I've had time to catch my breath, the elevator opens and I step cautiously into the hallway. It's empty except for a lone cleaning cart at the far end of the corridor, although there are no custodians in sight. At random, I turn left and slink toward the first doorway. Praying the security camera on this floor isn't being monitored too closely, I press my ear against the door and close my eyes. I hear voices, then canned laughter. It's Chandler, Monica, and Joey. It's just someone watching *Friends*.

I check the subsequent four rooms, which are all deathly quiet, but on my next try, I hear Zara's voice. I squish as close to the door as possible as I try to decipher her words. Dammit. I can't make it out. Everything sounds muffled. All I can tell is that she's pissed off.

After a moment, a male voice interrupts her. It's low, very low. My brow furrowing, I try to identify it. It's not Caleb in there—I would recognize his voice anywhere—but could it be Sean? Maybe Mr. Joshi—

The door flies open. I recoil back from the shock of Zara suddenly inches away.

"I can hear you breathing from inside," she snaps. "What the hell, Shay?"

Words fail me as my eyes widen with surprise. Before I can come up with an answer, Zara smirks and flicks the brim of my sun hat.

"And who do you think you are—Ms. *Marple*?"

Despite myself, my lips curl upward at the Agatha Christie reference. Slowly I take off my hat and sunglasses, stalling as I try to peek in to see who else is in the hotel suite. Zara notices and quickly shuts the door behind her.

"Do I need to call security?" She huffs impatiently. "What are you doing here? I thought Joshi got rid of you."

"Yeah, well." My jaw clicks as I prepare myself for this conversation. "I'm still here. And I would appreciate if you didn't tell him."

"That all depends on why you're stalking me." Zara cocks her head to the side and stares. "Now that you're done with the big bad Joshi, are you here to research all of my dirty little secrets?"

I bristle at Zara's mocking tone. One of the others must have told her about my history at the watchdog, my vendetta. Suddenly, I hear a noise behind the door. A cough. My eyes track to the opening in the doorway.

"I'm sorry I misled you," I say, careful to keep my voice strong. Shoulders straight. "But would you mind if we discussed this inside?"

"I do mind, actually. You still haven't told me why you're here."

My eyes dart to either side. When I'm sure no one's around, my voice low, I tell Zara that "Hector," the Blush Continental owner Raj had been meeting with, threatened Daniela to keep quiet, and how it's an open secret that Blush Continental is controlled by the cartel. I tell her about Blush El Paraíso, Raj's photo at the black hotel, and that I think the Joshi Group may have been laundering money through their hotels too.

Zara's jaw is hanging off her face by the time I finish. Her eyes watery, she presses the back of her hand to her mouth, shaking her head as she stares at me. After a beat, she drops her arm and laughs.

"You've got to be kidding me," she whispers hoarsely. "You've *got* to be kidding."

"I'm not."

I cross my arms, trying to decide where to go next. If I'm going to get her to open up to me further, then I have to pretend I've ruled her out as a suspect.

"Can I come in?" I check over both my shoulders with a flair. "Caleb or Sean betrayed Raj and Radhika to the cartel. It's the only explanation I can come up with.

"I need you to tell me what really happened the night Radhika died, what you saw, and what Radhika told you about the Joshis. You could know something that helps put this whole thing together."

I pause as Zara frowns at me skeptically. After a moment, she asks, "What's in this for you?"

I hesitate, thrown off by the question. I was expecting resistance—but not like this.

"You could wash your hands of us and go home right now," Zara says, eyeing me. "Why not leave this mess for us?"

"Because . . ."

I hesitate, leaning my weight against the doorframe, wondering what Zara wants to hear. Wondering what's even the truth.

Because I have a vendetta against Mr. Joshi.

Because I want to help bring your sister's murderer to justice.

Because I need to know that Caleb's innocent. That I didn't sleep with a murderer.

I grimace as the last thought pops in and out of my head. Is that even true? I don't trust my own feelings when it comes to Caleb, my sense of what is right and wrong. Nothing makes sense, and no reason I come up with feels like the right one.

So instead of bullshitting, I tell her the truth. I tell her I have no fucking idea.

"OK," Zara caves, afterward. "I'll talk to you—but not now. Meet me in a half hour at the Oceanside Bistro."

She rolls her eyes, seeing my face.

"It's fine. Caleb, Sean, and the *big man* are out to dinner with the US ambassador. That scary-looking security guard went with them. You're safe for a few more hours."

I check my phone. Daniela's meeting is over, and although we still have to review the security footage from the outdoor cameras, that's just going to have to wait.

"Sure," I say, flicking my eyes back up to Zara. "But first, I want to know who you're talking to in there."

"Is that relevant?" she asks crisply.

"You tell me."

Zara smiles at me drily.

"I'm telling you, Shay, it's not relevant."

I hold her gaze, refusing to blink, to back down on this. After a moment, she finally gives in.

"Archer?" she calls out sweetly, pushing open the door. "Archer, be a doll and come to the door, would you?"

My pulse pounds as footsteps approach us.

Archer? Why does that name sound familiar?

A moment later, a middle-aged man appears in the frame, round-faced and as harmless-looking as my father. He looks as baffled as I must appear. Who had I been expecting? Sean? Mr. Joshi?

The murderer standing right in front of me?

"This is Archer Nguyen," Zara declares, hooking her arm

through him. "Archer is an early investor in Lustre, deputy chair of the board, and a *pain* in my ass."

She smiles down at him sweetly. "Even though my sister just died, you couldn't wait to talk business, could you, pet?"

He clears his throat, not looking at either of us.

"Zara, who is this?"

"A curious friend of the family." Zara drops his arm, her voice souring. "You can go now, Archer. That'll be all."

I rack my brain as he shuffles out of view. It dawns on me how I know of him. Archer Nguyen is on the guest list. I ran a background check on him earlier this afternoon—and he's just as Zara said. Deputy chair and an early investor in Lustre. A run-of-the-mill Silicon Valley venture capitalist. Now that I think about it, even Radhika mentioned that Zara had forced her to invite a few "key" investors to the wedding. But why did he come to Blush, even when all guests were specifically sent away?

"You're really doing business right now," I say incredulously. "When did he arrive?"

"I don't just run a business, Shay. I run an empire, and not all my investors have the compassion gene." Zara sighs. "Archer flew in early this morning, even though we specifically told all the guests *not* to come. The man doesn't take no for an answer."

I nod, slightly deflated. He must have been who she was rushing off to see this morning when I heard her talking on the phone by the pool.

"I'm nearly done with him," Zara says, backpedaling into the hotel suite. "I'll see you at the bistro?"

She tries to close the door on me, but I wedge my foot in the frame just in time. The door bounces off my sneaker and nearly hits her in the face.

"Can I have your phone number?" My voice shakes as she glares at me. "In case of an emergency."

"An *emergency*," she echoes.

"You never know."

"Sure. Fine. Just take my card."

Zara lets the door fall open as she moves to the entryway, on which perches a designer white leather bag. I step toward her as she rummages through it, but when I'm just a few feet away, the light catches on something in the wide lip of her purse.

"Here."

Zara thrusts a business card in my direction. I take it, my eyes still on the bag, gravity pulling me toward it. There's something in there. Glimmering. Sparkling, even.

I feel Zara's hot hand on my wrist, yanking me away, just as it dawns on me what I'm looking at.

Radhika's missing cellphone.

24.

My mother didn't speak to me for two weeks after I dropped out of school."

The audience collectively held its breath as Zara paused at the podium, slowly rolled up the sleeves of her perfectly oversize blazer.

"I was twenty-five and halfway through my MBA at Stanford. But I knew in my gut"—she tapped her flat stomach—"that was the right thing to do. And for the first time in my life, I didn't listen to her."

Smiling, Zara stepped away from the podium and paced the front length of the auditorium, her polished gaze meeting the eager eyes of the students in the front row.

"This is a single mother who left her abusive husband and raised three kids on her own while working a crappy job in a research lab." Zara paused again, letting the words resonate. "A mother who valued education so much, she managed to complete her PhD in organic chemistry on evenings, weekends, and public holidays."

Zara pointed to the projector screen behind her, which displayed a list of Lustre's business, scientific, and media awards.

"A mother who would create and patent a chemical formula that would revolutionize the skincare industry."

Zara flashed her white teeth at the crowd, which was hanging on to her every word. "You see, my mother, Dr. Simran Singh, is an organic chemistry *genius*. And I"—she changed the slide to a flashy photo of the Lustre product line—"am a *marketing* genius."

The packed auditorium laughed appreciatively, including Shay, even though Zara's guest lecture at USC was supposed to be for students. Shay listened closely as Zara went on to dive into the nitty-gritty of what it was really like for her to launch a biotechnology start-up from scratch and create the most well-known luxury skincare brand in the world.

Business plans. Market analysis. Pitching investors. Securing funding from venture capitalists. Brand building. Scaling the product lines. Board governance. Strategy.

"Considering most of you in the room can't afford our products, you'll be pleased to know that we're going after the drugstore market."

She threw her head back and laughed as dozens of people in her audience broke into applause.

"Hold your horses. We're still in clinical trials." She switched the slide to a pictograph illustrating the demographics, income, and skincare preferences of her existing and target customers. "Although, *very* soon, we'll be able to manufacture our proprietary ingredients at a fraction of the cost . . ."

Despite the fact Shay believed capitalism to be the root of all evil and antiaging creams products of the patriarchy, she found herself listening in rapture along with the rest of the students.

She couldn't deny how refreshing it was to see a woman like Zara, who was also the daughter of Punjabi immigrants, take the world by storm. Refuse to be humble about her achievements. Project the type of confidence any man would in her position. Watching her speak, Shay understood a bit better why the *Los Angeles Journal* was forcing her to frame her article around Zara. Even without the backlash and scandal, she had become the most talked-about tech executive since Mark Zuckerberg, Sam Bankman-Fried, and Elizabeth Holmes. When Shay's article was published—which Lexie had scheduled for two days after the Cabo wedding—*everyone* was going to read it.

As Zara offered the room her top tips on series A, B, and C investing; managing burn rate; and finding one's niche within the start-up ecosystem, Shay's mind wandered away. Wandered to Caleb.

She slept over the night before, and they'd stayed up late talking, among other things. Sometimes, when she was with him, she felt like she was regressing into the teenager she'd never gotten to be. Drinking and smoking too much. Procrastinating on Lexie's edits so she could meet Caleb for lunch, or drinks. The sex was pretty great too.

On nights like those, it would have been easy for Shay to forget their entire relationship was a lie. That Caleb wasn't really her boyfriend. Reveling in his touch, Shay could have closed her eyes, inhaled his signature scent, and imagined that life really was this simple. She was a grad student at USC, and he was the mostly nice, sweet (not to mention rich) guy who cared about her. Who always put in the extra effort. Who made her feel . . .

Shay squirmed, suddenly uncomfortable in the plastic auditorium chair. She shouldn't be thinking like this. She and Caleb would be over the second he read the article. On Lexie's strict instructions, Shay had added several paragraphs about the Prescotts, particularly the criminals, addicts, and alcoholics in Caleb's direct lineage. Technically, Shay agreed with Lexie's editorial note: readers would need to understand why Caleb became estranged from the Prescotts and was driven to earn his de facto status in the Joshi family. But morally?

Shay's anxiety was increasing as the wedding drew closer, and every time she started losing her nerve, she looked in the mirror and reminded the woman looking back she was doing the right thing. She *had* to take Mr. Joshi out. The end would justify the means, and Shay thought she'd resigned herself to Caleb being the collateral damage.

But taking advantage of their intimacy, their pillow talk, felt just plain wrong. This article was supposed to publicly crucify Mr. Joshi—not sweet, innocent Caleb. How could Shay throw him into the limelight like this? How could she justify using him?

"When are you taking Lustre public?" a student asked suddenly in the front row, interrupting Zara's take on market penetration. Shay sat up, remembering she was here to pay attention. Zara blinked at the student in disbelief as he waved his hand around to make sure he'd heard her.

"Why?" Zara sipped her water bottle demurely. "Does your daddy want to invest?"

The student laughed along with the audience, seemingly unaware he was the butt of the joke.

"Your critics think you're making a strategic mistake by delaying your IPO."

Zara raised an eyebrow. "And what if I never take it public? Some of the world's largest and best-run corporations remain privately held," Zara answered seriously. "Think Cargill. Aldi. Deloitte. IKEA."

She stepped toward the student, holding his gaze.

"While other corporations go public only to fail spectacularly. Think Vonage. The Blackstone Group. Pets.com and the other catastrophes of the dot-com bubble. Even Facebook—or should I say Meta—took over a year to recover after it bombed its IPO.

"Next time you ask a question," Zara told the student firmly, "don't interrupt. And certainly don't assume you know the answer."

Clearly pissed off by the student, Zara refused to answer any further questions, and after the lecture, students and professors alike swarmed her at the podium. Shay, who'd tried and failed to meet Zara at Radhika's bachelorette party, doubled back the way she came and decided to stake out the parking lot. As she zigzagged through the rows of expensive cars—Mercedes, Teslas, Range Rovers, and even a Bentley—wondering which one belonged to Zara, she spotted her hustling around the corner of the building.

Zara looked so elegant, even jogging in high heels, her long trench coat billowing behind her in the wind. Shay beelined to the pedestrian path and started walking toward her. When Zara was just a few feet away, Shay waved her down.

"*Zara?*"

She looked up from her phone, frowning at Shay as if trying to place her. Zara was model-gorgeous online and in the papers, but even more stunning up close. No makeup, and totally flawless. It was like the woman didn't have pores.

"I was at your lecture," Shay said, her legs suddenly shaky.

"You and four hundred others," Zara said impatiently. "May I help you?"

"Um." Shay faltered.

Shay had found out about Zara's lecture by chance only a few hours ago and hadn't expected to actually speak with her this afternoon, so she hadn't prepared any questions. And she'd only come because Lexie perpetually had her on the hunt for more "juicy details," and her latest editorial note—they were working on Shay's ninth draft—asked Shay to find out what Zara thought of Raj and the Joshi family.

As Lexie kept reminding her, as much as the article focused on Raj, Radhika, the wedding, and the corrupt Joshis, it was really a follow-up to Zara's profile. About the type of family *her* little sister was marrying into.

It was about how Zara Singh—chief executive, girl boss, celebrity entrepreneur, and icon—got *duped*.

"I didn't have a chance to speak with you at Radhika's bachelorette party," Shay said finally, confidently. "I wanted to introduce myself."

"You're friends with Radhi?" Zara brightened, bitchface to friendly like zero to sixty. "What's your name?"

"Shay. I'm dating—"

"Caleb." Zara's eyes widened. "You're the grad student. Interesting choice."

"Yeah," Shay said, unsure of the meaning behind Zara's words. "He's a nice guy."

"Are you still coming with him to the wedding?"

Shay hesitated. "Why wouldn't I be?"

"You know." Zara gave her a knowing look. "After your little tiff with Radhi at the bachelorette. Don't hold it against her. She was having a rough night. She wanted to yell at me, not you."

"Right." Shay smiled politely. She shouldn't have been surprised that Radhika told her sister about the incident, and although she thought Radhika was the one at fault, Shay knew the story didn't reflect well on either of them.

"I'm doing my masters in public policy," Shay said, changing the subject, indiscriminately gesturing toward campus. "My parents were hounding me to level up my education, but maybe I should drop out like you. Your lecture was incredible, by the way. I'm a huge fan. I can't wait until Lustre hits drugstores and I can afford some of your products."

"Thank you," Zara said flatly, her eyes already drifting back to her phone. "It won't be long now."

Shay shifted her weight between her heels, deciding how best to keep the conversation going, how to entice Zara to reveal her feelings about the Joshis.

Flattery? Zara would be used to younger, ambitious women fawning over her, hoping to hitch a ride on her coattails. Shay pursed her lips, the wheels turning. No. Zara wouldn't respond to flattery. She was a businesswoman.

She would respond to competition.

"I'm really looking forward to the wedding," Shay said cheerily. "I can't believe someone I know is marrying a *Joshi*. It's like a fairytale, isn't it?"

Zara tensed.

"One of my uncles is a manager for a Joshi Group hotel chain in Kuala Lumpur," Shay continued chattily, lying. "I can't remember which one, but he won't shut up about how proud he is to work for the family. He got all my cousins jobs there too."

Zara's face had fallen to somewhere between distaste and amusement. Encouraged, Shay doubled down.

"Like you said in your lecture, some of the world's greatest corporations are still family run," Shay said slowly, her eyes locking on Zara. "And the Joshi Group? I hear they're the best of them all."

Zara smiled tightly before averting her gaze. Had Shay struck a nerve?

"I suppose," Zara said after a moment, pulling her coat closed. "They are quite prominent in *Asia*."

"Just Asia? I thought they had hotels all over the world, and their office here in LA—"

"That sham of an office?" Zara spat. Immediately, her cheeks flushed. "I'm just kidding. Ha!"

Shay's heart pounded. That didn't sound like a joke.

"Anyway, I'd better be going." Zara's tone was off as she steered around Shay. "See you in Cabo."

"Do you have time for a coffee?" Shay asked, scrambling. "There's a cute place around—"

Zara waved over her shoulder without bothering to reply, and defeated, Shay watched her sashay across the parking lot.

That sham of an office.

What did she mean by that? What does Zara suspect about the Joshis?

25.

Saturday, April 27
6:22 p.m.

> Meeting finally over. Heading to your room
> now with the laptop. Did you find Zara?

Give me a chance to explain, would you?" Zara calls after me.
"No, thank you!"

I speed up from a panicked brisk walk into a run as I hightail
it down the corridor. *Zara* has Radhika's phone. Radhika's *missing* phone. What possible explanation is there? I know better
than to stick around and find out.

I screech to a halt at the bank of elevators and slam the button twice. A beat later, the doors open, but before I can throw
myself inside, Zara catches up.

"Stay away from me," I spit, backpedaling away from her. I
look up and down the hall, but no one else is around.

"I'll scream," I warn.

"God, you're being dramatic." Zara sets her hands on her
hips. "Just let me talk—"

"*I'm* being dramatic?" I stammer. "You're hiding your dead sister's phone!"

"True." Zara clicks her teeth. "But I have a good reason."

She steps forward slowly. My whole body tenses.

"Would you just hear me out? If you're not satisfied, you can call in the cavalry."

My heart races as she smiles over at me as if nothing is wrong. As if she has this situation totally in her control.

"I won't try and stop you."

My mouth twitches as I weigh my options, my muscles on standby to fight or flee.

The rational thing would be to hand her and the phone over to the National Guard. But if Zara has a valid reason for hiding Radhika's phone, then turning her over will only make her look guilty. The authorities might try to pin this whole thing on an innocent woman.

It's a risk either way, and ultimately, my curiosity overrules the rational side of my brain. I walk ten feet behind Zara as we make our way to the Oceanside Bistro. The host recognizes her and gives us the best table, apologizes for the inclement weather that will prevent us from sitting outside or enjoying the sunset. Out the window, rain clouds loom large on the horizon, threatening to split at any moment.

"Radhi was so young when Lustre took off," Zara says after she orders us two skinny margaritas. "Mom and I wanted to give her an equal share, but we were worried about handing her too much too soon—"

Zara stops, clocking my notepad as I reach for it.

"This has to be off the record."

"As long as you don't tell me anything incriminating, sure, it's off the record," I say testily. "But I'm still taking notes."

She purses her lips at me. She and I both know she doesn't have much bargaining power right now, and after a moment, she keeps going.

"My family has a controlling stake in Lustre. Mom, my brother, Radhi, and myself each own fifteen percent of the company. That's sixty percent. Our investors own forty. Whenever we make big decisions as a company, my family's collective votes always overrule the investors. We control the company. Are you following so far?"

I nod, even though I find corporate structures and governance confusing. "Yes," I say, scribbling. "Keep going."

"And like I was saying before, Radhi was really young when we launched the company. We were worried about the pressure on a young girl having to make big business decisions. We ended up setting up a trust whereby Radhi would inherit her shares when she turned twenty-five."

Zara looks at me, her eyes filling with tears.

"Next month she would have celebrated her twenty-fifth birthday."

Zara pauses again as the waiter drops off our drinks. My legs thrum as I wait on the edge of my seat and take notes. Once the waiter is out of earshot, Zara continues.

"As Radhi's trustee, I've always voted on her behalf at board meetings, but by the next one, Radhi would have cast her votes herself.

"Most of our investors want to take the company public. My family doesn't want to, and we've shot down every motion to start the IPO process. Archer, that motherfucker, isn't just here to talk business, Shay. He wants to know what's going to happen to Radhi's votes."

I race to write everything down as Zara explains that, with

Radhika's fifteen percent shares, Archer and the investors—who currently have forty—would have the majority they need to overrule the Singh family and take the company public. I don't know where I expected this conversation to go—but this isn't it.

"So why exactly do you have Radhika's phone?" I ask, still confused.

"Because I'm protecting my business," Zara says gravely. "Don't you get it? Radhi was weeks away from joining Lustre's board of directors. From controlling *fifteen* percent of the company. She has highly confidential documents and emails on that phone. I can't let them fall into the wrong hands.

"You know what this country is like," Zara continues dismissively. "If I hand her phone over to the Mexican authorities, God knows what'll happen to Lustre's proprietary information. But I promise you, as soon as I'm back in the US, I'll take that phone straight to the FBI."

I set down my pen, trying to push past her prejudices. Trying to decide if I believe her.

"You and your mom hold the same amount of shares as your brother and sister, yet . . ." I pause, remembering her lecture that day at USC. "*You* recognized the potential of your mother's invention. You made Lustre what it is today. Were you really OK with being an equal shareholder to your siblings?"

"I fib a little in my lectures," Zara says, smiling sadly. "It's not much of a brand highlight to tell the public that my mother was never home, and when she was, she was studying, working, or crying over our deadbeat father.

"I raised Radhi and our brother. I helped them with their homework. I drove them to school and packed their lunches. I gave them the sex talk, because I certainly never got one.

"I only wanted what was best for Radhi," Zara says as tears start leaking down her cheeks. "She wasn't just my sister; she felt like my child too."

My own eyes mist as Zara goes on to explain how protective of and close she is with her family, and how she always imagined Lustre as a family-run business with all four of them equally involved. Their mother, Dr. Simran Singh, is head of research and development, and their brother, a dermatologist, works on her team. Zara, with her business and marketing prowess, is the chief executive. And when Radhika grew bored of influencing, Zara says, she'd have had a job leading Lustre's data science team right there waiting for her.

"I've been begging her to come work for me ever since she graduated from MIT," Zara says as her emotions level off. "But she was dead set on being an influencer, which, if you ask me, was a waste of her potential."

"That's what you were fighting about at her bachelorette," I interrupt, suddenly remembering Radhika's tirade when I'd underestimated her.

I could be running the data science team at Lustre if I wanted . . . I could be president, Shay, if I wanted.

"You told me Radhika was upset with you that night, not me," I remind Zara. "And that you should have told her more often you were proud of her."

Zara nods, her cheeks flushing with color.

"I was too hard on her. Being an influencer made her happy. Getting married at twenty-four, to a guy she'd only known for a few years, made her *happy*. I should have just let her be."

When Zara doesn't volunteer any further information, I ask, "Were you jealous of her?"

Zara laughs.

"I have to ask. She's over a decade younger than you. Her life was a lot easier than yours. And she was about to get married—"

"You have to ask," Zara echoes, rolling her eyes. "Of course you do. Because I couldn't possibly be happy without a husband by my side, could I? And seeing Radhi getting married must have sent me into a murderous rage?"

My cheeks burn. "I didn't mean it like that."

"It's fine." Zara smiles tightly. "I get it. You have to cover your bases—but the answer is no. I was not jealous. I have a great life, a great job, and great sex, when I feel like it. As I learned from my mother, husbands just hold you back."

Zara reaches into her bag, pulls out Radhika's sparkly phone, and slides it decidedly toward me.

"I have nothing to hide from you, Shay," Zara says, gesturing for me to take the phone. "Take the phone, for all I care. We're locked out anyway."

Curious, I lean forward and inspect the sparkly phone case. It's definitely Radhika's. Covering my pointer finger with a napkin, I click the side button and wake up the phone. The home screen photo is a selfie of Raj and Radhika kissing in bed, and there are eighty-nine WhatsApp message notifications, three new voicemails, and twenty-two iMessage alerts. The sender information, message contents, and timestamps are all hidden.

As Zara tells me how she's spent the last few days trying and failing to guess the passcode, suddenly, I get the sinking feeling that I'm looking at the wrong family. The wrong company. Radhika was about to turn twenty-five and gain full rights to her stake in Lustre. Could *she* have been the target, and Raj the collateral damage, rather than the other way around?

"Why didn't you want to take the company public?" I ask, changing the subject back to Lustre.

"You came to my lecture," Zara answers. "Control. Mom and I are determined to make the product line more affordable, so everyone can benefit. That's why we're investing so much right now in clinical trials.

"But Archer and those other bloodsuckers have no interest in doing what's best for the product line, for our customers long-term." Zara sighs. "They just want to cash out on their investment."

I scribble more notes as fast as I can and quickly do the math.

"What happens to Radhika's shares now?" I ask, the wheels turning. "Do you think it's possible one of your investors wanted to take Lustre public so badly, they killed Radhika over it? With her fifteen percent stake, plus the investors' forty—that's a fifty-five percent majority. They'd overrule your family on the vote."

"Sure, *but*"—Zara blows air through her teeth—"Radhi had a will. Her shares, her votes—everything goes back to our mother. My family still retains control."

"But as of her wedding day . . ." My eyes widen as I think through another possibility. "Would Radhika's shares have still gone to your mother? Or would *Raj* have inherited them?"

Before Zara can answer, I ask, "Isn't it odd Radhika was killed just a few weeks before she had full rights to her shares in Lustre?"

"It's a little strange," Zara admits. "But you're forgetting one thing."

"And what's that?"

"We're wealthy. Nobody of our caliber even says the word 'marriage' without locking in an ironclad prenup."

Zara stares off into the distance, her eyes heavy.

"If my sister was still alive," she says gravely, "after marriage,

Raj could not have touched her shares in Lustre. And Radhi wouldn't have gotten a cent of the Joshi fortune either."

* * *

ZARA ORDERS US two more skinny margaritas as we go over everyone's whereabouts the day and night leading up to the murders, and, encouragingly, her version of events lines up with my timeline. But what I'm most curious about is what happened at the club in Cabo San Lucas: was anyone fighting? Did she notice someone outside their group watching Raj and Radhika or acting suspiciously? Unfortunately, Zara doesn't have any answers. All she knows for sure is that everyone drank to excess except for Sean, who was sober and frequently stepped out to take work calls. Raj and Caleb did a lot of cocaine too. Recalling the security footage from the resort lobby, in which Raj was uncharacteristically quiet when they returned to Blush, I ask Zara what his mood was like that evening. If he'd had a disagreement with anyone. Blushing, Zara tells me she didn't recall; she says she drank a little too much and the specific details of their night out were hazy.

"I heard the club's bouncer nearly kicked you all out," I say next. "What happened?"

"Oh—*that* I remember. Radhi was dancing on our table. Of course she convinced me to get up there with her." Zara smiles, shaking her head. "Let's just say we're lucky the manager recognized me. Which reminds me. I need to get my assistant to send him some free samples."

"I see." I sigh. I was hoping for a lead.

"I'm sorry, Shay. But from what I could tell, everyone had a great night.

"Like I said before, I followed Radhi back to her villa and

helped her with her skincare routine," Zara says after we move on to their return to Blush. "I was going to walk her over to Raj's, but I was so tired. I was falling asleep standing up. Around 2 a.m., she kicked me out and told me to go to bed."

"And you went straight back to your own villa." After Zara nods, I ask, "Do you have any idea what time Radhika went over to Raj's?"

"I have no clue. Shortly after, I'm guessing. If only I'd—"

Without warning, Zara bursts into tears again, and although I'm desperate to keep the conversation going, I give her some breathing room. It must be painful for her to go over that fateful night, and the weight of her grief and regret sits heavy on my chest.

Zara's story checks, and I don't believe Zara could have betrayed her sister to the cartel; I can't come up with a single reason why she even would. Still, I'm not sure I can trust her. Zara has this veneer about her that feels false and inauthentic. It could just be her celebrity, her robotic-level determination, but for some reason, I can't shake the feeling that she's not being totally honest with me.

"Who do you think betrayed Raj and Radhika to the cartel?" I ask after she's composed herself. "Which one let the killer into the villa: Sean or Caleb?"

Zara blows her nose. "Well, it certainly wasn't me."

I nod. I believe her.

Don't I?

"Sean's a lovely guy," Zara says after a beat. "I like him a lot. He's ambitious. Intelligent too. Way too intelligent to do business with a drug cartel."

"So you think it's Caleb."

"Maybe." She shrugs. "But guys like him are a dime a dozen,

and I'm not sure he has the guts for something so heinous. So maybe not. Shay, I really don't know."

I remind Zara about her comment to me after her USC lecture, when she called the Joshi Group's LA office a sham. "Why did you say that? Did you suspect someone at the Joshi Group was involved in criminal activities?"

"Oh, that." Zara blushes. "I didn't mean to imply anything. I find it irritating when companies set up offices for show. Sean, Raj, Caleb, and maybe two dozen other people work in LA. The rest of the Joshi Group's corporate staff are stuffed into some sad office park back in India."

Zara says the word *India* as if it leaves a bitter taste on her tongue. Doing my best to ignore her prejudice, I tap my pen against the table and study her face carefully. Does she know more about the Joshis than she's letting on?

I remind her of my theory that Raj's business meetings with Hector and Blush Continental were a cover, that he was being sent down to Cabo at the behest of Mr. Joshi.

"If Raj was laundering money for the cartel," I say carefully, "it's hard to believe Radhika was in the dark."

Zara's face hardens.

"Did she—"

"If Radhi knew her fiancé was a drug trafficker," Zara hisses, "she wouldn't have agreed to marry him—and she definitely would have told me about it. You're barking up the wrong tree, Shay, and you're *really* starting to piss me off."

I bite my tongue, chastised, but not totally convinced. As Zara stands up, she glances at her phone. Her face drops.

"Archer's hounding me. I have to go."

"OK." I nod. I have more questions, but Zara's reached her limit with me. This will have to do for now.

"Thanks for answering my questions." I rise from the table too. "Let's touch base later tonight?"

"Of course." She hesitates. "Actually, I, uh . . ."

"Yes?"

She shakes out her hair and winces.

"I'm sorry for jumping down your throat. You're trying to help."

Zara smiles at me then. Her entire face transforms.

"I just miss her. You know?"

Zara gives me whiplash. One minute she's a celebrity bitch committing microaggressions against other people of color, the next she's a robotic Silicon Valley tycoon, and the one after that?

She's human. She's just a big sister—grieving a big fucking loss.

As I watch Zara walk away, I can feel all my doubts and follow-up questions vanish into thin air. Zara didn't do it. She may have her secrets, but she didn't betray Raj and Radhika to the cartel. Right?

My hands trembling, I search my pockets for a cigarette, anxiety swelling in my throat. Because if Zara didn't do it, then there are only two other people who could have.

26.

Saturday, April 27
7:31 p.m.

Just saw this! Long talk with Zara.
Even more confused, but I don't think
it's her. Where are you? Let's go over
the outdoor camera footage?

I left my laptop in your room. Don't be
upset, but I just got to Blush Continental's
HQ in San Jose. I know you said we
should leave Hector alone, but there
has to be paperwork somewhere that
contains his real name. Maybe we
can connect him to the cartel.

Daniela . . . Going after Hector is
dangerous! What if someone catches
you??

> It's Saturday night. The office is
> empty and I have the file cabinets to
> myself. Don't worry, I'll be fine.

> ☹

> Just to be safe, can you text me
> every ten minutes to check in?
> And send me your location?

> Daniela???

t's pouring rain outside. When did it start? How long have I been talking to Zara?

Disoriented, I linger beneath the bistro's awning and decide to wait out the storm. I'm not supposed to smoke here, but when I read Daniela's texts, I take the chance and sneak a cigarette anyway.

She's gone after Hector. What is she thinking? What would happen to her and her family if the cartel finds out she's working with journalists? I grimace as my imagination takes hold, and even though I'm terrified for her, my body hums in anticipation. Eric Santos has a paper trail connecting several Blush owners to the cartel. If Hector's one of them, then, by virtue of his meeting with Raj, we can prove the cartel's connection to the Joshi Group. To Mr. Joshi himself.

Sheets of water pour down from the sky and, ten minutes later, show no sign of letting up. I shift my weight between my heels, deciding whether or not to make a run for it, and just as I'm about to step forward, the hairs on the back of my neck spring upright.

I whip around to face the bistro. It's moderately busy, guests finding shelter and amusement during the rains, but I don't see anyone I recognize. Still, I scan the face of everyone inside as I wrestle with the same sinking feeling I experienced this morning on the beach. Last night on the stairs behind the villa. Yesterday morning when I found my laptop on the desk.

A feeling like someone is watching me.

Has someone been following me?

I check the time. Shit. It's getting late. Mr. Joshi, Sean, Caleb, and Brown Hulk Hogan might already be back from dinner; I need to get out of here. I make a run for it through the rain and am completely soaked by the time I reach the doors to the shopping piazza. So are my cigarettes.

The gift shop is still open, so I quickly buy a new pack and then bolt into a side corridor to get off the main drag. There must be a way to get back to my hotel room without going through the lobby and risking being seen. I take a series of side corridors and staircases, and even dart through an employee-only section of the hotel, but somehow end up right where I started. The Oceanside Bistro.

Dammit. Through the double doors just ahead, there's a straight shot through the lobby to my hotel room. Do I risk it? Conflicted, I scan the resort's outdoor area, where several guests in the pool splash around in the rain, and search for another option. My eyes land on the back patios of the ground-floor hotel suites. My patio is one of them. If only I could hop the railing and sneak back into my room. Unfortunately, the door is locked from the inside.

My only way back is through the lobby, and I'm about to take my chances when I catch a whiff of something strong directly to my left. Someone's smoking marijuana. Instinctively, my eyes drift in that direction—

I freeze in terror. It's Sean. And he's staring right at me.

It's too late to run; he's already seen me. I sneak a look to either side. I think he's alone, and, rattled, I take a moment to calm my nerves before walking over to him. He's about twenty feet away, sheltered beneath the awning that runs the length of the Oceanside Bistro and other resort amenities. He grins stupidly as I approach. He's the one smoking the joint.

"Ladies and gentlemen, it's the source close to the families!"

"Sean—" I stop. I have no excuses. I have nothing to apologize for.

"You're very good." Sean exhales smoke from his nostrils, and I step away so as not to inhale. "I hadn't the foggiest idea. Although I should have known something was off. You and Caleb were a proper match made in hell."

I notice a glint in his eye, raw and fierce. I don't know what to say or do in response. There's no point questioning him about the murders. He hates me, and Sean could very well be the one responsible. He's more likely to hurt me at this point than he is to help.

"I forgot my wallet here earlier," I lie, keeping my voice as steady as a rock. "I'm leaving right now. I would appreciate if you didn't tell your uncle—"

"You're obsessed with him. Aren't you?" Sean spits. "You don't have a life of your own, and so you want to ruin ours?"

"Sean, it's not—"

"I bet you feel so clever, don't you, getting this far. But let me tell you something—"

"No," I interrupt firmly. I won't take this abuse. "I don't want to hear it. I'm leaving, and if you're lucky, you'll never have to see me again."

I dash into the rain toward the lobby, my pace brisk, my cheeks and ears red with humiliation. But when I'm just a few steps away, I feel a hand firm around my elbow. Gasping, I whip around and shake my arm free.

"Did he do it?" Sean breathes, the rain falling in torrents around us. Gently, he retracts his hand and wipes water from his brow.

"Tell me the truth. Did my uncle do it?"

Our eyes meet, and an understanding passes between us. A temporary ceasefire. He wants to know about the fire in Mumbai. He wants to know if Mr. Joshi is guilty.

"There were seven eyewitnesses," I say after careful calculation. "Eighteen people died, Sean. Five of them were chil—"

"No," Sean whispers, his voice catching. "No. I don't believe you."

"You don't have to believe me," I say. "It's still the truth."

The rain beats down around us, hard and unrelenting. Sean didn't know about Mr. Joshi's role in the fire. I see the good in him, the kindred friendship we could have had, and yet again, I must resist the urge to believe Sean couldn't have killed Raj and Radhika. Sean's innocence of the fire doesn't rule him out now.

"Sooner or later, your uncle is going to get exactly what he deserves," I say before turning to leave. "Feel free to pass along the message."

* * *

LEAVING SEAN, I dart through the lobby with my head down, unable to breathe until I've made my way back to the suite and have switched on the "do not disturb" function. There. Now the only other person who can unlock that door is Daniela.

The room is freezing cold. I turn off the AC, and while I change into fresh clothes and towel-dry my hair, I take a moment to process my exchange with Sean. Is he going to rat me out to Mr. Joshi? Am I safe continuing to stay on at Blush? I need to take my chances that he'll keep quiet. Sean seemed a little off-kilter this evening, either from the marijuana or the possibility his uncle killed eighteen people. I've always believed Sean (and Raj) didn't know Mr. Joshi started the construction-site fire, and after Sean's reaction, I've never been more certain.

But that doesn't mean he's innocent of all charges. Thank god the Joshis don't know I'm on their scent about their involvement with the cartel. Who knows what Sean would have done to me just now.

Without skipping a beat, I hop onto the bed, where Daniela's laptop is waiting for me. There's a pink Post-it Note affixed to the top with her passcode. I smile. I can get started on the outdoor security footage without her.

After I log into the system, I check the cameras with a view of the footpath connecting the main resort with the Villas and watch the footage from Wednesday night and early Thursday morning, around the time of the murders. But it doesn't tell me anything I don't already know. It just confirms the timeline and the exact timestamp of when each person left and then returned to the Villas.

The footage from Thursday morning, 1:36 a.m. onward, I pay particularly close attention to. As Zara said, the group splits up on their return to the Villas. Zara and Radhika walk ahead of the men, but nobody's body language raises any further red flags. And except for Daniela's brief appearances on her way to and from her rendezvous with Caleb, nobody else appears in the frame until after six in the morning, when gardening staff start tending to the plants.

Next, I check the cameras facing the pools, outdoor bars, and cabanas. It takes much longer to go through the footage, as it's harder to spot the people I'm looking for among the other guests and staff. I first catch sight of the Singh family on their way to brunch on Wednesday at 11:00 a.m.: Zara, her mother, brother, and sister-in-law. An hour and a half later, they all return together to the Villas. Around 12:30 p.m., Caleb, Raj, and Radhika wander into the frame and claim three deck chairs by one of the outdoor pools. I cross-check their movements with the timeline. It checks out. They must have come straight from the gym.

I watch them closely as they horse around in the water, order drinks from the swim-up bar. At one point, Radhika splashes Caleb in the face. Annoyed, Caleb stalks off and starts swimming laps, and immediately, Raj wraps his arms around Radhika in a fiery embrace. None of this behavior is unusual; for them, it's par for the course.

I fast-forward through the footage as Raj and Radhika make out in the pool. They seem so happy together, so free, so in love. I almost smile watching them. They were always like that. Kissing. Touching. They really cared about each other, didn't they? They would have been really happy together.

After about fifteen minutes, they pull away from one another and start to talk. I resume the playback at normal speed. They're too far away from the camera for me to attempt to read their lips, but I can tell from their body language it's a spirited discussion. Are they arguing? Maybe. Maybe not. They were passionate people. Often this was just how they spoke to each other. As they converse, she looks over Raj's shoulder a few times and watches Caleb swim, but his face is in the water and he doesn't seem to notice.

When Caleb's finished swimming around 2:30 p.m., the three of them leave the pool and return to the Villas. I keep trolling through the footage, but no one I'm looking for appears on that camera the rest of the day, and so I switch to the camera positioned above the swim-up bar in the infinity pool. From this angle, I can see the backs of the bartenders, guests ordering drinks, half the width of the pool, and the beach just behind.

I rewind the footage until dawn breaks on Wednesday morning—around 6:00 a.m., just over twenty-seven hours before Raj and Radhika's bodies were discovered—and sit back. On ten-times speed, I watch as Blush staff come and go, clean the pool, prepare the bar, and tidy up the deck. At 7:00 a.m. on the dot, a beach attendant in a beige uniform strolls into view, pushing a cart of beach towels. I narrow my eyes in recognition. It's the Backstreet Boy with frosted tips, the one who brought me my coffee and helped me track down Sean in the spa earlier today.

Not much happens for the next few hours. A few guests swim in the infinity pool, and those who wander down to the beach are helped by the Backstreet Boy, who hands them towels, brings them beverages, and makes them laugh.

I'm just starting to get restless and am considering playing the footage at twenty-times speed when I see a familiar blur of movement. I tap the keyboard, rewind it back thirty seconds, and then replay at normal speed. And, at 11:04 a.m., Sean strolls into the frame.

He seems to be coming from the direction of the main resort, not the Villas. I take a peek at Sean's movements in the timeline; he must have come straight here after his appointment in the spa.

I watch closely as he paces along the edge of the infinity pool, hands in pockets, and stares off into the horizon. At one point, he sits down on the pool ledge and dangles his feet in the water. He must just enjoying the amenities. The view. I move to fast-forward—

I pull back my hand. On screen, the Backstreet Boy, who was helping out a guest, suddenly makes a beeline toward Sean.

I can feel my stomach twist into knots as I watch Sean and the beach attendant walk up to each other and engage in conversation. Is Sean asking for a towel? For directions? I squirm. That doesn't feel right. There's something familiar here. It feels like they know each other. But the Backstreet Boy told me in the lobby earlier that he *didn't* know Sean; he was just forced by his boss to memorize the names and details about this weekend's VIPs.

I watch closely, shaky, as the two of them exchange words. Sean seems normal, calm, very much like himself, but it's the Backstreet Boy's body language that's throwing me off. With me and the other guests, he played the role of the enthusiastic, perhaps overly flirtatious, resort staff member, standing to attention. But with Sean, he's different. He's stiff, even anxious. He's far more serious.

I watch the clock closely as a minute passes, and then another. They *must* know each other. But how? And what on earth could they be talking about? The conversation seems to be wrapping up by about 11:11 a.m. The Backstreet Boy steps back from the towel cart around which they were huddling and scans the beach behind him. Sean nods, quickly glances toward the infinity pool, and then—

Wait. *What?*

The movement is so quick, so out of the blue, that I don't think I see it right. I rewind the footage and replay it at a quarter of the speed. My heartbeat reverberates through my body as I study their movements. The way Sean moves in, as if for a handshake—but on slower inspection—it's not a handshake he's offering.

It's an envelope.

I freeze the frame and, my heart beating wildly, take a picture of it with my phone. The envelope appears to be no bigger than the length of Sean's hand. It could be cash. It could be a note. For all I know, it could be a birthday card.

But why would Sean give the Backstreet Boy anything, let alone talk to him. Let alone *know* him?

I stand up from the bed and pace around the room, breathing through the jitters.

At 11:11 a.m., the day before Raj and Radhika were murdered, Sean handed an envelope to some random beach attendant. A beach attendant who works for Blush Continental. Which is a hotel group allegedly controlled by the *cartel*.

I don't want to jump to conclusions, but holy shit. This could be big. This could be the beginning of the end.

> Hey, you haven't checked in . . . Are you okay?
> Any luck? You'll never guess what I found . . .

I text Daniela the photo of Sean handing the Backstreet Boy an envelope.

> Who's the beach attendant with Sean?
> American, early twenties, frosted tips, a
> little full of himself. Do you know him?!?!

I toss my phone to the side and, hands shaking with trepidation, return to the footage. After Sean hands over the envelope, he immediately leaves in the direction of the Villas, and the Backstreet Boy returns to his beach duties. Nothing else suspicious catches my attention as I speed through footage from the next few hours. At 3:30 p.m., Backstreet Boy is relieved from his post by another staffer in a beige uniform and, from there, disappears into the resort. I check several other cameras—indoor and outdoor—but can't tell where he goes, or if he leaves the premises.

I look up when I notice the deafening silence. I open the blinds. The rain's stopped, abruptly. I slide open the window, and as a rush of cool, wet air billows inside, I start to worry that Daniela hasn't texted me back. I hope she's just busy digging through paperwork at the office, but I need to speak to her. I've exhausted my search of the security cameras and desperately need to figure out the identity of the beach attendant. Maybe there was a reason he didn't give me his name earlier and wasn't wearing a name tag. Does he work for the cartel? Maybe the envelope Sean gave him contained cash, and he killed Raj and Radhika at Sean's bidding. Sean had a lot to gain from Raj's death; his cousin gone, Sean is the only one who stands to inherit the reins of the Joshi Group.

I check the time and note that I haven't heard from Daniela in nearly an hour. Has it really been that long? I try calling her, and when she doesn't pick up, I push past the worry building in my chest and decide to poke around her computer. First, I scroll through her emails, but they all seem to be with her staff, team members, and wedding clients. After, I click the icon on her desktop for what appears to be Blush's staff management system. It's complicated to get around in Spanish, but after a while,

I get the lay of the land. There are interfaces leading to reservations, accounting and billing, and special events, and another "employee management" tab. I click it, which flows me through to another dashboard. There I find Blush's employee schedules.

I click on the drop-down menu for Wednesday, April 25, the day before the murders. The day Sean handed the beach attendant an envelope. I'm shocked by the number of staff Blush has on duty at a single time. Managers, concierge, bellhops, and valet. Housekeepers and custodians. Waiters and bartenders. Chefs and other kitchen staff. Activities and outdoor crew.

I click on the last tab, which takes me to a roster of all staff who were stationed outdoors. I scroll through the list until I find the position that roughly translates to "beach attendant." The timeslot 7:00 a.m. through 3:30 p.m. belongs to . . .

Greg Clancy.

Greg Clancy? I don't recognize the name. Is it the Backstreet Boy I'm looking for?

And why the heck hasn't Daniela texted me back?

My shoulders tight with worry, I type *Greg Clancy Blush Los Cabos* into Google, drumming my fingers on my thighs as I wait for Daniela's computer to spit out the answer.

It feels like an eternity—not mere seconds—when the results finally appear. The very first webpage is a Greg Clancy LinkedIn profile. Could it be the same one? I hold my breath as I click through and then squint at the profile picture. The guy in the photo has solid brown hair, not bleached-blond tips, and he's clean-shaven, younger. But it's almost certainly him.

The education section states he graduated from a liberal arts college in California three years ago, which would make him about twenty-five if he graduated on time. My breath bated, I scroll down to his employment history, where he's listed as

"Outdoors Coordinator" at Blush Resort & Spa Los Cabos. He started working here only two weeks ago. Chewing my lip, I sift through his past positions. He has over ten roles listed, seemingly switching jobs every few months, including—

Oh god. *Oh god.*

I press my palm over my face as I blink at the screen. As my limbs start to shake with fear.

Between his brief stint as a Verizon customer service operator in downtown LA, and his time as a bartender somewhere in Beverly Hills, it's listed right there in front of me.

Greg Clancy, the beach attendant who accepted an envelope from Sean the day before the murders, is a former intern of the Joshi Group.

27.

'm in," Shay declared into her phone. She dropped her cross-body bag to the floor and knocked the front door closed with her hip. "Do I need to switch off the alarm?"

"I already turned it off in the app," Caleb answered. On the other end of the line, he honked his car horn rapidly four times in a row. "Sorry about that. Some punk just tried to cut me off."

Shay jangled the key she'd found beneath the flowerpot as she placed it on a ledge in Caleb's front foyer. Before venturing into the kitchen, she stepped out of her loafers. Caleb's five-bedroom in Silver Lake was strictly a No Shoes House.

"I can't wait to see you, babe," Caleb said after a moment. "I miss you already."

Shay walked a lap around his kitchen island before continuing on toward the living room. "You do not."

"I do too," Caleb said playfully.

"You do *not*." Shay laughed. "Anyway, how far away are you?"

"I'll be about forty minutes."

"*Forty* minutes," she echoed.

"Do you think you can entertain yourself for that long?" Caleb teased.

"I think I'll manage," she answered, scanning the living room. This was her first time alone in Caleb's house, and she decided to do what any normal fake undercover girlfriend would do in her situation.

Snoop.

Not that she expected to actually find anything useful. Caleb's house felt like a super-swish Airbnb; it was well stocked and artfully decorated, but it didn't contain any of the clutter that made a house feel like a home. Caleb's housekeeper cleaned up after him daily, laundered his clothes, shopped for groceries, and also functioned as a personal assistant. Even if Caleb had left anything helpful lying around that Lexie might deem a "juicy detail" for the article, it was likely already recycled, thrown out, or filed appropriately away.

Besides, Shay's article was basically finished. Lexie had finally approved the draft, and the editorial board had confirmed the date and time of publication. They'd even licensed Shutterstock photos of the Singhs and Joshis that were earmarked to be the featured images. All Shay had to do now was attend the wedding and whack in a last-minute paragraph or two about Raj and Radhika's big day.

All Shay had to do now was enjoy the time she had left with Caleb.

She drifted from room to room as a feeling of melancholy washed over her. She'd come to like this house, despite the extravagance it represented. She'd come to like how she *felt* in his house. Shay lay down on one of the guestroom beds and rubbed her hands over the buttery linen duvet. In Caleb's gym, she did a sun salutation on his yoga mat, then, sitting in his office chair, she admired his view of the reservoir and surrounding parklands.

Ten more days and this is over.

She wandered into Caleb's en suite and peered into his medicine cabinet, fully stocked with Lustre's product line, shaving cream, deodorant, cologne, and rows of prescription pill bottles.

Ten more days and you'll finally expose Mr. Joshi for who he truly is.

Shay slammed the mirrored door shut, her mind elsewhere, barely registering her surroundings.

Shay was so close to reaching her goal. *So* close. Then why did she still feel so empty, so—

"Hello?"

Shay's stomach lurched. Someone was home.

"Caleb?" she called quietly. No one answered. Pulse racing, she checked her watch. Only fifteen minutes had passed since they got off the phone; there was no way he could have driven home that fast.

Quickly, Shay retraced her steps downstairs. Maybe it was the housekeeper. But when she padded into the kitchen, instead she found Raj.

"Oh!" His eyes bulged as he clocked her. "It's you."

Inexplicably, Shay blushed. "Hi."

"Is—uh—Caleb home?"

She shook her head. "He's on his way back from Malibu." When Raj looked at her curiously, she added, "He took the morning off. Apparently, the surf conditions today were perfect."

Raj had a leather folder in his hands, and he set it carefully down on the kitchen island. It was embossed with lettering, but Shay was standing too far way to make it out.

"Shouldn't you be at school?" Raj asked her.

"No classes today." Shay looked up. "Shouldn't *you* be at work?"

Raj scrunched up his face but didn't respond. His eyes skirted around the kitchen, as if searching for anything to look at but Shay. She wondered if she should make an excuse to go upstairs, tell him she had to use the restroom so they could both wait for Caleb in peace. She wasn't imagining the awkwardness between them; it *was* awkward. Despite the number of times they'd hung out as a group, Raj never actually talked to Shay directly. He patently ignored her.

"I need a drink," Raj mumbled, darting to the fridge. He grabbed a bottle of Caleb's go-to light beer from the door and then hesitated. Staring into the fridge, he said, "You want one?"

Shay's eyes widened, realizing the question was directed at her. She'd never known Raj to get himself a drink, let alone offer one to someone else. Especially to *Shay*.

"Sure." She smiled. "I'd love one."

They took their drinks to the living room. Although it was sunny outside, it had rained last night, and the cushions on Caleb's patio furniture were sopping wet. She expected Raj to stare at his phone silently, but he barely touched it. Sipping his beer, he crossed and uncrossed his legs, a pensive look about him. Shay tried to catch his eye and smile a few times, find a way to launch into a conversation, but she could tell Raj's mind was far away. He seemed agitated, even upset, but then again, maybe that was how he behaved when sober. Shay usually saw him on the weekends.

"Are you on your lunch break?" Shay tried half-heartedly, unable to take the silence a moment longer.

Raj turned to face her, as if stunned to find her in the same room. After a moment his face relaxed.

"Something like that." He caught her staring at his embossed leather folder, which he'd brought with him to the living room. He swallowed hard. "I need Caleb to help me write my vows."

"You're doing vows?" Shay had heard they were having a Hindu ceremony, which didn't call for the recitation of the personal vows typically seen in Western weddings. "That's cool."

"I think so," Raj agreed. "Although our *pandit* isn't too happy about the idea."

"God forbid the *pandit* isn't happy."

Did she detect a hint of a smile?

Emboldened, she sat forward on the couch. "What do you have so far?"

Raj's eyebrows furrowed. "So far?"

"For your vows."

"Oh. Right." Raj sipped his beer, swished the liquid between his cheeks before swallowing. "I'm thinking I'll tell the story of how we met."

"How did you and Radhika meet?" Shay already knew, but it was a good opening.

"It's not that good of a story, come to think of it." Raj grimaced. "Or wedding appropriate."

He took another swig of beer before continuing.

"About four years ago, Caleb and I were out clubbing. He started chatting up a few of Radhi's friends and brought the group back to our booth."

"So it was Caleb who played matchmaker." Shay smiled.

"Yep. Thanks to him, I met the girl of my dreams," Raj quipped. "And, if I'm remembering correctly, Caleb got pretty lucky that night too."

"Well, I'm looking forward to your wedding," Shay said, ignoring the jab. "I've never been to Cabo."

"No shit. Everyone's been there."

Shay smiled at him tightly, sipping her beer.

"Where are you going to honeymoon?" she asked breezily.

"I'm not sure yet. We have a few weeks blocked off in May, but Radhi still has to confirm her schedule. She has a few summer collabs on the go."

"And you?"

"What about me?"

"I know how busy you are," Shay cooed. "Does taking time off affect your work?"

Raj regarded her wearily.

"Sorry. Stupid question." She shrugged. "I still don't really get what you do. Business something?" She laughed, not missing any chance to pry about the Joshi Group. "I don't know anything about the corporate world . . ."

Raj grunted in annoyance but couldn't seem to resist the chance to mansplain something to her, just as she'd intended. Raj went on to explain how he was in charge of meeting with and vetting potential business partners across the Americas and Europe, other hospitality companies with whom the Joshi Group might enter into joint ventures, invest in, or even acquire.

"What kind of investments are we talking about?" Shay asked in a Barbie-doll voice. *"Stocks?"*

Raj smiled at her condescendingly. "Not exactly."

"Because the stock market is another thing I don't understand . . ."

Raj waved her off, eager to clarify.

"No, no, nothing like that. In layman's terms, my job is to think of new ways for our company to make money. New investments. New partnerships. Have you taken an economics class?"

Shay shook her head, even though she minored in the subject.

"Right. Well, basically . . ."

Raj set down his beer with purpose as he started to explain the ins and outs of his job, and then the market at large. Shay listened closely as Raj rambled on about synergies, core competencies, and returns on investment. Granted, Shay didn't have the strongest business acumen, but still she could tell nothing Raj was saying was groundbreaking. Unlike Zara, who had kept a four-hundred-person auditorium in bated breath as she demonstrated her mastery of the corporate world, all of Raj's hot takes sounded like a bunch of corporate jargon.

"That's fascinating," Shay said after Raj finished his monologue. "Maybe I'm in the wrong field."

"Right?" Raj was clearly pleased by her flattery. "If you decide to sell out, you can come work for me. The LA office is *sick.*"

"I can think of worse places to work," Shay lied.

"I do all the hiring. We're a rowdy bunch."

"I bet," Shay simpered, remembering the two Joshi Group marketing executives she'd spoken to at Raj's party, and the amount of cocaine inhaled by the both of them.

"Don't you run that office with your cousin Sean?"

Shay trailed off before she could fish for details about Sean's role and responsibilities; Raj's face had gone dark the instant she mentioned Sean's name.

Raj stood up slowly, slamming the beer bottle down with a thud.

"Why are you asking me so many questions?"

"I'm just making conversation," Shay stammered as Raj's eyes flashed with anger. "I'm dating your best friend and want to get to know you—"

"You're dating him today. Don't pretend like he's going to keep you around much longer."

Shay felt a sharp jab in the chest as Raj glowered at her.

"You think you know Caleb, but you don't," Raj spat. "He just wants everyone to love him, and the moment they do, he's gone before they wake up.

"And who says you have the right to know me?" Raj said next, his shadow looming large as he approached her. "Do you know who the fuck I am?"

"I'm sorry," Shay wavered, her bottom lip wobbling. "I just—"

"Tell Caleb I need to talk to him. It's urgent."

He stared down at her like she was stupid.

"Think you can remember that, or do I need to write it down for you."

Shay cleared the lump in her throat, indignant and shocked by his behavior in equal measure.

"I'll tell him," Shay said firmly.

After, Shay stood at the front window and watched Raj storm down the driveway toward his bright red Bugatti and pressed her hand against her chest. Her heart was still beating rapidly.

She'd pissed him off. But how?

Shay racked her brain as she replayed their conversation in her head. They talked about his vows, and how he met Radhika. They talked about business. And then, for whatever reason, his temperament flipped like a switch when she asked about Sean.

From: Shaylee Kapoor
To: Eric Santos
CC: Lexie Dubois
Time: 8:43 p.m.
Subject: EMERGENCY!!

Dear Eric (and Lexie),

A lot has happened since I was last in touch. I'm still in Cabo and fear I've gotten in over my head. Maybe I should have listened to you both and gone home earlier today, but we're so close now and I can't leave any stone unturned.

I now believe more than ever the Joshi Group was laundering money for the cartels, using Raj's business meetings with "Hector" at Blush Continental as a cover. I also believe that Sean used the Cabo wedding to have his cousin murdered so he could solely inherit the Joshi Group, and that Radhika was collateral damage.

See the photo below timestamped eighteen hours before the murders: Sean passes an envelope to Greg Clancy, who started working at Blush two weeks ago and was formerly an intern at the Joshi Group. (Is he on your radar at all? Does he work for the cartel?)

Those questions aside, I have an urgent favor to ask of you. Daniela Munoz, Blush's events director, is missing. She went to Blush Continental's HQ to find paperwork confirming Hector's full name, but she's failed to check in and I haven't heard from her in over an hour.

I'm very worried something's happened to her. Do you have police contacts you trust who can check on her well-being?

I've attached all my research notes to this email for safekeeping. I'm sorry to ask so much of you, but should something happen to me, the truth still needs to come out. The people responsible for these horrific murders need to be held accountable. I hope it doesn't come to it, but if it does, thank you—and best of luck.

Sincerely,
Shay

PS: Lex, I love you. And I'm really, really sorry.

From: Eric Santos
To: Shaylee Kapoor
CC: Lexie Dubois
Time: 8:45 p.m.
Subject: RE: EMERGENCY!!

Remain calm. I'll drive over to Blush HQ right now and will touch base asap.

Sent from my iPhone.

From: Lexie Dubois
To: Shaylee Kapoor
CC: Eric Santos
8:46 p.m.
Subject: RE: EMERGENCY!!

Eric. I'm on the phone with our Mexico City desk. They might have contacts who can help you track Daniela down. More soon.

Shay, I'll dig into Greg Clancy and report back. Are you thinking Sean paid him for the hit? Be careful. And don't be a dumbass, all right?

Lex

PS. I love you too.

28.

I tell myself to stay calm as I pull on my sneakers and double knot the shoelaces. I secure a cross-body bag firmly around my hips and stuff in all my cash, credit cards, ID, passport, notepad, pens, and—

Shit. I forgot to charge my phone this afternoon. The battery is only at twenty-two percent.

I stuff it into the bag anyway, and then create a mental checklist before I leave the room. Should I never have the chance to return to Blush, I have everything I need to get myself back to LA. My eyes linger on my laptop; it's an old Acer computer, heavy, and I ultimately decide to leave it behind. If it gets into the wrong hands, at least Eric and Lexie have everything they need to keep this investigation alive. I don't know if my messages to them are an overreaction, but Daniela's gone AWOL, and given that I'm about to do something incredibly stupid, I can't take any chances.

I thought seriously about reporting Daniela missing to the authorities, like to Tobias at the US Consulate, but Daniela's

Mexican and I'm Canadian, and so we're not his concern. Daniela's lack of faith in local law enforcement also gave me pause about sounding the alarm to the authorities. What if I call for help and the officer assigned to the task is on the cartel's payroll? *No.* I stretch out my calves, preparing myself for the journey. Eric is the person most equipped to go after Daniela right now; he's a local, he has contacts. Lexie trusted him, and so I trust him too.

Leaving my hotel room door locked, I make my escape through the ground-floor patio. Once I'm over the railing, I skulk toward the beach. The rain has let up, but there are barely any guests in sight, just a few people drinking in one of the hot tubs, and luckily Sean's disappeared from his spot earlier beneath the awning. I hesitate slightly when I catch sight of three security guards stationed next to the infinity pool who seem to be guarding the access points between the public beach and the resort. I slow my steps as I approach, but I quicken them again as soon as I notice they're all huddled in fixation around someone's phone.

I think they're watching a soccer game; when I slip by them to the beach, the security guards don't even notice.

Once I'm on the sand, I walk west, stopping and starting until I'm confident no one saw me leave. There isn't a star in sight tonight. It's still humid—the storm isn't finished with us yet—and my skin is slick with moisture. Blush's lights slowly recede behind me, and as I draw closer to the next resort over, my mind races in confusion over how all the new pieces of this puzzle fit together. How they all point toward *Sean.*

This makes sense, but I'm still having trouble believing it. Sean had the strongest motive: Raj was his competition to be the next chief executive of the Joshi Group. I think back to all my conversations with Sean about his desire to change the company's policies to make it more sustainable and in line with international best practices, how he loved Raj as a brother and planned to take care of his uncle and aunt as they grew older. His shock over the possibility his uncle started the Mumbai fire. Was any of it genuine? Is Sean just as ruthless a criminal as Mr. Joshi?

Sean came across as so kind, so moral; he pulled the wool over my eyes. But now having seen that video of him and Greg Clancy, I don't believe a single word he's told me. It's too big of a coincidence that a former Joshi Group intern just happened to join Blush Continental's staff two weeks before these murders. Sean must have instructed Greg Clancy to get a job at Blush, and then paid him to get rid of Raj. Sean was staying in the villa next door, and Greg Clancy, as a staff member, has access to the resort's premises. Sean could easily have let Greg Clancy into Raj's villa in the middle of the night.

But why would Sean have Raj killed the day before his destination wedding?

And did Sean act alone—hoping the police and public would pin the murders on the cartel—or was he acting alongside the cartel itself? Did Sean conspire with them to go against Mr. Joshi?

Maybe. Maybe not.

I don't have all the answers. I haven't yet asked all my questions.

About a mile up the beach, I pull out my phone, which is now at nineteen percent battery. Bracing myself, I call Caleb. He declines the call, sends me straight to voicemail. I call him thirteen more times until I finally get a response.

Stop calling me.

My heart lunges as his text comes through. I reply instantly.

> I need to talk to you. Can we meet?

No.

I smile. Despite his answer, I'm encouraged. I know Caleb's temperament, and if he really meant it, he'd block my number and simply stop answering. A beat later, another text comes through.

Uncle told me everything. You used me to get to him. Our relationship was a lie. What more do I need to know?

> I could ask you the same thing. How many were there, by the way?

Caleb sends through three question marks. I roll my eyes.

> I'm talking about Daniela. How many times have you cheated on me? You lied too, Caleb.

That shuts him up. I circumnavigate a tide pool as I carefully craft my next message.

> I think I figured out who had Raj and Radhika killed. I'm sorry for what I did to you. I really am. But right now, we have to set that aside. You could be in danger.

Caleb's loyal to the Joshi family. He's the finance director of their company, may be helping them launder money for the cartels, and he's lied to me repeatedly. About his drug problem. Daniela. Whatever it is he won't let me see in his villa's safe. I don't believe he's entirely innocent, but I don't think he's involved with Raj and Radhika's murders either. Sean must be behind this—and Caleb's life could truly be at risk. If Sean betrayed Raj and Mr. Joshi, his own family, then he won't think twice about double-crossing Caleb too.

> You're not serious.

> I'm dead serious.

> Sorry. No pun intended.

I text Caleb the name and address of a dive bar in Cabo San Lucas, ask him to meet me there in an hour. It's Saturday night, and the town will be teeming with tourists and college kids out partying, plenty of police and security monitoring the crowds.

Plenty of eyewitnesses.

Because I'm cognizant of the fact I don't always think clearly when it comes to Caleb. And there's still a chance—however small—that I'm wrong about Sean. That the one I should be after is *Caleb*.

I accelerate my pace as a cold wind whips up from the beach and thunder rumbles steadily toward the shore.

If Caleb murdered Raj and Radhika, and that's a big *if*, it must have been in a narcotics-fueled rage. I don't believe he would have hurt them on purpose, and I'm about to bet my life that he wouldn't intentionally hurt me either.

* * *

THE NEXT RESORT over is throwing a beach party featuring belly dancers, Persian carpets, hummus, and other Middle Eastern stereotypes. They don't allow me on the property because I'm not a guest, but the security at a resort farther along the Tourist Corridor is much laxer. I manage to trespass through the grounds undetected and catch a taxi out front without anyone realizing I'm wearing the wrong wristband.

Twenty-five minutes later, I arrive at my destination. The dive bar is busier than it was on Wednesday during my meeting with Eric. I grab a barstool toward the back and, after ordering myself a Pepsi, scope out my surroundings. From here, I have a clear view of the door, the only way to get in and out of the bar except for the fire exit, which is immediately to my right. If Caleb isn't alone when he walks through that door, if at any point I feel I'm being lied to or threatened, I'm getting the hell out of here.

As I wait for Caleb to show up, I try calling Daniela two more times, and a wave of nausea rocks me as I realize it's now been over two hours since I've heard from her. She might have a good explanation for going dark; maybe she found something and is busy following up on a lead. But she would have texted me to check in, confirm that she's safe, wouldn't she? Thank god Eric and Lexie are on it; I hope they'll find a way to ensure her safety.

At the appointed time, Caleb pushes through the door, and I catch sight of him before he notices me, which gives me a moment to steady my breath. He's still wearing the same T-shirt he slept in last night, and he has dark circles under his eyes. His hair is greasy and slightly tangled; he looks like the walking dead. Still, I'm overwhelmed to see him.

His mouth is tense as his eyes track across the bar, and I wait until his gaze reaches me before I stand up and wave. As he weaves through the crowd toward me, my gut flip-flops like a dying fish.

Be careful, Shay.

Stay on your guard.

"Hi." I smile, as nervous as I was for our first date back in LA. An indie rock concert at the Hollywood Bowl.

He stops short in front of me and grimaces. "Hi."

"You want a Pepsi?" I ask lightly. "I'm buying."

Caleb pulls up the chair next to me. "Got anything stronger back there?"

"Um—" I stop short. "Actually, can you *not*?"

"What's that supposed to mean?" he asks evenly.

I mean, *Are you sober, Caleb?*

I shake my head, and without me having to say it, I see the lightbulb go off. Caleb's cheeks go scarlet. I order another Pepsi from the bartender, and as we wait for her to bring it over, I look into Caleb's eyes—gray and glassy—and wonder how many drinks he's already had. How high he is at this very moment. How the hell I didn't see it.

"Where do I even start?" I say after his drink appears.

Caleb's back is to the bar entrance, and instead of answering, he swivels on his stool a full one hundred eighty degrees and stares at it for a beat.

"Expecting someone?"

He quickly turns back around and stabs a straw into his drink. "Why don't you start from the beginning."

I've already decided to show Caleb all my cards. It's worth the risk. He alone could provide the information we need to get to the bottom of this. Alternatively, if Caleb is the one who betrayed Raj and Radhika to the cartel, then I'm hoping I'll be able to see through his lies talking face-to-face. Quickly I fill him in on Mr. Joshi's role in the construction-site fire, my mission to bring him to justice, and how I never intended to leak the news about Raj and Radhika's murder. And then I spring on him my theory that the Joshi Group is in bed with the cartel.

I stop talking when I realize Caleb appears not to be breathing. I wave my hand in front of his face, and eventually, he unfreezes and meets my gaze.

"That's a lot to process."

"Did you know?"

"Of course not! I only joined the company a few months ago—"

"But you've been a part of that family for a long time," I press, even though he seems genuinely dumbfounded by the news. "Plus, you work in the finance department. Did they hire you to help them with the money-laundering scheme?"

"Shay, I barely have all my company login credentials," he stammers. "I'm not in on this. And how are you so sure they're working with the cartel? They're a good fam—"

He trails off as he abruptly swivels around on his stool, and for the second time since he arrived, stares at the front entrance.

"Is this an ambush or something?" I joke.

Caleb frowns as he rotates back and takes a swig of his Pepsi.

"What's going on?"

"Nothing, I'm just on edge," Caleb mutters. "All day, I've felt like . . ."

He catches my eye. My heartbeat quickens.

". . . someone is following you?"

His Adam's apple bobs up and down as he nods. Someone's following Caleb too?

"I'm not here to make amends with you." He leans away from me, and my cheeks heat up as I realize how close I was sitting to him. "You said I might be in danger. Am I?"

Keeping an eye on the door, I speed through the rest of the story. Raj's selfie in front of Blush El Paraíso, and how I believe he was being sent to meet Hector at Mr. Joshi's behest. Eric's paper trail connecting Blush Continental and the cartel. And then I show him the photo of Sean handing Greg Clancy an envelope less than twenty-four hours before the murders.

"Do you know him? He used to intern for the Joshi Group in LA."

"It must have been before my time." Caleb shakes his head, his eyes wide and full of fear. "Shit. I *knew* Sean was hiding something. But this?"

"How did you know exactly?" I say carefully. "You've been suspicious about him from the beginning. Why?"

Caleb swallows hard, unresponsive.

"By all accounts, Sean loved Raj. Yet, from the very start, you doubted his innocence. What aren't you telling me? Why don't you like him?"

I keep going when Caleb doesn't speak up, my fists clenched. "Here's what I think: You, Sean, and Raj were conspiring with Mr. Joshi. He did you a big favor by expunging your record when you nearly killed that guy at the music festival—"

Caleb stammers in protest, but I forge ahead.

"—and now it was your turn to repay the favor. Mr. Joshi forced Sean to hire you so you could help with the money-laundering scheme, but Sean hates your guts. I gather the new work arrangement didn't go well, considering Raj and Radhika are dead. What happened? Did Sean give them up, or was it *you* who betrayed your best friend—"

I stop when Caleb breaks down, his tears wet and raw and, seemingly, very real.

"No." He shakes his head after he catches his breath. "You're wrong. I'm not lying to you—"

"You've lied to me before."

"About a stupid one-night stand, Shay. Not *murder*."

Caleb dries his eyes before speaking again.

"I never told you this, but I slept with one of my old coworkers last summer. A junior coworker. It got messy real fast. I needed to get out. You're right that Sean didn't want to hire me, but I didn't join the Joshi Group to help them launder money, or anything else you're accusing them of doing. I needed a fresh start.

"Sean's never liked me, and he's always made that perfectly clear," Caleb continues. "When I joined the finance team, he made it his mission to make my life a living hell. The guy bullies me at the office, belittles me in front of our coworkers. He treats me, and all of his employees, like servants. Like *dirt*."

"Sean's good-guy act isn't real," Caleb says, his breath hitching. "You shouldn't trust him."

"But I should trust you?" I whisper.

"Look at me," Caleb says, squeezing my hands. "Look me in the eye."

My stomach strains into knots as I dare to meet his gaze head-on.

"Shay." His voice cracks. "I'm innocent."

I needed to see Caleb face-to-face to know, and now, I think I do. I think he's telling me the truth. I don't know everything about this man—I don't think I want to—but I know his heart. Don't I? Caleb isn't the killer.

Sean's good-guy act isn't real.

And isn't everything Caleb's saying lining up with the evidence? I'm not just working off a half-baked theory anymore, a gut instinct, or a grudge. Sean handed an envelope to a former Joshi Group intern, and current Blush Continental employee, the *day before* the murders. It must be Sean behind this, performing grief and confusion when all along he's been pulling the strings.

But why? Just so he could take the reins of the Joshi Group?

"What now?" Caleb whispers after a long moment.

Swallowing the bile in my throat, I reluctantly tear my eyes away from him. I still feel unsettled, but I don't have a choice. I have to keep going.

"Tell me what to do," I hear Caleb say. "I want to help."

"If Eric and Lexie don't find Daniela in the next hour, we need to go to the authorities," I say after explaining she went missing looking for the real name of Raj's contact, Hector.

"Sure." Caleb peers over his shoulder at the door. He must still be spooked.

"Do you think anyone followed you here?" I ask, reaching for my notebook. "I have so many questions for you, but maybe we should go somewhere more discreet."

"What kind of questions?"

"For starters. Do you know why Sean would betray Raj to the cartel?"

Caleb comes up blank. Even though he hates Sean, he can't offer me a single reason.

Frustrated, I flip to a fresh page of my notebook and look through my prepared questions, unsure what to tackle first.

What really happened at the club in Cabo San Lucas? Why was Raj so quiet?

At the end of the evening, what did he say to you that he didn't want Sean to hear?

What are you hiding in the safe?

My body stiffens as the last question registers, and suddenly, the wheels click into place. I turn back to Caleb.

"The safe!" I whisper.

"Hmm?"

"The safe," I repeat. "You're hiding something, aren't you?"

Caleb stutters in protest. I gently press my fingers to his lips and shake my head.

"You're hiding something for *Raj*."

Caleb's mouth stops moving.

"How did you know?"

I flick my eyes to the front door, adrenaline masking my terror.

"Do you remember when we got back to the villa on Friday morning, and my laptop was out on the desk?"

Caleb nods as I explain how the room was cleaned that morning, meaning the "do not disturb" function was switched off and anyone with a master key could have entered.

"At the time, I was worried Mr. Joshi had found me out and sent someone to go through my research. And even though that wasn't true, ever since, I've had the feeling that someone's watching me. But now I think I've just been paranoid."

"Why?" Caleb asks.

"Because they weren't looking for something *I* was hiding, Caleb. Nobody's following me. Don't you get it?"

I was right to come here, to warn him, to trust my gut from the beginning that Caleb is innocent.

"Someone's after *you*."

From: Eric Santos
To: Shaylee Kapoor
CC: Lexie Dubois
Time: 10:24 p.m.
Subject: Re: EMERGENCY!!

Update: I'm with a police friend outside of Blush's headquarters. No one appears to be inside.

However, there's a Volkswagen Vento in the parking lot, and I'm sorry to say that the car is licensed to Daniela.

I don't know where she is, but trust me when I say I'll do everything I can to find out.

Eric

Sent from my iPhone.

29.

N ot too long ago, Raj had an argument with Uncle." Mr. Joshi.
"A big one."

Caleb looks over his shoulder suspiciously before continuing
with his story. "I don't know what happened, but Raj was really
upset. He said he'd stolen his father's folder and he needed me
to hang on to it and keep it with me at all times. That's why I
brought it with me to Mexico. It's in my safe right now. He told
me not to tell anyone—not even Radhi."

I furrow my brows. "Was it a leather folder?"

"Yeah," Caleb says. "Embossed with Uncle's initials: *NJ.*" *Narayan Joshi.*

Quickly, I tell him about that day when he was stuck in traffic
on his way home from Malibu, and how Raj showed up unexpectedly.

"He had a leather folder with him. When he caught me staring at it, he claimed he needed your help to write his wedding
vows."

"Raj never talked to me about his vows," Caleb breathes. "But that's the folder. He dropped by again later that evening to give it to me."

"*Well*. What's in it?"

Caleb shrugs. "I never looked."

He never *looked*?

"I figured it was sensitive." Caleb runs a hand through his hair. "He trusted me not to look. Our friendship is like that, but—shit. I should have looked."

Yes. He should have looked! Instinctively, I check the front door of the bar when someone new enters, but it's just another rowdy college kid.

Someone has been following Caleb and even broke into his villa trying to get that folder back. But the question is *who*. If the information is harmful to Mr. Joshi, he could have asked Brown Hulk Hogan to retrieve it and keep on Caleb's tail. But if it's Sean who desperately wants that folder, then maybe he was willing to kill Raj over it. To get his hands on that folder, would Sean take out Caleb too?

"What do you think is in there?" Caleb asks me after I say all of this out loud.

"Raj snapped at me that day when I mentioned Sean's name," I say, my mind whizzing. "And according to Sean, Raj had been pulling away from him in recent weeks. The information must be about *Sean*," I rationalize.

Right?

I don't know what to believe anymore. Or what the hell is going on among the Joshis. Raj's offhand comment at the house party suddenly comes to mind, how he was "running point" on an Americas deal and wished Mr. Joshi gave him more credit.

And then there was Sean's remark about how Raj stood up for him whenever Sean butted heads with Mr. Joshi. Everyone also knew that Mr. Joshi exerted control over the LA office, even though Raj and Sean were technically in charge, and so logic points to the conclusion that Raj and Sean were allies in the Joshi Group corporate politics.

And maybe they were. And then maybe Raj found a good reason to break that alliance.

"Was there any infighting in the family?" I ask vaguely as I try to imagine what the hell is in that folder. What information it might contain that could drive the two brothers apart.

Caleb shrugs. "There were certain things Raj and I didn't talk about."

"Such as?"

"Girl problems. Money problems. Family problems. *Work* problems."

Dammit. So the two best friends didn't actually talk about their problems.

I press my fingers into my temples, totally baffled. Caleb's revelation that he's been hiding Mr. Joshi's folder this whole time—a folder Raj very well may have stolen—offers zero clarity on the situation; it only makes it more confusing.

What's in that folder that upset Raj so much? It must be serious. Is Mr. Joshi looking for it as we speak? During the first family meeting, he asked Tobias if anything had been stolen; did he mean the folder?

"I think we should get out of here," I say hurriedly. "There's a hotel next door—"

"No," Caleb interrupts. "We're going back to Blush to get that folder."

"That might be dangerous."

"I don't care." Caleb stands and downs his Pepsi. "I need to see it before anyone else does."

My gut twists at the suggestion.

"Really? Why?"

"Because you and your fucking friends at the *Los Angeles Journal* are implying Raj was some sort of Indian Pablo Escobar. If there's anything in there that will damage his reputation, anything that implicates him, I need to get rid of it—"

"But—"

"But nothing." Caleb gives me a look, and I know better than to fight him on this. "Raj is dead. What does it matter if he was guilty too?"

* * *

CALEB AND I leave via the fire exit and then speed walk through two back alleys until we're at the center of town, hoping that if Caleb does have a tail, we'll lose them in the crowd. It's peak season on a Saturday night, and when we eventually find a free taxi, I ask the driver to take us to the resort west of Blush, the one with lax security where I caught a ride into town. Caleb says law enforcement is no longer guarding the crime scene, so our best shot at getting to Caleb's undetected is to sneak up the beach stairs behind his villa.

When we arrive back at Blush's neighboring resort, Caleb and I get lost, and on our way through the hotel grounds, we pass by a banquet room hosting an Indian wedding reception. Instinctively, we both stop in front of the door.

Just inside, the DJ is blaring *bhangra* music from the sound system, strobe lights flashing to the beat. There are at least a hundred people in *saris*, *lehenghas*, and *kurtas* partying on the dance floor. These days, it's quite common for South Asian families to host weddings at all-inclusive resorts in Mexico. But seeing one tonight, right now, on the same night Raj and Radhika should have been celebrating their own . . . It feels like a slap in the face.

When I look over at Caleb, I can tell he's thinking the same thing. That he's fighting back tears. I place my palm on his shoulder, but before I can think of what to say, how best to comfort him, he shrugs it off and tells me we need to keep going.

We stay silent until we're back on the beach. It's drizzling again, darker than it was earlier, and so we use the flashlight on Caleb's phone to light up the beach. My phone is nearly out of juice, and when Caleb asks me to turn my light on too, I tell him I can't. That I need to save my battery in case Eric contacts me with news of Daniela.

"I'm worried about her."

My words come out soft, barely audible over the wind, the waves crashing onto the shore. She's missing. Her car is in Blush Continental's parking lot, and she's fucking missing.

"I shouldn't have let her help. It was too dangerous."

"Daniela's a grown woman," Caleb says. "She can make her own decisions."

He stops, seemingly understanding his double entendre. After a moment he adds, "I'm sorry, by the way. For Daniela."

He turns to me, but I don't dare look over.

"I was on a lot of drugs that night, but that's no excuse. I was an asshole, doing that to you. I take full responsibility."

A wave comes in, stronger, and I dart up the sand as the water catches my right foot.

"I don't want to talk about that." I pause, push myself forward. "Tell me what happened the night Raj and Radhika died."

His story of their night out in Cabo San Lucas matches Zara's and Sean's. Everyone partied hard except for Sean, who was working from his phone. Nothing unusual happened, and everyone seemed to be in a good mood. I ask Caleb why the bouncer nearly kicked their group out, if it was because Radhika and Zara were dancing on their table, but Caleb says he doesn't even remember that. He was too coked out.

"Sean told me you were the last person to see Raj alive," I say, after. "That you two were talking outside Raj's villa at the end of the night, and that he seemed to be confiding something to you. Is that true?"

Or was Sean lying to me? Trying to steer me off course?

"That rings a bell." Caleb hesitates a long moment. "If memory serves me, and I'm not sure it does, Raj wasn't happy about something. It might have had to do with Radhi."

I recall the footage of them from the pool Wednesday afternoon. They made out while Caleb swam laps. And then stopped and started talking to each other in earnest.

"Were they fighting that night or something?"

"I don't think so. And even if they were, it wouldn't have been a big deal. They rarely fought, and only ever about stupid stuff."

"Such as?"

"Radhi didn't like how much Raj and I partied. And Raj thought Radhi was a bit immature sometimes. We all did. He didn't like how she acted one way for her followers, and totally different in real life."

Remembering what Zara had told me, I ask, "Was Radhika planning to give up influencing to work for Lustre?"

"She was undecided." Caleb pauses. "Radhi liked the idea of joining Lustre's board of directors when she inherited her shares next month, but she wasn't thrilled about having to work for Zara."

"No?"

"She thought it might ruin their relationship." Caleb glances over at me and rolls his eyes. "You know what Zara's like. She's a great sister to Radhi. But imagine having her as your *boss*."

I smile in agreement and then think of how Radhika's shares would soon give her a fifteen percent control over Lustre. Zara and her family didn't want to take the company public, but if Radhika—for whatever reason—had voted along with Archer Nguyen and the other investors, her family would have lost the vote. Radhika, alone, had the power to decide the future of Lustre.

"Do you think Radhika could have ever betrayed her family?" I ask next. "Would she ever go against Zara?"

Caleb looks over at me, dismayed. "Never," he breathes.

"So you don't think that Zara might somehow be involved in this? Maybe if she found out Radhika was going to vote against her—"

"Radhi would never do anything to hurt Zara." Caleb laughs. "She couldn't hurt anyone if she tried. Radhi was a good person. She made Raj return all the expensive gifts he tried to buy her. She even donated all of her influencer money to charity."

My heart feels a pang. "Really?"

"Really." He smiles. "She was a little childish at times, but she was a good person."

I go quiet, yet again overwhelmed by sadness over Radhika's death, for my judgments against her while she was alive. Because she was an influencer, I assumed her to be shallow and materialistic, but by Caleb's account, she was the opposite. What kind of person donates her earnings to charity and turns down gifts from her billionaire groom? As Caleb said, a good person, someone who wouldn't betray her own family. Someone who would never place money and power over love.

So is it all just a horrible coincidence that Radhika died only a month before she stood to inherit her shares in Lustre?

When we pass by Blush's main resort, I spot the three hotel security guards chatting animatedly to one another behind the infinity pool, having moved on from the soccer game. They don't pay us any attention as we trudge by and make our way toward the Villas another half mile ahead.

This is the darkest stretch of beach, and even with Caleb's phone light, we can barely see the rocks or where the sand ends and ocean begins. I keep my eyes on the ground ahead of me as we draw closer, and I'm so focused on my footing, on my thoughts swirling about Radhika, that I barely register it when Caleb turns off his light. A beat later, he grabs me—so hard it knocks the air out of my lungs—and pushes me to the ground.

"Caleb! What the—"

He presses his hand over my mouth as we land in a pile on the sand.

"Quiet."

It's just a whisper, a signal. The hair on the back of arms springs upright as Caleb crawls on all fours up the beach and plants himself behind a rock. I follow him, blinking, my eyes starting to adjust to the lower light. When I'm safely next to him, he points east. Toward the beach stairs behind the Villas.

"Someone's there."

My pulse pounds as I peek around the rock face. At the base of the stairs, a figure looms large.

"The National Guard?" I whisper.

Caleb shakes his head, and then I remember: there are no officers stationed at the crime scene anymore.

"Who is there?" the voice calls suddenly. It's throaty, undoubtedly male. Accented. My stomach lurches as the figure switches on a flashlight. It's Brown Hulk Hogan.

"Shit," Caleb whispers. "*Shit!*"

He sits back against the rock, and his head drops to his knees. I shakily crouch down next to him, trying to keep calm. What is Joshi's bodyguard doing down on the beach?

"He has a gun," I tell Caleb, my voice quaky. "He tucks it into his hip. I don't think he'll use it but—"

"You don't *think* he'll use it," Caleb mocks, a little too loud. I tell him to quiet down and let me think.

Leaning back, I assess our surroundings. We're just fifty feet away from Brown Hulk Hogan, who's blocking our route up the stairs to the Villas. We can't run past him or keep heading east either. The beach here is too narrow. He'd catch us.

I sit back on my butt and face west the way we came. The beach is wider, the terrain more varied with tide pools, rocks, and cliff faces. There are even tall grasses at the top of the beach.

"Listen to me," I whisper.

My eyes dart to Brown Hulk Hogan, who's on the move, his flashlight flicking back and forth as he walks in our direction.

"We don't have much time." I reach for Caleb's hands. "I'm going to make a run for it and distract him. You hide here until—"

"Not a chance," Caleb says. "No. I'll run. Or we *both*—"

"Caleb," I say quietly but firmly. "Right now, Mr. Joshi just thinks I'm a nuisance." I quickly remind him how Mr. Joshi dismissed me and the accusations about the building-site fire as if he was swatting away a housefly.

"But if his bodyguard sees us together after what I did to you, then he'll know something's up." I swallow hard. "Mr. Joshi might figure out we know about his links to the cartel. Do you understand?"

He does.

"I'll meet you in your villa," I tell him. "I'll find another way."

Caleb's fingers intertwine with mine, tugging slightly.

"What if he catches you?"

"He won't," I say lightly. "I'm fast."

"You smoke."

"I've been cutting back."

I can feel Caleb smiling at my lie.

"Call me when you're safe?" Caleb whispers. I nod and quickly check my phone. I have six percent battery. Hopefully, just enough to light up the beach when I lose the Hulk, or for an emergency phone call. I resist the urge to hug Caleb as I pull away, double check the laces on my sneakers. Brown Hulk Hogan is less than thirty feet away now, and I need to time it perfectly. I need him to get close enough so he sees my face, but not so close that he catches sight of Caleb or that it puts me within range of his gun.

The Hulk won't *actually* shoot me, right? He just thinks I'm a nuisance, I tell myself. As far as the Joshis know, I am an imposter, a leak. A shoddy nobody and nothing investigative journalist. I don't know anything that can hurt them.

I creep forward on hands and knees as Brown Hulk Hogan draws closer. When I can hear him breathing, I stand up and kick a pebble. He turns, and for a brief moment, his flashlight shines directly in my eyes, shading him out of view. I'm blinded.

"Boo."

Wedding Reception

From the bottom of our hearts, thank you for being here with us this weekend. We know the last few days have been a whirlwind, but we're confident the memories we've made this weekend will last us all a lifetime!

Today, our wedding celebration will reach its pinnacle, and, at the appointed time, someone will fetch you from your villa to whisk you away for the big finale.

Although the details are under strict lock and key, we can promise you a night full of wonder and amazement, entertainment and panache.

You thought the last three days were exciting? Honey, you haven't seen anything yet.

Love,

RAJ & RADHIKA

Dress code: Black Tie
Location: Top Secret

30.

S haylee Kapoor."

I duck out of the light, backpedaling in a zigzag so Brown Hulk Hogan can't blind me with his flashback.

"Out for a stroll?" I ask brightly.

"We warned you."

"Did you?" My breath quickens as Brown Hulk Hogan starts to trudge after me, his density sinking into the sand with each footstep. "Honestly, uncle-*ji*," I deadpan, "this vacation has been *such* a blur. I can't remember half of—"

He makes a move for his left jacket pocket—his *gun?*—and so I spin on my heels and make a run for it.

Fuck.

It's dark as hell. I sprint toward the ocean. There's less cover down there, but the wet sand is easier to run on and there are fewer rocks to trip me up. I can hear him barreling after me, grunting. The thud of his footsteps. But I don't dare turn around to check how close he is. He could aim and fire at any moment. Every second counts.

Within a minute, I'm sucking air, and every time I gasp for breath, it feels like something sharp is being rammed into my chest. As fast as I can, I place one foot in front of the other, trying to keep low. My movements unpredictable. The waves crash at my feet, soaking my shoes. I feel the weight of the water, hear the squelch, but I won't let it slow me down.

Is he still behind me? Now I can't hear anything but my shoes. Still, I force myself to keep up the pace, my cheeks and neck burning red. As I approach Blush's main resort and catch sight of a pair of lovers out for a late-night stroll, I chance a look behind me. Brown Hulk Hogan is still behind me, but—he's slowing down.

And then he stops.

Winded, I come to a halt and rest my hands on my knees, gasping for breath. He's watching me, but he won't come any closer. There are witnesses. But would he have shot me if he had the chance? And what would he have done if he saw Caleb with me?

I stand back upright, shaky at the thought of how close we'd come, and wave at him until he turns around and starts walking back toward the Villas. I sigh in relief. I'm safe, for now, and the distraction worked; with the Hulk chasing me, Caleb would have had plenty of time to get up the beach stairs to his villa.

The security guards are more alert back at Blush's main resort. After I show them my wristband and they warn me against venturing out at night by myself, I head straight for the Villas, breaking into a run as soon as I'm out of the security cameras' view. Once inside the villa community, I take the walking path to Caleb's, staying light on my feet and close to the empty villas. If Mr. Joshi, Sean, or Brown Hulk Hogan make an appearance, I'll have to quickly find a place to hide.

I slow down as I near Caleb's villa and crouch behind a massive cactus. All his blinds are drawn. My spine shivers as I wonder if he made it back safe.

The path between us is lit, and if I were to run—and someone at the Joshis' happens to be looking out his window—they'd see me. I'd be through.

I breathe out hard, sit back on my heels, and just as I try to text Caleb, the battery dies.

Shit.

Somewhere across the villa community, a door slams, and I snap back to ready position. I know I need to move. Brown Hulk Hogan is probably making his way back to the Villas via the beach right now, and the longer I stay here, the more chance I have of coming face-to-face with him. I wait one more moment, summoning up the courage, and then break into a sprint. Within a few seconds I'm at Caleb's door. I try the knob. It's locked, and so I softly tap on the door with my fingertips.

Is he there? Is he OK?

Standing out front like this is too risky, and so I dart around the side of the villa and wait. After what feels like an eternity, I hear the lock click. I spring upright and curve around the house, sighing in relief when I see Caleb's strained face peeking out from the doorway. I race inside, slam the door shut behind me, and then deadbolt the lock. Panting, I turn around to face Caleb. He's standing in the foyer, just a few feet back from me, a look on his face I've never seen before.

"What is it?" I smile, catching my breath.

"I thought you were dead."

Caleb closes the gap between us, and, without thinking, I wrap my arms around his neck as he pulls me into him.

"I thought I lost you too."

His words are a hot breath on my ear, and I feel limp in his arms as he holds me. I close my eyes, briefly, remembering what it felt like to be with him, why I let this go so far.

And then—I let him go.

"The folder," I say, a reminder to us both. We need to stay focused.

Caleb backpedals away from me, nodding. He won't look me in the eye.

"The folder," he echoes.

I show him my phone. "Can I borrow a charger? Battery's dead."

"Go for it." He gestures to the bedroom. "I'll meet you upstairs."

I plug my phone into the nightstand charger, and although I'm desperate to know if Eric's tracked down Daniela, I get impatient waiting for my phone to power on. I walk out of the bedroom, and as I pass by the en suite, I spot Caleb's toiletries bag on the counter. It's open, and half its contents are spilled out.

I take a step closer. Next to a bottle of Lustre's bestselling rejuvenation serum and his aftershave is an empty pill bottle. I look at the label and immediately tense. I'm not a doctor—I don't know what this medication is for—but the prescription was filled less than a week ago—and it's totally empty.

How much has Caleb been taking? How high is he right now?

I race upstairs, my nerves frayed by the time I reach the second level. Up ahead, the door to the wellness space is ajar.

"Caleb?" I call.

When no one responds, I pad toward the room and push open the door with my hip. Caleb's on a yoga mat, cross-legged, the embossed brown leather folder limp in his hands. *NJ.*

"Hey."

He flinches and then looks up, dumbfounded. As if he's

shocked to see me in his villa. After a moment, his face relaxes. I'm worried about him, but I'm more concerned about whether or not he'll be functional enough to help me find what's so important in that folder.

"Have you opened it?" I ask him carefully.

"I was waiting for you."

I run my fingers along the edge of the leather folder. It's about three inches thick. I pick it up, feel its weight, and then hand it back to Caleb.

"You should do the honors."

One by one, Caleb unearths loose pages from the folder so we can read them together. There's a memorandum addressed to company executives penned by Sean, outlining the detrimental findings of an environmental impact assessment on a proposed hotel site. Invoices for wedding expenses such as flowers, catering, decorations, and the venue rental, issued by Blush Continental and addressed to Mr. Joshi. A stack of printed emails between Mr. Joshi, Raj, and several of their colleagues, in which they discuss the regulatory filings for a new European acquisition. We read them closely. We read everything twice.

"Nothing?" Caleb asks me afterward.

I shrug, feeling discouraged. There's nothing unusual here. Nothing that stands out. I toss the papers to the side, and Caleb retrieves the remaining documents from the leather folder: two thick manila envelopes. Could this be it? The first one is in tatters, either with age or coffee stains. I hold my breath as I tug free the papers, but when my eyes start scanning the top page, I can't read it.

"What's that?" Caleb asks.

I blink, confused. I must be more exhausted than I think. It takes me a long moment to realize they're written in Hindi.

"What does it say?"

"I don't know," I stammer, flipping through the pages. "I speak Hindi, but I never learned to read it."

"Raj could."

"Really?"

Caleb nods. "His mom made him learn."

I repack the documents, kicking myself for having never learned the script. We'll have to go through those later. Next to me, Caleb dumps out the contents of the second envelope.

"It's in English," Caleb tells me. "It's their prenup."

My ears perk to attention. Raj gave Caleb his prenup? I sidle closer as Caleb's fingers absently flick through the document. It's more than thirty pages long, and when he gets to the last one, I see it's an original. It's notarized and has been signed by both Raj and Radhika.

"Did you know they had a prenup?" I ask him. After he nods, I pose the next thing that comes to mind. "Was it contentious?"

"Not at all," Caleb says, leafing through the pages. "Their families called all the shots. Raj and Radhika were just the ones to sign it."

I nod. That's what Zara had implied too. We start flipping through the pages, stopping on Raj and Radhika's respective declarations of assets and liabilities. I balk at the numbers. Neither were in debt, and Raj had six million in cash, in addition to his cars, real estate, and stock portfolio. (Not to mention whatever he would inherit down the road as Mr. Joshi's son.) Radhika too was well-off. She owned her house outright in West Hollywood, had seven hundred thousand dollars in the bank, and then her shares—

My mouth gapes. As of January this year, her fifteen percent stake in Lustre was worth four hundred fifty million dollars.

"Holy shit."

Caleb's eyes land on the figure a moment later. He turns to me, equally dumbfounded.

"That would make Lustre worth . . ." I do the math. "Three *billion* dollars."

"I had no idea it was worth that much."

"Me neither."

I think back to the profile of Zara and Lustre in the *Los Angeles Journal* last summer, where experts estimated the value of the company to be in the tens of millions. Not *billions*.

"Company valuations are partially based on projections," Caleb explains to me. "This number must take into account Lustre's expected growth once its antiaging products are more affordable."

I nod, remembering the clinical trials Zara talked about in her lecture. "They're going to release a new, cheaper line. Still, that number is *nuts*. Could Raj have been after *Radhika's* money?" I suggest. "One day, her shares will be worth even billions more—"

"Stop." Caleb grimaces. "Raj loved her. That's not possible. Besides, even if this valuation is right, the Joshi family is still much wealthier."

I bite my lip and look back at the prenup, and when my eyes skim over the next clause, I realize he must be right. I can't make perfect sense of the legal jargon, but it seems to match another thing Zara told me earlier: the prenup is ironclad; Raj and Radhika's respective fortunes are tightly protected from the other party.

Then what was Raj hiding here in this mess of a folder?

And does it have anything to do with the envelope Sean handed their former intern?

"I'm even more confused than I was before."

Caleb doesn't respond as he flicks through the prenup. After a moment, he tosses it to the side, stands up from the floor, and starts to pace.

"Was that everything Raj gave you?"

"Mmh."

I glance over at the safe, wondering if there's anything in there I haven't seen yet.

"Really?"

"Yes, really," Caleb snaps. "Do you not trust me, or something?"

He walks over to the safe and points inside. I sit up on my heels to get a better look. My chest tightens with embarrassment. He's right. There's nothing else in there.

"I'm sorry," I say, stuffing all the documents back in the leather folder. "I just don't understand why Raj went to such great lengths to hide this random stack of papers. It's as if he emptied the contents of a desk drawer and handed it over."

"Maybe it's the documents in Hindi," Caleb suggests, but I'm not convinced.

Something's off with Caleb. I can't put my finger on it, but I can't help but feel that I'm missing something.

From: Lexie Dubois
To: Shaylee Kapoor
CC: Eric Santos
12:21 a.m.
Subject: RE: EMERGENCY!!

Background check just came in. Greg Clancy is a busy
guy . . . Trespassing, vandalism, possession with intent
to distribute, petty theft, disorderly conduct. But
none of his crimes have been violent, and he's never
served time. He strikes me more as a dumb kid than a
hitman . . .

You hanging in there, Shay?

I've tried calling Eric a few times. No news.

Lex

From: Shaylee Kapoor
To: Lexie Dubois
CC: Eric Santos
12:40 a.m.
Subject: Re: EMERGENCY!!

Thanks, Lex.

I'm really worried about Daniela. I think it's time to call the
authorities.

From: Lexie Dubois
To: Shaylee Kapoor
CC: Eric Santos
12:43 a.m.
Subject: RE: EMERGENCY!!

I think you're right.

Lex

31.

Caleb sprawls out on the living room floor for a power nap while we wait for Zara to walk over. He didn't seem too thrilled when I called her, but the three of us need to present a united front when we go to the National Guard. I let them believe I wasn't in Cabo the night of the murders and failed to tell them I was an undercover journalist with potentially relevant information about their case. Zara and Caleb obstructed justice by hiding Radhika's cellphone and Raj's stolen folder, respectively. But we need to come clean about everything, regardless of the consequences. There's been no news from Eric. Daniela could be in danger. We can't wait a moment longer.

In the kitchen, I dump boiling water and a few tablespoons of coffee into a French press and wait for it to brew. I can't deny how disappointed I feel right now. I really thought that folder was going to contain the proof we needed to connect Sean to the murders, or, at the very least, help explain why he might have betrayed Raj to the cartel. All we have to hand over to law enforcement is circumstantial evidence, an unproven theory. A theory about which I'm feeling less and less confident with each passing minute.

The water slowly darkens, and I watch passively as the coffee grounds sink to the bottom of the French press. Just a few hours ago, after I saw footage of Sean handing over that envelope to Greg Clancy, I became convinced that he gave up Raj and Radhika to the cartel. Sean's interaction was extremely suspicious—and his role as the betrayer fit with my overall conviction that the Joshi Group is laundering money for the cartel. But now I don't know what to believe. Greg Clancy has a criminal record and ties to both the Joshi Group and Blush Continental, but Lexie's right; he seems like a dumb kid, and none of his crimes appears to have been violent. Do I really believe that *he* killed Raj and Radhika at Sean's behest? I think so. But I'm not so sure anymore. I feel like I have the whole picture, that the answer is right there in front of me, but it's just out of focus. Just out of my reach.

Racking my brain, I run over each folder document in my mind, wondering if I've missed something obvious. The prenup. Lustre's billion-dollar valuation. The papers in Hindi. The wedding invoices from Blush Continental. Sean's memorandum on the environmental impact assessment.

Which of these documents had Raj asked Caleb to protect? And, just as importantly, *why*?

There's a quiet knock on the door while I'm pouring myself a cup of coffee. Caleb doesn't get up, and so I peek through the blinds and, after confirming it's Zara, quickly let her in.

"You going to tell me why the hell you woke me up?" she asks as I slam the door shut behind her. "You were so cryptic on the phone."

"Coffee first. It's going to be a long night."

I hand her the cup I just poured. She sips it, makes a face, and hands it right back.

"That's disgusting. Tell me you have real milk, not this plant-based crap."

I'm too tired and frazzled to be annoyed. I fetch her cow's milk from the fridge, pour her a fresh cup, and then herd her toward the living room. She doesn't see Caleb on the floor and nearly trips over him.

"Do you mind sitting up and acting like a grown-up?"

Slowly, Caleb heaves his body upward in response.

"Do you mind not being a bitch?"

Zara shoots him daggers as she folds herself into the sofa.

"Thanks, Caleb. I've been called a bitch so many times, I now consider it a compliment." She sips her coffee and winces. "Seriously, this tastes like *Starbucks*."

Caleb opens his mouth to defend me, but I shake my head. A signal not to engage. I take the seat opposite Zara and get right to it.

Quickly, I explain to her what's happened since I saw her earlier this evening. I show her the photo of Sean handing his former intern Greg Clancy an envelope on the beach the day before the murders and tell her how I reviewed all the security footage on Daniela's computer. I tell her about Brown Hulk Hogan having chased me down the beach, and that Daniela's missing. And then I show her Mr. Joshi's folder—which is lying open on the coffee table—which Raj had asked Caleb to hide a few weeks before his death.

"We need to go to the National Guard tonight," I say afterward. "Daniela went missing at Blush Continental's head office, looking for Hector's real name. What if the cartel found out she was on to them and . . ."

I'm too shaken up to finish the sentence.

"This is so fucked up," Zara says, her voice shaky. She turns to Caleb. "I can't believe Raj gave you something to hide and you didn't tell anyone. What were you thinking?"

"Zara, you're not one to talk," I chide.

Caleb bristles, still on the floor.

"What's that supposed to mean?"

I give Zara a look, one that says *tell him*. With a sigh, she reaches into her purse and tosses Radhika's phone onto the coffee table. Caleb balks.

"Yeah, yeah," Zara groans. "Spare me the lecture—"

"You . . . *you* had Radhi's phone this whole time?" Caleb spits at Zara. He turns to me next, red in the face. "And you knew?"

"She has a good reason—"

"Oh yeah?" Caleb hisses. "And what's that?"

"Radhi was about to join my board, you halfwit," Zara says evenly. "There are trade secrets on that phone, and I wasn't about to let those Mexicans leak—"

"Zara," I snap. I don't have the bandwidth for her not-so-casual racism. "We get it. All right?"

I turn to Caleb, who's still shaking in anger. His eyes are glued to Radhika's phone.

"We all lied to the police," I say, my voice rising. "All of us. I don't know what the fuck is going on"—I gesture to the folder—"or what that means, but an innocent woman is in danger. We have to come clean about *everything*. Now."

I let the words hang there as I look from Zara to Caleb, and then back to Zara.

"Deal?"

"Fuck—*whatever.* Deal." Zara sighs irritably. Before Caleb can confirm, she adds, "But we're calling Tobias first. The National Guard is going to come after me the hardest for hiding Radhi's phone. I need the consulate's protection more than either of you."

Zara grabs her cell. Within thirty seconds, she has Tobias on speakerphone.

"Ms. Singh?" he says groggily.

I chew my thumbnail as Zara lies down on the couch and places her phone on her stomach.

"How can I help you?" Tobias clears his throat. "Are you all right?"

Zara looks over at me and sighs.

"No, I'm not all right," she tells him. "We're going to need you to come down to Blush right now. We have some—you know what? It's better if we explain everything in person."

"But it's the middle of the night—"

"And you're in the middle of a double-homicide investigation," Zara snaps. "This is important. I'm here with Caleb and his girlfriend, Shaylee. We're in Caleb's villa. We need your assistance urgently."

"What kind of assistance?" Tobias pauses. He sounds tired. "I was planning to stop by tomorrow afternoon to check in—"

"Check in?" Zara mocks icily. "Unfortunately for you, as I said, this is *urgent* and related to my sister's *murder* investigation, so if you could get your fake-tanned overpaid *lazy* government *ass*—"

Tobias interrupts Zara's tirade to confirm he'll be over within the hour. After Zara hangs up, she puts a pillow over her head, screams into it, and then sinks farther into the couch.

Zara is a bitch, but at least she's efficient.

I look over to Caleb, who's still lying on the floor, eyes half closed, his face lacking in emotion. I want to go to him, I want to know what he's thinking, but I feel frozen to my seat. Help is on the way. I should feel better. But then why am I still feeling panicky?

Why can't I shake the feeling that something is desperately wrong?

32.

'm stuck in my head, practicing what I'll say when Tobias gets here, spinning scenario after scenario over how all the puzzle pieces fit together. Caleb and Zara seem equally uninterested in group conversation. Very quickly after getting off the phone, Zara's eyes fluttered to a close. She must be exhausted. We're all exhausted. I rest my head against a throw pillow and wonder if I should also rest while I have the chance. I take a deep, meditative breath, hoping to ease the tension in my body. I barely notice when Caleb stands up and mutters something about going to the bathroom.

Breathe, Shay. Just breathe.

I inhale and exhale over and over and remind myself that I've done everything I possibly can. But is that true?

I open my eyes. Caleb's still in the en suite, and although I'm worried about what he's doing in there and what he's taking, that isn't a responsibility I can take on right now. I glance over at Zara, who's passed out on the couch.

I can't just sit here and do nothing. Not when Daniela's at risk.

Not when the truth could still be in my reach. I kneel in front of the coffee table and start flicking through the contents of Mr. Joshi's folder, stopping at the documents in Hindi. They're the only pages in here that Caleb and I didn't thoroughly review, and as I'm wondering what on earth they might say, I notice something.

I flit my eyes down to the coffee table, expecting to see the signature sparkle of Radhika's phone case.

My heart catches in my throat. Her phone isn't there.

I stand up slowly, my pulse pounding a thousand miles per second as I try to make sense of it. But it *doesn't* make sense. Zara placed Radhika's phone on the coffee table. I saw her do it. And it was there just a few minutes ago when she called Tobias. Which means . . .

I swivel around to face the bedroom, the en suite.

No.

I shake my head and nearly smile. No. This can't be happening. I must be mistaken. My whole body vibrating, I tiptoe into the bedroom. The en suite door is ajar, a wedge of cold yellow light shining through the crack. A shadow passes across it.

"Caleb?" I whisper.

It's dead quiet. No running water. No toilet flushing. No response.

But I know he's inside, and when I gather the strength to push open the door, I find him crying on the floor.

Radhika's phone is in his hands, which are held up as if in prayer. I look at the screen and gasp.

The phone is unlocked.

"What did you do?"

Tears well in my eyes as I drop to my knees beside him, ignore every cell in my body that's screaming at me to run.

"No." Caleb shakes his head, bawling. "Nothing—"

"What did you do?" I whisper again. "Tell me."

Caleb cries harder, convulsing. I reach forward and take the phone from him, half expecting him to stop me. Hit me. *Kill* me. But he doesn't.

Shaking, I tap on Radhika's phone, which is open to her voicemail. A beat later, her voice assistant announces she has a new message.

A message left early Thursday morning at 2:25 a.m.

"Radhi?"

Caleb's voice rings out on the phone. Loud. Clear. Drunk. Drugged. My eyes move up, toward Caleb. I listen to his voice as I watch the puddle of a man drowning right in front of me.

"Are you awake?"

Caleb pauses on the voicemail, grunting. He's the most fucked up I've ever heard him. And, if I'm remembering the timeline correctly, this call took place shortly after Daniela left his villa.

"Are you and Raj fighting or something?" voicemail Caleb says next. "He told me you're staying in your own villa tonight, and that he's sad because you guys never sleep apart, and I just wanted to say . . ."

Voicemail Caleb breaks down into tears too.

". . . I'm sad too, Radhi."

Gasps sputter from the phone, as if he's literally choking on his words.

"I love you so much."

My chest tightens as my vision blurs, the phone dropping with a smack to the tile below.

"I'm sorry. I'm so sorry—I didn't mean it. You're getting married. And Raj is my best—" Voicemail Caleb laughs through the tears. "I'm so happy for you guys, you hear me? I'm *happy* for you. I'm—*fuck*!"

Caleb cries harder in the voicemail. On the floor right next to me. But all I can hear is my pulse firing like a machine gun in my ears.

"You loved her," I say blankly.

My cheeks are on fire, and I gasp as the burning sensations spread down my neck, my limbs. Tears run down my face, and I don't bother wiping them away. He loved her? She annoyed him. He called her childish, immature. He was keeping her at a distance.

"But, if you loved her," I whisper, turning to him. "Then why did you . . ."

Kill her? Kill them both?

I don't recognize the man next to me, but suddenly, I remember his capacity to lose control. His violence. And even though every fiber of my being is telling me to leave—*run*, call for help—I don't. Reason and rationality leaving me, I stay rooted to the ground.

"End of message."

We both look down at the phone simultaneously, which lies between us on the floor. The voice assistant speaks again, her clipped tone reverberating through the en suite.

"Next message."

I look over to Caleb. Did he leave her second voicemail?

"Received Wednesday at 2:46 a.m."

"Hey, it's me."

Caleb's eyes widen, but it takes me a moment to realize who's speaking. That it's Raj's voice now on Radhika's voicemail, not Caleb's.

"I can't sleep, Radhi. Are you really not coming over?"

I sit back on my heels, watching Caleb instead of the phone. He seems just as shocked as I am. He hasn't listened to this message before either.

"I'm sorry about what happened tonight. You know I'm sorry—but, come on, this is *our* life. We get to decide what we make of it. Not my dad. And not your fucking sister either."

Staring at me, Caleb opens his mouth to say something, but I shush him and wave him off.

"Just come over and we'll talk about it, all right?" Raj pleads quietly. "Money is money. And family is *family*. And now you're *my* family . . ."

My hands tremble as I reach for the phone, bring it closer to our ears.

"I'm just sick and tired of everyone telling us what we can and cannot do!" Raj sniffs in the phone, anger dripping from his voice. "We're never going to be happy if we're just their pawns, Radhi."

My stomach twists in confusion as Raj raves on in the voicemail.

"This is *our* time, babe. We need to do this."

Raj's voice cracks on the other end of the line.

"We'll sell your shares, and we'll make a name for *ourselves*. You and me. *You* and *me*!"

Raj continues on his rant. He's drunk, and it grows more senseless with each passing moment. I look to Caleb for clarity, but he's staring at something above my head.

"No," he whispers, his eyes bulging.

"End of message."

"Caleb?"

He won't look at me, and suddenly, I can't breathe.

I drop the phone.

I don't get it. What's going on? And what was Raj trying to say in the voicemail?

Behind me in the doorway, I feel something move.

That's when I hear a loud click above my head. And the cool metal of a gun firmly against my jaw.

From: Lexie Dubois
To: Shaylee Kapoor
CC: Eric Santos
Time: 1:24 a.m.
Subject: EMERGENCY!!

Shay. The Scoop just leaked the craziest video. I've copied the article below.

What do you think it means?!?

Lex

THE SCOOP

EXCLUSIVE

RAJ JOSHI AND RADHIKA SINGH CAUGHT IN EXPLOSIVE SHOWDOWN HOURS BEFORE MURDERS

In security footage exclusively obtained by *The Scoop*, Raj Joshi and Radhika Singh can be seen in a screaming match at the Baja Beach Club in Cabo San Lucas late Thursday night, just hours before they were allegedly murdered by a drug cartel.

In the exclusive video, Raj, the son of a billionaire hotelier, and social media starlet Radhika can be seen yelling at one another while Radhika's sister, Zara Singh (yes, *2W* Zara Singh), watches aghast.

Approximately three minutes into the heated exchange, Raj grabs Radhika's wrist. As she shakes him off, Radhika falls to the ground. A club bouncer notices the fight and appears to attempt to kick Raj out, but Radhika quickly stands up and seemingly explains away the misunderstanding. Zara looks pissed (and fabulous, we might add) as she shoots daggers at Raj from the sidelines.

Such a tragedy to know there was trouble in paradise right before the lovebirds' untimely demise. We hope they made up. Click on the link to watch the full video.

33.

"You *bitch*."

Caleb's voice sounds far away as he stares up at the figure holding a gun to my head. Blinking away tears, I tilt my chin to the side and catch sight of her the very moment she laughs.

"You and your compliments," Zara deadpans. She flicks her eyes down to me, and my heart catches in my throat at the severity of her gaze. The searing realization that *Zara* is behind this.

No. *No.*

"How could you?" I whisper.

Ignoring me, she extends her free hand toward Caleb. "Radhi's phone. Now."

Caleb stares at the phone laying next us on the floor but doesn't move. After a moment, Zara sighs sarcastically and yanks my ponytail until my head's flush against her thigh.

"Don't hurt her—"

"Then don't make me hurt her," Zara snaps, shoving the gun harder into my cheek. "Give. Me. The. Phone."

Caleb complies. The screen has locked itself, and Zara nods approvingly after Caleb tells her the passcode and she punches it in.

"I had a feeling you would know the password." She smiles. "That you would try and get into her phone the moment we looked the other way."

She slips it into her back pocket and beams at him cordially.

"Now, be a good little boy and run along to the bedroom." Zara twists my ponytail again, so tightly I squirm from the pain. "And keep your hands where I can see them. Don't even think about trying anything."

Zara marches me, in a daze, into the bedroom, Caleb just ahead of us, palms up. She instructs us to sit on opposite sides of the bed, our backs against the headboard. My heart racing, I dart my eyes toward Caleb, trying to make sense of what's happening, how we're going to get out of this alive.

It's been Zara this whole time. *Zara.*

She never planned on coming clean to law enforcement, telling them she had Radhika's phone; she insisted we call Tobias to buy herself some more time. To wait until we'd let our guard down.

But why? She was Radhika's sister. She looked out for her. She *loved* her.

Didn't she?

"How could you?" I ask again, only realizing that I've been crying when I lick my lips and taste salt and snot.

"How *could* you—"

"Protect myself?" Zara snaps. "How could I protect what *I* built?"

The gun's still pointed at me, and my stomach drops as Zara's hand quivers unsteadily.

"I should really be thanking you," Zara says, her voice suddenly sickly sweet. "My plan to pin this on some lowly maid really went to shit when I found out about that fucking 'do not disturb' function. I didn't know Raj and Radhi had given only three people special access to the villa.

"But lucky for me," Zara continues, smiling at me so brightly it almost looks genuine, "you're an undercover journalist going after the Joshis! And that family might actually be laundering money. When we talked earlier today, Shay, I was on cloud nine. Honestly, why do you think I wanted to do this while we were *here*, in Mexico?"

My chest tightens as the realization sinks in. Zara was the first one to suggest the drug cartels were involved, on the drive home from the morgue. *She* was the one who told everyone about Raj's meetings with Blush Continental, insinuated that his frequent business trips were a cover.

Zara staged the murders to look like a cartel hit, to steer the authorities in the wrong direction.

"Now things are a bit more complicated, huh?" Zara asks rhetorically.

I think I'm going to be sick. I watch her closely as she curves the gun and her gaze back toward Caleb.

"I'm still working out the details, but I figure I'll delete Raj's voicemail and let the National Guard find your little love note to Radhi when they get here. I'm thinking . . ."

She pauses dramatically, her tone light, her eyes pure fucking evil.

"Shay figured out you murdered your best friends, which prompted you to go stark raving mad and kill her and then yourself. *I* was just so damn lucky to get away." She pauses, frowning at Caleb. "Pretty believable, huh? Radhi told me how you nearly killed a guy once. She told me everything."

I grip his hand, shaking uncontrollably as he looks over at me. She's nuts. And she's going to kill us both.

One of us needs to do something, but what? And how? We're powerless, weaponless. We don't have a chance.

"Anyway, by the time Tobias gets here," Zara continues, "this whole place will have another double homicide to reckon with, and so much contradictory evidence they won't be able to touch me.

"They'll very quickly rule out Sean." She bats her eyelashes toward me. "You know that footage Blush supposedly has of him hiring that kid to be his 'hitman'?"

Greg Clancy. The beach attendant with the envelope.

Zara smiles to herself. "That's just Raj's dealer from LA. He got him a job here so the kid could supply him and his buddies during the wedding."

I shudder.

"Poor Sean." Zara sighs. "A total insomniac ever since his family died in that car crash. He wasn't hiring a hitman, Shay. He was just buying a little weed to help him sleep."

I can't breathe. Sean's innocent. I was wrong this whole time—and it's going to cost Caleb and me both unless I can find a way for us to escape. A weapon. Anything to help us take Zara down. I watch her watching me and wonder if—when the moment reveals itself—the only chance we have is to charge her. She's tall, and strong. She has a gun. But there's two of us. It might be our only shot.

"I'm going to make this whole thing fall on you, Caleb," Zara says next, a touch of pride in her voice. "The woman of your dreams was just about to marry your best friend. And even though you screwed *everything* that moved, it still didn't fill that void in your chest, did it? I hear unrequited love can cause anyone to snap."

"Fuck you," he whispers, but she just laughs in response.

"You don't think that's the first time you left her one of those pathetic coked-out voicemails, do you?"

Caleb hesitates. "She knew?"

"Of course she knew, you idiot," Zara says. "*Everyone* knew—" Zara stops, flits her eyes toward me. My cheeks go red.

"Well. Maybe not *everyone*," Zara says coyly. "But for the record, Caleb, Radhi liked you a lot. She just didn't love you as much as Raj—"

"How could you?" Caleb interrupts, sobbing. "How could you kill your own sis—"

"Is it not obvious?" Zara snaps, her voice shaking, dropping down to a whisper. I brace myself as she steps closer to the bed and grips the gun so hard her arm starts to shake.

"Radhi wasn't supposed to be there."

Her eyes, devoid of emotion until now, suddenly well up with tears.

"They got into an argument at the pool that afternoon. I thought they resolved it, but then Raj started going at her again while we were out at that club. They fought so hard the club bouncer nearly kicked us out."

"I don't remember that," Caleb breathes.

"Of course you don't," Zara snaps. "You were off in la-la land dancing by yourself, and Sean was taking a call.

"Radhi swore to me she wasn't going to stay in his villa that night. I even tucked her into her own bed and waited for her to fall asleep . . ."

They were fighting. That's why Raj was so quiet in the lobby upon their return. Zara walked Radhika back to her villa; only she knew they were fighting. She was the only one who assumed Radhika *wouldn't* be in Raj's villa that night.

"Raj called her to apologize," I finish, remembering the voicemail. "She must have woken up and gone over after you left."

"She's so tiny," Zara says quietly, as if she didn't hear me. "They were spooning, sound asleep beneath the covers. I didn't know she was there until it was too late."

Zara starts to cry, right there in the bedroom, while holding us at gunpoint. This is so deranged, so unimaginable. Zara's affection and love for Radhika *was* genuine. She only meant to shoot Raj, and killed Radhika too by mistake.

"I loved you," Zara sobs, staring at us as if we were Radhika. "I did this *for* you. I swear, I didn't mean . . ."

I turn to Caleb as Zara cries harder, tilts further off balance. *We need to do something.*

Caleb nods, his chin moving almost imperceptibly. *We need to get out of here alive.*

"You killed your sister by *accident*?" I goad, as an idea takes shape that hopefully won't get the both of us killed. "That's the stupidest thing I've ever heard."

Zara freezes mid-sob. A beat later, she straightens her shoulders and glares back at me.

"Excuse me?"

"You killed Radhika on purpose. You were jealous. She had the perfect life, reaping the benefits of all your hard work—"

"Shut your mouth," Zara spits. "It wasn't like that. It was an *accident*."

"Was it?" I provoke.

Zara gawks at me, her mouth dropping open in disgust.

"Do you know why Raj and Radhi were fighting? Do you know what he was forcing her to do?" she hisses. "She was going to sell her shares in Lustre. In *my* company!"

My stomach squeezes as she glowers at me. "This is about the shares?"

Radhika's shares. Her fifteen percent stake in Lustre worth four hundred fifty million dollars.

I feel Caleb tense next to me, his temper flaring. He's preparing to pounce, to make a move. I grab his fingers and squeeze. *No.*

Zara's still on her guard, ready for us.

Not yet.

"Raj had been hounding her, *manipulating* her, to sell her shares to Archer and the other investors. Raj was after her for her money—"

"That's bullshit," I goad. "I read the prenup myself. Raj couldn't have touched Radhika's shares."

"*If* the shares were in Radhi's name, then they were safe. But if she sold them during the course of their marriage?" Zara swallows angrily. "If they used that money to start a new business—which that useless piece of shit wanted to do? That's a whole different story."

I think back to the voicemail, Raj's drunken angry voice pleading with Radhika.

We're never going to be happy if we're just their pawns, Radhi.

We'll sell your shares, and we'll make a name for ourselves. You and me.

"They wanted to use Radhika's shares to create something of their own," I whisper.

Raj needing more credit from his father. Radhika refusing to work for Zara at Lustre, wanting recognition in her own right.

"They didn't want to live in their families' shadows."

"That's what *Raj* wanted, and one day, Radhi would have followed him off a fucking cliff," Zara snaps. "She was brilliant, but like our mother, a total idiot when it came to love.

"Radhi could have anyone, and she picked *Raj*? She was going to marry a guy who, the moment he found out how much her shares in Lustre were worth, tried to convince her to *sell them*?"

Zara scoffs.

"He was so proud of himself, being 'VP Business Development.' In reality, his daddy gave him money to play with, knowing full well he'd never get a cent back. Raj had his whole life handed to him. He was a fool, mediocre at best. They would have crashed and burned, lost all my money—"

"All *your* money?" I interrupt, sitting forward on the bed. "You keep calling it *your* company, Zara. News flash. Your *mommy* invented Lustre. You just designed a pretty website for it. You were handed your life, just like Raj!"

Zara's eyes bug out at me and, just as I hoped, she finally turns the gun on me.

"What did you say?"

Out of the corner of my eye, I see Caleb leaning forward on the bed, preparing to make his move. She's an egomaniac. I need to keep her talking. I need to distract her.

"You heard me, bitch." I smile at her confidently, although inside, I'm screaming. "I said your mommy—"

"*I* made Lustre what it is today. *Me*. And I did what I needed to do to save my company. If Radhi had sold her shares, the investors would have had majority control and taken the company public. Lustre isn't ready."

She smiles at me demurely, wipes away the last of her tears.

"I can tell you—since you're going to be dead in a minute—that our clinical trials are not going as well as we anticipated. Our investors have no idea."

The clinical trials that would make Lustre's antiaging formula more affordable and accessible to the masses. The ones Zara talked about in her lecture.

"If we go public now, our valuation will plummet. We'll be back where we started—"

"So you're lying to everyone?" I spit, drawing her in. "Elizabeth Holmes did that too, And Theranos didn't exactly work out for her—"

"She didn't even have a viable product," Zara says, glowering. "*I* do. We just need more time. I need to get those clinical trials *working* before—"

"Look at you. You're about to kill me, and still all you can think about is work. About yourself. You didn't do this to save your sister from Raj, or because you loved her. You bitch. You did this to save yourself—"

It all happens so fast. Caleb charges at Zara, launching himself off the bed toward her, his arms out like a linebacker.

My breath catches in my throat as, for a moment, he seems to hang there. Suspended in the air. Suspended in time.

As if in slow motion, Zara swivels toward him. Eyes bulging.

But then time speeds back up.

She sees him—and then she fires.

34.

'm stomach-down on the floor when I realize the sound I just heard was Zara's gun going off. I've never heard a gunshot before. I expected the noise to be louder, for my ears to be ringing. It takes me a beat to realize the gun must have had a silencer.

I combat crawl toward the edge of the bed and peek around the corner, deathly afraid of what I'll see. Did she get Caleb? Is he dead?

I propel my body forward, until Caleb comes into view.

My heart gives out.

He's on the floor, bleeding. Zara's seated next to him, panting. Her gun is still pointed in his direction, but her limbs are shaking wildly. She's spooked.

I take a deep quiet breath as I stretch my body backward. I have just a few more seconds before she gets a grip and comes for me next. I want to go to Caleb. I don't know where he's been hit—if he's even alive—but if either of us is going to survive, I have to move *now*.

Mustering every ounce of strength, I hop off the ground and race to the bedroom door, slam it behind me.

"*Shay.*"

Zara's voice, back in the bedroom. Shit. My phone's in there too. Now what do I do?

The front door. The terrace door.

I don't have time to think. I just need to move, and so I race for the latter. Out on the terrace, I break into a run as I head toward the footpath behind the Villas. Behind me, I already hear Zara barreling after me, tripping over the ledge of the door. I stay low to the ground as I throw my legs one after the other.

"Help!"

I scream as loud as my lungs will permit. "Help me!"

But the villa next to us—Raj's—is empty, and the Joshis' villa beyond that one is too far away. Mr. Joshi and Sean are probably sleeping. By the time they hear me and answer the door, it might too late.

I veer toward the beach stairs. Zara is tall and athletic and has a gun. If this is a simple game of tag, then I've already lost. But a game of hide and seek? For that, I have a fighting chance.

I can hear her feet pounding on the pavement behind me, drawing closer and closer as I gasp for air, knowing every second could be my last. That she could fire at any moment.

At the top of the stairs, I grab the railing and swing my body around as my feet play catch-up. The lights from Caleb's dim quickly, but still I take the steps two at a time, praying I'll keep my footing. It's drizzling outside, the sky dark and starless. Down below, I can hear the waves crashing onto the beach, the tide rising toward the rocks.

Is she following me? How close is she? The staircase zigzags back and forth, and just as I round the corner to double back,

I feel Zara's footsteps shaking the metal stairs above. She's only one switchback behind me. If I slow down or hesitate, even just for one second, she'll catch up and have a clear shot.

"This might work out even better for me," she calls as we race down the stairs, her voice taunting. "*You* killed Caleb after you realized he murdered his friends. After you found out he was in love with Radhi."

I shake my head as I round another corner, propelling myself down the stairs. Caleb's not dead. He can't be. She's trying to mess with me. She's trying to get me to stumble.

"After killing him, you chased me down these stairs and I had to defend myself," Zara yells again. "How does that sound to you? Believable?"

I'm running out of steam. Both my courage and my breath are faltering. Is Zara right? Is this how it ends?

She'll concoct some story for the National Guard, point fingers at me, or Caleb, or the both of us. Lexie will tell my family the truth, won't she? That I chose to be here. That it wasn't my fault. But now, as I force myself down the stairs farther into the darkness, I don't know if that's true. I don't know how I'm going to survive.

I don't dare look over the railing. Are there any people on the beach? Is anyone out there to help? My mind flashes, creating a picture of what happens when we reach the bottom: I sprint from the base of the staircase to the rocks, to hide, but by then our eyes have adjusted to the low light and she fires.

And it's over.

We're still high above the sand, and when I round the next corner of the staircase, on an impulse, I stop. I stay very still. I feel Zara slowing on the staircase above me just around the corner.

"Can we just get this over with?"

She sounds annoyed, as if I'm an employee who's brought her the wrong coffee order.

"Go fuck yourself, Zara."

She laughs, and I can almost picture her head thrown back. Her ponytail swishing. Her confidence riding high. Our standstill can't last forever, and she knows eventually she'll win. But I can't let that happen.

"I have a question for you," I say loudly, crouching down butt to heels. "Did Radhika know you hated her fiancé?"

Zara hesitates. She senses a game. But she's grieving. As fucked up as this is, she's been alone in this. And I know she won't be able to resist.

"Come on, Zara," I deadpan. "It's still your *villain monologue*. Spill the tea, girl—"

"My disapproval would only have hurt her, or pushed her to him," Zara says icily. "It was best for Radhi not to know."

"I think you should have told her," I call up. "About Lustre's failing clinical trials too. Maybe if you were just honest with her, if you didn't treat her like a child, then she'd still be alive."

Zara doesn't respond, and I sense I hit the nail on the head. She doesn't like being goaded. Talked to like this. She's not used to it.

"Was it a peaceful death at least?"

I hate the words I'm spewing, but angry people are more emotional. Their decisions less rational. I need Zara to go off base.

"Did you kill her first or second—"

"I didn't know she'd be there." Zara's voice quakes with fury. She's moved closer to the bend. "The bullet I used on Raj went straight through, and . . ."

She trails off. Is she crying?

"Oh," I say sharply. "The first bullet killed them both. So the second you put through your *baby* sister's *head* to make it look—"

Zara rounds the corner in a blind rage, her gun flailing, and without thinking, I spring up from the ground and rush her. She fires the gun and I wince, preparing myself, but she misses. A beat later, I throw my body weight against her. We both crash down hard onto the landing. And then I hear the metal ding of the gun hitting the railing.

I've never been in a fight before. Not even as a child. But I feel my animal instincts kick in as Zara fights to push me off her.

I feel the ocean roaring below. A fall from here would kill us both. I straddle her body with my knees, trying to keep us low to the ground, blocking her hands as she throws upward punches. One gets through, and the blow knocks me off balance. My jaw burning, I fly to the side as she pushes me off her.

And then it's a race to find that gun.

On hands and knees, Zara crawls away from me. I look ahead and see the glint of the barrel. Ignoring the pain, I roll on my side to cut her off, kick her in the stomach. She cries out, her body jerking back, and then I kick her again.

She's gasping for air, her head forward as if in child's pose. Wincing, I pull myself off the ground and move toward the gun. She reaches for my calf and grips it tight, tugs me back down. She's clawing at me, doing everything she can to hold me back. But I persevere. I crawl forward, and I stretch, and I fight, and finally—

My fingers brush the barrel of the gun.

"It's over, Zara," I pant as I clutch the grip and point the gun at her. She freezes.

"You're going to pay for what you did."

I shift onto my butt and wrap my other hand tight around the grip, holding my arms straight out. Her eyes flick to the gun, and then back to me. She smiles.

"Shoot me, then," she challenges. She's breathing hard, winces as she sits higher on her knees.

"Don't move—"

"Then *shoot* me." She shrugs in defeat. "One of us isn't leaving here alive, Shay. The choice is yours—"

"You're coming with me," I say forcefully, unsure what I'll do if she disobeys. "We're calling the National Guard. And your ass is going to jail—"

"I'm not. I won't."

Zara smiles sadly, and then uses the railing to pull herself off the ground.

"Don't move!" I bark.

She freezes. Somehow, I find the strength to stand up too.

"Are you going to kill me, Shay?"

I've always believed there was a clear and finite difference between right and wrong, but yet again, I find myself at an impasse, and facing what feels like an impossible choice. I can't let her go. My throat burns even at the thought. She killed Raj and Radhika—murdered them in cold blood. I won't let her get away with this. But I don't want her to die either. I want her to be punished by the full force of the law.

"I'll shoot you if I have to," I answer finally. "So don't move—"

"Then just do it already," Zara hisses.

My hands shake from the weight of the gun, the decision at my fingertips.

"No one's going to blame you," Zara laughs. "So just kill me already! Just fucking kill—"

But then Zara charges me without warning, and I don't have time to aim, or think, and I don't even process that I've pulled the trigger until I feel the kickback in my arms and shoulders. A burst of heat and light, and a dull pain that crashes over me like a wave. The wind knocked out of me, I fall back against the railing, and, for a moment, I can't see or hear anything.

"Zara," I pant, blinking furiously. "Zara!"

Slowly, my vision sharpens as the shock wears off. She's not on the landing.

Where is she? Did I kill her? Is all of this over?

The gun still firmly in my hand, I hobble to the edge of the landing and look down the stairs.

"Zara, are you—"

I stop when I see blood. Dark pools splattered all the way down the stairs. There's a trail leading down to the beach.

She's injured. She won't get far. And just as I'm about to go after her, I hear a siren.

LOS ANGELES JOURNAL

BREAKING NEWS ALERT
ZARA SINGH ARRESTED IN CABO WEDDING MURDERS
Sunday, April 28

Los Cabos—The celebrity chief executive of revolutionary skincare brand Lustre has been apprehended on suspicion of murdering her sister Radhika Singh and her sister's fiancé, Raj Joshi.

The *Los Angeles Journal* first reported on the double homicide Saturday morning after a source close to the families confirmed the fatal shootings and that the investigation had been taken over by a special task force within Mexico's National Guard that combats drug cartels.

Mexican security forces have declined to comment on the details of Singh's arrest, the evidence against her, or if they still believe the murders to be cartel related.

This story is developing.

THE SCOOP
Monday, June 10

SHOCKING! ZARA SINGH UNRECOGNIZABLE IN PRISON GARB!

The former Lustre beauty queen behind bars in Mexico for allegedly killing her sister and future brother-in-law is not so lustrous these days, sporting unkempt hair, a dull complexion, and even a few wrinkles.

In pictures obtained by *The Scoop*, Zara is seen jogging in the courtyard of the minimum-security prison in Los Cabos where she is awaiting trial and news of her application to be extradited to the United States. Why Zara allegedly killed Radhika Singh and Raj Joshi on the eve of their Cabo wedding is still a mystery . . . although a source familiar with the fallen Silicon Valley darling claims Zara was "totally obsessed with her sister's man" and "super in love with Raj and must have killed them both out of jealousy."

Zara certainly looks a little down in the dumps these days. Just six weeks into what could be a decades-long prison stay, Zara's infamous "Lustre" is fading. If only she had access to her own products behind bars.

TWO VISIONARY HOTELIERS JOIN FORCES TO REDEFINE LUXURY TRAVEL

BLUSH CONTINENTAL—THE JOSHI GROUP JOINT PRESS RELEASE
Thursday, July 25

Blush Continental and the Joshi Group today revealed they have signed an agreement to develop an ultra-luxury resort near Los Cabos, Mexico, a strategic partnership anticipated to transform the region's high-end tourism landscape.

Javier Hector Gonzales, a co-owner of Blush Continental, says: "We are thrilled to be expanding our luxury offerings with an innovative industry leader like the Joshi Group. The forthcoming resort's east-meets-west design concept represents our blended signature styles."

Narayan Joshi, chief executive of the Joshi Group, says: "The new resort will offer unparalleled guest experiences, gourmet dining, and state-of-the-art spa and wellness facilities. We expect this to be the first of many projects together."

Blush Continental and the Joshi Group celebrated the launch of their joint venture earlier this week with a cocktail party at Blush's Los Cabos location, which Gonzales says has "bounced back" since the tragedy on the property three months ago.

Image alt text: Blush staff members sipping champagne in the iconic Atlantis Banquet Room as Events Director Daniela Munoz delivers a toast.

For immediate release.

35.

M s. Kapoor?"
I look up from my phone. The receptionist is smiling at me over horn-rimmed glasses. Her lips curl upward, slowly revealing two rows of too-white teeth.

"He's ready for you."

The receptionist directs me to a conference room with floor-to-ceiling windows, a mahogany table for ten, and bar. After she leaves, I help myself to a glass of water and stare out at the smoggy LA skyline I'm becoming rather fond of. I squint. I can almost see my apartment building. I moved out of my shitty rental, obtained the right to work in the US, and have been officially calling this city home for months, but a lot has happened this summer. Sometimes, it feels like an eternity has passed since I flew back from Cabo. It's as if I've lived a whole other lifetime.

Zara spent six whole hours as the most wanted fugitive in the western hemisphere before the National Guard apprehended her several miles east of Blush, bleeding and slightly delirious. The bullet I fired only grazed her shoulder, and she appeared to be as right as rain by the time American paparazzi descended on Cabo and documented her first court appearance. She turned down all media requests and, in the weeks that followed, Hollywood worked itself into a frenzy bidding over the rights to her story, hoping to turn her case into the next big true-crime documentary or blockbuster.

But sources say Zara continues to turn down every offer, and she's refused to speak up even to quell the hilarious rumor that she was in love with Raj and killed him and Radhika out of jealousy. Her strategy of staying silent is working. Zara's reached an even higher level of celebrity as an alleged criminal than she did as chief executive of Lustre. The media can't get enough of her, and filmmakers, podcasters, TV hosts, book publishers, and journalists have been hounding all of us involved to tell our side of the story. Everyone wants the salacious details about what really went down in Cabo at the infamous destination wedding that never happened.

Different versions of events are out there. Shortly after Tobias quit his job at the consulate, he ramped up his TikTok presence with content on the investigation from a procedural perspective and is now a surfer/true-crime influencer. The Joshi family issued a short, terse statement stating they never approved of the marriage to begin with and were considering a civil-damages suit against Zara for emotional distress. Meanwhile, several of Radhika's influencer friends have created an active Reddit community that pores over publicly available evidence, like that club security footage leaked by *The Scoop*, hoping to prove Zara's innocence.

Only Caleb and I know what really happened, which is why the media is desperate to speak to us the most. Court documents have been leaked—yet again by *The Scoop*—that Zara's prosecutor is calling us as her prime witnesses.

The National Guard showed up ninety seconds after I shot Zara and went after her, so thankfully, I didn't have to. Caleb had survived and called for help; Zara's bullet went straight through his chest, but luckily failed to hit his heart, lungs, or any major arteries.

In the days that followed, I stayed by Caleb's bedside, and together, we watched the media circus unfold on the small television in his hospital room. We told the police everything—we didn't hold anything back—but both of us have refused to speak to the press. Caleb's too heartbroken; he just wants to put this sad chapter behind him, and I . . . Well, I think the Singh family has suffered enough. There's a rumor going around that the mother, Dr. Simran Singh, overcome with grief, has taken an indefinite leave of absence from Lustre. Zara and Radhika's brother— quiet, bookish—has been forced to take charge of the company. The sibling who stayed behind the scenes and out of the spotlight, who has a wife and a child on the way, has been forced to take on Zara's role of holding the family business together.

Despite Zara's murder charges, Lustre remains as popular as ever, market experts continue to exaggerate its valuation, and a columnist at the *Los Angeles Journal* recently opined that the brand would continue to disrupt the skincare industry and emerge all the stronger. There was a time not so long ago when I would have reveled at the chance to bring a company like Lustre to its knees, and I would have told the world Zara's family secret: clinical trials to create a cheaper version of her antiaging formula are on the verge of disaster, the company is overvalued, and Zara's relentless corporate pursuits turned her into a murderous monster. I would have screamed "I told you so." *This* is what happens when all we care about is how we look, how much we have, how much of the world we can take for ourselves.

But now?

It's occurred to me that I don't have to take the burden of the whole world on my shoulders, that right and wrong, good and evil, don't only exist in black and white. And although I'm still foolishly, hopelessly working toward a better and more peaceful world, I'm also working on finding some inner peace too.

I've stopped smoking, a few times. I've cut down on caffeine and alcohol, and have swapped out almond milk for oat. I have a new job I'm passionate about, but over which I'm determined not to lose my sense of identity. I pay thirty-seven dollars every Saturday morning to practice yoga with an instructor whose voice doesn't annoy me and whose class actually helps me recharge. I call my family at least once a week. I've made up with Lexie. And, for the first time in my life, I'm in a healthy relationship.

I'm seeing a therapist.

I was lost before my vendetta started against Mr. Joshi, and long before I met Caleb. But those three months working undercover, pretending to be someone I was not, steered me even further off track. My therapist has helped me understand that I'd unwittingly turned to nicotine, caffeine, and alcohol as coping mechanisms. How having to blend into Caleb's lifestyle forced me to question my beliefs and values even more than I already was. How the conflicted feelings I developed for Caleb blinded me to his addiction, his love for Radhika, and even to the role he played down in Cabo. Thinking back, I put myself in a dangerous situation by trusting him: I returned with him to the Villas for that folder, even though I still hadn't confirmed Caleb's innocence.

I smile, thinking of him, and decide to send him a text.

I'm here. Any second now . . .

He replies immediately.

> Good luck today!

We've decided to stay in each other's lives, although we're taking the friendship slow. We've gone for coffee twice since his twenty-eight-day stint in a drug treatment facility in Monterey, which he checked into of his own volition. Caleb's doing a lot better, but it's a long road to recovery and, in a bid to start over, he's made some big life changes. He's resigned from his job at the Joshi Group, sold his house, and is looking for something a bit smaller in Malibu. He says he wants to be closer to the ocean, to nature. He's not sure what he'll do yet for work, but with his sizable trust fund, he's not exactly in a rush to figure it out.

The second time we met up, I worked up the courage to ask him about Radhika. Without much encouragement, he opened up about the depth of his feelings for her, how he never intended to play matchmaker that first time they all met; Caleb noticed Radhika first, apparently, but stepped aside upon realizing his best friend liked her too. Like Zara said, everyone but me knew how Caleb felt about Radhika. As I've since learned, this was in fact the biggest source of tension between Sean and Caleb; Sean was worried that Caleb would act on his feelings and Raj would wind up hurt.

He just wants everyone to love him, and the moment they do, he's gone before they wake up.

Remembering what Raj said to me once, I found myself wondering if Caleb only loved Radhika so much because he couldn't have her; if he would have discarded her too in a different set of circumstances. It shouldn't matter to me, but it does. I'm still getting over my hurt feelings, although, surprisingly, the heartbreak is healing more quickly than I thought. My therapist has helped me come to the slow-burn realization that my feelings for Caleb weren't as strong as I believed them to be.

When I met Caleb, I was just really, *really* lonely.

Twenty-five minutes after the meeting was supposed to start, the boardroom door swings open. Even though I was expecting him, my heart jumps into my throat at the sight of him.

"Shaylee," he grunts.

"Mr. Joshi."

He frowns at me, clocking the chair I'm sitting in at the head of the table. It's his chair. But I don't stand up to trade places, or shake his hand, and instead gesture to one of the nine less powerful seats. A team of slightly younger men file in after Mr. Joshi. Lawyers, presumably. Mr. Joshi takes the chair immediately to my right, massaging his brow as one of his minions hands him a document to read and sign. I smile at him pleasantly, waiting for him to finish up his other business.

Waiting for the other shoe to drop.

"*So.* Shaylee." Mr. Joshi's eyes widen as he looks up from his work and intertwines his fingers on the table. "I heard the *Los Angeles Journal* hired you as their newest investigative reporter!"

He's heard.

Of course he has. For the past four months, Mr. Joshi's been having me followed.

"Your parents must be so proud of you for soldiering on in a dying profession," he deadpans. "Traditional journalism is not what it used to be. If I felt like it, I could buy the *Los Angeles Journal* and sell it for parts."

I smile at him through tight lips, stalling, allowing him one more moment to feel like he's in charge.

"Let's get started, shall we?" He leans back in his chair and crosses one leg over the other. "Tell me. What sort of disreputable article does your employer plan on publishing this time?"

"In a moment," I say crisply. "Not everyone is—"

I spot Sean through the frosted glass wall, hustling toward the boardroom.

"Good. He's here."

Mr. Joshi swivels to face the door as Sean enters, frowning at the sight of him. "*Beta . . . Tum yahaan kyon ho?*"

"I asked him to be here," I answer on Sean's behalf. "My meeting invitation was for the both of you."

Sean won't meet my gaze, or Mr. Joshi's, as he takes a free seat—the chair at the opposite end of the table. Now that Sean's here, I can feel my nerves catching up with me, and, keeping my hand steady, slowly raise my water glass to my lips.

Breathe, Shay. Breathe.

Mr. Joshi believes I'm here to cause a fuss because I've written an article that takes him to task about the Mumbai construction-site fire. Neither of us have forgotten about my work at the human rights watchdog, when my coworkers and I gathered evidence that proved Mr. Joshi ordered the fire to claim the insurance payout, that his actions led to the death of eighteen of his workers. He's been having me followed as an intimidation tactic and has surely brought his legal team with him today to try and put a stop to me. To threaten legal action, or a defamation suit, should the newspaper choose to publish it.

I gently set down the water, forcing myself to relish this moment of anticipation. Although I'm still working on a draft of that particular article, and the world will know soon enough about his role in the fire, that's not why I'm here today.

"Mr. Joshi," I say firmly. "I suspect you're about to have a busy afternoon, so let me get right to it."

I reach into my backpack and retrieve his leather folder. *NJ.*

"Where . . ." He stammers, red-faced. "That's *mine*."

"I know." I unzip the folder and pull out photocopies of all the documents he'd stored in it. "Raj took it from you. And then he asked Caleb to keep it safe. But you already knew that."

I turn to the last pages in the pile, the ones written in Hindi. Mr. Joshi's face reddens at the sight of it.

"Did you have your bodyguard follow Caleb around Cabo hoping to get these back?" I ask him, knowing full well the answer. "After your son and Radhika were murdered, during our first meeting with Tobias and law enforcement, *you* asked if anything had been stolen from Raj's villa. You were worried a certain document in here would fall into the wrong hands—"

"I have no idea what you are—"

I wave him off, leaning forward in my chair.

"I'm speaking right now, Mr. Joshi. Don't interrupt me," I spit. "Raj gave these papers to Caleb after a fight with *you*. After he discovered something about you."

I place my hand firmly on the table, my whole body vibrating in hatred for the man sitting from me.

"After he found out *you* killed Sean's parents."

36.

Someone in the boardroom gasps—one of the lawyers—but I don't dare look away from Mr. Joshi. The man is a murderer, several times over. Long before the fire, he killed his own brother, Jackie Joshi, with whom he had started the Joshi Group, and his brother's wife.

"This is the original police report." I point at the pages, and then pull out the two that follow. "And *this* is the police report you had doctored."

Mr. Joshi's mouth gapes as he scrambles for the papers, and the lawyer next to him looks over his shoulder in worried confusion. I don't need to explain the rest out loud. The car crash that killed Sean's mother and father when he was only sixteen years old: it wasn't an accident. It was murder.

A police officer by the name of Prakash Kumar Anand—who I still think of as my darling Brown Hulk Hogan—arrived at the scene of the crime. Initially, he made note of the fact that the car's brakes and airbag mechanism appeared to have been tampered with and filed the necessary paperwork. A few days later, he then doctored his own report to state the car crash was an accident. Mr. Joshi bribed police officials to look the other way, and perhaps as a reward for Brown Hulk Hogan's loyalty, brought him to the US to be his personal bodyguard.

"I . . . I . . ."

Mr. Joshi is speechless—not that I expected him to fill in the gaps. I don't know if I'll ever get the full story, but somehow, Raj found out about the doctored police report. Upon realizing what it meant, Raj confronted Mr. Joshi about his actions, stole the folder, and then went over to Caleb's to ask him to keep the documents safe. That was ten days before Cabo; the exact same time he started pulling away from Sean. Raj was unable to face Sean knowing the truth about who Mr. Joshi had stolen from him.

This is our *time, babe. We need to do this.*

We'll sell your shares, and we'll make a name for ourselves. *You and me.* You *and* me.

Raj's voicemail to Radhika.

His words haunted me, continue to haunt me, and during a recent lunch date with Radhika's best friend from math camp, Mei Lin confirmed to me that Raj started hassling Radhika to sell her shares in Lustre only ten days before the wedding. Which was around the same time he discovered his father killed Sean's parents.

Upon learning the truth, Raj didn't want to have anything to do with his father—or his fortune. He didn't want to use Radhika's money simply to assuage his own ego and make a name for himself, but to escape the financial shackles that kept him tied to Mr. Joshi.

"*Beta*," Mr. Joshi stammers into the silence. "Sean, my boy. You don't actually believe this *bitch*."

"Thank you." I smirk, thinking of Zara. "I'm taking that as a compliment."

"You are unbelievable," Mr. Joshi spits. "Sean has been through so much, Shaylee, and to accuse me of this out of nowhere"—he shakes his head—"it's abhorrent. My son doesn't deserve—"

"Enough."

Sean's voice, booming across the table.

We all turn to look.

My part in this meeting is over, and I sit back and relax to watch the rest unfold.

I would never accuse Mr. Joshi of something so heinous without having warned Sean, or obtaining his permission. After our team at the *Los Angeles Journal* translated the police reports and dug up corroborating evidence that Mr. Joshi orchestrated the murder of Sean's parents, I handed everything over to Sean. And after sleeping on the information for only one night, Sean gave us his full blessing to bring Mr. Joshi to his knees.

The news that his uncle killed his parents wasn't as big of a shock to Sean as I thought it would be. He said he was also old enough to remember his father and uncle had been in a heated years-long dispute over the future direction of the Joshi Group, and, just a few hours before the accident, Mr. Joshi had uncharacteristically taken his father's car "out for a spin."

"Would you have had me killed too, uncle?" Sean asks now, staring over at him calmly. "I was trying to change this organization, revert things back to the way they were before my father died. What would have happened if I'd succeeded?"

The environmental impact assessment penned by Sean. His belief in corporate social responsibility.

There's more I could be doing.

Do you know my father studied public policy too? . . . I'm just trying to make him proud.

"I don't know what you are talking about." Mr. Joshi's voice wavers, as if hurt. "She's lying, *beta*—"

"Don't call me that," Sean stammers, his eyes reddening. "I am *not* your son."

He stands up, pulls out a stack of papers from his briefcase, and hands it to the man next to him. The man frowns at it and then continues passing it along. When the papers get to Mr. Joshi, he laughs briskly and crumples them into a ball.

"You can't do that," he says sternly. "This is my company—"

"This is *our* company."

Another thing on which Sean enlightened me: Mr. Joshi only owns fifty percent of the Joshi Group, while his dead brother bequeathed the other half to Sean. Mr. Joshi was never *fully* in charge. All these years, Sean had simply gone along with his uncle's decisions and never challenged his position as the chief executive out of respect for his elder.

"I called an emergency board meeting earlier this morning," Sean continues, his voice strained and raw with emotion. "I raised a motion to terminate Narayan Joshi as chief executive of the Joshi Group effective immediately."

He swallows hard.

"The motion passed unanimously. And they elected me as the next chief executive."

Mr. Joshi's face drains of color. He squeezes his neighbor's shoulder and yanks him closer,

"He cannot do that. The board *cannot*—"

"Don't respond to him," Sean snaps at the man. "You work for the Joshi Group. For *me*."

Sean turns to his uncle then. It's clear he's holding back tears.

"We can do this. And we just did."

The next ten minutes are a blur as building security shows up and attempts to escort Mr. Joshi off the premises. He protests and resists like a guilty child, barely registering my official request for comment; my *Los Angeles Journal* article breaking the news that he's been deposed as chief executive of the Joshi Group goes live in fifteen minutes.

Eventually, two security guards are forced to physically drag him out of the conference room kicking and screaming. I've imagined this moment so many times before, and it's even more pathetic to watch in real life than in my fantasy. But as I wave Mr. Joshi goodbye, a smirk plastered across my face, I'm not sure how I'm supposed to feel.

Vindicated? Validated? Nothing at all?

Mr. Joshi is still a billionaire and has the funds to fight the litany of indictments, lawsuits, and other legal actions that are about to come his way. Raj, Radhika, Sean's parents, and eighteen of the Joshi Group's construction workers are still dead. The world is still round.

And there are plenty more bad actors who must be made to face the consequences for their crimes.

The meeting over, I sluggishly gather up my belongings and check my phone. I have missed calls from my mom and Lexie—both of whom will be anxious to hear about the meeting—and another from a private number.

Daniela.

That fateful night in Cabo, around the time Zara was holding Caleb and me at gunpoint, Eric finally managed to track Daniela to a holding cell at a San Jose police station; she'd set off a silent alarm while searching for Hector's name at Blush Continental's headquarters, and, unaware that she was an employee of the company, local police had arrested her for attempted burglary.

I was so relieved to learn she was safe, and that her employer believed the incident to be a simple misunderstanding. But my anxiety returned a few weeks later when Daniela called me out of the blue and said she was still determined to help us prove that the Joshi Group—and Blush Continental—are laundering money for the cartel. She told me she was back to work at the resort—and that she'd dug up some paperwork on her boss, Javier "Hector" Gonzales.

Eric quickly confirmed this man was one of the Blush co-owners in his paper trail leading back to the cartel. An hour later, after I explained to Lexie this was the same Hector who Raj had been meeting with monthly the year before his death, she greenlit our article.

Eric is the lead journalist on the ground; I'm the coauthor running background and liaising with our primary source, Daniela; and Lexie, our editor, is making sure we're being cautious so none of us winds up dead. Especially Daniela, who's risking the most. She's working this story from inside Blush Continental.

I stare at the embossed leather folder still in my hands—*NJ*—wondering whether I should leave it here or give it back to Caleb. I no longer need it. We've made multiple photocopies of every document inside, including the invoices Blush Continental issued to Mr. Joshi for the wedding expenses; it wasn't just the doctored police report that turned out to be valuable.

Why did Raj and Radhika decide to get married at Blush?

Upon closer inspection of those invoices, we realized that Blush's charges for flowers, catering, and other expenses were ten times the amount Daniela said she originally quoted Mr. Joshi; someone had later gone into her accounting system and raised the prices. We're still looking for more proof, but we suspect holding the wedding at Blush presented the conspirators with another money-laundering opportunity. Mr. Joshi was never going to pay full price; the cartel could have "paid" the balance in cash and cleaned up some of its dirty money.

We know this is just the tip of the iceberg, especially now that the two "visionary hoteliers" are publicly going into business together. We suspect they will try and funnel dirty money by inflating the construction costs of their new resort. Eric's sources also claim Blush Continental and the Joshi Group will use their joint venture as a vehicle to build more black hotels for the cartel.

As I ready myself to go, I notice Sean holding court from his chair opposite me as the new chief executive of the Joshi Group. The remaining lawyers in the room are huddled around him, whispering at him in tense, hushed voices. Sean looks so handsome, so much like Raj. When he catches me staring, he looks over at me and smiles.

"Can I walk you out?"

He abandons the lawyers, and, together, Sean and I take the elevator thirty-five floors down to street level. We don't say a word to each other. Sean looks like he hasn't slept in weeks; his insomnia must be acting up, and I . . .

I don't know what to say to him right now. He only helped us take down Mr. Joshi because he believes we're on the same side. Not that Sean has any idea, but we've been investigating him too.

Sean's good-guy act isn't real.

At first, I didn't want to believe that Sean could have known and stood passively by as Mr. Joshi and Raj climbed into bed with the cartel. Sean, like me, has a utopian vision for the world in which everyone gets along, shares resources, and collectively works toward the betterment of humanity and our planet. He *is* a good guy, I thought. I *still* think. He's working on changing the Joshi Group for the better from the inside. A man like that would never do something as heinous as working with a drug cartel.

But we all contain multitudes, don't we? We are human. Walking contradictions—myself included—and Sean's paradox is that he also has some not-so-good qualities. According to my latest research, he has a history of cheating—his romantic partners, and three exams at Cambridge. He has a giant portfolio of personal investments in fossil fuels, weapons, and arms manufacturers. He enjoys the company of high-end sex workers. And, as corroborated by Greg Clancy and several former Joshi Group employees, Sean indeed treats his employees, housekeepers, and other people he deems beneath him like dirt.

"I guess this is it," Sean says to me when we're outside on the steaming-hot pavement.

I squint at him until I wrestle my sunglasses free from my purse. "I guess so."

"Will I ever see you again?"

"If you're lucky, then no. You won't."

Sean's mouth crinkles upward. He thinks I'm joking, and so I smile too.

"You should have this," I say, holding out his uncle's leather folder. "It belongs to the Joshi Group."

He regards the folder before taking it.

"How does it feel to be the new chief executive? Congratulations."

Sean frowns at me as I offer him my hand. I hold his gaze firmly as he shakes it.

"Oh." I feign confusion. "And isn't a second congratulations in order? I read your joint press release with Blush Continental."

A shadow crosses Sean's face, a flicker of good and bad. Light and then dark.

Maybe Sean knew all along Mr. Joshi and Raj had gotten the Joshi Group involved with a drug cartel. Maybe he didn't. But if it's the latter, as the new chief executive, then Sean will find out very soon.

"Good luck," I tell him. "You're going to need it."

He raises an eyebrow at me as he withdraws his hand. Does he sense that I'm testing him? Does he know that we'll be watching?

Because if Sean doesn't come clean to the authorities, if he doesn't immediately pull the Joshi Group out of its operation with Blush Continental and the cartel, then Eric, Lexie, Daniela, and I are going to find out. And we are sure as hell going to make him pay.

I smile at Sean then, friendly, direct. And as the sun beats down around us, hard and unrelenting, yet again I find myself drawn to him. We could have been friends in another life. Kindred spirits. Allies.

It's too bad we're destined to be enemies in this one.

Acknowledgments

Every book takes a village. I am hugely appreciative of everyone at William Morrow and HarperCollins Canada for their support of *The Plus One*. A big thanks to my editors Jennifer Lambert and Asanté Simons for brilliantly guiding me through each draft and helping me come out on the other side. A special shout-out as well to Neil Wadhwa, Cindy Ma, Brianna Benton, Liz Psaltis, Amelia Wood, Kaitlin Harri, Kelly Cronin, Amanda Hong, and Yeon Kim.

I want to thank Martha Webb, my champion; Paige Sisley; and the entire team at CookeMcDermid Literary Management.

As ever, thank you to my family and friends for their love and encouragement. And to Simon. Thank you for brainstorming *The Plus One* with me the entirety of our "romantic" Cabo vacation.